# Conjured

# Conjured

## SARAH BETH DURST

WALKER BOOKS
AN IMPRINT OF BLOOMSBURY
NEW YORK   LONDON   NEW DELHI   SYDNEY

First published in the United States of America in September 2013
by Walker Books for Young Readers, an imprint of Bloomsbury Publishing, Inc.
www.bloomsbury.com

For information about permission to reproduce selections from this book, write to
Permissions, Walker BFYR, 1385 Broadway, New York, New York 10018

Bloomsbury books may be purchased for business or promotional use. For information on bulk purchases please contact Macmillan Corporate and Premium Sales Department at specialmarkets@macmillan.com

Library of Congress Cataloging-in-Publication Data
Durst, Sarah Beth.
Conjured / by Sarah Beth Durst.
pages       cm
Summary: Haunted by disturbing dreams and terrifying visions, a teenaged girl in a paranormal witness protection program must remember her past and why she has strange abilities before a magic-wielding serial killer hunts her down.
ISBN 978-0-8027-3458-7 (hardcover)  •  ISBN 978-0-8027-3459-4 (e-book)
[1. Supernatural—Fiction.   2. Magic—Fiction.   3. Identity—Fiction.   4. Memory—Fiction.]   I. Title.
PZ7.D93436Co 2013       [Fic]—dc23       2013007847

Book design by Nicole Gastonguay
Typeset by Westchester Book Composition
Printed and bound in the U.S.A. by Thomson-Shore Inc., Dexter, Michigan
2 4 6 8 10 9 7 5 3 1

All papers used by Bloomsbury Publishing, Inc., are natural, recyclable products made from wood grown in well-managed forests. The manufacturing processes conform to the environmental regulations of the country of origin.

*For Andrea*

# Conjured

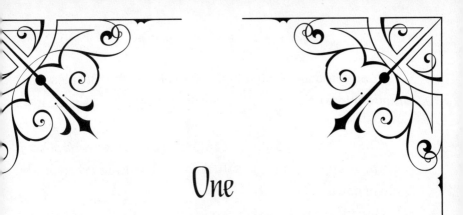

# One

"YOUR NAME IS EVE. Remember that."

She was supposed to call him Malcolm. Pressing her forehead against the cool glass of the car window, she stared at the house. Yellow and narrow, it loomed over the lawn. She traced the outline of the house on the window: a peaked roof, two windows with shades drawn, a front door dead center. "It's a face," she said.

The man and woman in the front seats checked their phones and then their guns. "You can't give her kiwis," the woman said to the man. Malcolm. And she was Aunt Nicki. "She'll think they're mice."

"Kiwis are nutritious," Malcolm said. Twisting in his seat, he leveled a finger at Eve. "I walk first, you second, Nicki last. Understood?" He didn't wait for her response, and she didn't give him one. He stepped out of the car and stretched.

"Start her on apples," Aunt Nicki said, opening her door and stepping out into the street. "Or bananas. Oranges."

"*You* could have shopped," Malcolm said. "Besides, it is impossible to eat an orange without it spitting at you. It's a hostile fruit."

"Oranges are classic. For centuries soccer moms have been carting orange wedges to refuel their charming tykes on the field of battle."

Outside, they shut their doors. Eve let the blissful silence wrap around her for three seconds until Malcolm yanked open her car door. "You push the red button to release the strap." His voice was kind and soft, as if he expected her to cower or bolt. He pointed next to her, and she located the red button. It clicked, and the seat belt snapped out of her hands and flattened onto the seat behind her. "It's going to be okay," he said, and she was certain he wasn't talking about the seat belt. Not wanting to see pity in his eyes, she stared at the seat belt contraption for a second before she climbed out of the car and followed Malcolm toward the house.

The sky was a matte gray that washed out all shadows. She couldn't tell where the sun was—or if this place even had a sun. A single brown bird perched on a scraggly tree in the middle of the front lawn. Eve watched the bird warily until her toes hit the front stoop. She looked up at the house. She still thought it looked like a face, intent on swallowing her whole.

"Inside now," Malcolm said. "Gawk later."

Aunt Nicki ushered her in.

"Wait here," Malcolm instructed. Gun drawn, he disappeared through a doorway. Eve strained to listen to his footsteps as he moved from room to room. She felt Aunt Nicki's hand on her elbow, as if the woman expected her to bolt. *As if I had anywhere to bolt to*, Eve thought.

The hall was as dreary as the outside world. It had faded, brown-striped walls and a worn carpet. A picture of a dead tree by a canyon hung on one wall. "Homey," Eve commented.

Aunt Nicki squeezed her elbow, and Eve fell silent.

She waited until Malcolm reappeared. He holstered his gun. "Clear," he said. "I like clementines. Easy to peel. But you can only buy them in crates. No other fruit comes in crates. What the hell do I need with a crate of fruit?" He tapped Eve's arm and then pointed. "Living room. Kitchen. Bathroom. Your room. Hers."

She memorized the layout. "Which is yours?"

"I won't be staying."

A sudden wave of panic crashed into her, and she wanted to grab his arm and say, *Stay!* But she didn't. Instead, she pushed the wave back, back, back, and said, "Oh."

"Clementines are a wussy fruit," Aunt Nicki declared.

"So says the champion of soccer moms."

"I'd rather face six drug dealers and an irate bookie than one overtired soccer mom with a screaming toddler in a minivan who has just been denied her parking spot."

"Point taken," Malcolm conceded.

He had been with Eve every day at the agency. She hadn't imagined that he'd abandon her with a woman she barely knew. Not wanting to listen to more banter, Eve left them in the hall and wandered into the living room. Green couches lined the walls. The cushions were worn with indents shaped to strangers' bodies. The coffee table sported rings from dozens of glasses. She stood in front of the cold fireplace and studied the photos on the mantel.

Her by a lake.

Her with Aunt Nicki at a restaurant.

Her in front of this house.

She had the same hair and makeup in each photo, but at a glance you wouldn't know that they'd all been taken the same afternoon inside a studio. She'd never stood in any of those places, never been here, never met Aunt Nicki before today.

Or at least she thought she hadn't.

Closing her eyes, she called up the memory of taking these pictures. She'd waited in a cold room with a few metal chairs and a magazine full of pictures of women with parted lips. A photographer had arrived with Agent Harrington—Malcolm—and they'd set up a screen behind her. . . . Yes, that felt like a real memory.

"Lake Horace," a woman said behind her. *Aunt Nicki*, she reminded herself. "You spent summers there as a kid. Maybe you loved to canoe. Or swim. Or catch tadpoles. Whatever. You decide. That one, that's Mario's. Brilliant pizza."

"I like pizza," Eve said. She'd had it at the agency. Also, chicken lo mein.

Malcolm smiled at her warmly, approvingly, his eyes crinkling. She thought about smiling back, but then the moment passed. "You moved here . . ." Malcolm paused so she could fill in the blank.

"Three weeks ago," Eve supplied. "My parents had a job

transfer to South America, but they're not ready to move me yet, so Aunt Nicki offered to take me in for the summer."

"South America, how interesting," Malcolm said. "Where in South America?"

Eve bit her lower lip. He'd drilled her on this. She should know it. Began with a P . . . Two syllables . . . "Pernu?"

"Peru," Aunt Nicki said. "And don't phrase it like a question." To Malcolm, she said, "I'll work with her. Stop mother-henning us." Her face brightened with a smile, and she wrapped her arm around Eve's shoulder. Eve stiffened. "Eve and I will be just fine. We'll be buddies. Rent movies. Pop popcorn. Flirt with the pizza delivery boy."

Eve held as still as stone. She reminded herself that she trusted them, sort of. Or at least she had no choice but to trust them, which was close enough.

Aunt Nicki released her.

Eve staggered back. "Do you mind if I just . . . I'd like to see my room."

"I'll show you—" Malcolm began.

She held her hands up, palms out to stop him. "You don't have to. I remember." She skirted around the coffee table and then backed out of the living room.

In the hall again, she felt as if the striped walls were leaning in toward her. She hurried to a plain white door and put her hand on the knob.

"Eve." Malcolm.

She didn't move.

"Eve, you'll be safe here."

She looked at him.

"I want you to feel safe here." He did. She could see it in his eyes. And for an instant, she felt as if he'd wrapped her in a cocoon and nothing could hurt her. But then she remembered he wasn't staying. She pushed the bedroom door open and entered.

Malcolm didn't follow.

Inside the bedroom, half of her expected a rush of familiarity to fold around her like a homemade quilt. But of course, it didn't. She studied the room: a bed with a checkered blanket and one flat pillow, a wooden dresser, a tiny desk with a chair. Eve closed the door and then sank down on the bed. Hugging her knees to her chest, she stared at the wall. The wallpaper had a swirl of leaves with birds perched on branches and caught mid-swoop in patches of blue. It was a nice bedroom, even if it didn't feel like hers.

She wondered how she even knew this was a bedroom when she didn't remember ever having one. She'd known what a car was too, though the seat belt had felt unfamiliar. She could recognize a few kinds of birds. For example, she knew that these painted ones on the walls were sparrows and the live one outside had been a wren. She didn't know how she knew that. Perhaps Malcolm had told her in one of her lessons.

Or maybe it was a memory, forcing its way to the surface of her mind. But the sparrows she remembered flew. She pictured their bodies, black against a blindingly blue sky. She didn't know where that sky was or when she had seen it. The birds had flown free.

Eve raised her hand toward the birds on the wall. "Fly," she whispered.

The birds detached from the wall.

The air filled with rustling and crinkling as the paper birds fluttered their delicate wings. At first they trembled, but then they gained strength. Circling the room, they rose higher toward the ceiling. They spiraled up and around Eve's head. She reached her arms up, and the birds brushed past her fingers. She felt their paper feathers, and she smiled.

Then she heard a rushing like a flood of water, and a familiar blackness filled her eyes.

❊

*I am alone in a carnival tent of tattered red. Music, tinny and warped, swirls around me. Fog teases at my feet as if it wishes to taste me. A trapeze swings empty above me, and then it's not empty. A broken doll dangles from it.*

*I hear a man's voice. Loud, as if to an audience, he says, "Choose a card."*

*The trapeze vanishes, and I am standing in front of a table covered in red velvet. Cards lie in front of me: seven of spades, queen of hearts, jack of diamonds, a castle caught in thorny vines, a man hanging from a tree . . .*

*"Choose a card," the Magician says.*

*He's a shadow in the mist.*

*I study the cards. Perhaps the castle, I think. I reach for it.*

*The Magician catches my wrist. "Not for you." His voice is soft, nearly a purr in my ear, and I want to ask why not. No sound*

*comes out of my mouth. I touch my throat. I feel bumps in my skin,*
*even, in a row, straight across my neck.*

*My scream is silent.*

❧

Lying on the bed, Eve sucked in air. Her hands flew to her neck. Smooth skin. She swallowed and felt her throat throb as if she had screamed it raw.

The birds were on the floor, lifeless as paper.

She heard a knock on the bedroom door. "Food's ready, if you're hungry." It was Aunt Nicki. "Sandwiches. Microwave soup."

Eve jumped up and scooped the paper birds off the floor. They lay limp in her hands with feathers spread and beaks open. She shoved them into a dresser drawer just as the doorknob turned.

Aunt Nicki stuck her head into the room. "You okay?"

Eve nodded. Leaning against the dresser, she wet her lips and wondered if she could speak. *Worst vision yet*, she thought.

The woman sighed. "This is the part where I say something all touchy-feely about how it's all going to be okay and this will feel like home in no time and you have a wonderful opportunity to reinvent yourself and your life . . ."

"You can skip that speech if you want," Eve said. Her throat felt rough, as if she'd swallowed sand. She licked her lips again.

"Awesome," Aunt Nicki said. "Come out and eat so you don't faint."

Eve's eyes slid to the bed. Anyone could see she'd been lying there. She didn't know if Aunt Nicki noticed. "In a minute, okay?"

Aunt Nicki closed the door.

Eve sagged. After a moment, she recovered and peeked in the dresser drawer at the limp birds. The branches in the wallpaper were bare now, and the leaves fanned out against an empty blue sky. "Sorry," she whispered to the birds. She wondered if they'd liked their taste of freedom or if they'd been scared. She shut the drawer again, gently this time.

Eve left the bedroom before Aunt Nicki could return to fetch her. She found the two agents in a tiny kitchen. They sat at a table squeezed between the refrigerator and a wall.

"Ham, chicken, or turkey?" Aunt Nicki asked without looking at Eve. She pointed to bags of cold cuts on the kitchen table. "Or do you want to be a vegetarian?"

Eve selected a roll and picked at the crust. She sat at the table, a little closer to both of them than she liked, but there wasn't much choice.

"Vegetarians don't eat meat," Malcolm explained. "No hamburgers. No sausage. No steak. No bacon. No pepperoni." He helped himself to a stack of ham slices and shoved them into a roll. "Instead, they eat a lot of beans. Also, fruit. This is a kiwi, by the way." He speared a slice of green fruit with a fork and ate it.

He was being kind again, acting as if he could heal the holes inside her if only he were helpful enough, and Eve had to look away, studying the kitchen instead of him. The kitchen was sparse but clean. The yellow walls were nice. The counter had been scoured bare in spots. Not all of the cabinets hung straight. The lace curtains drooped over closed shades. She interrupted a discussion of the pros and cons of vegetarianism to ask, "Can we open the shades?"

Malcolm and Aunt Nicki exchanged looks.

"We could," Malcolm said slowly.

"You said I'd be safe here," Eve said.

Both of them nodded. "So long as you follow the rules," Aunt Nicki said. "No witness who followed the rules has ever been harmed in the history of the witness protection program."

Malcolm studied her with narrowed eyes. "Repeat the rules."

Eve put down her roll. The crumbs felt like dry dust in her mouth. "No contact with anyone I used to know. No phone calls. No letters. No smoke signals. And if telepathy miraculously becomes possible, no telepathy either."

"And?" he prompted.

"Don't tell anyone about my past," Eve said.

"And?"

"Don't discuss the case."

Malcolm nodded. "Good."

Eve crossed to the window and raised the shades. She looked outside at the brown lawn with the crooked tree, the black agency car with the tinted windows, and the dull gray sky.

"Feel better?" Aunt Nicki asked.

Eve didn't answer.

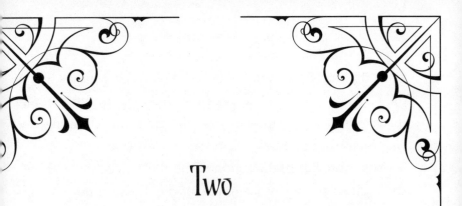

# Two

*445 . . . 446 . . . 447 . . .* Eve counted the cracks in the plaster ceiling as she lay in bed and waited for dawn. *451 . . . 452 . . .* Shadows clung to all the furniture. Occasionally, a car's headlights swept across the room, erasing the shadows, but then they returned, smothering the room. She listened to the clang and snap of the pipes in the walls and thought of hands playing the pipes as if the heating system were a carnival organ, like the one that played in her visions.

*492 . . . 493 . . .*

Slowly, the shadows in the room faded from black to slate, then from slate to dove gray. The branches in the wallpaper still looked bare and bereft without their birds.

Eve heard a door open and close, and then footsteps. She counted them instead of the cracks . . . ten steps between Aunt Nicki's room and the bathroom. Another door creaked open and shut, and then she heard the water *whoosh* on in the shower. This sent the pipes clanking and rattling in the walls so loudly that Eve got out of bed and placed her hands flat on the walls to feel as well as hear the shaking. She felt like that inside—as if she were rattling, clanging and clanking and snapping like the pipes.

She waited until the sound of the shower ceased, and then she found a set of clothes in one of the dresser drawers. Malcolm had left them for her—socks, underwear, bra, jeans, and a T-shirt. She touched the cotton T-shirt to her cheek. He'd asked her in the agency, the day before they came here, what colors she liked. She'd picked a few at random. These shirts were those colors. Poking her head outside her room, she checked the hall. Aunt Nicki had already returned to her bedroom. The bathroom door was open. Eve darted inside and slid the lock.

Staring at the lock, she started to shake. She held her hands in front of her, and they trembled. Inside *and* out, she was like the water pipes.

She unlocked the door.

That was better.

Her ribs loosened, and she could breathe deeply again. She dumped the clothes in a corner, used the toilet, and brushed her teeth. She kept her eyes firmly on the sink and did not look up at the mirror until after she had spat. Then she steeled herself . . . *Black-brown eyes. Straw-yellow hair. Pink lips. Round face.* Fixing the image of herself firmly in her mind, she raised her eyes to see her reflection.

She almost looked familiar this time. She'd forgotten the shape of her chin and that her eyebrows were straw-yellow too. Also, the length of her eyelashes.

Eve showered and tried not to look at her body too much. It kept surprising her too. She couldn't keep it all in her head: her toes with the freshly trimmed toenails, the goldenness of her skin, the shape of her knees, and the smoothness of her hands. She studied her hands in the shower. The flesh on her fingertips was puckering from the water, and her skin felt soft and squishy, waterlogged. She wondered if she'd ever be used to this flesh.

The doctors had said she would. They'd said the changes were all cosmetic, adjustments so she wouldn't stand out, so she wouldn't be noticed by those who shouldn't notice. A necessary precaution, given that the suspect in her case had not yet been caught. Since she couldn't remember what she looked like before, she couldn't compare. It all felt new, and it all felt as changeable as clothes.

She dried herself and dressed. As the steam in the mirror faded, it tossed bits of her reflection back at her. Hair. Shoulder. Cheek. In a clear corner of the mirror, her eyes stared back at her, and she touched the image and then touched next to her eyes. "You should be green," she said, suddenly certain. "Be green."

She heard a rushing in her ears as black-brown drained out of the eyes in the mirror. Green infused the irises, spreading out from the pupils.

And then her legs folded underneath her.

❄

*I feel a brush in my hair.*

*"It always begins with 'once upon a time,' my dear. That is how*

*it is, even if 'once upon a time' is now." Gnarled hands separate the*
*strands of my hair and wind them around knuckles. "A witch . . .*
*for of course there was a witch. There always is, isn't there? She had*
*stars in her eyes and dust in her hair. She heard the sounds of the*
*forest when she moved and the ocean when she spoke." The Story-*
*teller tilts my chin up. "Such pretty eyes. Such a pretty, pretty girl."*

*The Storyteller is not pretty. Her face is shrunken in wrinkles,*
*as if her skin were a squeezed dishrag. Her eyes are milky red,*
*clouding out whatever their true color was. Her knuckles on the*
*hand that holds my chin are knobs that curl her fingers. But*
*she smiles at me, and it is like sunshine.*

*"There's a girl too," she says, "in a tower, and it doesn't matter*
*whether she wakes or sleeps, for she's locked inside with a world*
*laid out before her that she cannot touch."*

*She threads a piece of yarn through a needle. It's straw-yellow*
*yarn.*

*"And so the girl sleeps and dreams wonderful dreams of horses*
*in sea foam and birds that carry her to the tallest mountain. Lovely,*
*lovely dreams of a pretty, pretty girl."*

*Her fingers wrap around my wrist, and she smiles at me.*

*Then she plunges the sewing needle into my arm.*

✳

Footsteps echoed from outside in the hall. "Eve, is everything
all right?" Aunt Nicki called through the door.

Splayed on the floor, Eve clutched the wet towel against
her chest. She hugged it tight as she concentrated on breathing.
In, out. In, out. In . . .

The doorknob twisted.

Eve tried to find her voice to answer. "F-fine."

The doorknob stopped.

"Just . . . slipped. I slipped. I'm fine." Eve rubbed her arms. Goose bumps prickled her skin. Everything ached. She winced as she touched her elbow. She must have hit it hard.

"Come to the kitchen when you're done," Aunt Nicki said. "We need to talk about what you're going to do while you're here." Footsteps retreated from the door. Eve counted them— nine to the kitchen—and then pried herself off the floor. She used the sink to pull herself up and peered into the mirror.

Green eyes stared back at her.

"Such pretty eyes," she whispered, touching her face. Shuddering, she backed away from the mirror. She staggered out of the bathroom. By the time she reached the kitchen (nine steps later), she felt steadier. Taking a deep breath, she entered.

Aunt Nicki stood in front of a toaster. She was dropping bread into the slots. "Orange juice is in the fridge," she said without looking at Eve. "That's a typical breakfast drink. You aren't old enough for coffee."

Eve nodded. She didn't bother to question the statement, not without Malcolm here. She didn't think Aunt Nicki would be so patient with explanations. Aunt Nicki hadn't even turned around, not to greet her, not even to notice her eyes. *I should have changed them back*, she thought. But green . . . felt right.

The shade was up again, or still, in the kitchen, and she was drawn to the window. Outside was the same matte gray as yesterday. For an instant, she thought that maybe it was still yesterday and she'd imagined the dark, silent night with the sounds of cars and the cold streetlight outside her window. But no, she could feel the damp hair on her neck from her shower, and her elbow ached from the fall.

"Malcolm isn't here," Eve said. She knew as soon as the words left her mouth that it was true. She didn't hear any other sounds in the house. It was just the two of them, squeezed into the cramped kitchen. She'd thought she would like it with fewer agents around, but she didn't. It made the house feel tight around her, as if it had shrunk in the night.

She shouldn't miss him. Just because he'd chosen shirts in her favorite colors. Just because he explained seat belts and cameras and pizza and television. Just because she knew him better than anyone else she could remember . . .

"He'll be here for you any minute," Aunt Nicki said. With a butter knife, she gestured at a stack of papers on the table. "Read those. You need to choose one."

Eve sat down in one of the chairs. It swayed under her, and she planted her feet on the ground, though she wasn't sure how that would help her from falling if the chair decided to break. She picked up the papers and read "Job Description" at the top and "Duties and Requirements" underneath. Each sheet followed the same format. "A job?"

"Yes, a job," Aunt Nicki said. "A summer job. Work for money. It's what ordinary teenagers like you do in the summer." Eve noticed that Aunt Nicki hadn't looked at her yet. She fixed her eyes everywhere but at Eve—the table, the papers, the sink, the counter, the toaster. Yesterday's friendly hug must have been for Malcolm's benefit. Eve bet that popcorn and movie night wasn't about to happen.

Eve flipped through the papers: pet shop clerk, hostess, library assistant . . .

"You can't sit in the house by yourself all day," Aunt Nicki said. "And I can't be here to babysit you all the time. I have other responsibilities too."

As Aunt Nicki fetched the margarine from the fridge, Eve scanned through the pet shop clerk description. Cleaning cages, feeding animals . . . She imagined cage after cage of birds and rodents, all watching her. She set that job aside. Next one was a hostess at a restaurant called the Firehouse Café. She didn't remember ever having eaten in a restaurant. Malcolm had described one once, but that hardly qualified her.

"You need structure to your day," Aunt Nicki said. "You need interaction and experiences. It will help." The toaster popped, and she spread margarine on the browned bread. "Do you understand me? God, who knows if you do? It's like talking to a brick."

Eve had no idea what to say to that. She considered asking if Aunt Nicki normally talked to bricks. But the agent didn't seem to have much of a sense of humor, at least not where Eve was concerned.

Choosing not to respond, Eve picked up the next job description. Library assistant. She ran her fingers over the words as she read. Shelving books, assisting the librarians with patrons, reading at children's story hour. "Libraries . . . they're the places with stories," Eve said. Closing her eyes, she tried to summon up a memory of a library. Shelves of books. Sunlight falling across a table. She saw spiral stairs. It could have been a real place, or Malcolm could have shown her a picture at some point. It *felt* like a real place. She poked at the memory, but her mind didn't yield anything but that image.

She opened her eyes to see Aunt Nicki watching her. Eve glanced down quickly at the job description—she didn't know how the agent would react to her changed eye color. Aunt Nicki laid a plate of toast in front of Eve. "Good choice. You won't disturb many people there." Narrowing her eyes, she continued to study Eve as if she were cataloging her faults. "Fidget more. You hold yourself too still."

Eve didn't move. Heaving a sigh, Aunt Nicki grabbed the orange juice and poured a glass. She set it down hard on the table. Juice sloshed over the edges, and drops spattered the papers. "Serve yourself from here on in," Aunt Nicki said. "I'm not here to wait on you. Just to watch you and guard you. Understood?"

Eve took a sip of the orange juice. It stung her tongue and tasted sweet at the same time. She set it back down. Aunt Nicki seemed to be waiting for a response. Again, Eve didn't give her one.

The doorbell rang.

Aunt Nicki slapped a napkin on the table next to Eve's untouched toast. "About damn time." She marched out of the kitchen, and Eve listened as Malcolm entered the house.

Their voices drifted into the kitchen. "How is she?" Malcolm asked. Hearing his voice, Eve felt lighter. The muscles in her shoulders and neck loosened.

"Unreadable. Unreachable. Unchanged."

"You need to give her time."

"It's been seven months already."

Eve frowned. She knew she'd had memory losses while she'd been in the agency. Her mind had erased chunks of time here and there—hours, days—but still, she didn't think the lost time added up to months. Weeks maybe. Of course, she had also lost additional weeks in the hospital before that. Days and nights had blurred together inside the hospital room while she'd recovered from the procedures, the surgeries that gave her this new body and face. But seven months? Her hands strayed to her face, near her eyes.

Months. Days. Years. Did it matter how much time she'd lost if she couldn't remember anyway? It didn't. She filled her lungs with air and then exhaled, as if she were flushing it all away. Postprocedure, one of the nurses at the hospital had showed her how to use the toilet and shower. Later, Eve had taken off the toilet tank cover and watched the chain mechanism raise the cap in the tank, and she'd waited while the float rose up until the water stilled. She liked the idea of sending what you didn't want away from you and then waiting to be filled with clean water.

"You were fine with this yesterday," Malcolm said. "What happened?"

"I hate being alone with her," Aunt Nicki said. "She freaks me out."

"Keep your gun on you, and stay alert."

Eve picked up the piece of toast and nibbled at the edges. It felt as if she were swallowing sandstone. Crumbs scraped her throat, and her tongue felt slick from the margarine. But at least she could eat it. Bread always seemed to stay down. Her name was Eve, and she liked bread. *That's enough for now*, she thought.

Malcolm and Aunt Nicki entered the kitchen, and the room felt crowded again. Eve shrank into her chair and put down the toast. "Did she select a job?" he asked Aunt Nicki.

"You can ask me directly," Eve said.

Malcolm smiled as if he were proud of her, and Aunt Nicki looked at her as if the family dog had spoken.

Without meeting their eyes, Eve handed Malcolm the library assistant job description. "I like stories."

"Good. That's . . . good." Malcolm accepted the description. "All right then, let's go. I'll tell you about libraries on the way. Unless . . ." He looked at Aunt Nicki.

Aunt Nicki shook her head. "We talked about orange juice."

Eve took another sip of the acidic juice. At least she hadn't had to explain why her eyes were green. Eyes down, she picked at her bread.

"Are you sure about this?" Aunt Nicki asked Malcolm.

"A routine will help her," Malcolm said. "More stimulation."

Since this was exactly what Aunt Nicki had proclaimed earlier, Eve wasn't surprised when she nodded. "Again, you could talk directly to me," Eve said.

"Will you say anything interesting back?" Aunt Nicki said. "Because you haven't so far. This could all be a colossal waste of valuable time and resources."

Eve studied her for a moment. "I don't think I like you."

Aunt Nicki raised her coffee cup as if toasting her. "Mutual."

"Because I freak you out."

"You eavesdropped," Aunt Nicki said. "How industrious of you."

"Drink your coffee, Nicki," Malcolm said, sounding amused. "Eve, grab your coat. The library opens soon, and I'll need to talk with the director before you can begin. We have an arrangement with her to place someone there as needed, but we'll have to settle on the specifics. Nicki, let her know to expect us."

Outside was yet another black car. This one lacked the tinted windows and hulked low to the ground. Malcolm checked up and down the street and also inside the car before he allowed Eve into the passenger seat. She fastened the seat belt as she'd been shown and looked back at the house. Aunt Nicki had locked the door behind them. It occurred to Eve that she didn't have a key.

"Your address is 62 Hall Avenue," Malcolm said as he climbed into the driver's seat. He locked the door and then checked the rearview mirror as he pulled out of the parking spot. "You should memorize that. Also, I requisitioned a cell phone for you. It's in the glove compartment." He pointed. "If you need help, call. If you feel unsafe, call. If you even feel uncomfortable, call. I'll come."

Eve opened the glove compartment. A gun lay there. Next to it was a rectangular black box. She took the box out and closed the glove compartment. Inside the box was a sleek black phone, like the ones she'd seen the agents use.

"Keep it in your pocket at all times," he said. "I've already programmed in my number and Nicki's. But don't use it to call anyone else. We monitor the call record."

She had no one to call, or at least no numbers she remembered. She slid the phone into her jeans pocket. It dug into her hip.

"It also has a special tracking device," Malcolm said. "In other words, it lets us find you at all times. Even if you don't think we're there, we'll be there. You *will* be safe."

Eve shrugged. She already knew they watched her at all times. It was what they did. They watched. So she watched them. She knew the muscles in Malcolm's cheek twitched every time he concentrated. His forehead pinched when he was about to speak. He smiled with only half of his mouth. She knew his face better than she knew her own. If that freaked out Aunt Nicki, then so be it.

"You said you'd tell me about libraries," Eve said.

He brightened. "Yes! Of course. Libraries are public buildings . . ." He launched into a full explanation—their history, their structure, their purpose. She watched his mouth move as he talked. It was always soothing to listen to him. Like the hum of a refrigerator.

Interrupting, she asked, "Why are you so kind to me?"

Startled, he shot her a look, but then he fixed his eyes back on the road, switching lanes to avoid a parked car. "You're my case."

"I'm Aunt Nicki's too."

"You were mine first." He pulled into the parking lot of the

East Somerville Public Library. More softly, he said, "Besides, you need someone to be kind to you. I don't think anyone ever has been."

She stared at him. For all the explaining he did, he never hinted about her past. Doctor's orders, he'd claimed.

He parked, then turned to face her. "Remember, you'll be in public. It's imperative you follow the rules. Stay inconspicuous— Your eyes. They're different." His own eyes bugged, the whites startlingly white against his dark skin.

"I changed them," Eve said. She looked down at her hands, twisted tight into a knot in her lap. She should have changed them back before he saw.

"You changed them," Malcolm repeated. "Did you know you could do that?"

Eve thought about it. "I didn't know I couldn't."

She watched him wipe his expression to carefully neutral. "It's a good discovery. From now on, though, please limit your discoveries to when you are safe inside the agency. You can't do that in public." He held up his hand as if to forestall her reaction, though she hadn't intended to respond. His voice was soft and gentle. "You can't do any magic here. There is no magic in this world—that's why this place is safe for you."

She held her face still. Another hint about her past. He had told her so much in those few sentences, more than he'd ever told her before. *There is no magic in this world*, she thought. *I'm from another world?*

He clasped her hands in his. "Eve, I am serious. If you aren't capable of this, if you don't feel ready, let me know and we drive away right now. You don't have to work here. You don't have to stay in that house. We can return to the agency and wait until you're ready."

The kindness was back, filling his eyes, and for an instant she wanted to cling to his hands and say, *Yes, take me back. Keep me safe. Stay with me.* But she thought of the girl in the tower with a world laid out before her that she could not touch. "I want to be here."

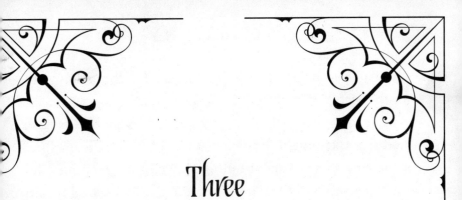

# Three

EVE LIKED THE LIBRARY at once. She and Malcolm walked into the lobby, and she inhaled the smell of paper and dust—it reminded her of Malcolm's office at the agency. Books lined the shelves behind the circulation desk, and a bank of plants filled the windowsills.

A woman bustled up to them as they stood in the lobby. "Mr. Harrington? I'm Patti Langley, the library director. I'm afraid there's been a bit of a mix-up regarding your request."

Malcolm scowled, which on him was a formidable expression. His bushy eyebrows lowered to shade his eyes so they looked like dark craters.

Patti smiled so brightly that her eyes crinkled up until they nearly disappeared. "As I attempted to explain to your associate on the phone before she disconnected me—I'm sure accidentally—I know we told your office we had an assistant position available, but I'm afraid it's been filled. We simply don't have the funding for two assistants. Believe me when I say that our budget is out of my hands. I'm so terribly sorry for the inconvenience this may cause you."

Eve looked at each of them, their expressions so exaggerated that they might have been dolls mimicking real expressions. She thought about telling Malcolm never mind. They could just leave. She could pick another job. But Malcolm didn't so much as glance at Eve.

"This position doesn't require funding, ma'am," Malcolm said. "Surely the office told you that? Budget constraints aren't a concern. We will handle the financial aspect."

Patti's face turned pink. "Oh!" She sounded like a mouse that had been squeezed. "Still, we only have work enough for one assistant."

"Surely there are things to shelve." Malcolm continued to scowl. "Eve will be an asset. She follows direction well. Never makes trouble. She's the quiet type."

"Perhaps we should discuss this in private," Patti said. "It's . . . The board has concerns. *I* have concerns. *Security* concerns."

"Very well." Malcolm leveled a finger at Eve. "You have your cell phone. Use it if you need to. Don't leave the library." He followed Patti behind the circulation desk, and then they disappeared through an office door.

For an instant, Eve didn't move. She touched the lump in her pocket that was the cell phone and wondered if this was a test. She looked at the windows, expecting to see Aunt Nicki watching her from outside. All she saw was the parking lot. She glanced at the office door. It stayed shut.

Quickly, she scooted into the main library, past the reference desk, past the computers, and into the stacks. Stepping in between bookshelves, she felt as if the library were enveloping her. The smell of books swirled around her.

Selecting a book at random, Eve pressed her nose against the pages and inhaled. She smelled dust and paper, a hint of coffee like Malcolm drank, a little overly sweet scent like Aunt Nicki wore. Eve pictured a woman curled on a couch with this book, her cup of coffee beside her, her perfume fresh on her wrists. Eve wondered if she left behind smells on the things that she touched too. She imagined tracing her smells out of the library, into Malcolm's car . . . Her smell would be thick in the bed where she'd lain with the sheets tucked tight around her as she stared up at the ceiling and tried not to dream. She'd trace the smell back to the agency, but what if she followed it farther? Had there been books in her past that she'd touched? Had she felt safe with them? Just holding this book made her feel as if arms were wrapped around her.

"Smell okay?" A male voice. Very close.

She felt as if ice water had been poured into her veins. Freezing, she didn't breathe. She had the phone, she reminded herself. Plus, Malcolm wouldn't have left her if there were any real danger.

Forcing herself to inhale and exhale, Eve lowered the book from her nose. On the other side of the book was a boy her age. He had brown eyes with green flecks, and unlike Malcolm, he was closer to her height, so those eyes peered directly into hers as if pinning her to the bookshelf.

He scooped a book off the shelf next to her and sniffed it. "This one smells like bacon." He picked up another. "Cigarettes." A third. "Just book. I like the smell of fresh books best, especially just-processed books with the slick plastic covers." He stuck out his hand. "I'm Zach, library page, at your service." After a second's hesitation, she shook his hand. It was warm and soft. "I think it's a shame that it's customary to shake hands upon greeting when what I really want to do is kiss your lips and see if you taste like strawberries."

She released his hand. "I'm Eve. I've never eaten a strawberry."

"Allergies? I'm allergic to cats. Not cats themselves, per se. Hairless cats are fine. It's the cat dandruff, caught in the fur. Need serious anti-cat-dandruff shampoo." His hair had slid over his eyes as he talked; he shook it back and smiled at her. "Glad you didn't freak when I said I want to kiss you. I'll wait for an invitation, of course, but I believe in being up front about these kinds of things. Prevents misunderstandings later. I don't want you thinking that we can ever be just friends. Unless it's friends with benefits."

Eve stared at him. "Are you a friend of Malcolm's?"

"Don't know a Malcolm," Zach said. "Not a common name. Never met an Eve, either, come to think of it. I will resist the obvious apple jokes, promise."

So he wasn't sent by Malcolm to watch her. "Apples?"

"Little-known facts about apples: apples are members of the rose family, it takes energy from fifty leaves to produce one fruit, and humans have been eating apples since at least sixty-five hundred BC. Bet you're asking yourself how a handsome guy like me who can't seem to stop talking ended up working in a library where the talking thing is not so condoned."

She continued to stare at him, blinking once.

"Or perhaps you're wondering about hairless cats. They're less cuddly than you'd think. Also prone to sunburn. And oddly prone to more earwax, due to less ear hair. But I'm boring you. Cardinal sin when talking with a beautiful girl. Not to be confused with the original sin . . . And I promised no obvious jokes. Sorry. Don't hate me."

"I'll try not to," she said gravely.

"Now you're just being polite." He heaved a sigh.

Eve's mouth twitched into a smile. "I'm not good at polite. I'm told I need to practice more."

"You could decide to embrace a policy of total honesty, like I have. I don't lie."

She'd thought that was what people did. Malcolm and Aunt Nicki lied all the time. Right now, Malcolm was in Patti Langley's office, undoubtedly lying to her. "That's wonderful."

"My parents think it's annoying."

"Do they lie?"

"It's the only language they speak." His voice was cheerful, but his eyes were sad. She wondered if that contradiction counted as a lie. "Hyperbole and sarcasm totally don't qualify as lies," he said. "There is truth in my pain."

"Everything about me is a lie," Eve said. She thought for a second and added, "Except my eyes."

"You have pretty eyes," Zach said.

"So I've been told."

Sitting in a cracked leather chair in the library lobby, Eve flipped through the books that Zach had picked for her: a history of bread, a biography of a nature photographer, a book on bird migration, another on skyscrapers. Malcolm had taught her to read. She remembered him patiently showing her a few words. After that, the lessons were a blank, but they must have happened and they must have stuck. Or maybe she'd learned to read long ago, and he'd merely reminded her. Regardless, if she could remember the words, she should remember learning them. If she knew what a skyscraper was, she must have seen one. She thought of the flock of sparrows, black against the brilliant blue.

*Stop*, she told herself.

She couldn't think like that. Worrying about what she did and didn't know would only eat her up inside. She knew things but couldn't remember how she knew them—the doctors said that was common with memory loss like hers. They said she had long-term memory loss, punctuated by bouts of short-term memory loss. But knowing it was common didn't help. Eve stroked the book covers, their slick plastic wrapping sliding under her fingertips. She wondered how much truth was in these books, and if any of them featured girls who could change their eyes or cause birds to fly off wallpaper without knowing why.

Malcolm and the librarian, Patti, emerged from her office. ". . . very well, and I appreciate your frankness, Mr. Harrington."

"And I appreciate your flexibility."

Crossing the lobby, Patti beamed at Eve. "Congratulations, and welcome. You'll start tomorrow." She asked Malcolm, "Is nine to three acceptable for her schedule?"

"Perfect," Malcolm said.

Eve stacked Zach's books beside her and stood. "I like your library."

"That's nice, dear," Patti said. "Just please remember, this is a safe haven for our patrons, and we'd like it to remain so. I will be watching." Patti checked to make sure no one was looking at them, and then she reached up to her neck and flicked open the top two buttons of her blouse. She pulled the collar open. Two eyes were embedded on her sternum. The extra eyes blinked at Eve.

Eve clasped her hands together tightly so they wouldn't shake. Her skin felt as if spiders were crawling all over her. But she kept her voice even and calm as she stared at the extra eyes. "Oh."

Patti calmly rebuttoned her shirt.

Malcolm placed a hand on Eve's shoulder. "We will return tomorrow."

A few more words, a nod, a handshake, and then Malcolm steered Eve across the lobby. Looking over her shoulder, Eve gawked at Patti until they exited. Malcolm led her outside and down the ramp. Parked diagonally in a handicapped spot, Aunt Nicki waited in another agency car. The motor was running.

Malcolm opened the back door, and Eve climbed inside. She fastened her seat belt without fumbling, and Malcolm patted her shoulder approvingly.

As Malcolm squeezed into the passenger seat, Aunt Nicki said, "Meeting rescheduled to today. Lou wants us in. We can pick up your car later."

Malcolm sighed. "Today?"

"Poor baby. Busy day," Aunt Nicki said. "How did it go in there?"

"Fine. Everything's been arranged," Malcolm said.

"The librarian has two extra eyes," Eve said.

Aunt Nicki raised both of her eyebrows. "She showed that to Eve?"

"She was making a point," Malcolm explained.

"Huh," Aunt Nicki said.

Eve looked back at the building. She bet that Zach didn't know about the extra eyes. She imagined what he would have said about them. She thought he might recite facts about flies or other multi-eyed creatures. "Is she from another world too?"

"Can you swing by Dunkin' Donuts?" Malcolm asked, his voice mild. "What do you know about other worlds?"

"Nothing." She stared at the library until it disappeared behind the trees.

No one spoke until Aunt Nicki turned into the Dunkin' Donuts parking lot. As she parked, Malcolm twisted in his seat to look at Eve. "Eve, would you like any coffee?"

"She's too young for coffee," Aunt Nicki said. "It'll stunt her growth and make her boobs tiny. Get me a medium espresso, no milk or sugar."

"She could have decaf," Malcolm said.

"It's a bad habit to start."

"Smoking is a bad habit to start," Malcolm said. "Chewing your fingernails, bad habit. Obsessively quoting eighties music, also bad. Decaf is nothing."

"I'm fine," Eve said. "Is she from my world?"

"You tell me," Malcolm said.

"If I knew, I wouldn't ask."

Aunt Nicki laid her hand on Malcolm's sleeve. "Just get the coffee."

He didn't move. "You might like a jelly donut. Remember, we ate them in the agency last week. You licked the jelly off your fingers. Lou wasn't impressed with your manners. Said we should work on that."

"Lou isn't impressed by anything," Aunt Nicki said. "He's the only person I know who's totally unimpressed by level five."

Eve tried to dredge up a memory of a donut or Lou or level five. But she couldn't. She reached inside her mind, and the thoughts skittered away like sand or mist. She concentrated harder, reached deeper . . . Blank.

"It's an act," Malcolm said to Aunt Nicki. "Thinks if he's jaded, we'll respect him more. Absolutely nothing wrong with displaying a little amazement or showing a little compassion. You ought to try it."

"I am as warm and fuzzy as a kitten," Aunt Nicki said.

"Toward her?" Malcolm asked.

"She just sits there. Doesn't she know—"

"Don't," Malcolm said. "We agreed."

"If she knew why—"

"End of conversation," Malcolm said. "We are not talking about this here and now. Or ever, really, but expressly not here and now. Pick another topic. Weather report said it was supposed to rain, but it's not raining yet."

"Scattered showers," Aunt Nicki said. "Mostly cloudy tonight."

"See? Not so hard," Malcolm said. "Stay here. And behave." He stepped out of the car and went inside the Dunkin' Donuts. Eve had thought she had all her recent memories of the agency. She should be able to remember something as specific and simple as eating a jelly donut last week. She felt her ribs squeeze tight together. Her hands balled into fists, and her nails dug into her palms. Aunt Nicki had said seven months. What else was in those seven months?

Aunt Nicki tapped her fingers on the steering wheel as they waited for Malcolm. In an overly bright voice, she said, "So, tell me, Eve, how did you like the library?"

Gulping in oxygen, Eve focused on what she could remember: the smell of the library books, the sound of Zach's voice . . . He let words spill out as if his brain were a faucet always turned on. She didn't think she said that many words in a week. But Aunt Nicki was waiting for an answer. "Fine," Eve said.

"Fabulous," Aunt Nicki said.

Eve concentrated on keeping her breathing even. She felt as if she were shaking inside, her organs rattling against her bones.

Aunt Nicki tapped her fingers on the steering wheel and watched the donut-store door. "You know that Malcolm is an optimist."

"You could tell me what you think I should know." Eve fought to keep her voice steady and mild. All the while she continued to dig her nails into her palms.

"You're Malcolm's case," Aunt Nicki said. "It's his call."

"I don't remember eating a jelly donut," Eve said, her voice a whisper.

Aunt Nicki was silent for a moment. "I know."

Malcolm returned with two coffees and a donut bag. He tossed the bag to Eve and positioned the two coffees in the car's cupholders. He looked from Eve to Aunt Nicki and back to Eve. "What did I miss?"

Eve clutched the bag to her chest. Her hands shook.

"Trading beauty secrets," Aunt Nicki said. She put the car in reverse, and they peeled out of the parking lot. Ten minutes later, Aunt Nicki pulled up to a featureless gray garage with a guard booth. There was nothing to indicate that this building housed a branch of WitSec, the Witness Security Program. A blue-uniformed guard checked her ID and Malcolm's and shined a flashlight at Eve's face, and then the garage door rattled up. Aunt Nicki drove in, and it lowered behind them. She pulled into a parking spot, diagonal again.

"You could straighten the car," Malcolm commented.

"You could have driven."

"Just saying, the next person is likely to think it's straight and pull out and—"

"Maybe have to turn the wheel. Yeah, that would be so terrible. I don't think so. Parking perfectionist. You have issues." Aunt Nicki and Malcolm both stepped out of the car. This time, Eve didn't get to enjoy the moment of silence when they both shut their doors; Malcolm yanked hers open immediately. She wished she had a moment to regroup. Or a day. Or a year.

Still clutching the bag with the jelly donut, she stepped out of the car. She regretted it instantly. *Cage*, she thought. Her eyes darted around the garage. Walls, close. Ceiling, low. She headed for the door, striding quickly.

"Look at that, she remembers the way," Malcolm said softly behind her.

"She's been here enough," Aunt Nicki said.

"Not this level. Usually we park on C."

"Whoo-hoo, it's a miracle," Aunt Nicki said. "You read too much into everything."

"And you have the patience of a five-year-old."

"Part of my charm," Aunt Nicki said. "Just for the record, I don't approve of any of this. You're taking too big a risk."

His mouth quirked. "Lou believes I don't risk enough."

"He just wants different kinds of risks, whereas I think you're both insane."

Eve halted in front of the door. She wanted in. Now! She pushed on the door. It didn't budge. Malcolm reached around her and waved his ID card in front of a panel, and then the door unlocked with a *snick* sound.

Inside wasn't much better.

Bright lights filled the hall and reflected off silver-and-white walls. The air tasted stale. She didn't think she'd ever noticed that before, but it felt like chalk on her tongue. Outside tasted damp. Home tasted mildewy. The library tasted like warm dust.

"Let her lead," Malcolm said.

"Lead where?" Aunt Nicki asked.

"Out," Eve said. She counted her steps—twenty-five to the elevator. She pushed the up button, then stepped inside when the elevator opened. Malcolm and Aunt Nicki scooted inside after her as she pressed five.

"Five?" Aunt Nicki asked. "But that's—"

"Shh," Malcolm said.

"Out," Eve repeated. She was certain of it.

The elevator doors slid open. Eve strode forward, trusting instinct or memory to lead her. She turned left and then right. She halted in front of a massive steel door.

Two armed guards on either side shifted as they watched her. She touched the elaborate gears of the lock. *Maybe I'm wrong. Maybe this isn't . . .* Malcolm flashed his badge. So did Aunt Nicki.

The guards twisted wheels on either side of the door, and Malcolm punched numbers into a keypad. The steel door rolled open. Eve hesitated for an instant and then walked inside. Immediately she felt the coldness suck against her skin. She walked through a blank corridor toward the next door.

Malcolm placed his hand on a pad. It scanned his palm, and the door slid open. The next door required a combination code, which Aunt Nicki entered. The fourth set of doors was guarded again. One of the guards radioed for permission, which was granted.

As the last door slid open, Eve prepped herself. *This is it*, she thought. She could feel it, her destination. Malcolm gestured for her to proceed, and she strode forward.

Inside . . . it was empty.

She halted in the center of the room. Spinning, she looked in all directions. The room was vast, with a silver ceiling far above them. The walls were bare silver, smooth and cold. The floor was spotless white. Except for the door they'd come through, the room was featureless.

All the certainty drained out of her, flushed away. She started to shake again. This wasn't . . . She didn't know this place. Or at least she didn't remember it. It was just a room, an empty room.

The two agents watched her.

Eve circled the perimeter of the room. Her reflection followed her, crisp on the silver. She saw no reason for this empty room to be guarded, and she didn't know why she'd been so sure this was her destination. This . . . this was nothing.

"You were expecting a big breakthrough, weren't you?" Aunt Nicki said to Malcolm.

Eve felt empty inside, as empty as the room.

Malcolm held his hand out to Eve. "Come with me." He sounded tired and sad. "There's still time."

"Not much," Aunt Nicki said softly. "Not much."

Eve crossed the room and took Malcolm's hand. His hand was warm, but she felt cold inside and out.

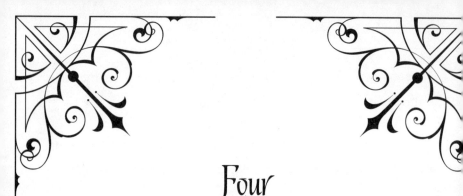

# Four

EVE LET THE AGENTS lead her out of the silver room. On her right, Malcolm cupped Eve's elbow gently. On her left, Aunt Nicki gripped Eve's upper arm so hard that Eve could feel each fingernail denting her flesh, as if Aunt Nicki's nails were coated in steel instead of wine-red nail polish. Eve felt numb inside, as if every ounce of energy had been drained by her failure.

As she and the agents exited, Eve saw that the security guards were staring at them. Both Aunt Nicki and Malcolm ignored the guards, but Eve stared back. One guard flinched and looked away. Surveillance cameras swiveled to record them as they passed through the other doors. The second set of guards did not react.

Aunt Nicki stabbed the elevator button with her index finger. In silence, Eve watched the numbers flick up to five. The doors slid open, and the two agents shepherded Eve into the elevator. Pivoting in sync, they flanked her, and Malcolm pressed number three. The elevator doors slid shut. Neither agent looked at her.

The elevator lurched downward, and tinny music echoed. Eve listened to it and pictured a carousel, shrouded in fog. A memory? A vision? Neither?

Aunt Nicki said to Malcolm, "Lou is going to rip out one of your balls."

"So long as it's not the right one," Malcolm said. "Right one's made of steel."

"He'll rip it out, pickle it, and display it at the holiday party between the poinsettias."

The music swelled. A thin, sour flute squeaked the melody. Eve tried to think of something, anything, to say to the two agents, especially to Malcolm, who had believed in her.

"Man of Steel Balls or not, Lou has your kryptonite," Aunt Nicki said. "You can count on it. Whatever it is, he'll have ferreted it out. It's his modus operandi."

"She is my sole concern," Malcolm said. "He knows that."

The elevator lurched to a stop, and the doors opened. Eve saw drab brown walls. A plaque directed visitors to the reception desk. "I remember this place," Eve said. She meant it as a peace offering—at least her mind hadn't utterly betrayed her.

"Fantastic." Aunt Nicki shoved Eve forward into the hall.

Malcolm strode past her, and Eve trailed after him. She did remember the third floor. She'd spent days here before they'd moved her to the house on Hall Avenue. She knew the blue carpet, worn in spots and patched with duct tape. She knew the fake plants, brilliant green and coated in dust. Several office doors were shut, but a few were open, and she saw file cabinets and chairs, framed diplomas on the walls, family photos and coffee mugs on the desks—all familiar.

Eve stopped outside Malcolm's office. A brass nameplate was nailed next to the door: MALCOLM HARRINGTON, US MARSHAL. A red, white, and blue flag on a toothpick was wedged into the top of the nameplate. She touched the flag.

"You put that there," Malcolm said.

She nodded. "It was on a cake."

"Yippee-ki-yay. She remembers desserts." Aunt Nicki pushed past Eve into Malcolm's office and flopped into the desk chair. Head back and eyes closed, Aunt Nicki spun the chair in a circle.

The cake had been served at a party for Malcolm. Red, white, and blue frosting. Vanilla inside. He'd brought Eve a piece with the toothpick flag on it, and she'd eaten it in his office curled up in one of the worn leather chairs. She'd saved the toothpick.

"You're in my chair," Malcolm said to Aunt Nicki.

"You won't be able to use it for a while," Aunt Nicki said. "You are about to be spanked." She dropped her feet hard on the floor to quit spinning, but she didn't open her eyes.

Eve heard footsteps in the hall behind them. She started to turn to see, but Malcolm propelled her into the office. He shut the door behind him. "You shouldn't take such glee in this," Malcolm said, again to Aunt Nicki.

"I take zero glee." Opening her eyes, Aunt Nicki looked at Malcolm. Her expression was serious. "I know as well as you what's at stake."

Eve wanted to ask what was at stake, but before she could, Malcolm knelt in front of her. "It will be okay," he said. "No one blames you. You shouldn't be afraid." She hadn't been until he said those words. Now, her heart thumped faster and her throat felt tight. Across the office, the door was thrown open. Rising, Malcolm blocked Eve, but she saw around his elbow. A bald man in a gray suit with suspenders filled the doorway. His tie was loose, and his scalp had a sheen of sweat that reflected the fluorescent lights. This was Lou. He was a foot shorter than Malcolm and a foot wider, but he seemed to loom over the office. Eve shrank back.

Lou spoke, his voice mild. "Agent Harrington, are you trying to give me an aneurysm?"

Malcolm straightened. "No, sir." His voice was as sharp and crisp as a salute.

"Because my wife—you know, the doctor with the fancy degree—demands that I cut out all stress from my life," Lou said. Listening to his voice, Eve began to shake. She knew his voice. Oh, yes, she knew it deep, the way she knew the pulse in her veins and the breath in her lungs. "Already cut out red meat, red wine, sausage, and bacon. And you know how I feel about bacon. There's no other food with a scent more perfectly designed to trigger the appetite than bacon. You could pump the smell of bacon into a room full of vegetarians after a veggie-burger-eating contest, and every one of them would crave cooked pig before the end of an hour. So explain to me exactly why you are rendering my no-bacon sacrifice moot by giving me an aneurysm."

"I took a calculated risk," Malcolm said. "It was mine to take."

Lou's voice was still as soft as a cat's purr. "If we lose her, we lose the case."

Eve had heard his voice in the background while medical equipment beeped in rhythm with her heartbeat. She'd heard it when she'd woken with tubes shoved down her throat and her skin feeling as if it had been burned from her bones. Even though she wasn't in the hospital anymore, Eve felt her heart thump fast and wild like a chased deer, and she retreated from him and his soft voice. She bumped into a table, and papers spilled onto the floor.

In one smooth movement, Malcolm scooped the papers back onto the table and guided Eve to the closest leather chair. "Breathe," he said. "Deep breaths. In and out."

She looked into his warm brown eyes and obeyed. Breathing, she sank into the chair. She wished he were next to her all the time, reminding her to breathe, making her feel safe. She kept her eyes fixed on his, trying not to see Lou looming behind him.

Malcolm kept his eyes on her as he said to Lou, "I'd like to discuss this elsewhere."

"You think she understands?" Lou asked. He'd ordered the surgeries, she remembered. He'd said when it was enough or not enough. She heard him in her memory, clear in the haze.

He'd never spoken directly to Eve, only to the doctors and nurses. Remembering, Eve gulped in air. She'd spent days, weeks, in that hospital room.

"Yes, I do," Malcolm said. He fetched a computer tablet off his desk and handed it to Eve. "I'll be back soon," he told her. She heard the reassuring promise in his voice. "You can look through the photos again."

She ran her fingers over the dark, cold screen of the tablet as she watched Malcolm follow Lou out of the office. Picturing the operating room, she wanted to call him back—*don't go with him!*—but she didn't move or speak. She saw Malcolm's silhouette through the beveled glass window. And then he was gone.

"What's Lou going to do to him?" Eve asked.

"Flay him, fillet him," Aunt Nicki said. "Since when do you care?"

"I care." Saying it out loud felt like a jolt of electricity through her body. She shouldn't care. But she did. She wanted to shoot out of the chair, chase after Malcolm, and make sure he was safe.

Aunt Nicki snorted. "Look at the faces if you care so damn much."

Eve looked down at the screen, a dark mirror. Her own green eyes stared hollowly back at her. The left side of her face was obscured by the glare of the fluorescent lights. She thought she looked like a ghost staring out at herself.

He'd said to look through the photos again, but she didn't know what he meant. She had no memory of this tablet or any faces. She felt as if a fist were curled inside her stomach. She could remember a piece of cake but not this, the operating room but not level five, this office but not her home before it.

Aunt Nicki shoved her chair back and stood. Without a word, she stalked around Malcolm's desk. Leaning over Eve, Aunt Nicki tapped a button on the tablet, and it flashed on. A photo of a teenage girl appeared. She had sour lips and hostile eyes underneath a rainbow of eye shadow. Aunt Nicki slid her finger across the screen and a new face appeared, a teenage boy with a single braid in his hair. He had dark skin and black eyes, and he wore an embroidered gold shirt. His expression was serene.

"Should I recognize them?" Eve asked.

"Never have before," Aunt Nicki said. "But let's be optimists and say sure! Your best buds, all in high definition. You used to share lunches, have sleepovers, trade homework answers, play truth or dare, borrow one another's clothes."

Eve slid her finger across the screen the same way Aunt Nicki had. There were dozens of photos, all close-ups. Half were male, and half were female. Most looked to be Eve's age, or close to it. She tried to conjure up memories to match the photos, but she felt nothing as the faces flickered past. "You're lying."

Aunt Nicki leaned in close. Her face was inches from Eve's. Her eyes bored into Eve's. "Prove it. Prove you're worth all he did to find you, all we are risking to keep you. Remember them."

In the photo on Eve's lap, a girl wore a smile with crooked teeth. She had freckles on the bridge of her nose, and antlers that sprouted in the midst of her limp red-brown hair. Eve studied her and shook her head. She didn't know her.

Eve slid her finger to bring up a new face, a sandy-haired boy with a pointed chin. Next, a boy who needed to shave. He wore a black chain around his forehead. Next, a girl with a pale-green face. She had pearly scales on her neck. Next, a gangly teen with the face of a Doberman on his bony shoulders. And then back to another human face, a girl with jet-black hair and sorrowful eyes. Frozen in their photographs, the faces stared out at her with accusing eyes. *Know me*, their eyes seemed to say. *Remember me.* But Eve didn't. She scanned through face after face, one after another, as Aunt Nicki returned to Malcolm's desk. Green eyes, brown eyes, red eyes, cat eyes, black eyes, milky eyes, blue eyes. Her hand shook as her finger slid across the screen, summoning more faces of strangers. "I don't know you," she whispered at the screen. "I don't know you!"

A hand caught her wrist.

Her hand was gently lifted up, her fingers lifted from the screen. Eve raised her face to look up at Malcolm. She didn't read any blame in his eyes. Just pity.

Eve swallowed hard once, twice. Her throat felt thick.

He touched her cheek with one finger. He studied the damp remnant of a tear as if it were a jewel glittering in the fluorescent light. Eve touched her own cheek. She hadn't felt herself crying, but her skin was damp.

In a hushed voice, Aunt Nicki said, "Is she . . . ?"

"Just for the record, I *am* right, no matter who approves or doesn't." Malcolm put his hand protectively on Eve's shoulder.

"Huh."

Coming around the desk, Aunt Nicki peered at her as if

Eve were a strange new bug. Eve turned away, but Aunt Nicki caught her chin and tilted her face up. Pulling away, Eve spun toward Malcolm.

"Didn't her eyes used to be brown?" Aunt Nicki asked.

Ignoring her, Malcolm said to Eve, "Lou wants you to meet a few people. Kids your age. They're waiting for us in the cafeteria."

Aunt Nicki jerked to attention. "Them? She can't!"

"He insists," Malcolm said, his eyes on Eve.

"Damn, Lou has balls," Aunt Nicki said. "Stolen from all his prior employees. You have to talk him out of it. You know what they're like—"

Malcolm rubbed his fingertip against his thumb. "We have no choice. He's curious, he said. And the other options were worse."

Aunt Nicki shook her head vehemently. "She's not the same—"

"She can handle it." He squatted so their eyes were level. Eve felt herself caught in his intense brown eyes. "Can't you?"

Eve ignored Aunt Nicki. Malcolm's eyes were warm and encouraging, as if he hadn't noticed how she failed him again and again and again. "Of course," Eve said.

His mouth quirked in a half smile, an expression she'd seen so often on him that she'd memorized it. She remembered all of his expressions. "Good girl," he said.

❋

As Eve trailed after Malcolm through the halls and between the cubicles, she listened to the *whoosh* of the air conditioner, the hum of the server room, and the churn of a printer as it spat out pages. *This isn't right*, she thought. She knew this place better than she knew any place, and it didn't . . . sound right. She should hear the receptionist's radio. At least one TV should be tuned to the local news. The police scanner should be crackling with voices. More important, the offices should be filled with marshals and their staff. Their conversations on the phone, to witnesses, and to one another should have drowned out the air conditioner and the computers.

The quiet made her skin prickle.

After she passed the third empty interrogation room, Eve asked, "Where is everyone?"

Malcolm pointed to a red light that flashed on the ceiling. "High profiles on the floor. Only essential personnel in the office. Best to limit exposure."

"Is that who I'm to meet?" she asked. She wondered what "high profile" meant and why it was important to limit exposure.

"It's 'whom,'" Malcolm said.

"Whom," Eve repeated dutifully.

"Never met anyone who didn't sound pretentious saying 'whom,' though. Best to just imitate what people say and not overthink it. If you start thinking about it, English doesn't make much sense. For example, the plural of 'tooth' is 'teeth,' but the plural of 'booth' isn't 'beeth.' The word 'abbreviation' isn't short. Neither is 'monosyllabic.'"

He halted outside the cafeteria, and the lecture abruptly ended.

"Did you teach me everything I know?" Eve asked.

"No," he said.

"Who did?"

"You did," he said. "You listened; you learned." He rapped her forehead lightly. "You. Not me. Not Lou. Not anyone." He glanced at the cafeteria door. "That's something not everyone understands. You know more than you think you do, more than you believe you remember."

*But I don't remember!* she wanted to shout. She didn't. It wouldn't have helped. Instead, she followed Malcolm's gaze, looking at the cafeteria door. It was blue, with a notice that read INTERAGENCY BILLIARDS RESCHEDULED, TUESDAY, 4:00 P.M. It also had a no-smoking sign, a poster with instructions for what to do if someone were choking, and a reminder to follow security protocol. Eve heard three voices through the door: two male and one female. She noticed that the muscles in Malcolm's neck had bunched up.

Eve listened to the voices, but they were muffled by the door. She couldn't distinguish individual words. "Are they connected to my case?" she asked. "Will they help me remember?"

He didn't answer. Instead, he said, "After this, I'll take you for pizza. Garlic knot crust. Kills your breath for hours, but worth it." He pushed open the cafeteria door and then added in a low voice, "Don't provoke them. Don't question them. Don't trust them."

Inside was the cafeteria: yellow-and-green floor, round metal tables with chairs, refrigerator, water cooler. Before she'd moved in with Aunt Nicki, Eve had eaten here, either food that the agents brought for her or food from the vending machines that sold vacuum-sealed sandwiches, wilted salads, and hard-boiled eggs of dubious freshness.

It felt a little like she was home.

She decided that was the saddest feeling she'd had yet.

Opposite the vending machine and kitchenette was a lounge area with a pool table, a TV, and a brown couch. The couch was backed against a wall-size mirror that Aunt Nicki had once said was designed to make the cafeteria look larger than it was—a stupid effect, she'd said, since it made you feel as though you were being watched. Eve tried to remember when they'd had that conversation, but she couldn't.

Two boys, each about sixteen or seventeen, were at the pool table. One leaned on the table, and the other lounged against the wall. Both had the same studied ease as models at a fashion shoot. Their faces were sculpted and smooth, as if carved from marble or ice, and she could see the curve of muscles against their shirts.

On the couch was a girl, also sixteen or seventeen, with blue-black hair. Her tanned legs were tucked under her and her head was cocked to the side, resting on her hand, as she flipped through a book. She was as beautiful as a statue, too, and if it weren't for the way she turned the pages, Eve would have thought she was made of molded plastic.

Malcolm propelled Eve into the room in front of him. "Kids, this is Eve."

All three of them swiveled their heads to look at her.

Instinctively Eve shrank backward. She bumped into Malcolm. Solid as a wall, he didn't budge. All three sets of eyes stared at her without blinking. She stared back. Looking at them felt like looking at herself in the mirror. Like her new face and body, they were all too perfect.

One of them—the boy who was leaning against the pool table—broke into what looked like a well-rehearsed smile, wide enough to seem friendly but with enough of a twist to convey boyish charm. "Welcome!" he said. His blond hair fell lazily over his eyes, and he pushed it back as if aware that the gesture made him look even more handsome. He was holding a pool cue in his other hand. He twirled it in a circle and then laid it down on the pool table. "We were about to play a new game. You can join us, Eve."

"Can she?" the other boy asked. He raised one eyebrow in a perfect arch. Again, it looked like a rehearsed expression, or like he was a marionette whose master had twitched a string. He had brown hair that was so perfectly still it looked as if it had been carved out of wood. She wondered how she knew what a marionette looked like—did Malcolm show her one, or had she learned on her own?

"Aw, Big Scary Agent Man looks nervous." The girl's lips curved into a smile, which she aimed like a weapon at Malcolm. "Don't worry. We'll play nice."

Eve felt Malcolm squeeze her shoulder as if to reassure her—or warn her. "I have a report to file for Lou," he said. "I'll be back in an hour. Eve . . ." His face tightened, as if he wanted to say something and then changed his mind. "I will be back." He exited before Eve could formulate a reply other than *Don't leave me with these people.*

Plastering a smile on her face, Eve took a step backward

toward the door. She thought of the look on Aunt Nicki's face and the red light in the hall that had emptied out the agency. She shouldn't have said she could handle this, at least not without clarification. It wasn't at all comforting to think that this was Lou's idea, not Malcolm's.

The boy with the purposefully tousled hair left the pool table and strode across the cafeteria with his hand outstretched. "I'm Aidan. You must be scared. This is all so different, and Mr. Strong Silent Type—"

"His name is Big Scary Agent Man," the girl corrected.

"—didn't explain much, I bet, when he extracted you from your home and family." Aidan clasped Eve's hand. She started to shake his hand as Malcolm had taught her, but Aidan twisted her wrist and kissed the back of her hand. His lips felt cool, like water.

The black-haired beauty on the couch spoke again. "Aidan, quit flirting with the new girl. You'll scare her off, and I need someone new to talk to. The last batch of innocents bored me to tears. Really, they need to set higher standards—he only targets the best of the best." She uncoiled herself and laid her book, a slim volume with the title *Metamorphosis* by Franz Kafka, on the couch. She crossed to Eve but didn't offer to shake hands. "Except for your eyes, you could pass for my sister. The younger one, not the dead one."

Up close, Eve could see her eyes were golden, the color fading into the white so only thin crescents of white framed the gold. Her pupils were like black lightning strikes in the center. She had lion eyes. Or snake eyes. Not human eyes.

Eve tried not to let any reaction show on her face.

"I've chosen the name Victoria," the snake-eyed girl said. "I think it has flair."

Aidan continued to smile. "I'm Aidan, as I said, and that's Christopher, though he prefers to be called Topher, which is idiotic but we tolerate it."

Topher still lounged against the wall. "I choose to be less generic." He had clean-cut hair and a chiseled jaw, and wore a V-neck sweater and khaki pants. He could have stepped out of any magazine in the agency lobby. "'Topher' is sophisticated yet casual."

"'Topher' is a douche," Aidan said.

"Enough." Victoria waved her hand lazily at the boys as if she were a queen silencing peasants. Topher tipped an imaginary hat at her in response.

"Excuse us. We love meeting people like us. You'll have to forgive our enthusiasm." Aidan's voice was lazy and smooth. He didn't seem enthusiastic. None of them did. The girl regarded Eve as if she were a potentially interesting specimen, and the other boy wore a sneer that bordered on hostile.

She found her voice. "That's . . . fine." People like us?

Aidan smiled again, as if they were already firm friends. "Of course, we can't ask the usual nice-to-meet-you questions, like where are you from and who is your family. That wouldn't be appropriate here. Rules, you know."

Eve nodded, grateful for the rules. She wouldn't have to explain why she couldn't answer simple questions like where she was from.

"But you *can* tell us a few choice tidbits," Victoria said. "Such as, what can you do?"

Eve thought of the birds on the wallpaper and the change to her eyes. Once, she'd caused a forsythia bush to bloom out of season. Another time, she'd lit a candle in Malcolm's office without matches. She didn't think she could talk about any of that. "I have a job at a library. I think that means I can alphabetize."

Aidan laughed. He had a cascading chuckle that filled the room. At least she'd succeeded in making one of them laugh, though it didn't seem to help. The air still felt stifling, and the room felt crowded with just the four of them.

"Harsh," Topher said. "They're making you work? Oh, tell me she doesn't come from peasant stock. Does she smell like a goat? I can't abide goats. Filthy garbage-eaters."

"I *don't* work, at least not for them." Victoria examined her nails and frowned at one. Her nail polish was infused with glitter. "You should have made that clear when you arrived. They are required to ensure that we're comfortable. Proper treatment was established decades ago, long before our case."

"It's fine," Eve said, thinking of Zach. She'd liked talking to him. Words seemed to tumble out of his mouth. She'd also liked being within walls of books. There, she'd felt as close to safe as she could remember. Here . . . she didn't.

She shot a look at the clock, but only a few minutes had passed since Malcolm left. Aidan noticed her gaze. "You're right, Eve," he said. "We should start our game before we run out of time."

Victoria slipped her arm around Eve's waist. "Think of it as a getting-to-know-you activity. Your chance to prove that you're cool enough to hang out with us. We all went through it."

"I don't . . ." Eve tried to step away, but Victoria swept her toward the pool table.

"Oh, you'll love it," Victoria said. In a conspiratorial whisper, she added, "It's so very invigorating." She passed the pool table and positioned Eve next to the mirror wall in one corner of the cafeteria.

"But I don't know the rules," Eve objected.

"There are no rules." Victoria wiggled her fingers at her and then scooted to another corner. "Except stay in your corner until I say 'go.'" Aidan and Topher chose the other two corners, one by the vending machine and the other by the water cooler.

"I don't—" Eve began.

"Ready?" Victoria said.

Topher raised his hands, palms out. Sparks danced between his fingertips as if his hands were electrified. Eve felt words die in her throat as she stared at the sparks.

Victoria clapped in glee, like a child. "Set? Go!"

Aidan vanished.

The air popped, sucking into the space he'd vacated. Half a second later, he reappeared next to the pool table. He picked up a pool cue, winked at Eve, and then vanished again. He reappeared between Topher and the vending machine.

Still smiling, Aidan jabbed at Topher's throat with the pool cue—hard, as if he wanted it to pierce straight through his jugular. Eve felt her entire body freeze at the sudden, unexpected violence of the gesture.

Before the tip touched his throat, Topher slapped his hands together and caught the pool cue between his palms. White-hot sparks leaped from his hands onto the wood. Aidan dropped the pool cue as electricity raced up and down it.

Victoria was laughing.

Eve flattened herself against the mirror. Her mind shrieked at her to run. But the door was beyond the two boys. Glancing at Victoria, Eve saw her transformation: first her body stretched and narrowed, and then her skin puckered into scales. Her mouth opened to expose needle-sharp fangs, and the snake that used to be a girl hissed at Eve. *Who are these people?* Eve wondered.

With his hand engulfed in white sparks, Topher threw a punch. Aidan vanished, and Topher's fist swept through the empty air in front of him. Aidan reappeared on top of the pool table. "Is that the best you can do, pretty boy?"

"Not by a long shot," Topher said.

Against the mirror, Eve didn't let herself breathe. She wanted to melt into the wall so they wouldn't notice her. This was their game? Watching, she waited for them to drop to the floor, caught in nightmares, ending this. But they didn't.

Victoria darted across the floor. Fangs extended, she aimed for Topher's ankle.

He pointed at her, and a bolt of electricity shot from his index finger. Hissing, Victoria curled backward. The bolt missed her and seared the floor, which blackened in a spattered star.

Aidan vanished again. He reappeared next to Eve. Casually, he leaned against the mirror. "Come on, new girl, play with us."

"I don't think I like this game," Eve said as neutrally as she could.

The snake swelled, transforming into the black-haired girl again. She rose gracefully in one movement and dusted off the front of her blouse. "But it's a delightful game, Evy. We call it 'Who's Next to Die?'"

*They're insane,* Eve thought. She glanced at the door. Most of the office was empty, but someone would hear her if she screamed for help, wouldn't they? Malcolm was out there; so were Lou and Aunt Nicki.

"Aw, how cute," Victoria said. "She's looking for a rescue."

Topher wove his hands back and forth in front of him, and the sparks danced and grew between his palms. "You can't depend on them. First lesson. He left you to play with us."

"Don't be shy, Evy." Victoria smiled encouragingly. "Each one of us has our specialty—that's why we were brought here. We're all special treasures. Prove that you're special, Evy." She lunged forward and transformed again while in motion. This time, her torso remained human while her legs fused into the tail of a massive snake. She smiled, revealing snake fangs. She flicked her forked tongue over her lipstick-coated lips.

"She's poisonous," Aidan commented, still conversationally. He vanished with a *pop* and reappeared again on top of the pool table. "Use your magic, Green Eyes. Show us what your talent is."

Eve climbed onto the couch, her back against the mirror.

The half snake, half girl reached the couch. Hissing, she coiled, prepared to attack.

Casually, Aidan picked up a billiard ball, and then another and another. In rapid fire, he hurled them at Eve. She ducked and dodged on the back of the couch. The balls hit the mirror, cracking it. "Fight if you want to live!" he called.

"Come on, new girl," Topher said. "Prove you won't be the next to die." His hands were ashen. White-hot sparks burned on his fingertips. He picked up one of the metal chairs, and electricity danced over it. Fangs wide, Victoria sprang onto the couch, aiming for Eve, as Topher threw the electrified chair at her.

She veered to the side, and the chair crashed into the mirror.

The mirror shattered.

Eve swept her arm over her head and then out, and the shards flew through the air like knives toward Aidan, Topher, and Victoria. As they broke from the wall, the remaining bits of the mirror fell away to reveal a hole in the wall. Eve glimpsed Malcolm and Lou standing on the other side, watching them from a room beyond. Malcolm's fists were clenched, and he was glaring at Lou. *A one-way mirror*, she thought.

And then the inevitable vision claimed her, and she collapsed.

❉

*I touch the stripes of moonlight that crisscross my skin. Silver, dark, silver, dark.*

*The box tilts, and I slide to the side. I brace myself but it's not enough, as the box shifts the opposite way and then back again. My flesh feels tender from banging against the walls, and I wrap my arms around my chest and curl tighter into a ball.*

*Sometime later it stops, and I lie still. I smell burned popcorn and urine. Outside, I hear the tinny music of the carnival. And then voices.*

*"She's broken." A woman's voice.*

*"She's perfect." A man.*

*And then I am outside the box—the box is the size of my palm, and I am restored to my true size. I feel dirt and patches of grass under my back. Neon lights blink above me, words that I can't read because they are reversed and twisted. They blink out and don't return. It's black. After a while, I see stars.*

*I watch the stars and then realize they are on a string. They're not stars at all. They're boxes dangling from a silk ribbon, like charms on a necklace. Inside them, I see faces, shrunken within their tiny cages. I reach out my hand toward them, and they scream.*

*"Shut her up," a voice says. The same man? Maybe. Maybe not.*

*A hand clamps over my mouth, and I realize that I am the one who is screaming. My throat aches, and I fall silent. The hand is gnarled and soft like a slice of withered fruit. It smells sour. I know this smell. I relax against the hand.*

*"Once upon a time," the Storyteller whispers in my ear, "a man wanted the stars. And he wanted them with such an awful want that it ate him from the inside."*

*With her hand on my mouth, I watch the magic boxes swing back and forth. The boxes are decorated with jewels. Sapphires, emeralds, and diamonds. Each edge is gilded in silver, and each clasp is unique—on one, the clasp is curved in the shape of a cat; on another, it's split into branches of a tree. Within the boxes are eyes. Blue eyes, brown eyes, black eyes, cat's eyes, red eyes, all watching as the Storyteller lifts me into her arms.*

*I see her face—and she is young. Her cheeks are smooth. Her wrinkles have been washed away. Her eyes are clear, with ivory whites and brown irises, as if her old milky-red eyes were glasses that she removed. Her hair is silk-soft and black. Only her hands are still old. She places one of her hands over my eyes.*

*I am again within a box. This time, I am carried for far longer. I knock from side to side as if being tossed from hand to hand. I see moonlight through the slats of my box. I see sunlight. And then I see moonlight again.*

*I hear the click of the lock, and the lid of the box is pried open.*

*"She's broken." A woman's voice again. Familiar, soothing.*

*"She's perfect." Again, a man. Familiar, frightening.*

*I squeeze myself tighter into a ball as he reaches in to touch me.*

# Five

EVE'S HANDS WERE WRAPPED around a glass of orange juice. She blinked at the pulp that swirled in the orange. Aunt Nicki was talking as she buttered toast. ". . . doesn't matter. If Lou says jump, we fetch the trampoline. You *have* to try harder."

She didn't remember coming into the kitchen, sitting down at the table, or drinking the orange juice. She didn't remember anything since the cafeteria and her last vision. Her hands tightened around the glass. *Calm*, she told herself. *Stay calm.* She looked out the window. Outside was bathed in pale yellow, as if it were morning.

"Are you even listening to me?" Aunt Nicki asked.

The clock over the refrigerator said 7:05. She swallowed. It was hard to breathe. Her lungs felt constricted, and the air in her throat felt as if it had hardened. It *was* morning. It had been late afternoon at the agency. She'd lost all her memories of last night, plus any memory of what she'd done since she woke—everything since her last vision.

She was wearing a pale-purple T-shirt and jeans—different clothes from yesterday. This shirt had a picture of a bird on it. She didn't remember putting it on, but she must have. She must have slept, woken up, showered, and dressed. Aunt Nicki snapped her fingers underneath Eve's nose. "You have work at seven thirty," Aunt Nicki said. "Pretend to care."

About to reply, Eve looked at her, and the words died in her throat. Aunt Nicki's black hair was cropped short above her ears, and her face was a deeper tan. Slowly, afraid of what she'd see, Eve twisted in her chair to look at the rest of the kitchen. Dishes were piled on a drying rack, enough to have been used for multiple meals. A collection of cereal boxes lined the counter. A half-eaten loaf of bread was shoved on top of the refrigerator. Photos were stuck to the fridge—more of her and Aunt Nicki. One of them had Aidan, the blond boy from the agency.

She crossed to the fridge. With shaking fingers, she eased the photo out from under a "Remember to Recycle" magnet. She and Aidan were next to each other in a booth. A pizza was on a checkered table in front of them. Both of them were smiling, and Aidan's arm was draped around her shoulder. She put the photo back on the fridge. She straightened it, shifted the magnet, and straightened it again before she finally stepped backward and inhaled.

Aunt Nicki was watching her.

"I . . . ," Eve began. She didn't know how to finish the sentence. "I need to get ready for work." She fled the kitchen for her bedroom. Shutting the door behind her, she leaned against it.

She saw little differences. Her sheets were rose-striped under the quilt instead of blue, and a stuffed monkey was propped up on one pillow. She'd never owned a stuffed animal as far as she knew. Leaving the door, she crossed to it and picked it up. The monkey's head flopped to the side. Clutching the monkey, she examined the rest of the room.

The birds were still missing from the wallpaper. She checked the top drawer—still there. But the other drawers were full of socks, underwear, shirts, and sweaters. She opened the closet. A few skirts and pants hung from hangers, and a few pairs of jeans were piled on a shelf. There was a mesh hamper half-full of dirty clothes that she had no memory of wearing. Eve closed the closet and hugged the monkey.

She hadn't forgotten a few hours. She'd forgotten days. Maybe weeks. *Bouts of short-term memory loss,* the doctors had said. Her mind had betrayed her. Again.

She started to shake so hard that her knees caved, and she sank to the floor. Closing her eyes, she tried to summon up any memory of the time between when she'd collapsed at the agency and this moment. Just one conversation. Or one breakfast. Or one sleepless night. She must have done *something*— the photo of her and Aidan with the pizza proved that. She remembered every detail of the moments before the vision: the white-hot sparks on Topher's fingers, the lazy smile on Aidan's lips, the flat stare of Victoria's snake eyes. Victoria's eyes had been golden. The billiard balls had been purple, blue, and red. The cafeteria had smelled faintly of pepperoni pizza and coffee, and the air had tasted stale, pumped in through the air-conditioner vents. She could resurrect every moment in her mind, including the vision of the silk ribbon with silver-edged boxes that shook as the wagon was pulled over bumps, cracks, and potholes in the road. After that . . . there was nothing. A blank, empty swirl in place of her memories.

Eve heard the door to the house open and shut. She listened to heavy footsteps in the hall. Outside her door, Aunt Nicki greeted Malcolm. Eve knew she should stand, but she felt as if the weight of the lost days held her to the floor. How many days? Or was it weeks? Months? *Weeks*, she guessed. Judging by the clothes and the trees outside, it was still summer. She could stand, open the door, and ask Malcolm . . . but she couldn't face the sight of his eyes, of the disappointment she'd see there.

A knock on the door. "Ready, Eve?" Malcolm called.

*No*, she wanted to say. But then she remembered the door had no lock. He could open it. She peeled herself off the floor and called, "Coming!" She laid the monkey on the pillow and crossed its arms so it looked as if it were defying the world, and then left the room.

Malcolm waited for her in the hall. Eve pasted a smile on her face, but he only glanced at her and then headed out the door. She followed him out of the house.

Outside, it was humid. The sticky air prickled on her skin. Eve sucked in a breath and smelled overripe trash. She heard a dog bark once, but didn't see anything move in either direction. Even the leaves were motionless on the trees.

The car was red with a gash on the back door. She'd never seen Malcolm in anything but a black car. She thought about teasing him, saying the car was blushing in embarrassment at the gouge in its paint—that seemed like something he'd like her to say. But maybe she'd already made that joke. It wasn't a very good joke anyway. She climbed into the passenger seat without saying anything.

Malcolm got into the driver's seat and locked the doors. His muscles were tense. He hadn't been this tense before. She wondered what had changed in the missing weeks.

Anything could have happened. Or nothing. She didn't know which would be worse.

Eve tried to think of what she could ask that would give her clues but wouldn't reveal her memory loss. She rejected every question she thought of. In silence, she watched him as he leaned forward, hands tight on the wheel.

He drove into the library parking lot. She suddenly wanted to be inside, surrounded by objects whose memories were permanent and unchanging, right there in black and white. Better, they wouldn't care how much of her own story she knew or didn't know.

But there would also be people inside. She wondered what she'd said to them, what they'd said to her, what she'd done. She thought of the boy Zach and wondered if he'd be there.

Malcolm parked near the entrance. He rubbed his hand over his eyes. He looked tired, as if he hadn't slept well in days. She wondered where he did sleep. She didn't know where he lived, if he had a family, what his life was like outside WitSec.

He must do more than shepherd her from home to work to the agency and back—if that was indeed what he'd been doing during the missing weeks.

"He won't stop," Malcolm said. "He'll find another way. I know the type. He believes he is justified or invincible, or he simply wants. If we don't catch him, it will begin again."

"I . . ." She searched for words. He must have meant the suspect in her case. Eve hadn't known the suspect was a he. And what would begin again?

"We can protect those who match the profile, but it's all guesswork. And he could simply change whom he targets." Heaving a sigh, he looked at her for the first time today. She saw thin red veins in the whites of his eyes, and the circles underneath were dark, almost bruises. "You are the key, Eve," he said. "I know it."

She swallowed hard and knew she couldn't tell him about her memory loss. Her eyes shifted away from his, and she focused on the clock. Seven thirty. She remembered the librarian, Patti Langley, saying her shift would start at nine o'clock. She must have been switched to an earlier shift. So much could have changed.

She felt Malcolm's hand on her shoulder. "I don't mean to pressure you, Eve. Lou's methods, though . . . I don't think either of us wants a repeat of that. We *have* to make forward progress."

She nodded. She couldn't think of any other response. She thought of the hospital—the drip of the IV, the beep of the monitors, the pain that gouged like a fork in her veins, and his orders for more, more, more. "I'd better . . . I have work." She put her hand on the door handle.

He squeezed her shoulder. "Don't let anyone know that you've forgotten again."

She froze. Her heart fluttered in her chest. Air roared in her ears. She hadn't . . . He couldn't . . . "How did you know?" Her voice sounded thin.

"I know you," he said simply.

"How often . . . ?" She licked her lips. She knew this had happened before, in the agency, in the hospital, but she didn't think it had happened here before. Maybe it had.

"Often enough."

"Why?"

He hesitated, as if considering many answers. "Your magic makes your mind unstable," he said at last.

"Can you fix me?"

The pity in his eyes made her throat feel tight. She blinked fast, her vision suddenly blurry, watery. "We're trying," he said. "All of this . . . Believe me, we're trying."

"Will my memories come back?"

"Maybe. I don't know."

"What do I do?" She meant about her memory, herself, the case, the lost weeks, all of it.

"Lie," he said. "Lie to everyone until you know the truth."

The door slid open.

She followed him inside, and the door slid shut behind them, erasing the sounds of outside that she hadn't even noticed: cars on the road, wind in the trees, a lawnmower hum in the distance. In the lobby, the clock ticked extra loud in the silence.

The lobby was coated in shadows. Bookshelves blocked the thin light from the windows, and the circulation desk created its own pool of darkness. Eve wondered why it was okay with Malcolm for her to enter an empty building with a boy she barely knew (or thought she barely knew)—especially a public building with shadows that could hide anyone. Before she'd entered the house on Hall Avenue, Malcolm had checked every room. He always watched the street as she got into his car. Yet he had simply dropped her off here.

She tried to tell herself that meant this place was safe.

She still didn't like the shadows or the silence.

"You get the lights, and I'll switch on the computers, okay?" Zach didn't wait for her to respond. Instead, he headed for a bin beside the door. It was positioned beneath a slot in the wall, and it overflowed with books.

She didn't know where the light switches were. She couldn't ask. Instead, she chose a direction and walked toward that wall, hoping she'd see the switches before Zach noticed that she was aimless. At least she could remember what a light switch was. Zach rolled the book bin toward the circulation desk. A few books toppled off the top, and he bent to pick them up— buying her time to spot a bank of light switches by the corner.

She lunged for them and flicked them on. Yellowish light spread across the lobby. The shadows faded somewhat, washed away, and she exhaled in relief.

With the lights on, Zach ducked behind the desk and turned on the computers. One after another, they hummed to life. She watched him, glad he hadn't asked her to do that, trying to memorize which buttons he pushed in case she had to do it later. As if he'd felt her watching him, Zach raised his head. "You okay? You seem . . . quiet today. Not that you aren't usually the antigarrulous type. And that was an impressively convoluted sentence, if I do say so myself."

"Very impressive," she agreed.

"Like the New York pretzel of sentences. Or croissant. And now I'm hungry." Finished with the computers, he set the paper bag that she'd seen him carrying on the desk, and he pulled out a bagel with flecks of pepper, onion, sesame seeds, and poppy seeds. "Your bagel, my lady." It rained seeds on the desk. His was plain.

She picked up the bread—"bagel," he'd called it. With all the seeds, it looked like a feast for a bird. But she must have eaten one before. He was acting as if this was their routine. Out of the corner of her eye, she watched him split his bagel in half, spread cream cheese on both halves, and then close them back together like a sandwich. She mimicked him and then took a bite. The seeds stuck to her teeth.

"Despite legends to the contrary," Zach said, "bagels have nothing to do with the shape of the King of Poland's stirrups."

Eve heard a soft thump. "Did you hear that?" she asked. The bagel suddenly tasted like cardboard in her mouth. She quit chewing and listened. She'd thought the sound had come from Patti Langley's office. But her door was shut, the light was off, and the sound didn't repeat.

"Hear what?" Zach asked. "The agony of a dozen legends, condemned to history's 'false' list, crying out at once? Also false: Twinkies having an infinite shelf life, and Caesar salad having anything to do with Julius Caesar."

She stared at the office door until she'd convinced herself she'd imagined the noise.

Finishing his bagel, Zach swept the crumbs into the bag. She handed him her partially eaten bagel. "I'd say you eat like a bird, but birds eat half their weight in food every day," he said.

"Just not hungry today."

"Too many factoids sour your appetite? Sorry. It's just that you . . ." He trailed off. "Right. Okay. We should process the returns."

After disposing of the bag, Zach set himself up at one of the computers. He typed a few keystrokes and then began to scan the items from the bin. Mimicking him, Eve stationed herself at a nearby computer, and her fingers froze over the keyboard. She didn't know what to type. In fact, she had no memory of ever having used a computer, though she knew she had spent many hours watching Malcolm and Aunt Nicki use theirs. A screen blinked, demanding a user name and password.

She glanced at Zach. He continued to pluck books out of the bin and scan them with a handheld scanner. Every few books, he'd type numbers into the computer. *Lie*, Malcolm had said. She'd have to lie with actions as well as words, she realized. "I'll pass you the books," Eve offered. "It'll go faster that way." She scooted around him and picked books out of the bin.

"Uh, okay. Good idea."

They worked side by side as the clock ticked closer to 8:00 a.m.

At a few minutes to eight, the library door slid open, and Eve jumped. Waving at them, a man strode into the lobby. "Good morning, Zach. Eve." He headed for the Children's Room without slowing. A librarian. She forced herself to breathe normally.

"Eve, you sure you're okay?" Zach asked. "You seem jumpier than a cat on a hot tin roof, which I have never personally witnessed but must be spectacular, at least for the observer if not for the cat."

"Fine." She plastered a smile on her face and did her best to keep it there as other librarians drifted in. All of them greeted Zach and Eve by name. Eve knew none of them. After each hello, she pretended to be absorbed in her task and hoped no one would try to talk to her. Soon patrons began to arrive. Eve dug through the books in the bin until it was empty and all the books were sorted onto carts. At last, she looked up.

Patti Langley was watching her.

Eve bit back a yelp. She hadn't heard her arrive. She glanced over her shoulder at Patti's office—the door was open. How had she slipped by? *Never mind*, Eve told herself. Patti was here now. Eve forced herself to breathe evenly, and she summoned up a smile for the library director. At least hers was a face that Eve knew.

Patti did not smile back. "I told you I want you in the stacks. No interaction with patrons."

"Oh. I . . ." Eve couldn't think of an excuse. A hush had fallen over the lobby, as if everyone had slowed to look at her. She shot a glance at the other librarians and the patrons. None of them were paying any attention to her. Still, she felt eyes on her. Shivers crept over her skin.

"Done!" Zach announced as he added the final book to a cart. "Don't worry, Ms. Langley. We're going." He snagged Eve's hand and pulled her out from behind the circulation desk. She continued to feel watched as he led her through the lobby and into the main library, hurrying past the reference librarians, a man in a gray suit with a newspaper, and a woman with a toddler.

Soon they were within the stacks. She felt as if the shelves were folding around her protectively. At last, the feeling of being watched began to fade.

"Safe now," he said. She noticed he still held her hand. He seemed to realize it at the same moment. He dropped her hand and then cleared his throat. "Someday you'll have to tell me what you did to get under Peppermint Patti's skin."

Eve shrugged and looked at the bookshelves. It was hard to look at him while she lied. "She didn't like me from the beginning." She supposed she could be telling the truth, for all she knew. *I don't know enough*, she thought. *I'm going to make a mistake.* Or more mistakes. She'd reach a critical mass of mistakes, and then . . . She didn't know. She wished she could claw at the empty places inside her until she ripped through to expose what she *did* know.

"Well, I liked you from the beginning." He grinned at her. Startled, she stared at him. "Hey, you usually laugh when I flirt like that. You sure you're all right?"

She clung to that clue of what she'd forgotten: he'd flirted, and she'd laughed, even if she couldn't remember it. "Tell me why you like me."

His grin vanished. He had a crease in his forehead between his eyebrows, and his lips were pursed as if he were worried. "You're fascinating. You're . . . like a closed-up flower. You're a shell with mother-of-pearl inside. You're a cloud that hasn't formed into a shape yet, but could. You're shadows layered over shadows."

"You mean that."

"Every word." Zach didn't break eye contact. His eyes were brown, as warm as Malcolm's. "Even the stupid poetry clichés, which, let's face it, were pretty much all of them. You are the mystery and excitement that I have been craving my entire life."

"I'm not an unformed cloud. I'm a cloud that's broken open, and my insides are pouring out like rain." As she spoke, the feeling of safety dissipated. The stacks weren't hiding her; they were hiding others. She imagined eyes between the books, peering out at her. The shelves could hide a dozen listeners.

"Okay, that's way more poetic than mine." Zach caught her hand. "Hey, I'm not mocking! Okay, I am mocking a little. You are obviously having a bad day. And that is obviously an understatement. If you don't want to talk about it, I understand. But if you do . . . I'm your guy. Always."

She stared at her hand in his. His fingers twisted around hers, locking their palms together as if they were two halves of a broken whole. She wanted to believe him. "What do you want from me?"

"Undying affection?" Zach suggested. "Passionate love? But I'll settle for a little trust. You never talk about yourself or your life. I want to know you, Eve. Is that too pushy? I don't want to be too pushy. But you did ask."

"And you don't lie." Eve felt a smile creep onto her face, but it vanished in an instant as she heard voices near their shelves: a librarian guiding someone to a nearby section.

Zach dropped her hand and jumped back. His cheeks were tinted pink. "Patti will be by to check on us. We should, um, look useful."

Eve turned away from him and toward the shelves. "So . . . we shelve?"

"Or we select a book, mock it relentlessly, and then put it back on the shelves, which is pretty much the same thing that you said."

She supposed that's what they'd been doing these past weeks. That seemed nice.

Side by side, they scanned through the books, shifting those that were out of order. She was aware of his movements, taking a book down, shifting others over, and reshelving. Shelf by shelf, they worked through the section.

She wished she could remember this. She wished it so hard that her fingers shook. She had to squeeze the books to hold them steady. Yes, she'd lost memories before, but this time . . . This time it felt so much more immediate. She'd spent hours, days, in these bookshelves with this boy. She felt like if she reached out she could pull the trace of her lost self from the air around her. The memories should linger here, like ghosts. Ghost memories, all around her. Eve spread her fingers out and stared at them as if she could will them to catch and hold her lost memories.

She wondered if she'd lose today too, the next time her mind betrayed her. She didn't want it to slip through her fingers. She wanted to do something, something momentous, that would fix it in her memory so it couldn't slip away into nothingness, erased in a single, arbitrary moment.

"Zach?" Eve said.

"Hmm?"

Eve leaned toward him and pressed her lips against his. His eyes flew wide, and she felt him freeze. But as she was about to pull away, he kissed her back.

She didn't know she knew how to kiss. She had no memory of kissing anyone. But still, it felt natural, and it felt right. Eve wrapped her arms around his neck and wove her fingers into his soft, soft hair. She tasted his breath; still a hint of cream cheese. Close to her, his body felt warm, and his lips moved gently against hers as if whispering silent secrets.

She closed her eyes, shutting out the view of the books around them. The sound of distant voices, footsteps, the hum of computers, the rustle of pages, all faded. She could no longer feel the carpet beneath her feet. The solid ground had melted away, and she felt as if she were floating.

It felt both unreal and wonderfully real at the same time.

"Enough," a woman's voice said.

Zach broke away.

And then they fell.

Their feet hit hard on the carpeted floor. Zach staggered backward, catching himself on the shelves. Eve reached forward, steadying herself on him. He gripped her elbows. "What was—" he began. His eyes widened as he looked beyond Eve's shoulder, and he released Eve. "Ms. Langley!"

Catching her balance, Eve pivoted to face Patti Langley. The librarian looked pale, and Eve thought she saw a hint of fear. But it vanished fast, hidden beneath a scowl.

"Did you see that?" Zach asked her.

"Unfortunately, yes." Patti placed her hands on her hips. "This is not appropriate behavior for a library. I'd expected better of both of you."

Zach waved his hand at the ceiling. "No, no, I mean—we were flying! Seriously, feet off the ground! You must have seen it."

Eve opened her mouth and then shut it. She'd felt it too. But it wasn't possible. If she'd used magic, she would have fallen into a vision, not straight down onto the carpet, awake and alert. "We couldn't have been."

He looked at her. "You do sweep me off my feet in a cliché, metaphoric way. But this was literal! You must have felt it. We crashed down!"

Eve shook her head. She knew how it worked—if she used magic, she collapsed. It was the one constant. "It must have been your imagination."

"There was no flying," Patti said. "Or floating. Or even

hopping enthusiastically. There were only two library pages who weren't shelving." She waved at the shelves and the half-full book cart nearby.

"But—" Zach began.

Patti held up her hand. "Zachary, I'm going to have to ask you to work the front desk for the rest of the day."

He turned to Eve. "Eve—"

"It was a nice kiss. So nice it made me dizzy." Eve withdrew from him. "But my feet didn't leave the floor, and neither did yours."

"I was sure—"

"Zachary," Patti said. "Now."

Eve forced herself to smile at him. "You should do what she says." Shooting glances over his shoulder, Zach retreated through the shelves.

Both Patti and Eve were silent until Zach was gone.

Patti leveled a finger at Eve. "I can see the wrongness gathering around you like a storm." She tapped her sternum above her extra eyes as she said "see." "When your storm breaks . . . don't catch that boy in it. And don't use magic in my library ever again."

She left before Eve could think of a reply.

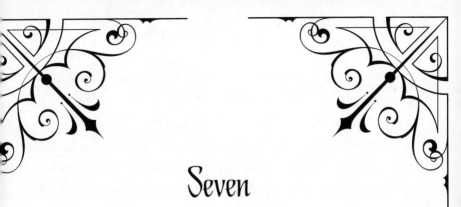

# Seven

FLUORESCENT LIGHTS BATHED THE library shelves in a sickly yellow. In several rows, the lights flickered or had already died. Eve avoided those. Aimless, she drifted deeper into the stacks.

Any time she heard footsteps, Eve veered into a different row. It wasn't difficult. The library patrons strode through the bookshelves with purpose, often lugging already-full book bags, and they zeroed in on one section of shelves. Sometimes they'd linger there, opening and shutting books, murmuring to themselves, and sometimes they'd strike, selecting a single volume and taking off with it. She watched them through the gaps in the books several rows away, and then she'd continue on, alone again.

As she passed by books, she ran her fingers over the spines. Bits of dust clung to her fingertips, and she wiped them on her jeans. She didn't open any of the books. It was enough to know that the words were there—that at least someone had remembered enough moments and facts to fill a book. Occasionally she noticed a book that had been misshelved and moved it. Oddly, that act made her feel better, calmer.

*If my insides were a bookshelf,* she thought, *I'd be a jumble of volumes, stacked in random order and filled with blank pages.*

She wandered deep into the library, going to the end of every row. Each row ended in a brick wall with a faded print of a cracked oil painting: a garden or a pond or a fruit bowl. Studying one, she decided that it was hideous and that she liked it. The scene was so motionless that it felt as though it were outside of time; there was no past or future to it, just a garden with blurred purple flowers and a too-blue sky.

"Eve?" A woman's voice.

Eve jumped and then pivoted to face a woman she didn't know. The woman was dressed in a mud-brown blouse, her gray hair held in a twist on her head. She wore slipper-like shoes that were soundless on the carpeted floor. She didn't hold a gun or look threatening in any way, but still Eve's heart pounded wildly.

"Your shift ended fifteen minutes ago," the woman said.

"Oh," Eve said.

"Your ride's outside, and he's impatient." She gestured toward the front of the library.

"I must have lost track of time." Eve winced at her own wording. In truth, she had no idea when her shift was supposed to end. Malcolm must be worried. He was always worrying—it was part of his job description. She was surprised he'd waited fifteen minutes instead of marching in to find her.

"Overachiever. You make the rest of us look bad." The

woman smiled as she said it to soften the words, and Eve attempted a smile back.

She headed through the stacks, past the reference desk, and into the lobby. Eve didn't see Zach. At the circulation desk, Patti watched Eve with her two visible eyes. Feeling Patti's eyes on her, Eve walked quickly out the sliding glass door.

She halted on the welcome mat.

A boy with tousled hair leaned against a fiery-red sports car. He raised his hand in a wave when he saw her. She scanned the parking lot, looking for Malcolm's car or even the SUV that had been parked there earlier. She didn't see anything that looked like an agency car.

Aidan could not be her ride.

"You coming, Green Eyes?" he called to her.

"With you?" Eve asked.

For an instant, he tensed—and Eve suddenly pictured a different boy, tensed like that, alert and listening, in the darkness. He'd worn an embroidered gold shirt. The image was so vivid that Eve was certain it was a memory, but she didn't know from when or where. And then Aidan relaxed and smiled lazily at Eve, destroying any similarity to her memory. "Yeah, with me. Unless you want to walk, which I wouldn't recommend since it looks like rain. You don't have the right complexion for 'drowned rat.'"

The memory didn't sharpen. She could picture the set of the boy's shoulders, the tension in his legs—as if he were caught between fight or flight—but she couldn't see his face. He was a shadow, and the world around him was a blur.

"There's nothing wrong with my complexion," Eve said.

Fact, not arrogance. The surgeries had left her with perfect skin.

"Of course not," he said smoothly.

She looked at the parking lot again. Still no Malcolm or Aunt Nicki. *This could be the routine,* she thought. The woman in the brown blouse had said "her ride" as if this were normal.

She continued to hesitate, glancing over her shoulder at the library lobby. From the circulation desk, Patti Langley watched her. Her hands were on the books, scanning them and handing them to patrons, but her eyes were unblinkingly fixed on Eve.

If this was the routine, she couldn't let Aidan guess she'd forgotten. And she couldn't let Patti think anything was wrong.

Malcolm's voice whispered in her memory. *Lie to everyone.*

Eve walked down the stairs.

Aidan opened the passenger door. "Your chariot, Princess of the Perfect Pores." He executed an elegant bow. "Get in. I'm starving, and everyone's waiting."

Climbing into the passenger seat, Eve wondered who "everyone" was, and whether they planned to try to kill her again. She looked once more at the lot and then the library.

Patti watched her from one of the lobby windows.

Aidan hopped into the car, turned on the ignition, and cranked up the radio. She felt the beat of the bass drum thump through the seat and into her thighs. "Ten points for each pedestrian; fifteen for the cyclists," he said over the music.

She kept her face impassive, as if his statement made sense.

"It's a joke. Hit them; rack up points. Like a video game. Really, you should try to absorb some of the local culture. It's fascinating stuff."

Eve fastened her seat belt as he slammed his foot on the gas. His tires squealed as he peeled toward the street. He slammed on the brakes at a stop sign as a woman walked her dog across the street. The woman glared at him as he inched forward, and he smirked. "Never can impress you, can I?"

"Her or me?"

"Don't play dense, Evy. It doesn't suit you."

"What does suit me?" she asked.

"Me, of course." He flashed a dazzling smile at her. Reaching over, he took her hand and laced his fingers through hers. He held her hand so easily that she was certain this was not the first time he'd done so. Eve felt the muscles in her body tensing as if they were braiding themselves together.

It was easier to swallow the loss of stretches of nebulous memories than to face the absence of a single specific memory. Aidan, holding her hand. Zach, shelving books beside her.

As he drove with his other hand, he played with her fingers, running his thumb across her knuckles. His hand knew hers. She looked away, and her eyes fixed on the side mirror— a black car with tinted windows was behind them.

She saw a street sign: Hall Avenue. She tensed even more. "You missed my turn," she said as evenly as possible. *I made a mistake*, she thought. *I shouldn't have gotten in this car. It's a trap.* She eased her hand away from his.

"Pizza, Green Eyes," Aidan said. "Like yesterday. And the day before."

"Oh." Eve felt her face flush red.

He was studying her instead of watching the road. She didn't like how speculative he looked, as if he knew what was wrong. She pointed at a traffic light as it switched to yellow. "Watch the road."

He sped through the red light.

The black car sped through it behind them.

She twisted in her seat to look backward, trying to see the driver's face through the tinted window. Savior, enemy, or chaperone?

"You want to lose our tail?" Aidan asked.

He'd seen the car. Eve couldn't tell from his statement if the car's presence was normal or alarming, and Aidan didn't wait for her to decide how to answer. He swung the car onto a side street, roaring past houses and dodging garbage cans.

The black car followed.

Aidan zigzagged through the town, choosing one-way streets that fed into others, until he peeled out onto the main road without pausing at the stop sign. He barreled over the median and reversed directions.

And all of a sudden, a memory bloomed in her mind. A city, at night. She'd been carried through the streets, skyscrapers' dark silhouettes blotting out the night sky. She'd felt the rapid heartbeat of the person who carried her. His feet were silent on the pavement; his breath was loud in the silence. She'd felt the wind in her face and through her hair. And she'd felt a laugh inside her as they'd escaped . . .

Eve, without meaning to, laughed out loud.

Grinning at her, Aidan floored the gas.

*Keep running*, her memory whispered to her. *Don't stop!* "Go there," she ordered. She pointed to a parking lot. The lot was empty, the pavement broken with tufts of withered grass in the fissures. "Left," Eve said, trying to chase the memory. "And then left again."

Aidan careened left.

The lot opened onto another street. At the light, Aidan yanked the wheel to the left again. "And we're behind him," Aidan said. "*That*, Green Eyes, is why I love you."

*He . . .* She felt as if her brain stalled at those words. The memory evaporated. Music from the radio pounded in her head. It had to be an expression—just something he said in the moment, right? Her brain couldn't have forgotten something as momentous as falling in love.

He drove up behind the black car and leaned on the horn. He then pulled around the black car, waved, and drove slowly and sedately to the parking lot of a restaurant with a neon sign that read MARIO'S HOUSE OF PIZZA. He parked and turned off the engine.

The black car parked beside them.

The window rolled down, and Malcolm glared at them.

Unclipping his seat belt, Aidan shot out of his seat and planted his lips on Eve's. His lips were hard, and his breath was warm. Eyes open wide, Eve didn't move.

Laughing, Aidan climbed out of the car and stretched. Slowly, Eve got out of the car. She trotted to Malcolm's window. Before he could speak, she said, "You could have warned me." She meant about everything: Aidan picking her up, whatever relationship she had with him, the fact that Malcolm would be following her.

"You asked to come here," Malcolm said.

"I did?"

"Lou told you it could help, exposure to others."

She digested that. "What do you think—" Before she could finish the question, Aidan put his hand on her shoulder.

"One slice of pepperoni," Malcolm said. "Extra cheese." He rolled the window back up again.

"Come on, Green Eyes. Garlic knots won't eat themselves." Aidan trotted to the door of Mario's House of Pizza. She glanced beyond Malcolm's car toward the traffic light and the strips of stores. She had, for an instant in the middle of the chase, touched her past.

Maybe exposure to Aidan would help her remember more.

Eve followed Aidan into the restaurant.

Inside, Mario's House of Pizza reeked of burned bread, like Aunt Nicki's toast, but tinged with the faint sting of antiseptic, like the hospital. The floor was sticky, the décor was red and white, and the tables were mostly empty.

"Good," Aidan said. "They're still here."

In one corner, Topher and Victoria had staked out a table. The table was for eight, and three of the empty seats had used paper plates, napkins, and cups in front of them. Topher raised his hand in a half salute, half wave. Victoria looked up from her book and tossed her hair, clearly broadcasting that she'd registered their arrival and was unimpressed.

Aidan curved his arm around Eve's waist and deliberately patted her butt. Eve froze, unsure if this was a common occurrence or new, and also unsure what reaction was expected.

Topher's eyebrows shot up toward his hairline. Aidan strolled to the table as if nothing unusual had happened. He parked himself at the table and swept aside the used plates with his arm.

Feeling Victoria and Topher's eyes on her, Eve approached the table more slowly and slid into a seat next to Victoria. She wondered when and how they'd switched from trying to kill her to wanting to eat with her—and when and how Aidan had started to say "love."

"Sorry we're late," Aidan said to Topher and Victoria.

Victoria studied her. "You missed Nicholas, Melissa, and Emily. But that's okay—they weren't worthy of joining us anyway."

"Oh." Eve filed those names away in her head as Victoria and Topher exchanged inscrutable looks. Eve wondered how many others like them there were, as well as the wisdom of allowing them to meet. If they were all in WitSec, wouldn't it be safer to be separated? Again, a question she couldn't ask.

Aidan smiled broadly, and then he planted a kiss on the top of Eve's head. "One slice of mushrooms and peppers? Like usual?"

"Like usual," Eve echoed.

Victoria snapped her book shut. "Well, then."

Whistling, Aidan sauntered toward the counter. Eve watched him walk away, so sure of himself and who he was. She envied that confidence in a rush of jealousy so acute that it felt like a thumb shoved into her solar plexus. She turned back to Victoria and Topher to find them staring at her.

Both of them plastered smiles on their faces at the exact same time.

Eve twisted the corners of her lips upward in what she hoped resembled a smile. She was grateful that she'd sat on the side of the table closest to the door. She'd only have a few seconds' head start if she had to run.

"So . . . how are things with you and Aidan?" Victoria asked. Eve noticed that her eyes looked more human than they did before. The whites were wider, and the pupils were rounder. Her irises were still golden.

Eve shot a look at Aidan. At the counter, he winked at her and blew her a kiss. He then turned and spoke to the man at the cash register. She assumed he was ordering, but she couldn't hear his words. "Fine," Eve said vaguely.

"He's going to be insufferable now," Topher said to Victoria.

"Only if this works," Victoria said.

*Can I ask what they mean?* Eve wondered. *Or am I supposed to know?*

Topher called to Aidan, "Get an order of garlic knots!" At the counter, Aidan waved. He talked more to the man at the cash register, then pulled out his wallet to pay.

"What made you late?" Victoria asked. "Or am I prying?" Beside her, Topher smirked, and Victoria elbowed him. His smirk half vanished.

"I had work," Eve said.

"You"—Topher leveled a finger at her nose—"shouldn't be working so hard at that library. You should be spending time with us instead."

Eve tried to remember agreeing to spend any time with these people. She couldn't.

"Besides," Topher continued, "books lie."

Victoria whacked his shoulder with her book. "Philistine."

"Beyond the misuse of your time, if you spend too much time with the locals and their literature, you'll end up with vocabulary exclusive to this world," Topher said. "Case in point, 'philistine.' You need to be in a world with certain historical facts for that word to exist." He stretched his legs out and propped them on one of the empty chairs. "And most worlds differ so dramatically that that kind of historical overlap isn't even on the table."

"But that's why it's so fascinating! All the differences reveal the minute and not-so-minute differences between related realms," Victoria said. "Seriously, Topher, you can't tell me you don't enjoy the interrealm equivalent of the regional-dialect-comparison conversation. You know, the grander version of: some say 'soda'; some say 'pop.' Some call it a 'bubbler'; others a 'water fountain.'" Victoria made air quotes as she talked in her mocking lilt. Eve tried to keep her face blank. She wondered if this conversation would have made sense if she had all her memories.

"No one says 'bubbler' in any world," Topher said.

"You are in the heartland of 'bubbler,'" Victoria said. "Soak in the 'bubbler.'"

"I hate the people here." Topher scowled at the other customers. There were only three other occupied tables. Across the restaurant, by the window, a woman coaxed her three children to eat their pizza without stripping off the cheese. Their faces were smeared with orangish grease. In another corner, an older couple ate sauce-soaked sandwiches. The man stared out the window as he ate, and the woman continually checked her phone. The last customer was a middle-aged man in paint-stained jeans who had folded a piece of pizza in half and was shoving it into his mouth. Eve wondered what people in other worlds were like.

"They are pigs," Victoria said prissily.

One of the kids tossed his pizza on the floor and began to cry, a bleating sound.

"Sheep," Topher corrected.

Aidan laid a tray on the table. He slid a slice of mushroom and pepper pizza in front of Eve. She had no memory of eating that kind of pizza before. The mushrooms resembled dried slugs. "At least no one here is trying to kill us," Aidan said.

"Yet," Topher added.

He'd said it so casually, as if death could stride through the door any second and order garlic knots. Eve felt as if the grease-tinged air had turned rancid. Her eyes slid to the door, and then to the black agency car with the tinted windows. She hadn't thought . . . Of course she'd known that Malcolm and Aunt Nicki were her guards. She'd known she was in WitSec for her protection. All the security cameras. All the guns. But to hear out loud, tossed off in conversation, this easy talk of death . . .

Topher suddenly grinned. He rubbed his hands together, and sparks danced over his palms. "Let's have some fun with the sheep." Stretching back, he slapped his palms on the wall. The lights in the pizza place flashed.

"Cut it out, man," Aidan said. "I still have two slices cooking."

"Why don't you go electrify the urinal again instead?" Victoria suggested. "That seems to be suitably juvenile for you."

"If 'juvenile' means 'hilarious and awesome' in the local dialect, then yes, you are correct," Topher said. "But I'll quit if you fetch more Tabasco sauce." He picked up a nearly empty bottle and waved it in the air. He then uncorked it and chugged the remaining sauce. A shudder ran through his body, and he shook it off like a horse shaking its mane. "Fantastic stuff. Must remember to pack a case for home."

Eve's stomach churned, but not from the sight of the sauce. She tried to will it to steady. *Don't be sick*, she thought. *Hold it together.* She tried to breathe evenly. In and out. In and out. Malcolm had said "he" was still out there, and Patti had been concerned about security. She shouldn't be so surprised. She'd just had so much else to think about. Lately, it felt as if her thoughts were swirling and bubbling inside her. She didn't remember feeling like this before, but then, given her memory . . .

Aiden draped his arm around her, and Eve flinched. "Green Eyes, you okay?"

"You are looking greenish beyond your eyes," Victoria said. "Not an attractive shade."

Eve licked her lips and coughed. Her throat felt as if sand had been poured down it. She thought of what Topher had said and clung to the word "home." "After this is over . . . after we testify . . . can we go home?"

All three of them looked at her.

"Testify?" Topher asked carefully.

"We aren't witnesses," Victoria said, "despite the agency name."

"But I thought . . . ," Eve began.

"All the witnesses are dead," Aidan said. His voice was kind. She looked at him, into his eyes, which suddenly looked more serious and sad than she'd thought he could look. He stroked her cheek and brushed her hair back behind her ears. With pity in his voice, he said, "Didn't you know? We're merely likely targets."

"He only kills the best of the best," Victoria said. "The young and the strong."

"And that," Topher said, "is why we have to stick together."

Victoria smiled at her as if they were friends. "Strength in numbers."

Aidan brought Eve's hand to his lips and kissed her knuckles. "Together."

An hour later, Eve knocked on the window of Malcolm's car. He rolled down the window. She handed him a slice of pepperoni.

"Extra cheese?" Malcolm asked.

"Yes," she said.

"Everything okay?" he asked.

"Yes," she said. *No*, she thought.

"Aidan?" Malcolm leveled a look at him. "What game are you playing now?"

Behind her, Aidan placed his hands on her shoulders. "No game. I'll take her straight home. You can stay and eat your grease." His hands felt like shackles, chaining her to him. *Together*, she thought. *Safety in numbers*.

Malcolm snorted. "I'll be so close behind you that you'll think my license plate is yours. You'll wonder if I'm actually in your back seat, and then you'll realize, no, that's Malcolm, stuck to my rear like a bumper sticker."

Eve didn't have to look at Aidan to know that he was grinning. "Sounds like a dare," Aidan said. "What do you say, Eve? Up for some more fun?"

"Nuh-uh." Malcolm leveled a finger at Aidan. "You pull any of that stunt-car driving again, and I'll ram your car so fast that you won't know which happened first—your stunt or my crash." He looked at Eve. "Do you want to ride with me? Just say the word."

She must have had a reason to agree to these pizza dates. Her past self must have seen something in Aidan. "I'll be fine."

Aidan thumped her shoulders. "That's my girl."

She wanted to say she wasn't his girl. But maybe she was. Maybe it was safer if she was. She let him guide her to his car.

In the car, Eve leaned her forehead against the car window. She counted the parked cars and then the telephone poles as they drove past. Every once in a while, she checked for Malcolm's car in the side mirror. He kept behind them by exactly one car length.

"You're quiet today, Green Eyes. What's churning in that pretty head of yours?" Aidan reached over and ruffled Eve's hair. She tensed as the car veered toward the median. He corrected it, both hands on the wheel again. Behind them, Malcolm closed the gap until he was only a few feet from their fender. "Is it Topher? You know he gets in these moods." Before the end of lunch, Topher had shorted out one cash register and singed multiple tables. "Just think of him as a blond, blue-eyed version of an elephant transported from the wide savannah to a city zoo. Sometimes he sees this place as more cage than sanctuary."

"Are we safe here?" Eve asked.

He flashed a smile at her. "If we stick together."

"If then. Are we safe here?"

His smile faded. He said carefully, "They say we are."

"Do you think we're safe here?" She studied him, trying to read his face, trying to gauge whether he would lie to her. She thought of the who's-next-to-die game and the cavalier jokes about death. All the jokes didn't mean there wasn't something very real to fear. In fact, she thought they meant the opposite.

Aidan was silent for a moment, then said, "There's only one way in and one way out of this world. It's the safest place we could be. He should have explained this to you."

"He didn't," Eve said. Or maybe he did.

Aidan whistled low. "You should have been briefed like the rest of us when you arrived."

Eve glanced again at the side mirror. As Aidan braked at a traffic light, Malcolm braked too. The front of his car looked like a scowl. "Can you brief me?"

"Yeah, no, not my job," Aidan said. "Our tailgating friend would have my head on a platter. He's a bit protective of you, you may have noticed. He plays favorites. Only reason I'm allowed near you at all is that Lou insisted."

"But if I'm supposed to know already . . . ," Eve argued.

"There's no magic in this world, right? So, no portals. The only known one is in the agency—it was brought from another world. And don't ask me how that was accomplished if there were no portals here. Apparently, it happened decades ago— who knows, maybe centuries. The agents won't spill about that. And don't ask me where the portal is either. Close-lipped bunch of bastards."

*Level five*, she thought. She didn't know why she was so sure. She'd been in the silver room, and she hadn't seen any "portal," whatever that was. But still, she was certain. "You don't know?" Maybe he'd forgotten. Maybe he'd lost memories too. Maybe she wasn't alone. Taking a deep breath, she took a risk. "Do you remember coming here? Do you remember where you're from?"

"Tsk-tsk. Rules are rules."

"But do you remember?"

He looked at her instead of the road. Behind them, Malcolm honked as if saying, *Pay attention*. Aidan veered around a parked car. "Yeah, of course. It's only been a few months. And the only reason I don't know the portal location is because the agents blindfolded me—a security precaution, they said. They didn't want me popping in and out of there without their approval. I can't teleport to a location I haven't seen. Didn't they blindfold you? They claimed it was standard procedure."

"Yes, of course," she lied. She shouldn't have asked. She'd revealed too much. Eve laced her fingers together and then unlaced them. Maybe she was the only one with memory losses. Maybe she was the only one with visions. None of them had collapsed back at the agency when they'd used their power in the game. Topher hadn't collapsed in the pizza place when he'd used his. She'd been blaming the surgery for her problems, but from the perfection in their faces, it was clear they'd had the same surgeries that she'd had. Maybe the surgery was different for different people. Maybe hers had been botched. She spread her hands on her lap. Her hands looked perfect, her fingers smooth and even. She was perfect on the outside but broken on the inside. A voice inside her whispered, *She's broken.* But she couldn't tell if that was a real memory or a memory of a vision.

She noticed Aidan was watching her. He was trying to be subtle, but she caught the quick glances as he drove. She tried to figure out how she could salvage the conversation, but she couldn't think of anything to say. Instead, she looked out the window at the cookie-cutter houses and the mailboxes and the bleached, dry lawns. Her thoughts spun and spun as if caught in a blender. He'd said he'd been here only a few months; she knew she'd been here longer. Longer than

Victoria? Longer than Topher? Longer than the ones like them that she hadn't met (or had met but didn't remember)? She could have been the first, the experimental surgery, and they'd perfected it later.

Or maybe she was flawed in some other way. Maybe she always had been.

Aidan parked in front of her house. Malcolm parked on the opposite side of the street. A tree, heavy with branches, hung over the black car as if it wanted to hide Malcolm from view. "He's never liked me," Aidan said.

"I thought you charmed everyone."

Aidan flashed a grin at her. "Only those I deem worthy."

"Are you complimenting me or insulting Malcolm?"

"Both at once," Aidan quipped. "Aren't I impressive? I can also walk and talk at the same time." She could tell he wanted her to smile. She couldn't. Her cheek muscles wouldn't budge, so she looked at the house instead.

She heard Aidan open his car door. Out of the corner of her eye, she saw him scoot around the front of the car. He opened her door and held out his hand. She fumbled with the seat belt and stepped out of the car. She didn't take his hand.

On the sidewalk, she looked at Malcolm's car. "Why doesn't he get out?"

"Ignore him." Aidan drew her toward the house. "He's jealous because he's too old for you." She shot another look at the car. That couldn't be true—could it? "Or maybe it's the pepperoni pizza. By now, the smell should have permeated the car. He might be unable to resist it any longer and is busily stuffing his face."

"He could have eaten while driving," Eve pointed out.

"Possible," Aidan said. "But unsafe. Good thing you were with me." At the door, Aidan raised her hand to his lips and kissed her knuckles. His lips were soft. He turned her hand over and kissed her palm, then her wrist. "I'd never endanger you."

Eve extracted her hand. "Except for when you tried to kill me."

"Except for that," he agreed. He leaned closer, and Eve shot a look again at Malcolm's car. *Lie to everyone*, he'd said, *until you know the truth*.

She let him kiss her. But she didn't float above the cement steps, and when he stepped back and smiled at her, she had to remind herself to smile too. He left whistling. She stayed on the steps and watched him drive away, aware that Malcolm was watching her.

# Eight

AFTER AIDAN DROVE AWAY, Eve knocked on the front door. She still didn't have a key. Or if she did, she didn't know where she had put it. She might have to invent a lie for why she didn't have it.

The lies pulled on her like weights on her limbs, and she suddenly felt exhausted.

She wished she could simply walk down the street away from the house and keep walking until she was somewhere else where no one knew or remembered her any better than she knew or remembered them. But Malcolm's car sat dark and silent across the street, and she had already knocked.

She heard footsteps inside. Sharp, loud, close. And then the door swung open.

"Oh, it's you," Aunt Nicki said. "I was hoping for something more interesting. Like a delivery of soap." She waved her hand at Malcolm's car, and he drove away. The street was empty except for parked cars and recycling bins. Aunt Nicki checked outside and then waved Eve inside.

Eve lingered in the hallway, looking for other changes that she might have missed in the morning—other clues to what she was supposed to know. She flipped through a stack of mail scattered on a small table. Most of the envelopes were addressed to "resident" or "occupant." She supposed that was what she was, an occupant. She didn't feel like she was home. She was merely occupying space.

Aunt Nicki bustled past her. "Worst part about this babysitting duty is that housecleaning isn't included. Not enough cleaners with the right security clearance. Okay, obviously, that's not the worst part."

Eve faced the wall with the photo of a dead tree. She tried to force herself to picture "home," to remember what it felt like to be there. If she was so sure that this *wasn't* home, then what was? Did it have a smell, a sound, a color, a temperature? Anything? *Remember!* she shouted at her mind. Taking a deep breath, she closed her eyes. Her hands clenched into fists. She tried to focus on the single word "home."

A towel smacked into her stomach, and Eve flinched.

"You dust," Aunt Nicki said as she went into the living room.

Eve examined the towel. It had a smear of grease on one side, and the edges were frayed. She must have helped Aunt Nicki or someone clean before because she knew she was supposed to wipe down surfaces with it. At home? Or only here?

She peeked into the living room. The vacuum lay across the carpet. Aunt Nicki was squirting blue liquid onto the mirror and then wiping it away. Eve entered the room and began dusting the coffee table. It had a thin film of gray dust that smeared as she rubbed it with the towel. Coffee rings were permanently ingrained in the wood. She moved aside a stack of magazines: *Country Gardens*, *Better Homes and Gardens*, *Fine Gardening*, and *Guns & Ammo*. "You like flowers?" Eve asked.

Another squirt on the mirror. "I like guns. Malcolm likes flowers."

Examining the magazines, Eve tried to picture Malcolm in a garden. He'd loom over daffodils and crush any seedlings.

"He claims that weeding is therapeutic." Aunt Nicki wiped the mirror and then squirted again. "He has his entire backyard mapped out so the plants bloom clockwise from spring to fall. Plus an entire wall of rhododendron bushes in garish fuchsias and purples. I know, I know, you wouldn't think it to look at him. But he's a mush inside. Likes to nurture flowers and puppies and broken kids."

There was that word again. Broken. *She's broken.* Could it have been Aunt Nicki's voice? She hadn't caught the voice, but the memory of the rest of the vision was as strong as a real memory, maybe stronger. She could picture the box she'd been trapped in: a wooden box, encrusted in jewels, with a silver snake-shaped clasp. The box was the size of a person's hand. She'd been shrunk to fit inside it. Inside the box had reeked so badly that it had made her eyes sting. But she remembered worse smells: decay, a putrid and acidic stench that wafted through the air, and thick, cloying incense, overlaid to hide the odor. "If I'm not a witness, why do you want me to remember so badly?" Eve asked.

Aunt Nicki stopped wiping. Blue dripped down the surface of the mirror. "Who said you weren't a witness?" Her voice was careful, casual.

"Aidan. He said we're merely targets."

"Aidan isn't supposed to discuss the case."

Eve noticed she hadn't denied it. "So I am a witness?"

The blue pooled on the mantel. "That boy has never had a truly casual conversation in his life. He always chooses his words. He *doesn't* slip. What else did he say?"

Eve wished she hadn't spoken. She pointed to the mantel. "The blue is dripping."

"Yeah, and you missed a spot." Aunt Nicki waved her hand at the coffee table. "I can't imagine what he was thinking. You might be dense as a rock on an average day, but still . . ."

She remembered that Aidan had said, *Don't play dense. It doesn't suit you.* The same word. She wondered if that meant anything. "He said I wasn't. Dense. I'm not dense."

"Apparently not anymore. What is going on with you? Lately, you're asking as many questions as a toddler."

Eve shrugged and looked down at the towel that she was squeezing and twisting and strangling in her hands without realizing it. "Nothing." She didn't want to talk about herself anymore. "How was your day?"

Aunt Nicki's eyes bulged like a bullfrog's. "You have never once asked me that."

"Oh." Eve bent her attention to the coffee table, scrubbing

away every speck of dust that had dared to land on it. She artfully arranged the magazines like she'd seen the receptionist do in the agency lobby. She then paid meticulous attention to the coffee table legs. She didn't look up. After a minute, she heard the squirt of Aunt Nicki's cleaning supplies.

"My day was fine," Aunt Nicki said at last.

Eve couldn't think of a follow-up question. They cleaned the rest of the room in silence. Later, they cooked and ate dinner in silence.

At night, also in silence, Eve lay flat on her back in bed. A car passed by outside, and light swept across the ceiling. She counted the cracks in the plaster until the light hit the opposite wall and the room plunged into darkness again.

She listened to the curtains over the window flutter from the breath of the air conditioner. The dry, chilled air wormed between the sheets. Eve pointed her toes and then flexed them, counting as she did it: *ten, eleven, twelve . . .* She then considered what was keeping her awake:

One, Aidan.

Two, Zach.

Three, WitSec.

Four, the case.

Every time she tried to make sense of them, she felt knotted and sick. Maybe if she could sleep, it would all be clear tomorrow. Or not. Regardless, she told herself, tomorrow would come whether she slept or not, counted or not, remembered or not. She closed her eyes.

Eventually, she must have slept.

Next time she opened her eyes, her alarm was buzzing like it had ingested a beehive. She stared at it blearily for a moment, perplexed by how to shut it off, and then she slapped the silver button on top. It worked. She untangled herself from the sheets and got out of bed. Standing, she looked around the room. Everything seemed to be where she'd left it last night, including yesterday's clothes on the top of the hamper. She exhaled and felt the muscles in her shoulders unknot. She found a key on top of her dresser—she guessed it was the library key, or maybe the house key. She took it with her, as well as the cell phone from Malcolm.

She showered, dressed, and joined Aunt Nicki in the kitchen. Aunt Nicki was peering into the toaster at a piece of bread. She jostled the lever.

Eve opened the refrigerator and took out the orange juice. Holding the bottle, she hesitated. She didn't know which cabinet held glasses. She chose one at random. She got it on her second try, and poured herself a glass.

The clock over the trash can ticked. 7:10.

"Can I ask you a question?" Eve asked Aunt Nicki.

"I don't know. Can you?" Aunt Nicki shot back, then winced. "Sorry. I have a little brother. It's reflex. Go ahead."

"Say there are two boys . . ."

"You're asking a relationship question?" Aunt Nicki looked up from the toaster. Her eyes were doing their bullfrog impression again, Eve noted.

"You prefer kissing one of them, but the other insists you should be kissing him," Eve continued. "Which one should you continue to kiss?"

Still staring, Aunt Nicki sat down hard in the empty chair. "You're seriously asking me this. You aren't asking about . . . Never mind."

Eve wrinkled her nose. She smelled a hint of burned bread. "Your toast is done."

Aunt Nicki waved her hand at the toaster. "It just started. That's crumbs from yesterday's toast."

"Is it going to catch fire?"

"Crumbs are small. Besides, the char adds flavor. So these two boys . . ." Aunt Nicki folded her hands in front of her on the table. Eve had the sense that she wanted to take notes. "You're kissing both of them?"

"Not simultaneously," Eve clarified.

"I should hope not," Aunt Nicki said, and then she considered it. "Though that could be interesting . . . A-a-a-and that kind of statement is exactly why I shouldn't babysit children. You should *not* be kissing two boys at the same time."

She sounded so emphatic that Eve felt a grin tug at her cheeks. But she wasn't sure she should laugh at a woman who brought her gun to breakfast. Currently it was tucked into an embroidered leather holster that looked as much a fashion accessory as Aunt Nicki's layered fake-pearl necklaces.

"You said you're enjoying kissing one of them?"

"Is that unusual?" Eve asked. "I thought that was the point of kissing."

Aunt Nicki shook her head. "I cannot believe we're having this conversation."

"Would you rather I ask you why Aidan thinks I'm not a witness? And why he, Victoria, and Topher don't have memory losses and I do? And why I can't use magic without losing consciousness but they can? Or should I ask what the case is about? Or where I'm from? Or why I know some things but not others, like 'bread' but not 'bagels'? Or why I don't know what you want me to know? And what happens if I do remember? What happens if I don't? What then?" She said it all in one breath and then sucked in air. The air tasted burned.

A coil of smoke rose from the toaster, and Eve coughed. Aunt Nicki popped out of her chair and bustled over to the counter. She dumped the toaster upside down over a plate. Her toast, plus a shower of ember-like crumbs, fell onto the plate. "I think that's a record for number of words spoken by you at once."

"But you aren't going to answer me." Eve didn't have to phrase it as a question. She knew it was a fact.

"You should kiss the one you like kissing," Aunt Nicki said. "Don't kiss the other one."

"Okay." Eve sipped her orange juice. "Thanks."

Aunt Nicki stared at her again. "You're welcome."

❋

At 7:30 a.m., Eve stuck the key she'd found on her dresser into the lock on the library door and was mildly surprised when it worked. The door slid open. She hoped it was a sign that today would go well.

Behind her, Zach charged up the stairs. He had a paper bag—bagels, she guessed—in one hand. He skidded to a stop

next to her. "Hey," he said casually, as if he hadn't been running to catch her.

"Hi," Eve said.

The library doors slid shut and then open again as Eve and
Zach continued to stand, staring at each other, in sight of the
sensor. She knew what they were both thinking about: the kiss,
the flying.

A black car pulled into the library lot and parked under a
tree, the same one as yesterday. No one got out of the car. She
suddenly felt exposed. The library was tucked away from the
street. Trees blocked the view. With another glance at the black
car, she ducked inside. Zach hurried in with her, and the
door slid shut again behind them. Eve wished she could lock
it. But no, this was a public place. *A WitSec-approved place,*
she reminded herself.

Inside, the library was quiet. Shadows were layered in a
pattern on the floor. Eve headed for the light switches and
flipped them on.

Everything looked the same as yesterday.

*Good,* she thought. She wanted routine. Nice, safe, boring,
wonderful routine.

Zach fetched the overnight book-return bin and then
opened the bagel bag. "Breakfast?" he offered. She accepted
the everything bagel. Seeds rained on the circulation desk,
and Eve bit into it. She still didn't like it. She ate it anyway.
*This is what I need,* she told herself. *Normalcy.*

Zach didn't eat his.

"You don't want it?" Eve asked.

"All I want is to kiss you again."

"Oh." Eve wiped her lips with a paper napkin, cleared the crumbs from the desk, and straightened a few books on a cart. "You want to kiss me because you want to see if we fly." When he didn't answer, she looked at him. "You don't lie," she reminded him.

"Just think! If I'm right and we're, you know, magic together—"

"We're not," she cut in. Or at least *he* wasn't. He couldn't be. He was from this world, and Malcolm and Aidan had both said there was no magic in this world . . . unless they'd lied, but she couldn't think of any reason for them to lie about this.

"I didn't hallucinate," Zach said. "Yes, I read a lot. Watch a lot of TV. Play a few video games if I think the story line is worth it. But I've never had a problem separating reality from fantasy." He held up one finger. "One kiss. If we don't fly, I leave you alone."

Eve shook her head. Malcolm had told her not to do magic outside the agency—plus she didn't want to lose consciousness here. "It's too dangerous."

"Aha! You didn't say it didn't happen!"

"Zach . . ."

"Worst case, we hit the ceiling. Bash a few light fixtures. Plummet from the ceiling. So we'll kiss over carpet just in case. Or, ooh, we can make a landing cushion out of the pillows from the chairs in the reading room!" Grabbing her hand, he yanked her out of the lobby and through the reference area. He hit the lights for the reading room, an octagonal wood-paneled room with chairs in every corner. Zach began to toss the chair pillows into the center of the room.

"I don't think . . . ," Eve began.

"Cannonball!" He jumped into the air and landed on his butt on one of the pillows.

She laughed. She couldn't help it. His joy was infectious.

He stood up, his expression uncharacteristically serious. "Flying isn't the only reason I want to kiss you. You are all I think about. You are exactly what my life has been missing. You are what I have always wanted. You are magic, with or without the flying."

"But you'd prefer with the flying."

"It would be a cool bonus, that's all I'm saying."

She laughed again.

He crossed to her, close without touching. "Say no because you don't like me that way. Say no because you didn't enjoy kissing me. But don't say no because you're afraid."

She looked into his eyes, his warm, wonderful eyes, and wondered if she could trust him. "You don't know what I'm afraid of," she said softly.

"Then tell me. And I'll tell you why you shouldn't be scared."

It was such an innocent statement, said by someone who didn't know fear. His innocent fearlessness was beautiful, and she wanted suddenly to feel that fearlessness too. Stepping forward, she put her arms around his neck. He wrapped his around her waist. She felt her heart beat faster. Or maybe it was his. Both of their hearts beat fast through their shirts, against each other.

She touched her lips to his.

*No magic,* she thought to herself. *Don't fly.*

She breathed with him as they kissed—and then the feel of the floor faded away. His grip around her waist tightened. She broke the kiss and looked down. They were several feet above the pillows.

Floating like feathers, they drifted down. Landing on pillows, they lost their balance and toppled over, clinging to each other. Entangled, they lay silent for a moment.

"Whoa," Zach said, breathless. "Wow."

"Wow," Eve agreed. She hadn't lost consciousness. She hadn't had a vision. She hadn't even felt herself use magic at all. In fact, she'd focused on the opposite.

"Did you know you had magic kisses?"

"Last night Aidan kissed me, and we didn't fly." She watched his face as she said it, unsure if he'd be upset that she'd kissed someone else. But she didn't want to lie to him when she didn't have to—she already had to lie to him about so much.

His face didn't change, but she felt his arms stiffen around her. "Who's Aidan?"

"A boy who thinks I'm supposed to be kissing him."

Drawing away from her, Zach sat up in the middle of the pillows. "And what do you think?" His voice was careful, measured.

Eve sat up next to him. "I think I'd rather kiss you."

"Oh. Well, that's okay, then. But you'll excuse me if I'm still a little bit jealous. Is this Aidan good looking?"

Eve shrugged. "Yes."

"Well, this just gets better and better." Zach pushed away the pillows and stood up. He tossed the pillows toward the chairs. "Buff guy? Likely to beat me up? Not that I wouldn't fight for you. I totally would. You are completely fight worthy."

She put her hand on his wrist, stopping him from chucking the next pillow. "Zach?"

"Sorry, but it's somewhat of a shock to kiss the girl of your dreams and then find out she already has a boyfriend. I kind of wish you'd told me that earlier, except that I probably wouldn't have kissed you, and there goes fodder for my dreams for the next decade." He ran his fingers through his hair. "Did you mean what you said? You'd rather kiss me?"

She nodded. "You don't play games."

"Great. What a rousing endorsement next to Pretty Boy." He took a deep breath. "Sorry, sorry, sorry. Jealousy is ugly, isn't it? I'll stop. You're here with me. That's good." He tried a smile.

She saw him try, and she touched his cheek. "Kiss me again," she suggested.

A real smile lit up his face. "Yes, ma'am." He leaned in toward her. As his lips pressed against hers, she heard paper rustle, and she felt wind in her hair. Her feet stayed firmly on the carpet, but she felt something brush against her back. She broke away.

Books flew in circles around them.

Zach grinned wide. "It worked."

He'd worked this magic . . . through her? Using her magic? He kissed her again joyfully, and the books flocked to the ceiling.

Breaking the kiss, they watched the books fly. A pair circled and spiraled. A few flew in a line, rising and falling. One flapped closer to another, and a third dove toward them, opening and shutting its pages furiously, as if jealous. Eve laughed out loud. Zach was laughing too. Holding each other, they laughed as the bird-books flew around them.

At last, the books slowed, and they sank one by one toward the floor. They collapsed, strewn around the reading room, fluttering their pages up and down until at last they all lay still at Eve and Zach's feet.

One of the librarians halted in the doorway to the reading room. "What—"

Books had fallen everywhere, spine up onto pillows, pages bent, upside down.

Eve and Zach leaped apart.

The librarian's eyes were so wide that the whites were visible in a ring around his irises. He looked like a startled horse, Eve thought—and then she wondered when she'd been near a horse. She could picture one, yoked to a carnival wagon. Its eyes were wild, and it strained against its harness. Distracted by the memory, she didn't answer. Instead, Zach did.

"I can work magic when I kiss her," Zach said.

Blood began to rush to the librarian's face, tinting his neck and cheeks a ruddy pink. His mouth opened and shut, but words didn't come out.

Quickly, Eve said, "We tried a new shelving technique. It didn't work well."

Color faded from the librarian's cheeks, and he began to breathe again. "Okay. You . . . uh, clean this up before the patrons come in, or Patti will have your heads."

Eve nodded.

The librarian retreated, looking back at them several times.

"You lied easily." Zach bent to pick up the books. She joined him and didn't know what to say. He was right.

Halfway through cleanup, she saw a hint of movement outside one of the reading-room windows. She looked up to focus on it. Shrouded in shadows, a hooded face was pressed against the glass. Someone watching her. And then the face was gone.

Clutching the books, Eve went to the window. No one was there.

"Eve?"

She retreated from the window. "Nothing. Everything's fine." That lie was easy to say too.

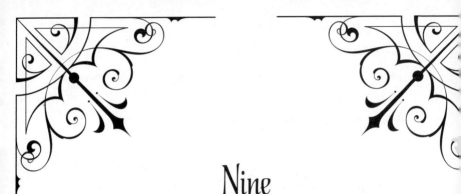

# Nine

SAFELY BEHIND A CURTAIN, Eve studied Aidan through the library lobby window. He was leaning against his car in front of the entrance next to a NO PARKING sign. His hands were loosely in his pockets, his ankles were crossed, and his face, eyes closed, was tilted up toward the sun. He looked entirely at ease, as if he belonged there.

"Is that Pretty Boy?" Zach was behind her. His breath was soft on her neck.

Aidan *was* Pretty Boy. He looked like an airbrushed model in one of Aunt Nicki's magazines. Seeing him, though, made her want to run in the opposite direction, which didn't make sense if she was supposed to be with him. "He's supposed to take me to lunch with his friends. I think."

"Are you going?" Zach's voice was neutral.

Malcolm had said she'd asked for the lunches. But she didn't remember. How could she be committed when she didn't remember? She thought of Aidan kissing her, and her fingers touched her lips.

Aidan stretched, pulling his arm across his torso and then over his head. His chest muscles flexed. He rolled his neck as if he were limbering up.

Eve stepped away from the window. She faced Zach. Behind him, she noticed Patti Langley at the circulation desk. Her hands processed books, scanning them, demagnetizing them, and handing them to patrons, but her eyes were glued to Eve, as always.

"No," Eve said to Zach. "I'm not."

"Are you going to tell him that you aren't going?" Zach's hands were shoved in his pockets, but he didn't look anywhere near as comfortable as Aidan. In fact, he shifted from foot to foot as if nails poked into the soles of his feet.

"No." She felt herself smiling, though she couldn't explain why.

"You can escape through the back door in the staff room," Zach said. "Get a couple blocks away and then call your aunt to pick you up."

"I want to go with you." She didn't plan to say it, but the words felt right—the same way it felt right not to walk out the door and go with Aidan, no matter what her past self had planned.

"I don't have a car. Or even use of my mom's lunchbox-on-wheels." But he seemed pleased. His eyes were bright again, and his cheeks were twitching as if he wanted to smile but thought he shouldn't.

"Where do you go after work?" Eve asked.

"Home. I live a few streets that way." He pointed in the opposite direction from Aidan. "Come home with me. For lunch, I mean." He blushed pink. "I make a mean egg salad bagel sandwich. Pickles and everything."

She thought that sounded wonderful. She was aware she was smiling goofily at him. He wore the same expression, his eyes full of her, as though drinking her in. "Can we skip the everything bagel?" she asked.

"You don't like everything bagels?"

She shook her head.

"Why didn't you ever say so before?"

"I'm saying so now." *I can't be bound by a past self I don't remember*, she thought. It was a freeing thought, and she felt her entire heart lift.

His smile faded as his eyes flicked to look over her shoulder and out the window. "So, Pretty Boy . . . He won't call your aunt and freak her out if you don't show?"

Her shoulders slumped. He would, of course, and Aunt Nicki and Malcolm would crash down on her with full wrath if she left with no word. Eve peered out the window at Aidan and felt as if a box lid were slamming shut on her and she were shrinking inside. And then she straightened as an idea occurred to her. "I'll tell Patti."

Without waiting for Zach to respond, Eve crossed the lobby to the circulation desk.

The librarian immediately looked down at her computer, as if she hadn't been staring at Eve for the past ten minutes. "Yes?" she said, like she'd expected a patron.

"There's a boy waiting for me outside. I . . ." She thought of how concerned Patti had been about security, of Patti's secret eyes, of her arrangement with WitSec. *She's hiding too*, Eve thought. "I don't feel safe with him."

Patti looked up sharply, dropping the feigned air of disinterest. "He's picked you up before. He must have been approved."

"I know." Eve couldn't explain it to Patti any more than she could explain it to herself. She looked down at her feet, unable to meet Patti's intense gaze, and thought that maybe this was a bad idea, maybe she should go with Aidan and not second-guess the agency.

"Intuition?"

Eve nodded, still studying her shoes. "I'd just . . . feel better if I went home with Zach. I can have Malcolm or Aunt Nicki pick me up at his house."

"You'll tell them about your unease with the boy?"

Eve looked up at Patti. There was sympathy in her eyes. "I will."

"Good. I'll take care of him for now." Patti smiled reassuringly at Eve. The smile transformed the woman's face, softening her by a decade.

Eve smiled back, though her cheeks felt stiff. "Thank you very much."

"You have to trust yourself," Patti said, and then her smile faded. "In the end—when they find you, when whoever you're running from catches up—that's all you can do."

Eve shivered and wondered if that was experience talking or prophecy. She backed away slowly, then quickly, and returned to Zach. She took a deep breath, looked one more time out at Aidan, who was checking his watch, and said to Zach, "Show me that back door?"

He led her through the library, deep into the stacks, to a door marked STAFF ONLY, tucked between the audiobooks and older magazines. He forced the door open—it was half-barricaded by books—and they slipped inside.

The staff room was stuffed with books. Stacks of books were piled on the floor as high as Eve's hip. Several work tables overflowed with books. Metal bookshelves that ran floor to ceiling were crammed with more books. In one corner a refrigerator hummed, and even it had books shoved on top of it. She wished she could burrow in between all the books and stay, but Aidan would undoubtedly find her here, as soon as he tired of waiting and came in to search the library. Following Zach, she zigzagged through the piles to a bright-orange door marked EMERGENCY EXIT ONLY.

Zach pushed through the door. No alarm sounded. He held it open for her, and she stepped outside. The back of the library faced the woods.

The woods were thick. Oak, maple, and evergreen trees clustered close together, obscuring any view of the streets or houses beyond. Vines twisted around their trunks, and the undergrowth was a snarl of green bushes. Anything or anyone could be hiding in them. Eve stepped back toward the door as it sucked shut. She squeezed the door handle—it had locked behind them.

"Come on," Zach said, "before Pretty Boy decides to look for you." He tromped into the underbrush. "As much as I'd love to fight for your honor, that guy could flatten me with his pinkie. I have a fine sense of self-preservation."

Eve doubted that. If he had, he wouldn't be anywhere near her. But she followed Zach anyway. As she stepped into the woods, she heard the crackle of tiny branches snapping under her shoes—and she remembered she'd been in woods before.

The memory slammed into her so hard that she had to steady herself on a tree trunk.

Woods.

But not like these.

She'd been in a forest of gnarled, ancient trees whose leaves blotted out the sun, leaving the forest floor in perpetual twilight. The roots had been so thick that she'd had to climb over them. Here, the trees were as skinny as her arm, and the sun poked through the canopy above. The underbrush was thick and green, tangling her feet and covering a fallen stone wall. "This is a young forest," she said.

"Used to be a cow pasture," Zach said. "All of this was farmland. Hence all the stone walls. Now it's just houses and trees. Must have looked really different."

"You don't remember?" Continuing after him, she remembered the sound of her feet crunching a layer of old leaves and needles as she ran. The mat of branches overhead had been so thick that only moss and a few ferns grew on the forest floor.

"It was a hundred years ago. Or, you know, some large number of years. Probably if we chopped down the fattest tree and counted the rings, we'd know. I don't, however, have an ax handy."

She couldn't remember where the other forest was or why she had been fleeing or who had been with her. She did remember the way the trees had towered above her, how the branches had battered her, and how the roots had slowed her escape.

Eve checked behind them. She saw no one, but still, she felt watched. Shivers traveled up and down her spine. Birds rustled in the branches above. A squirrel darted through the underbrush. She jumped at each sound, her ears straining to hear more.

"I used to come here when I was a kid. It was pretty much the best superhero secret lair ever. That was one of my forts." He pointed toward a fallen tree. "And that was my lookout." He pointed next to a massive boulder beyond the fallen tree. She tried to see it as a child's playground, not as the forest that loomed in her memory. "You know, to spot the supervillains that I'd proceed to defeat with my array of superpowers." Still in the same light voice, he asked, "So, how long have you had superpowers?"

She halted for an instant, looking across the woods at the boulder. She'd thought she'd seen . . . It had looked like the S-curve of a snake, sleek scales reflecting the bits of sunlight that filtered through the leaves. Victoria? Eve started walking again, faster.

"I mean, it's obviously not *my* power." Crashing through the underbrush, Zach hurried to catch up to her. "I have never been able to do a single thing like that before. Believe me, I tried. I was that kid who used to attempt the Jedi mind trick on his teachers in elementary school. For art class, I fashioned my own Harry Potter wand. Lacked a phoenix feather, though. But when I kissed you . . . I was thinking how kissing you was like floating on air—and we did. And the second time, I deliberately imagined us levitating."

"And the books flying?"

"I wanted to see what else we could do. So I imagined that. And it worked!" Up ahead, the trees were thinning, and she saw bits of roofs and corners of houses through the branches. "My current theory," Zach continued, "is that we're like the Wonder Twins, except with lips instead of rings. And you know, not related. Not at all related. Because that would be disgusting."

"Uh-huh."

"Alternately, and more likely, it has nothing at all to do with who I am. I could be anybody. You're transferring your magic to me, and then I'm using it. You're the only special one."

Eve looked back at the rock. A snake slithered down the face of the boulder and disappeared into the underbrush. "Can we walk faster?" Continuing to look backward, she didn't notice that they'd reached the edge of the woods until Zach stopped.

He pointed across a street. "That's my house."

Zach's house could have been plucked from the cover of a beautiful-homes magazine. On the left and right, the yards were parched yellow, but his was vibrant green, mowed to look more like carpet than a live plant. The house itself was pristine white and had a porch with two white rocking chairs and a wind chime that hung listlessly in the still air.

Eve took a step out of the bushes and then stopped as she heard a car turn onto Zach's street. She retreated and crouched behind a tree.

A blue car drove past them.

She emerged again and checked to the right and left, aware that she was mimicking the way Malcolm always checked the street. Several houses down, a neighbor was mowing his lawn. A few houses beyond that, a brown dog slept on a porch. Eve didn't see anything that seemed threatening or unusual. She started across the street.

Zach didn't move.

"What is it?" Eve asked. She turned back to him and was rocked with another burst of memory: she'd been fleeing with her family. Or maybe it wasn't her family, but she knew them well. At some point, she had fallen, and a man had picked her up and carried her over his shoulder as if she were as light as a jacket. She hadn't been left behind.

Zach pointed to a silver car in the driveway. "My mom's home."

"Oh." Eve tried to picture the people who had run with her. Family or not? The man who had carried her, had he been her father? Brother? Uncle? "Is that . . . bad?"

He still didn't move.

"Back to the woods or to the house?" She felt too exposed

outside the bushes. Anyone in any nearby house could see her. Out of the corner of her eye, she saw a red car speed past their street. She tensed, ready to run, but it didn't turn.

Zach shook himself. "Sorry. House."

Eve bolted across the street, down the slate walkway, and onto the porch. Zach's house had an antique door knocker and two baskets of flowers that framed the door. Several long seconds later, Zach joined her.

Slowly, so slowly that Eve wanted to grab the key herself, Zach drew a key out of his pocket. As he slid it into the lock, the front door opened. A woman in a pink shirt and white capris was framed in the doorway. "Yes?" She had pearls around her neck and a faded bruise on her left cheekbone, mostly obscured by makeup. She wore a layer of makeup over her face, her eyelids, and her lips, as if it were a thin plastic mask. "Oh, Zach! You're home! And you brought a friend."

*This must be Zach's mother*, Eve thought. He had her lips, though hers weren't curved into a smile like Zach's often were. Her cheeks were so smooth that Eve wondered if she ever smiled.

"This is Eve," Zach said. "She works with me at the library."

"How lovely," his mother said.

Eve checked the street as a blue SUV barreled by. For an instant, she couldn't breathe. But the car didn't slow, and she glimpsed a family inside it.

"I invited her to lunch." Zach was peering over his mother's shoulder as if he expected to see someone else with her.

"Delightful," his mother said.

Another car, a black one, turned onto the street. She had to get inside, or at least out of sight. She inched closer to the door.

"I didn't think you'd be home," Zach said. "Is everything okay?"

Zach's mother's eyes brightened. "Of course, Zachary! Don't be silly. Can't I have a change in plans without causing concern? Come in, please, both of you." She opened the door wider.

Eve darted inside. She flattened against the wall and watched through the window as a black car with tinted windows crept down the street. It rolled past the house without stopping. Her rib cage loosened, and she took a deep breath.

"I thought you had your museum meetings today," Zach said, coming inside too.

"Oh, I couldn't. Your father has some business associates coming for dinner. I need to prepare." His mother shut the door behind them, and Eve sagged against the wall. *Safe,* she thought.

Zach frowned at her. "You've been preparing for those meetings all month."

"I can catch up on the meeting minutes later." His mother dismissed his words with a wave. "Let's see what I can whip you two up for lunch!" She beamed at both of them, and her cheeks shifted shape as if they were molded plastic.

For the first time, Eve looked at the inside of the house. A staircase with white carpet swept up in a curve to a second floor, and a brass chandelier hung from the vaulted ceiling. To her right, she saw a living room with stiff chairs that faced an immaculate fireplace. To her left was a dining room with a banquet-style table decorated with a linen tablecloth, crystal candlesticks, and a bowl with orchid blossoms floating in water.

"I'll make us sandwiches," Zach said to his mother. "Don't worry about us. Mom, you—"

Her plastic smile erased as quickly as it had appeared. "Don't start, Zachary." She kissed him on the top of his head. "You and your friend go sit on the sun porch. I'll bring you something nice." She scurried into the dining room and then through a white door.

Zach sighed. "And that's my mother. Come on. We'd better sit on the back porch."

Eve followed him past the staircase to a hall filled with framed photos. Slowing, she looked at them. One was a bride, a younger version of his mother with coiffed hair and a smile that looked exactly like Zach's—a happy smile, not a plastic one. She wore a lace-encrusted dress and stood on a curved staircase. Another was a man in a suit, shaking hands with other men in suits. In another photo, the same man was in a boat on a lake in jeans and a plaid shirt. He held a fish that was as long as his forearm. Eve stared at the lake photo the longest. She knew this place. Another memory? Leaning closer, she peered at the shape of the evergreen-covered hills and the dock, all familiar.

"The fish that didn't get away," Zach said. "I caught a minnow that day, as Dad is very fond of reminding me. I threw it back."

"Lake Horace," she said, suddenly sure.

"You've been there?" Zach asked.

She felt herself deflate. "No." She'd seen it in a photo on the mantel, one of the fake photos that the agency had made. "I mean . . . yes. I . . . spent a few summers there as a little kid."

"You remember the bait shop on East Main? My father swears by their tackle. We'd stop there on the way up, buy Dr. Peppers and bait, and then we'd spend the afternoons on the lake."

She swallowed a lump in her throat. She didn't know why her eyes suddenly felt hot. "Sounds nice."

"Yeah, well, out of the four of us in that boat—me, Dad, his fish, and my minnow—I think the only happy one was that minnow. I set him free." He guided her to another photo, a boy and a man with hats and goggles who were bundled in pillowlike coats and pants. "Another of Dad's favorite activities, skiing. This shot is memorable as the 'before' image on the day I broke my arm." He pointed to another. "And this was my first day of first grade. Clearly, I would not have acquiesced to the tie if I'd had any choice."

From the kitchen, his mother called, "You looked adorable! And it was a hairline fracture."

"I looked like a tool. Sheer luck I wasn't saddled with horrific nicknames for all of elementary school. Do you have any nicknames?"

Eve shook her head. Aidan called her "Green Eyes," but she didn't want to think about him. She was safely inside Zach's house, away from him, away from the agency, away from anyone who knew who she used to be. She peered at another photo, a little girl on a swing. The girl was so clearly laughing that you could almost hear it through the picture. A boy—Zach, much younger—was behind her, also laughing. Sunlight was caught in his eyes. "That looks like a happy memory."

"My sister." Zach's voice was flat. "She died when I was eight."

"Oh." Eve was aware that she was supposed to say more. But her mind felt blank. He stared at the photo for a long time, as if he were trying to memorize the way her curls flew into the air with the wind.

"You're right, though," Zach said at last. "That day was happy."

Side by side, they looked at the picture.

Zach broke the silence. "Do you have any brothers or sisters?"

*Maybe*, she thought. She could have dozens or none. Her stomach felt as if it were squeezed tight. She couldn't remember one happy day or horrible day with her family, at least not with any certainty. "I live with my aunt."

"Right. I know." He looked as though he wanted to ask more. But he didn't. "Come on. Back porch has chairs you can actually sit on, as opposed to the living room, which is designed solely for Victorian women in corsets." He tugged on her elbow, and she followed him to an enclosed porch at the back of the house. The porch had windows on all sides, as well as three skylights. Flowering plants hung from each corner, and a fan turned overhead, stirring the warm air. Most of the windows were open. Screens kept the bugs outside.

Behind them, Zach's mom appeared with a tray holding two tall glasses filled with yellow liquid, lots of ice, and little plastic swords that pierced slices of lemon. "Lemonade?" she said brightly. She laid the tray down on a wicker table.

Zach sighed again. "Thanks, Mom. You really didn't have to."

His mom patted his cheek. "I like to. Don't deny me this." She scurried back inside and shut the door behind her. A stained-glass sailboat hung on the door. It swayed from the motion of the shutting door.

"Your mom . . ." Eve stopped. She couldn't say what she was thinking—that he was lucky to know his mother. She wondered if her own mother missed her, and she wished she could miss her mother. She couldn't ask what it was like to have a mother. *I'm broken*, Eve thought. Empty pieces were rattling inside her. She thought again of the forest. She remembered she'd felt safe when she'd been carried through the trees. Whoever he was—father, brother, uncle, friend—he had made her feel safe.

"I don't want to talk about her," Zach said, again in that flat voice. "Let's talk more about you, okay? How did you discover you can . . . you know? Does anyone else know?"

"My aunt knows. And her friend Malcolm."

"The guy who drops you off, right? Large, African American man with legs the size of sequoia tree trunks? Looks like a bodyguard, right down to the leather jacket and the shades?

Probably knows six kinds of martial arts and carries a knife in his socks?"

"It's a gun."

Zach's eyes widened. "I can never tell if you're serious or if you have the most awesome deadpan delivery of any person alive."

Eve shrugged and looked out at Zach's backyard. It was perfectly manicured. The grass was brilliant green like the front yard and looked as if it had been combed so that all the blades bent in the same direction. Flowering bushes framed the yard, and a patio with a table and chairs was in the center. Gardening supplies were artfully stacked in another corner. Everything had its place. Its precision reminded her of a hospital room. She shuddered and looked away. To hide her reaction, she took a lemonade and sipped it. The tartness felt like a pinch on her tongue. She set the glass down again.

"So, what can you do?" Zach asked. It was the same question Victoria had asked her. But unlike Victoria, he didn't stop there. Questions tumbled out of his mouth as if they were in a hurry to escape him. "How much magic can you transfer at a time? What are its limitations? What fuels it? Is it innate? Is it powered by something? Powered by kisses? Are you a succubus sucking my life force?" He sucked in a deep breath and then blew it out. Eve couldn't help smiling. "Yay! A smile, at last! Eve, what you have, what you can do . . . it's wonderful, amazing, incredible, worthy of a smile! And so are you. Even if you are a succubus."

He took her hand. She let him. Her hand was awkward in

his, as if his fingers weren't sure how to encompass hers. It didn't feel like holding Aidan's hand; it didn't feel practiced. Zach cradled her hand in both of his, and his hands shifted from position to position.

"Don't be afraid, Eve. Not of this. You can be afraid of spiders or snakes or airplane crashes or a zombie apocalypse . . . but don't be afraid of yourself."

He was right. She'd come here so she wouldn't have to be afraid. She looked out at the perfect lawn and tried to think of this house as a sanctuary. For one afternoon, she didn't have to be afraid of Aidan, the case, her magic, or her visions. Of course it wouldn't last, but for the space of a few moments, she could feel free.

"Eve?" Zach asked, a little hesitantly.

Eve looked into his warm, brown, hopeful eyes. She felt as if she were looking straight into his heart. She wondered if this was what it felt like to fall in love. She had nothing to compare it to. But she knew that more than anything else, right this moment, she wanted to make him smile. "Do you want to try to make it rain?" she offered.

She watched delight spread over his face.

"Think of rain," she ordered him. And then she kissed him. For that moment, it felt as if the rest of the world melted away. She let go of her worries, fears, memories, questions, all of it. She was conscious of the taste of his lips, the feel of his breath, and the soft smell of his skin.

She heard Zach's mother say, "Oh my!"

Eve and Zach sprang apart.

His mother stepped onto the porch carrying a tray of sandwiches, enough for six people, but she wasn't looking at Eve or Zach. She laid the tray on the table next to the lemonade. "It wasn't supposed to rain today. I'd better pull in the patio chair cushions." She scurried outside as the first drop of rain hit.

"Whoa," Zach said.

Rain fell fast. Drops hit the slate patio like bullets.

"Good thing I didn't think of a tornado," Zach said.

Eve agreed.

"You've never done this before?"

She shook her head, and then she jumped as her pocket buzzed and trilled. She pulled out the cell phone and stared at it as it shook and sang in her hand. Zach reached over and pressed the Talk button. She felt her face flush, and she put the phone to her ear. "Hello?"

"Are you safe?" Malcolm asked in her ear.

She looked at Zach. "Yes." She meant it. With him, she felt completely safe.

"I am coming to fetch you now," he said. "Stay exactly where you are, keep away from windows, and don't ever, ever do this again." She heard a click, and the phone call ended.

"Your aunt?" Zach asked.

She shook her head, staring at the silent phone. She'd never heard Malcolm sound like that, as if he were radiating anger.

"Big black guy with the gun in his sock?"

She nodded.

"Are you in some kind of trouble? I don't mean only right now. I mean, you look out the window a lot. You're jumpy. I just . . . Are you safe?"

She flinched at the repetition of Malcolm's question, and suddenly she didn't feel so safe anymore. The porch had windows on three sides. The flowering bushes could be hiding anyone.

Rain pelted outside. Zach's mother raced toward the porch, holding an array of pillows to her chest. Zach got to his feet. "I'd better help her."

Eve didn't move. Rain smacked the roof, loud as a hammer. She'd been stupid to come here, stupid to involve Zach. Zach shielded his head with his arms and ran outside to fetch more chair cushions. His mother dumped her batch of cushions inside and then ran back into the rain.

As they finished, Eve heard the squeal of tires from the front of the house. Seconds later, the doorbell rang. "Oh!" Zach's mother said. Her makeup ran down her cheeks, and her hair was flattened against her face. Her blouse was plastered to her skin, and her pants were stained with rain. She hurried to the door, poking at her hair to try to fix it. Eve heard the door open. "Yes?"

A deep voice answered in a familiar rumble. Eve stood. Without meeting Zach's eyes, she walked toward the voice, through the hallway of family photos.

Malcolm towered in the front doorway. Rain streaked his face and plastered his coat to the muscles in his arms. He fixed his eyes on her, but he addressed Zach's mother.

Behind her, so soft that only Eve could hear, Zach said, "You didn't answer me. Are you safe?"

Eve didn't answer. *I'm supposed to be*, she thought, looking at Malcolm. She thought of Aidan and the hesitation in his voice as he'd answered that question.

"You might want to learn how to lie," she said at last.

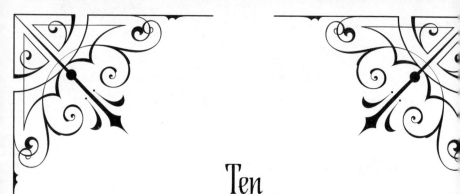

# Ten

EVE DUCKED INTO MALCOLM'S car. Rain spattered inside and beaded on the dashboard. Outside, it pounded the windshield. As Eve fastened her seat belt, Malcolm slammed her door shut. He then climbed into the driver's seat, squeezed the steering wheel so hard that she saw the veins in the back of his hands, and started the ignition. Eve watched the muscles in his cheek twitch as he backed out of Zach's driveway.

"You could yell at me," she suggested. "Seems to make Aunt Nicki feel better." She remembered Aunt Nicki shrieking at her once when Eve had tried to fetch the mail alone. Eve tried to identify when that memory was from and couldn't. One of the lost weeks? If she could reclaim those memories . . .

He backed onto the street and put the car in drive. Across from Zach's house, a black SUV pulled up and parked. Twisting in her seat, she watched a man in a suit step out of the car. He was pelted by rain as he strode toward the house. "Who's that?" she asked. "What does he want with Zach?"

"That's not your concern." Malcolm drove, a little too fast, away from Zach's house through the rain. Puddles sprayed as he hit them.

Yes, it was her concern. It was her fault! She'd brought trouble to Zach, exactly as Patti Langley had warned her— she'd caught him in her storm, both literally and figuratively. "If the agency hurts Zach in any way, I won't cooperate with the case."

Malcolm slammed on the brakes. The car squealed to a stop in the middle of the street.

"You don't make threats." His voice was quiet. She shrank against her seat. "You don't know how many have died. You don't know *how* they died. They were cut to pieces. Carved like drumsticks from a turkey. And each piece was kept in its own box until the ritual was complete." He turned back to the road and continued to drive. "You *will* cooperate, and we *will* catch him."

Eve's mouth felt dry. She nodded. She tried to push the image of severed body parts out of her mind, but couldn't. Her hands clutched each other on her lap. "That . . . that's the case? My case?"

He drove in silence as the rain pounded the car.

It wasn't like him to talk like this—the cold tone, the tight anger. At last she said, "You're just trying to scare me."

"Yes!" He hit the steering wheel with the heel of his hand. "You need to be scared!"

Eve stared at him. She'd never seen such an expression on his face, contorted as if she had stabbed him. His breathing was hard and fast.

"Don't risk yourself," he said. "Please. Stick to the established schedule. Stay with agency-approved people. Inform me immediately if there are any changes in your status. Please, Eve. I can protect you from everything but yourself. Do you understand?"

His voice caught on her name, and she had a sudden thought: *He cares about me.* She wanted to reach out and touch his arm, to reassure him or apologize or . . . she didn't know. She'd never had thoughts like these before. Besides, he was driving, and she didn't know how he'd react. So she only nodded.

Malcolm parked the car, breathed in deeply, and put on his shades. He then stepped out of the car into the rain, checked up and down the street, and crossed to her side. She unclicked the seat belt and climbed out. One hand on her shoulder as if he expected her to bolt, he guided her into the house.

Inside, Malcolm dumped her in the doorway to the living room. He then stalked to the kitchen without a word.

Eve stepped into the living room. A puddle formed around her shoes. Damp, her clothes stuck to her skin. She remembered Aidan saying once that "drowned rat" was not her look.

Aunt Nicki rose to her feet—she'd been sitting on the couch. Aidan, who had been by the window, vanished in a *whoosh* of air. He reappeared next to Eve, wrapped his arms around her, and folded her in against his chest. Aunt Nicki raised both her eyebrows at this.

Two hands on his chest, Eve pushed him away. He

staggered back. "I only . . . I'm just glad you're all right," Aidan said.

"I'm fine," Eve said.

Walking in a full circle around Eve, Aunt Nicki inspected her. "I assume Malcolm read you the riot act about never doing that again?"

"He hinted that it wouldn't be acceptable," Eve said dryly.

A cabinet slammed in the kitchen, and they all flinched.

"You'd think he'd be at least a little pleased," Aunt Nicki said. "Sneaking out with a boy is a very normal-teenager thing to do. I hope you at least made out with the boy."

Eve felt her face flush.

"I'll talk to Malcolm. You talk to *him*." Aunt Nicki pointed to Aidan. Snorting in what sounded suspiciously like a laugh, Aunt Nicki headed for the kitchen, leaving Eve alone with Aidan in the living room. Eve studied the carpet, the coffee table, the mantel, the wall.

"Can we . . . talk?" Aidan asked.

"I'd rather not." She wished she'd kept walking down the hall and into her bedroom. She wished she'd gone farther away than Zach's house. She wished she hadn't let Malcolm bring her back.

"Then I'll talk. You're special, Eve. You have to know that. You make me crazy, worrying about you all the time . . ."

"Why?" She looked at him. He was running his fingers through his artfully tousled hair. She noted that he had dark smudges under his eyes, as if he hadn't slept. She didn't know why—she hadn't been gone for more than an hour. "Who am I to you?" she asked, and then she took a breath and asked a question that she knew Malcolm wouldn't want her to ask. "Who are you to me?"

"You really have to ask that?" He looked hurt.

She should continue to lie about her memory, play along with whatever people dropped on her. "I do," Eve said firmly.

Aidan walked to the mantel as if to look at the fake photos of her. Eve suspected he didn't want to stand near her anymore.

"Who are you?" Eve asked.

He ran his fingers through his hair again. "Rules."

"Forget the rules. Why should I trust you?"

"Because I care about you, Eve." He held out his hand, as if expecting her to come to him. She laced her hands together in front of her and didn't budge. He lowered his hand. "Because you are the first thing in this world of vacant people, tasteless food, gravity-bound structures, and flaccid entertainment that I have found interesting."

"Uh-huh."

Since she hadn't crossed to him, Aidan came to her. "Or if you don't like that answer, then try this: because I've lost people. People I care about. In my world, there's a war . . ." His voice cracked, and for the first time, Eve thought she was seeing through his smiling facade. Then he controlled himself again. He clasped her hand and drew it to his heart. "You are the answer to a prayer. You are the treasure that I have been seeking. You are the prize that I am destined to win."

"That's nice." Eve wormed her hand away from his.

"I can be your knight in shining armor. I can make you happy. I can make you safe. I can make you whole, if you let me."

Eve opened her mouth to say he couldn't—she was broken with pieces missing, except that she didn't feel broken anymore, thanks to Zach.

"But you found someone else to do all of that. Tell me about him, Evy. Who is this human boy who caught your eye and captured your heart?" He caressed her cheek and then curled his fingers in her hair. His hand tightened into a fist. "What can he do for you that I can't?"

"He can make me fly." She pulled away, and several strands of her hair, still knotted around his fingers, yanked out of her scalp. She spun away from him and ran to her bedroom.

"Evy!"

She shut her door and leaned against it. She scanned the room—the only other door led to a closet, and the window was locked with a padlock. And she realized she'd spoken the truth. She'd flown with Zach—and she hadn't had a vision.

He'd fixed her. He'd cured her.

She didn't have to be the broken girl anymore, afraid of herself, afraid of what she could do, afraid of what was inside of her.

She strode to her dresser and opened the top drawer. "Go back," she told the paper birds. "Be as you were." Eve felt wind in her face as the paper birds fluttered in the drawer. They rose out in a spiral. Backing toward the bed, she watched them dive and soar around the room before flying toward branches in the wallpaper and settling against them. She saw a bird melt into the paper—before she pitched backward, unconscious.

---

*The Magician has a black felt hat. He flips it off his head and tosses it up and down his arms and across his back. He throws it into the air, and I can't see it against the glare of the stage lights. He catches it, plunges his hand in, and pulls out a bouquet of tissue roses, held by the severed hand of a girl. The hand is rigid and bloodless.*

*The audience laughs, but it's a tinny sound, as if it were an old recording. It cuts off abruptly. I can't see the audience from where I lie, wrapped in stage curtains like a shroud, but I see a girl step onto the stage.*

*She has freckles, red-brown hair, and antlers like a deer.*

*The Magician gives her the flowers, and the severed hand begins to bleed. Red flows down the antlered girl's arms. It pools at her feet.*

*And then she and the Magician are gone. I lie unmoving in the silence.*

---

Eve stumbled to the bathroom. She clutched the sides of the sink and tried to force the remnants of the vision out of her mind. *It's not real*, she told herself. *This is real.* This sink. This house. These people. This life. This body. She splashed water on her face.

*Breathe in*, she ordered herself. *Out. In.*

She thought of Zach.

He hadn't fixed her.

She pictured him next to her—if he were here, he'd be telling her facts about sinks or toilets or mirrors or toothpaste or whatever caught his attention. Closing her eyes, she listened to his voice in her imagination. It was like wrapping herself in a warm, soft quilt.

When her breathing was under control again, she listened for sounds of who was in the house. She heard a clatter and then sizzling from the kitchen. At least one person was here.

Leaving the bathroom, Eve followed the sounds to the kitchen. Aunt Nicki was at the stove, stirring hunks of meat in a skillet. She glanced at Eve and then shook pepper onto the meat.

"What's today?" Eve asked. "Have I forgotten again?"

"Don't know." Aunt Nicki stirred more. "It's the day you nearly gave Malcolm heart failure and broke Aidan's heart all in one fell swoop. I'd call that a twofer. You really dove into the traditional teenage rebellion with flair."

It was the same day. She hadn't lost any new memories, at least not yet. Eve exhaled heavily and sank into one of the chairs. "I saw an agency car outside Zach's house. Is he all right?"

Aunt Nicki twisted her head to look over her shoulder at Eve. "You actually care. Astonishing. This is not unlike discovering that one's cat has an appreciation for fine art."

"Did I endanger him?"

"Maybe. Maybe not."

"What do I do?"

Aunt Nicki's lips formed a perfect *O*. "You're seriously ask-ing me for relationship advice. Again." She laid down her spoon and sat in the second chair, opposite of Eve. "Well, if you were an ordinary girl, I'd tell you to spend as much time with him as possible doing ordinary things. See if you like being together, or if you drive each other nuts. But since you're *not* an ordinary girl . . ."

Eve waited.

"In your case, for his sake, you should stay the hell away from him."

"Oh," Eve said.

Above the refrigerator, the clock ticked loudly. The refrig-erator hummed, and the food in the skillet hissed. In a gentler voice, Aunt Nicki said, "The agency is taking care of it."

Eve felt her breath catch in her throat. Again, her ribs wouldn't expand. She clasped her hands together hard. Aunt Nicki couldn't mean . . . "Please don't let the agency hurt him."

"You don't—"

"I kissed him."

Aunt Nicki shrugged. "You kissed Aidan too."

"But it was different. Zach and I floated in the air. And this morning, in the library reading room, we made the books fly. And at his house, we made it rain. And I didn't black out. Not once. Until I was alone again." As the words tumbled out of her mouth, she thought she sounded more like Zach than her-self. Thinking about him in danger made her stomach clench.

Standing up fast, Aunt Nicki knocked her chair backward. "Stay here," she ordered. She darted out of the room as she yanked her phone out of her pocket. Eve heard Aunt Nicki say, "Lou, it's Gallo. It's about the boy . . ." and then her voice was too soft and muffled to make out the words. On the stove, the meat began to burn.

# Eleven

EVE WOKE UP THE next morning and knew she had seen the antlered girl before.

She kicked the sheets away from her feet and stood in front of the birds in the wallpaper. The birds were silent and still. One had its wing extended as if it were about to take flight. Another had its beak tucked beneath its wing, as if trying to hide.

She'd seen the girl's face somewhere other than in her vision.

Eve left her room and headed for the kitchen at a walk first, then at a run.

Aunt Nicki stood at the stove. She was stirring a glop of gray mush in a pot. Sniffing it, she wrinkled her nose. "Oatmeal is a terrible concept. Who cooked this, looked at it, and thought, 'Yummy'? Much more realistic to look at it and think, 'Great! This is perfect grout for my new bathroom.'" She looked up at Eve. "You're not dressed. Did you forget how to dress? I am not picking out your underwear. And I don't do socks."

"I want to look at the photos," Eve said.

Aunt Nicki's expression changed instantly. "I'll drive you."

Eve tossed on clothes and shoved her feet into shoes while Aunt Nicki pitched the oatmeal and fetched her car keys. Eve then followed Aunt Nicki to a black car that was tucked around the side of the house. She strapped the seat belt on and closed her eyes. She tried to fix the image of the girl's face in her mind: the curve of her cheeks, the freckles on her cheekbones, the shape of her nose. The girl had tousled brown curls that were striped with straw-blond strands. The deer antlers sprouted from between the curls. Each boasted six prongs covered in soft brown felt-like fuzz, except for the tips, which were bleached white.

Eve kept her eyes squeezed shut for the entire drive.

She heard the driver-side window roll down, Aunt Nicki talk to the guard, and the agency garage door rattle up. Eve was rocked backward as Aunt Nicki zoomed into the garage, and then forward as she shot into a parking spot and slammed on the brakes. Still, Eve didn't open her eyes until she heard her car door open.

Malcolm was standing there.

He didn't speak.

Eve strode through the parking lot. Malcolm and Aunt Nicki fell in behind her. Aunt Nicki used her ID card on the door, and Eve headed directly to the elevator. Inside, as the tinny music crooned and crackled, Eve covered her ears to block the noise.

"Shut it off," Malcolm growled to Aunt Nicki.

"The beauty of elevator music: no off switch," Aunt Nicki said.

Malcolm thumped the speaker with his fist but it had no effect. *Six prongs*, Eve thought. *Brown eyes. Soft brown. Like leaves in winter.* The elevator lurched to a stop at the third floor. The door slid open.

Eve walked out into the hallway and then into the reception lobby. Malcolm held up his hand to forestall any words by the receptionist. "Close your eyes," Malcolm told Eve. "I will guide you."

She obeyed and let Malcolm and Aunt Nicki guide her through the halls. Other marshals called out greetings. Grimly silent, neither Malcolm nor Aunt Nicki replied.

Eve heard a door shut, and the sounds of the agency were cut off.

She lowered her hands from her ears and opened her eyes. Malcolm was standing before her. He thrust the tablet at her. His hands were shaking, she noticed. Hers shook too as she accepted the tablet. She sank into one of the leather chairs and stared at her glossy reflection in the smooth surface.

For an instant, she couldn't remember how to activate it. She swiped her finger over the surface, but it stayed dark and blank. She tried pressing the button. The screen blossomed to life, and a face appeared. Looking out at her, the face filled the screen: a boy with black eyes and skunk-colored hair. She scrolled to the next face. And then the next.

A boy with pale skin.

A girl with piercings.

A yellow-eyed boy with gills in his neck.

A boy with blotches on his face, or tattoos—elaborate tattoos on his forehead and chin in swirls so dense they blurred into blotches—who stared straight out of the tablet.

*No,* she thought. *Not you. Or you.* She wondered if she was wrong. *Not you. No, no.* She could have imagined it. Or maybe seeing the photo had influenced her visions. *No. No.* Maybe her memories were warped or faulty. *Not you.* Maybe . . .

There.

There she was. The girl with the antlers. She smiled out at Eve with her crooked teeth and her round cheeks with freckles and her six-prong antlers and her brown curls with strands of blond. "Yes," Eve said out loud.

Malcolm sank into his chair. "Tell me about her."

Eve pictured the antlered girl in her vision. She'd reached out her hand for the flowers . . . Eve shook her head. She didn't know the girl's name or where she was from or why she was there or why she was in Eve's mind . . .

But Eve knew one thing.

"She's dead," Eve said.

❦

Several doctors scurried in, took Eve's temperature, took her blood pressure, and took a blood sample. Aunt Nicki fielded phone calls. Malcolm typed furiously on his computer. Other marshals shuttled papers in and out of the office. A bulletin board was pulled into the office, and a photo of the antlered girl was pinned to it, along with a collection of numbers.

Eve didn't move from the leather chair.

She didn't look at any of them. She continued to stare at the face of the antlered girl. She felt as if the office were tilting and rocking around her. *She's real*, Eve thought.

"She liked flowers," Eve said out loud, suddenly certain. The girl had had them in her room, daisies and peonies and flowers that Eve couldn't name shoved into vases and cups and jars on the dresser, bookshelf, and windowsill. She'd braided them around her antlers and worn dresses with patterns that mimicked vines and leaves.

The typing paused. "What else?" Malcolm asked.

Eve shook her head. Her fingers traced the shape of the girl's antlers. Six prongs. Exactly like in her vision. Exactly like in her memory. Eve pictured her with flowers . . . and on a hill. *Yes*, Eve thought. *I remember a hill.* The girl had been silhouetted, blue sky behind her, as if she'd been waiting . . . and then she'd run down the opposite side of the hill, disappearing from sight, her antlers the last bit of her to vanish behind the rocks and grasses. "There was a hill. But I don't know where. And I don't know why she was there or why I was there. Why do I remember her? Who was she?"

"Keep trying," Malcolm said.

"You said they were cut into pieces. Was she?"

Aunt Nicki let out a sharp hiss. "Malcolm!"

Malcolm didn't respond to Aunt Nicki. "You have to remember on your own," he said to Eve. "Your testimony won't carry weight if the jury thinks we fed you false memories. Forget what I said, okay?"

Her hands started to shake hard. Carefully, she laid the tablet on her lap, and she folded her hands together. "You think I saw . . . that?"

"We can't lead the witness."

"That isn't a yes," Aunt Nicki put in. "Keep it together, girl."

Hand still trembling, Eve picked up the tablet again. This girl. She'd been someone's daughter, sister, friend, niece, cousin. She'd had a name . . . but the knowledge of that name slipped away from Eve as if it were a minnow in a stream, bright and shiny in the sun but flashing by so fast that it was only a glimmer, then gone.

"Malcolm . . . ," Aunt Nicki began.

Malcolm cut her off. "It was necessary."

"It wasn't in your report," Aunt Nicki said.

"It doesn't change the result. Agent Gallo, do I have your support? You know what Lou's reaction to this morning will be."

Aunt Nicki was silent.

Eve's eyes flickered up. Aunt Nicki was rubbing her face as if she were tired. Her shoulders sagged, and she looked older than Eve had ever thought she was. "Yes," Aunt Nicki said. "She cares, you know. About the boy. I wouldn't have thought it possible."

Eve looked down at the tablet. The antlered girl continued to smile, forever cheerful. Staring into her warm eyes, Eve heard the door open and slam, and then a voice speak. Lou's voice. She felt her muscles squeeze into fists at the sound of his voice. "Anything else?" Lou demanded. Eve didn't look up. She kept her eyes glued to the face of the antlered girl.

She didn't hear Malcolm's response, but he must have shaken his head because Lou said, "Damn it. This proves we were right! *You* were right! If we could—"

"Patience," Malcolm said. "She's come so far."

"She has a boyfriend," Aunt Nicki put in. "And she's adjusted to the library. She's been helping me around the house as well."

Lou snorted. "Fantastic. She's a real prodigy. Next, you'll have her composing symphonies and writing sonnets. It's not what we need."

Still without looking up, Eve said, "You could tell me what you need."

She heard their surprise—a rustle of their clothes as they turned toward her or toward each other. She knew Malcolm's startled expression without having to see it.

"See, even she agrees," Lou said. "You are too damn cautious!"

"You push too far, too fast, you'll break her," Malcolm said.

Eve raised her head to look at Malcolm. Just Malcolm. She didn't want to look at Lou. "I'm already broken," she said. "And this girl is already dead."

Malcolm's mouth thinned. She knew that expression too. It crossed his face before he exploded—it was the moment before the backdraft. But he held in the firestorm. "You don't know what's best for you. I do. And you need a return to normalcy."

"Agent Harrington—" Lou began.

Malcolm slapped the bulletin board, the one with the photo of the antlered girl on it, and raised his voice, the first time that Eve had ever heard him do so to Lou. "This is progress! I have . . . *she* has made progress! So let us continue! My way!"

Lou was silent for a moment. "Very well. For now."

"Good," Malcolm said in his usual calm, measured tone. His chest was heaving as if he'd sprinted a marathon. "We're done here. *For now.*" He took the tablet from Eve. Hand on her elbow, he hauled Eve to her feet. Her knees felt solid, and she didn't shake, to her surprise. To Aunt Nicki, Malcolm said, "Call Patti Langley. Let her know we're incoming." To Lou, he said, "Short-term results don't justify jeopardizing the long-term goals."

"I said 'very well,'" Lou said, his voice still mild. "But if the situation changes, if he starts again . . . I will have no choice but to accelerate matters."

"Understood," Malcolm said.

He pulled Eve past the bulletin board. Dragging her feet on the carpet, she slowed to look at it. The board was vast, nearly the size of the office wall, and the photo of the antlered girl was tiny within the expanse of empty cork. Two dates were under her photo—today's date and five years' prior—plus a reference number and a case number.

The photo looked lonely on the huge bulletin board. She wondered . . . *No*, she thought. *Don't wonder. Don't think.* She let Malcolm lead her out of the office. Numbly, she walked through the halls. Other conversations—bits of phone calls, briefings, meetings—swirled around her in a meaningless mélange of noise. She barely saw the people who brushed past her.

Ahead, two marshals escorted a boy into an interrogation room.

That looked like . . . "Zach?" She rushed forward as the door to the interrogation room shut. Malcolm's hand clamped on her shoulder, stopping her. The door was closed, and the shades were drawn.

Spinning around, Eve faced Malcolm. "I saw Zach!" She thought of the phone call that Aunt Nicki had made to Lou. She'd assumed that had helped Zach, but what if it had made things worse?

"You didn't," he said firmly.

"But—"

"He isn't here." Putting his arm around her shoulder, Malcolm guided her firmly toward the elevator. Eve felt her rib cage loosen. She sucked in air. If Malcolm said he wasn't here, it must have been her imagination. "Come with me. There's nothing for you here."

"It wasn't him?" Eve asked.

"It wasn't." At the elevator, Malcolm pushed the down button. It opened immediately. Without looking back, Eve walked in with him. The tinny music crooned.

Eve clasped her hands behind her back and thought of Zach and of the brown-eyed girl with flowers woven around her antlers. She thought of them for the entire drive to the library, and tried to think of what to say to Zach when they were alone in the stacks again.

Malcolm let Eve off as usual in the parking lot, though it was hours after her shift had started. Wind blew in the branches of the trees, scattering drops of rain onto the pavement. The clouds had drifted apart, leaving patches of dull gray between them. Puddles filled all the crevasses in the asphalt. As she stepped out of the car, Malcolm handed her an umbrella.

"You did well today," Malcolm said.

"Thank you." Eve wasn't sure if she meant for the umbrella, his words, or more.

She put the umbrella over her head and ran for the lobby door.

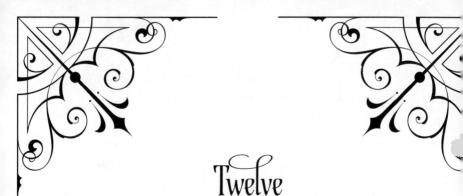

# Twelve

INSIDE THE LOBBY, EVE shook out the umbrella. Drops spattered on the carpet and the wall. Near her, a man seated on a bench lowered his book to frown at her umbrella and wet shoes. He wore a suit and had sunglasses tucked halfway into his coat pocket. She wondered if he was a marshal. As she wiped her feet on the mat, he raised his book, but she felt as if he were still watching her.

She expected to feel better once she was inside the library, but she didn't. *I'll feel better once I find Zach*, she thought. Talking to him, or listening to him talk, always made her feel better. She crossed to the circulation desk.

Two librarians were working the desk—an older woman with bobbed hair and a man with a tattoo on his neck. The woman clucked her tongue. "You're late, Eve."

The man was scanning returned books and adding them to a book cart. He didn't look up. "Patti is pissed. Very, very pissed."

Eve wished she knew their names. She was supposed to have known these people for weeks, but they seemed less real and less familiar than the antlered girl. "Have you seen Zach?"

"Not today," the woman said. "But he's probably in the stacks, where you should be."

Eve eyed the door to Patti's office. It was cracked open, and the light was on. She didn't want to be delayed by a conversation with an irate librarian. With her umbrella dripping by her side, Eve hurried out of the lobby and into the main library.

The reference librarians scowled at her umbrella—or at her. She didn't know their names either, though she thought they looked familiar.

Eve ducked into the stacks. She ignored the book carts full of books to be reshelved, and she steered around patrons. Systematically, she combed the aisles: reference, nonfiction, memoir, audiobooks, fiction, mystery, science fiction and fantasy . . . She checked the children's room and the teen section. She looked in the presentation rooms, the reading room, the staff room, even the men's room.

She didn't find Zach.

*He's not here,* she thought. Her heart thudded fast and hard in her chest. *He should be here.*

Maybe she'd missed his shift. Or maybe he'd stayed home sick. Or maybe that *had* been him in the interrogation room . . . Her hand reached for her phone and then stopped. If Zach had been there, then Malcolm had lied. And if he had lied . . . Standing in the middle of the stacks, Eve felt as if she were crumbling.

*Stop*, she told herself.

She didn't know that Malcolm had lied to her. Zach could have left to run an errand or taken a break. Or she'd simply missed seeing him as she'd scurried through the library.

*Patti would know,* Eve thought. Patti Langley was obsessed with security. She'd know whether an employee was here or not. Clinging to that idea, Eve walked out of the stacks . . . and then jogged . . . and then ran.

Reaching the lobby, she stopped cold.

Aidan leaned against the circulation desk. He waved to Eve and aimed his dazzling smile at her, as if the sight of her filled his day with delight.

"You," Eve said.

"Me," Aidan said. "And you."

She noticed that a line had formed behind a woman wrestling a toddler. If Zach were here, he would have been recruited to help at the desk. "I don't have time to talk right now." Eve started to march past Aidan. The man in the gray suit, she saw, was still there. He watched her from the bench.

"I know. And that's why we need to talk." The flirting lilt vanished from his voice. "We don't have the luxury of time anymore."

Halting, Eve stared at him. "Do you know where Zach is?"

"Zach? Ahh, Zach. So that's his name."

She felt her hands ball into fists. "Did you . . . take him anywhere?"

Aidan spread his hands to show his innocence. "I've never met him. I don't even know what he looks like. Besides, why would you think that of me? I'm wounded, Evy. Truly."

Eve couldn't say why she didn't trust him—and even if she could articulate it, she couldn't say it out loud with the librarians listening. And they *were* listening. The closest librarian feigned interest in her computer screen, but her eyes kept darting to Eve and Aidan, especially Aidan. Another librarian stared openly, as if watching a TV show.

"I have to talk to Patti." Eve brushed past Aidan. He caught her arm.

"You have to talk to *me*. And Victoria and Topher, of course. C'mon, we don't bite. At least not often. And never in public. I swear we'll be the model of decorum. We'll only talk." He tightened his grip.

"Let go of me," she said quietly.

The other librarians ceased typing. She didn't hear any pages rustle or books being stacked. Out of the corner of her eye, she noticed the patrons were watching also.

"I saw the photo on the bulletin board," Aidan said, just as quietly. "That girl . . . She was Victoria's sister. We *need* to talk to you."

Eve felt as if her blood were freezing, crystallizing in her veins. She shook her head. "You're lying," Eve said loudly. The antlered girl belonged to her memories, deep in the past and in another world.

One of the librarians piped up. "Want me to fetch Patti?"

Aidan released her. He took a step backward and raised

his hands as if in surrender. "You can trust me, Green Eyes, even if you don't know it yet. I have your best interests at heart. We all do."

Keeping an eye on him, Eve skirted around the circulation desk. The other librarians kept their eyes on Aidan as well. He didn't vanish or even budge. She felt shivers on her skin. If he was telling the truth . . . She couldn't think about that right now. She had to find Zach. Zach first, then she'd face Victoria.

She pushed open the door to Patti's office and stepped inside. "Patti . . ."

Patti's desk chair was swiveled to the side. A sweater was draped over the armrest. She'd just stepped out, Eve guessed. Her computer hummed softly, and her desk lamp was on.

On the desk under the lamplight, in the center of a semi-circle of books, was a small box. It had gilded edges, jeweled faces, and an ornate clasp.

Eve took a step backward slowly, carefully, as if her knees weren't fully functional. Her heart thudded so hard and fast that the sound of it filled her ears. She felt it beat through her chest and into her skull. Her lungs tightened, as if her rib cage were constricting. It was hard to breathe, and the air felt thick.

She'd seen this box.

In a vision.

It had a silver clasp in the shape of a tree. Rubies clustered like glittering apples in the silver leaves. It was the size of her palm and had slats on all sides. There was also a hook on the top so it could hang from a rope—or from a silk ribbon inside a wagon between feathers and painted skulls.

It couldn't be real.

And it couldn't be here.

She backed against the door.

As her back touched the door, she screamed, and she shoved her hands forward as if she could shove the box and all it meant away.

Books and papers blew off the table in a blast. The box flew against the wall and smashed into it. It crashed down, falling over stacks of books, end over end, and rolled onto the carpet. It lay on its side, and Eve kept screaming.

Behind her, voices were shouting. And then she heard shouts change to screams as magic poured out of her like water through a broken levee. Books flew from the shelves, and the computer monitor shattered into shards of plastic, glass, and metal.

Eve plunged into darkness.

※

*Dangling from a silk ribbon, the boxes sway as the wagon bounces over the road. I am tossed against the painted wood walls, and I feel my skin bruise.*

*Eyes in the boxes watch me, and I watch them.*

*Bottles clink together on the shelves. Skulls snap their mouths open and shut. The skull of a mouse, of a bird, of a cat, of a man. Across the wagon, the Storyteller knits a ribbon of red and blue and gold. It coils around her feet already. Still, she knits it longer and longer.*

*"Once upon a time," she says.*

*I want to speak, but my lips won't move.*

"A man and a woman wanted a child . . ."

*I touch my face with my fingers. My skin feels soft and pliant, but my lips are sealed shut. I tug at them, and then I tear. My fingers gouge my cheeks and chin and lips. My mouth will not open.*

*Across the wagon, the Storyteller continues to knit.* "So they made a child out of clockwork parts."

*I have blood on the tips of my fingers and under my fingernails.*

"And when it was older, it killed them."

*The pain in my fingers feels exquisitely sharp, like tiny needles, and I see the droplets of blood form perfect spheres that plummet toward the wood floor of the wagon. But they do not hit. Instead, I hear rain on the top of a tent. I am no longer in the wagon. I am in the tattered red carnival tent. Rain seeps through the holes in the fabric so that it seems as if the tent itself is crying.*

*The rain slides down the paint on the face of the clown who contorts himself in the center of the tent. He is alone, and his dance is beautiful, a slow ballet that crosses over the floor of wood shavings. There is no music except the rain.*

"Choose a card," *a voice says behind me. It is the Magician, and when I turn, I see he stands at a table of red velvet. Cards spin in the air around him as if they were birds. The cards float, twist, and then land in his open hand.*

*Four fall to the table, facedown.*

*One card flips over without the Magician touching it.*

*It's the image of a sword in a disembodied hand.* "The Ace of Swords," *the Magician says. Another card turns over on its own.*

*"The Wheel of Fortune." A third card flips, showing a man in a robe with a chalice, a sword, and flowers on a table before him. "The Magician." And then the final card. It is blank.*

*I look up at the Magician for him to explain, but he is gone, and so is the tent around me.*

*I am outside, and the stars are spread close and thick in the sky, so many little pieces of brightness that I suddenly understand the word "stardust" because it looks like the blackness has been dusted with specks of light.*

*I smell burned caramel and popcorn, and I hear the ring and clatter of carnival games. The prizes hang above the booths— delicate clockwork birds in golden cages, masks made of curved horns, a flute that plays by itself. And I realize that I am perched like the prizes, high above the ground.*

*From here, I can see the carousel. Its horses are wooden mermaids and winged cats, and its riders are as strange and magical as the mounts—men, women, and children who have wings of their own or clawed hands or faces streaked with feathers. I watch the carousel for a long time, until the mounts detach from their golden poles and ride across the carnival grounds, rising and falling as if they were still connected to the mechanism. The riders are laughing with delight as they are carried into darkness. I stare after them into the darkness—and then realize I am looking into a darkened audience.*

*I am within the tent again, on the stage. Streaks of moonlight filter through slits and holes in the fabric. The stage is ringed with candles. They shed their light upward, twisting the Magician's face into grotesque shadows, which he has highlighted with makeup.*

*"You are the blank card, of course," he says.*

*Behind him is a silver mirror as tall as he is. It's warped, and the curves elongate his reflection so that he stretches into a skeletal figure. His hat narrows into a slit.*

*I walk toward the mirror and stop in front of it. It is metal, not glass, and the candle flames flicker in it. I look into it, and a girl with brown hair and antlers looks back at me. I raise my hand toward the girl's face. She raises her hand. I stop. She stops.*

*It's me. She's me.*

But I have green eyes, *I think.*

*And then I am pushed into the mirror.*

*I melt into the silver. It swirls around me, and coolness sweeps through me. In an instant, it's over. I emerge from the mirror into a meadow. I am beside a lake that glitters in the sun. A wagon waits for me. On its steps is the Storyteller, knitting a red ribbon.*

Eve sucked in air, and her eyes popped open. Harsh white light filled her vision and flooded her mind as if it wanted to sear away every thought. Her eyes watered as she tried to see shapes in the whiteness. She couldn't move her arms or legs. She felt straps bite into her skin as she strained. She was lying flat on her back. She smelled antiseptic, and the smell triggered a memory—tubes in her veins, pain flowering over her skin, eyes burning. She heard a steady beep, shrill and insistent.

*Hospital*, she thought.

She remembered in a rush: The tubes. The pain. The voices. The dreams. The way her muscles had seemed to stretch until they snapped, the way her skin had felt peeled from her body like the skin of an apple, the way her blood had seemed to burn through her veins as if it were gasoline that had been lit on fire.

Last time, they had taken her old body and reshaped it into this new body, this stranger's body. She had woken with only emptiness inside.

*No!* Eve thought.

She couldn't lose herself again.

She tried to flail, but the straps held her down. She arched her back, and alarms began to wail. She heard footsteps race toward the hospital room.

*Out!* she thought. Out through the windows. Out into the world. Out. Away. Far away and never come back. Never be found. Never be unsafe. Never be lost. Never be broken again. She strained to the side and threw her magic at the hospital bed bars, the straps that held her, and at the windows with the drawn shades.

All the windows in the room shattered at once.

Darkness claimed her again.

❁

*I am sitting in the wagon, and the Storyteller's arm is around me. "Shh, shh," she tells me. "Hush." She strokes my hair. "It won't hurt. Not one bit."*

*The Storyteller smells of Vaseline and greasepaint. Her cheeks have been painted with red circles, and a clown's smile stretches over her real lips. The paint has cracked where her skin is wrinkled.*

*I lean against her and let her comfort me, a child in a mother's arms.*

*I think perhaps I sleep.*

*When I wake, she is gone.*

*The Magician squats in front of me. He doesn't wear his felt hat or his cape or stage makeup, and without them, he seems costumed—as if the ordinary pants and shirt of an ordinary man were a disguise.*

*I shrink away, and feel the wood slats of the wagon at my back. Behind him, the scarves from his magic act are strung on a line of silk ribbon, as if they were laundry drying. Between each jewel-colored scarf is the wing of a dove, pinned to the ribbon. On the wagon wall, he has skulls as well, bird skulls and mice and snakes. He's painted them in bright carnival colors. The boxes are stacked in a corner, all empty. I know I am looking everywhere but at him, and I know it will not matter in the end.*

*He smiles at me.*

*"Come now," he says. His voice is soft, soothing, even beautiful. "Whisper sweet nothings to me."*

*I cannot run.*

*He leans close. His lips are nearly touching mine.*

*I scream, and he steals my breath.*

# Thirteen

EVE PLACED A BOOK on the shelf.

She stared at her hands, at the book, at the shelf.

She wasn't in the hospital. She wasn't strapped down. She wasn't in a wagon or a box or a carnival tent. Eve pushed the book into its slot and looked down. She stood on a step stool. A book cart was next to her. It was half-full of books.

She didn't want to turn around. She didn't know what she'd see, what had changed, what she'd forgotten this time. Softly, she called, "Zach?"

He might not be here. She might have lost him; he might be only a memory. Or maybe he was never real at all. Maybe none of this was. Maybe she was still strapped to the hospital bed, and this library, this city, this world was only a vision. She'd never left the hospital, and Malcolm, Aunt Nicki, Aidan, and Zach were all a trick of her mind. Or she was trapped in a box on a string in a wagon, and even the hospital was false. Or she was Victoria's sister—the antlered girl, as the mirror had shown—and she was dead.

Eve didn't realize she'd crouched down, but she was hugging her knees and rocking back and forth on the library stool like a demented bird on a perch.

"Eve?" a voice asked.

Zach.

She heard his footsteps and then felt his hand on her arm. He knelt beside her. She leaned against him and breathed in the smell of him. He cradled her against his shoulder and stroked her hair with one hand. His fingers twisted in her hair, and she thought of the Storyteller. She shuddered. "Eve, are you okay?" he asked.

She turned and touched his face. *He's real*, she thought. Or at least he was real enough that it didn't matter. She let her fingers rove over his face and neck. She felt his breath rise and fall in his chest.

"Eve, you're freaking me out. Talk to me."

"I went to your house, and we made it rain." Eve thought of rain pummeling the manicured lawn and patio stones, and then she thought of rain seeping through a carnival tent at night and of rain breaking through a canopy of leaves and making a campfire hiss and spit. "It rained on your lawn and on the street. I saw a black car through the rain, and a man went to your door. What happened next?"

She felt him tense through his shirt. "Eve . . . I told you everything. I swear. I didn't keep anything from you. And you know I wouldn't lie."

"Please . . . Just humor me." She looked at him and put every ounce of pleading in her eyes. *Don't ask me why*, she thought. *Just tell me.*

Zach studied her for an instant and then adopted his usual light tone. "In retrospect, and only in retrospect, it was kind of cool. Stark interrogation room. One-way mirror. Hostile balding guy in suspenders, straight out of a cable-TV cop show . . ."

"Lou," she whispered. Malcolm had lied. She felt herself start to tremble. Her insides were a jumbled knot. She'd let herself trust Malcolm. She wasn't sure when she'd decided to trust him. It must have crept up gradually, but she'd believed him, and now . . . It was hard to breathe. Her mind kept repeating: *He lied to me.*

"Lou," Zach echoed. Gently, as if he were talking to a feral cat, he said, "And then you know what happened. You were the cause."

"I was?" She couldn't seem to do more than whisper. Her throat felt locked.

"Your aunt called, said she'd talked to you, and boom, the interrogation ended. I was led to a room with a bed and a bathroom and left alone. Next morning, I was briefed on the fact that your safety depended on my secrecy, which was all very cryptically worded. I don't know what they told my parents, but I was brought home, and everyone acted like nothing had ever happened."

"And then?" Eve asked.

"And then . . ." Zach stroked her hair again. "You were missing for two days. The others said you fainted in Patti's office during the earthquake."

"Patti! Is she okay?"

"Yes, of course. Why wouldn't she be?"

Eve sagged against him. "What happened next?"

"You showed up at normal work time with more cryptic comments. Have you changed your mind about explaining? Because an explanation would be rather awesome."

*Lie*, Malcolm had told her before he'd lied to her. She opened her mouth to deflect Zach's questions, but no words came out. She slumped on the stool, against Zach. She couldn't keep doing this, lying to everyone, pretending she was okay when she was in fact splintering so badly that she was only shards of a person. "I don't remember," she said, barely a whisper.

"Hey, if you don't want to tell me, that's okay—"

She twisted to look him full in the face and enunciated clearly and loudly, "I don't remember anything since that day." At least she didn't remember anything except for lying strapped to a hospital bed with tubes and machines and lights . . . or lying strapped to a bench in a wagon with wind chimes of magic boxes and old bones.

He tried to grin, as if wanting to believe she was joking. "Even the day in the basement stacks with the plants . . ." His smile faded. "You're serious. Whoa. Really? Eve, that was two weeks ago. *Two weeks.*" His arms tightened around her. "You need a doctor. A hospital."

Her fingers dug into his arm. "No!" She fought to control her breathing. "No hospital. No doctors. Doctors already know. I . . . I had surgery, and I woke with no memory of who I was or where I was from or why I was there." She thought of the thick forest, of the wagon, of the meadow by a lake. "Since then, I've had these memory losses. In the middle of shelving a book or drinking a glass of juice . . . I lose hours, sometimes days, even weeks. Maybe months. I don't know."

Zach's eyes were wide. "Do the doctors have an explanation?"

"I think . . . I think maybe the doctors caused it. Something went wrong in the surgery. I came out . . . wrong. When other people use magic, they're fine. When you use my magic, you're fine. But when I use my magic, I black out and have these nightmares—visions, I call them—and sometimes I wake from them and I talk and walk and live, and then it's suddenly all erased, everything I did or saw or thought since the vision."

He continued to stare at her, blinked twice as if he were processing her words, and then said, "Like a computer crash?"

"I don't—"

"Your brain resets to the last restore point."

Eve didn't know what that meant.

"You're not saving properly."

She shook her head. "What—?"

"Your magic is screwing up the way your brain transfers short-term memories to long-term memory." He leaned toward her, his voice eager as he explained his theory. "They're stored in different ways in different parts of the brain, and all this . . . stuff has to happen for a memory to move from the hippocampus to the temporal lobe. Or maybe it's lobe to hippocampus. Anyway, your magic must be messing that up."

He understood! Impossibly, amazingly, he believed her

and understood, even if she didn't understand his explanation. "Malcolm said my magic makes my mind unstable."

"So when your brain finally glitches, you lose everything back to before the memory transfer was messed up. Am I right?"

"I guess . . . Yes."

He rocked back on his heels and stared at her again. "Shit. That sucks."

Despite herself, despite it all, Eve laughed. It was a hysterical laugh that shook her so hard that she had to clutch Zach to keep from feeling that she was going to shake apart. Tears pricked her eyes. "Yes, exactly."

He waited while she shook and laughed. Gulping in air, she settled again in his arms. He resumed stroking her hair. She lay against his shoulder. "You never talk about your past," Zach said. "Ever. I thought . . . There are reasons not to talk about the past. I thought you had those kinds of reasons. How far back do you remember?"

"Living with my aunt. Starting work here. But then . . . it's patches."

"There has to be an explanation for what you're experiencing. Long-term amnesia plus problems with short-term memory. Sounds like a side effect of a stroke. Or you could have been injured. You were hurt in a car accident or mountain climbing or skydiving or . . . Wow, Eve." Releasing her, he rocked backward on his heels and ran his hands through his hair. "All this time . . . you've been hiding this from me, from everyone?"

She felt a lump in her throat, and she had to look away from him. Without his arms around her, her skin prickled, cold. She wrapped her own arms around herself.

"You're really brave," Zach said.

Another laugh burst out of her lips, still shrill.

"I'm serious. I can't imagine . . ."

She heard footsteps. Both of them froze. A patron wandered into the aisle. He browsed through two shelves, selected a book, and then left. Eve listened to his footsteps recede, soft on the carpet.

Zach drew Eve close again and resumed stroking her hair, a little faster and harder than was soothing. "Listen, it will be okay."

"You don't know that." Eve wanted to tell him what Malcolm had said—about how the unnamed "he" cut his victims into pieces. And how each piece was kept in a box. And how she saw those boxes in her visions. And how, in her visions, she'd been inside one, shrunken and trapped, in a box that stank of the old urine of other victims. And how she'd seen one of the boxes on Patti's desk in this very library . . . How had it gotten here? Was the Magician here? *Am I safe?* She pushed down a burst of panic. The WitSec agents wouldn't have brought her back to the library if it wasn't safe, she told herself. She'd still be in the agency or the hospital.

"Well, no, I don't know, but I think that's what you're supposed to say in situations like these. Not that I've ever been in a situation like this." He was trying to sound light, Eve could tell, but his voice sounded strained instead.

Another patron poked his head into their aisle. He retreated with apologies when he saw Eve and Zach intertwined. Eve listened for more footsteps.

Zach stood up and pulled Eve to her feet. "It *will* be okay. Because I said so. And I don't lie." He placed his hands on her shoulders so she'd look directly into his eyes. "You know, the moment I saw you, I said to myself—because all the great people talk to themselves, of course—I said, 'Zach, you have to meet that lovely lady, because she will make your life extraordinary.' I was not wrong." He took a deep breath and tried to smile. "I'm going to help you remember."

"You are?" Eve asked.

"You remember that you like to kiss me?" His eyes looked puppy-dog hopeful. "And what happened when you first kissed me?"

"We floated. And then the books in the reading room flew." She could count the number of good memories that she had on one hand—those were two of them.

"And after that?"

She shook her head.

"We experimented. We learned. We . . . had our first real date."

"I don't remember." Saying it out loud made her feel as if someone had reached inside and ripped away pieces of her. Those memories were supposed to be hers! She wanted them back.

"Then I will show you."

He sounded so confident that she nearly smiled in spite of everything.

Taking her hand, he led her deeper into the stacks to a corner where the books were matching yellow and the fluorescent lights flickered and buzzed.

"Relax. All you have to do is give me the magic, and I'll shape it." He leaned toward her. "You don't even have to kiss me. The magic is in your breath. I only have to breathe it in."

She kissed him anyway, eyes open.

Behind him, she saw books sail off the shelves and then stack themselves around them, interlaced like stones in a wall, closing off their row from the rest of the library. He breathed in her magic again, and green tips of plants burst through the worn carpet. They grew, thickening and sprouting. Curling, they wrapped around the bookshelves and spread across the ceiling tile. Leaves unfurled, and soon the bookshelves and walls were draped in lush summer green. Red buds popped from the bends in the green. And then the buds opened all around them, a riot of burgundy roses.

He picked one and handed it to her. She took it. It still smelled like dusty paper, but when he touched the petals, they changed color, shifting from red to purple to blue to pale yellow. "Lovely," she said.

"Not done yet," Zach said. "I can use the magic in multiple ways. I can even hold the magic for a little while before it dissipates. Watch this."

Again he kissed her, taking her magic through the kiss and then pouring it into the library shelves around them. She saw the painting at the end of the row shimmer. Ripples spread through the paint, and water spilled over the lip of the frame.

It soaked into the carpet below, and water lilies sprouted in the dusty fibers. Painted geese swam in circles. "And now," Zach said, "we dance." He placed one hand on her back and held the other. She scooted her feet out of the way as he danced forward and backward, and then slowly she began to follow the rhythm. "You taught me this dance, and you described this bower. You said you'd seen it once and had wished you were the one dancing."

She had? She didn't remember that. She didn't remember this!

Backward and forward. Their lips were almost touching, and she breathed with him as their feet danced. They rose into the air, spiraling up as they danced, and they swirled between the books and the roses and the pond on the wall.

She tried to remember . . . *Maybe, yes, maybe I know this* . . . The touch of his hand on her back. The feel of air beneath her shoes. This was familiar. Yes!

She could smell roses in her memory . . . But they were strewn on a stage. A woman in black and white scooped them into her arms and then waved to the audience. In Eve's memory, the woman had no face. Eve's feet faltered.

"What is it?" Zach asked. "What's wrong? You liked this before. Said you never expected to have made a memory as nice as this. You said that. Remember?"

"I can't." She shook her head, as if she could shake the faceless woman out of her memory. "Stop. It's not helping. Let's just . . . stop."

Gently, he kissed her again, and they drifted down. She

felt the carpet under her feet. Around them, the roses began to close. The vines withered and crumbled into dust. The painting stilled, and the water evaporated.

"Oh, don't stop," a voice drawled. "He still needs to serenade you or produce a marching band from his pocket."

Aidan.

Within the wall of books, Aidan lounged against a bookshelf as if he'd been there for hours. He hadn't changed since her last memory of him. His hair still dusted over his eyebrows, his lips were still curved in a mocking smile, and he was still lovely.

Zach stepped in front of Eve, as if to protect her. "You must be Aidan."

Aidan tipped an imaginary cap. "And you must be Zach. Kudos on your dedication to getting the girl. Seriously, animated painted swans?"

"You aren't welcome here," Zach said.

"It's a public place. By definition, everyone is welcome."

"She doesn't want to talk to you." In front of Eve, Zach crossed his arms, as if attempting to channel Malcolm.

Aidan raised his eyebrows and then looked at Eve. "Eve, does your aunt know what kind of shenanigans you've been up to? I hope you've been sensible enough to hide it from her. For one thing, she'd be appalled that you fell for this sappy, maudlin mush. For another, if she knew you've been transferring your magic to a civilian . . . How much else have you told him?"

Eve opened her mouth and then shut it.

"Aww, you don't remember, do you, Green Eyes?" Aidan said, ignoring Zach.

Eve felt as if her blood had turned cold. She couldn't imagine that she'd told him about her memory losses, though of course she couldn't remember if she had or not.

"But I'm not here about your extracurriculars. We have much more serious matters to discuss." Aidan held out his hand, as if he expected Eve to take it. "Come on."

"Don't," Zach said to Eve. "You told me you were warned not to trust him."

Aidan mimed being stabbed in the chest. "I'm wounded to the quick! Who would say such a dastardly thing about me? Of course you can trust me, Green Eyes. We're on the same side. This boy . . . He doesn't even know there *are* sides. You think it's a game, don't you, local boy? Who can win the girl? Believe me, there's a lot more at stake."

Stepping in front of Zach, Eve blocked him. "You're the one who plays games."

"It was a test," Aidan said, "as I have explained to you . . . and as you have forgotten. A test that you passed with flying colors." He stretched out his hand again, palm up. "Come with me, and this time, I will explain everything. And more."

"Everything?" Eve asked. If he had answers . . .

His smile broadened like a shark in view of a school of fish. "And more," he promised.

"Eve isn't going anywhere with you," Zach said.

"Cute. But naïve. I see why you like him, Green Eyes. There's such a sweet innocence about him. But it's time to put away the toys. There are grown-up matters to attend to now."

"You can't—" Zach began.

Aidan vanished.

Eve suddenly felt hands on her shoulders.

"Oh yes, I can," Aidan said.

And the library and Zach vanished around her.

White.

And then red.

And then white, red, white, red, until Eve's vision cleared and she saw that she faced a wall of red-and-white checkered wallpaper, mirrors, and plaster sculptures of women in draped dresses. Aidan's hands were tight on her shoulders. She yanked away and fell forward. She caught herself on a table with a red-and-white checkered tablecloth, paper napkins, plastic cups, and menus.

"Easy there, Green Eyes," Aidan said. "Takes a bit to adjust."

The floor swam at her feet. She steadied herself on the table. She inhaled the smell of pizza and heard the bustle of people in a kitchen—the clanging of pans, the closing of ovens, the sound of knives on plates.

Straightening, she turned to face Mario's House of Pizza. All the tables were empty except one. Topher and Victoria had staked out a round table tucked against the walls in the corner. It had three chairs. Seeing them, Victoria rose and dragged a fourth chair to the table.

"Take me back," Eve said to Aidan.

"I told you," he said. "It's time to talk."

She pulled the phone out of her pocket to call Malcolm. Aidan caught her wrist. He twisted the phone out of her hand and then slid it back into her pocket. She noticed that there was a mirror behind him. She could break it, make the glass fly at him . . . And end up in the hospital again, maybe lose even more days or weeks. She couldn't face that. She sagged, and Aidan guided her toward the table as if he were a polite gentleman. Topher smiled a languid smile that could have been mocking or could have simply been pasted onto his face. Eve didn't think for an instant that it was a genuine smile.

Victoria smiled at Eve too, showing her gleaming teeth. "Evy, relax. We want to be your friends. Believe me, we can be the most wonderful friends."

Eve looked away. She couldn't look at Victoria knowing that her sister—maybe even her sister's death—was lodged somewhere in her memory . . . if she believed Aidan's assertion that the antlered girl was Victoria's sister.

"We thought we'd have time to win you over. Aidan had such a lovely plan . . ." Victoria sighed, and then said briskly, "But plans fall apart and time moves on, and now you'll simply have to trust us."

"Really, in your position, you don't have much choice," Topher said lazily. He propped his feet up on the table and tilted his chair back.

"What position would that be?" Eve asked.

Aidan drew the empty chair away from the table for Eve. Gently, he pushed down on her shoulder, encouraging her to sit. She shifted away from his hand, but she took the seat.

"I'm sensing a bit of tension," Victoria said. "We need to remedy that with grease and garlic. Aidan, fetch the garlic knots. They should be ready by now." She smiled again at Eve. "I think all serious conversations are better with fat and carbs, don't you?"

Eve didn't smile back. "What do you want?" She didn't know what she was going to say when Victoria asked about her sister. She had no answers.

"Garlic knots. Weren't you listening?" She snapped her fingers at Aidan. "Aidan. Fetch. Now." Aidan looked amused, but he still trotted to the counter. "Nice boy," Victoria said, either approvingly or ironically—Eve wasn't sure which.

"He's not," Eve said. "He kidnapped me."

"For your own good." Victoria reached across the table and patted Eve's hand. "We have to stick together. It's dangerous these days." Beside her, Topher played with sparks between his fingertips. He kept his hands low, under the table, so as not to attract attention.

"I'm sorry about your sister," Eve said.

Topher rocked his chair forward, and it landed with a thump. His lazy smile had vanished. Victoria froze. She didn't move. She didn't breathe. For an instant, Eve thought her face was going to crack like an ice sculpture tapped with a chisel. "Thank you," Victoria said, a chill frosting her voice. "Someday, she will be avenged."

Returning, Aidan tossed a bowl of garlic knots on the table. The smell permeated the air and wormed into Eve's nose until she breathed garlic.

Across the table, Topher squeezed Victoria's hand. A smile flashed onto her face, too fast to be real. "Until then, there is one silver lining," Victoria said. "If events hadn't unfolded as they did, then we wouldn't have been sent to this world, and we wouldn't have met each other—or you."

"Destiny," Topher said.

"Ours and yours." Aidan clasped Eve's hand.

Eve extracted her hand from his. She didn't know why they were making this hard sell to befriend her. She'd expected questions about Victoria's sister or her visions or the case. "I'm not interested in destiny. I don't need your 'safety in numbers.' The marshals are keeping me safe. So if you'll excuse me—" She rose.

Victoria laughed, her voice a cascade. "Oh, Aidan, you are so right about her! She's so . . . sweet and wide-eyed innocent as a little doe about to be served on a platter with julienned carrots and a fat apple in her mouth." She mimed placing an apple in her mouth and then pretended to crunch into it.

Topher leaned forward. "You can't trust the agency."

"Funny," Eve said. "They said the same thing about you."

"Of course they did," Victoria said. "They aren't stupid."

"Just short-sighted," Aidan added.

"It's their nature." Topher tipped his chair back again. "They're sheep. They can't understand or appreciate the power and beauty of wolves. They try to tame us, of course, to use us, but in the end, they fear us."

Sitting next to her, Aidan smiled, a tender, encompassing smile. He stretched his arm against the back of her chair. She sat ramrod straight, not touching his arm. "We see your power and beauty, Eve, and we admire it. We treasure it."

"You will be our treasure, my dear sweet Eve," Victoria cooed. Aidan had called her a treasure before—a treasure that he'd been seeking, a prize to win. Eve didn't like the sound of that. She wasn't a thing. Eve glanced at the door and wondered how quickly she could reach it. *Not quickly enough*, she thought. Aidan could stop her in an instant.

"She doesn't look convinced," Topher observed. "In fact, she looks confused. We need to be clearer." He leaned forward again. "Once this is all over, once the 'case' is closed, you will be killed."

Eve stared at him.

"Your big, strong protector agent man will kill you him-self," Victoria said. "Or perhaps it will be more anonymous. A little poison. An injection. An IV in the hospital. Oh, how easy it will be for them, especially once you fall into one of your oh-so-precious fainting fits, which, by the way, are ever so charming—the wilting heroine."

Eve felt as if the ground were falling away beneath her feet. They had to be lying. The marshals were keeping her safe. Malcolm was devoted to her safety.

"Or perhaps it will be that aunt of yours," Victoria contin-ued. "She's always despised you. If that big mush is too soft to do it himself, perhaps beloved 'Aunt' Nicki will smother you with a pillow as you sleep."

"Or use a gun," Topher said. "You always think of such elaborate death scenes, Victoria. Really, it isn't as though they'll tie her above a pool of sharks. They're much more practical than that. When they're done using her, *bam*. Dead."

They'd given her a home, a job, food, even a name. They'd made it clear that they needed her and her memory . . . but what about after she remembered? What would happen after they had all they needed from her? Eve shook her head. She shouldn't listen to this. It was lies. Poisonous lies. "Why are you saying this?"

"You're special." Victoria smiled again. "We saw it when we first met, and our observation of you has only confirmed it." Eve thought of the snake on the rock in the woods. She thought of the times she'd felt watched in the library and elsewhere.

"You've been watching me?" Eve asked.

Topher popped a garlic knot in his mouth. His cheeks bulged as he chewed. "We'd like to offer you a choice. You could be a good little sheep, play along with your herders, let them fleece you, and then let them kill you like so much mutton. Or you could join with us, pledge to our world, and let us save you when the time is right."

Eve sank into the chair. "How can I trust you? You tried to kill me when we met."

"Only in jest!" Victoria said. Then she shrugged. "Okay, no, it was real. We did try to kill you. Lou promised that if we tested you, we could stay together. Believe me, until that afternoon, we had no idea who you were."

Her heart beat faster. "Who am I?"

"You're the one with the power!"

"You have power too," Eve pointed out.

"Obviously." Victoria rolled her eyes. "We all fit the killer's favorite profile. Otherwise, we wouldn't be here. But you . . . you are unique!"

"A freak among freaks," Topher drawled.

Victoria swatted him. "Amusingly, you don't even know how special you are. You don't know how rare it is to have even one power. To have more . . . No one has more! We are the best of the best, yet we have limits. Topher, for instance, only controls electricity. Aidan only teleports himself to places he's been. Me . . . you've seen me. But you—you defy every theory of magic ever written! You possess multiple powers. And even more, you can share them. That's unheard of! No one can do that. You have such incredible potential! You can't even imagine the wonderful future that lies ahead of you!"

"If they don't kill you first," Topher said, eating another garlic knot.

"But . . . but why . . ." Eve swallowed and tried again. "Why am I unique?" That was the core question, she thought, the key to everything trapped inside her mixed-up, broken brain.

Aidan patted her shoulder. "It's all right. You don't need to remember why. It's the future that matters, not the past, as far as we're concerned."

They all knew about her memory? Eve felt cold inside. Malcolm had cautioned her to lie—ordered her, even—yet they knew. "How . . . ," Eve began.

"How do we know you don't remember? Aside from it being blatantly obvious every time you show up here with another memory lapse?" Victoria said. "Aside from that . . . well, snakes do have ears, despite common misconceptions."

"Victoria makes an excellent spy," Topher said proudly.

"Which is also how we know what they plan," Victoria said. "Destroy you, and let my sister's killer live. They fear you, and they think they can use him. They have it backward."

Topher rolled his eyes at her. "This shouldn't be a tough call. They plan to kill you, Eve. We don't. Align yourself with us."

"You don't need to decide now," Aidan said. "Consider it. Watch your keepers. Decide for yourself." She noticed he was speaking faster. "If you decide you want to live a life of safety, grandeur, and purpose, then your choice is simple. When the time is right, come with us back to my world."

"But . . . ," Eve began.

"Enough," Topher said. "It's time for our 'treasure' to leave us."

"You're . . . letting me go?" Eve asked.

Topher nodded at the door. "So to speak."

Malcolm charged through the front door. He had three agents flanking him. He held his badge in one hand—he flashed it at the employees—and a gun in the other. The other three agents wore bulletproof vests and had their guns raised.

Victoria, Topher, and Aidan all raised their hands in surrender.

"Garlic knot?" Topher offered Malcolm.

# Fourteen

EVE HAD SPENT A lot of time in Malcolm's car, studying his expressions. She was more familiar with his face than any other in her spotty memory. She was an expert on the way his cheek muscle twitched before he laughed or the way his eyebrows lowered when he was upset or the way his lips moved ever so slightly when he was deep in thought. But she still didn't know if he intended to kill her.

As he drove out of the restaurant parking lot, Eve studied him anew. He had a scar in the shape of a crescent moon on his chin that seemed to darken when he was angry—and it was dark now. His jaw was tense, and that tension rippled to his neck, thickening it, and down his arms to his clenched hands on the steering wheel. He glared at the road as if it had insulted him.

"After the case is over, what happens to me?" Eve asked.

"You live your life," Malcolm said. "But you live it without fear."

Such a nebulous concept. Her life. "What's my life like?" She tried to picture her home, but all that came to mind was the little room with the quilt on the bed, the painted dresser, and the birds-and-branches wallpaper.

"You know I can't talk about your past."

"Can you talk about yours?"

She noted the way his eyes widened to smooth the creases by the corners of his eyes—he was startled. His face was easy to read. She wanted to believe that his was a face that would never lie to her, but she knew he'd already lied to her at least once. "Mine?"

"Yes."

He braked at a traffic light and watched a pack of joggers cross the street. Chests heaving, they glistened with sweat. One of them drooped more than the others, arms sagging by his side as if they pulled at his arm sockets. Still, Malcolm scanned the joggers, his eyes flickering as if calculating the distance between them and the car, in case they proved dangerous. It occurred to Eve that his job was full of lies—both telling lies and watching for lies in order to protect his witnesses. "I . . . um . . . what do you want to know?"

"Everything! I want to know about you—who you are, what made you who you are. I want to know what it's like to have memories inside you that make sense!" She realized she was shouting, and she clamped her mouth shut. She didn't think she'd ever shouted at him before—at least not that she remembered.

Malcolm was studying her with the same attention that

he'd given the joggers. He then faced the road and eased off the brake. The car rolled through the intersection. "All right. If it will help, ask me questions."

She wanted to release an avalanche of questions—all the things she wanted to know about herself but aimed at him. She settled on one. "Do you have parents?"

"Yes."

"What's it like to have parents?"

He drove slowly, as if the car were also thinking while he deliberated. "Your parents define the world for you at first. Right, wrong, normal, not normal. You know, you should have this discussion with Lou. He's far better suited for the philosophical stuff. Joint major in psychology and biology. Smarter than he seems."

"Tell me about them. Your parents."

"My parents were fine. Mom stayed home; Dad worked. He was a cop. And he was my hero. He was the one I looked up to and emulated. He was always trying to protect everybody. While Mom . . . she was the one who protected me."

"What did she protect you from?" Eve tried to picture a mother protecting her like a mama bird. She tried to remember what it must have felt like to have her say good night or greet her in the morning or ask about her day or comfort her . . . or whatever mothers did.

"Anything and everything. She was fierce. Also, she sang all the time. Had a terrible voice. Could not hold a tune. I inherited that from her. Birds take flight when I sing. Small children cower in fear. Once, I joined in singing with the congregation during a wedding ceremony and the woman in the pew in front of me turned around and said in a prim voice, 'You know, singing is not required.'"

Eve searched her memory for music . . . A cello, always at night. A fiddle and a flute and bells. She'd heard a soprano sing once in a voice that rose so high it became silent . . . The memories floated in the murk of her mind without time, place, or context. She couldn't tell if they were real memories or not.

"She'd sing on holidays. On birthdays. In the kitchen. In the shower. My father liked to tease her about it, but she kept on singing."

"Are they dead?" Eve asked.

"Yes."

"Are mine?"

He hesitated. "I can't tell you that. You have to remember your past on your own."

"Why?" Eve asked.

"Because it has to be from you."

"Why?" Eve asked again.

"Because you need . . ." Malcolm stopped and then said, "Because the case needs your uninfluenced memories." She was certain that wasn't what he had intended to say.

"What if I can't solve your case? What if I never remember? What if you never catch him? What if no one is ever safe? What happens then?"

He gripped the steering wheel. Eve noticed they were heading toward the agency garage. "That won't happen," he said.

"How do you know?"

"Because I . . . because *you* . . . won't let it." Malcolm drove into the garage, and the door slid shut behind them. Twisting in her seat, she watched it lower, watched daylight disappear.

❁

The elevator doors opened on level three.

Eve saw Lou.

*I can't face him*, she thought.

She pushed the elevator door button, and the doors started to close again. Malcolm's arm shot out, blocking the sensor, and the doors slid back open.

Lou grunted, pivoted, and stalked away, and Malcolm prodded Eve forward out of the elevator. "He hates me," Eve muttered to Malcolm. *He might want to kill me*, she wanted to say.

"He doesn't hate you," Malcolm said.

Lou called, "Actually, I do." His voice drifted over the cubicles. "I hate everyone universally. It saves time. You have any idea how much time is wasted on polite pleasantries?" He was waiting for them when they rounded the corner. He wore a tie, but it was loose and the top button of his shirt was undone. Eve glimpsed a corner of a tattoo on his collarbone. "Don't start thinking you're special because of me." He walked into Malcolm's office.

*No*, Eve thought, *I'm special because I'm a freak.* A freak among freaks, as Topher had said.

Malcolm steered Eve inside and then shut the door.

Eve checked Malcolm's expression. It was guarded, as if he were thinking thoughts that he'd decided should not be said out loud. She wondered if those thoughts were directed at her or at Lou.

The bulletin board had changed since the last time she remembered being here. Instead of the one photo of the ant-lered girl, the board was covered in multiple photographs. All of the photos were of teenagers. They were arranged in a spiral, with lines and arrows drawn between them, and were labeled with numbers and dates.

She halted in front of the board. There was a circle around the number one next to the antlered girl. Beside her was a boy with tattoos on his cheek. He was labeled number two. Beside him was another boy . . . She recognized their faces from the photos on the tablet. But why had they been added to the board? She reached to touch one photo, the boy with the tattoos. There was something familiar . . .

"You remembered them," Malcolm said quietly behind her.

She hadn't.

She didn't.

It was hard to breathe. Her rib cage felt as if it had knitted together, squeezing her lungs until they were shriveled rai-sins. She heard her breath loud in her ears, ragged and harsh. Her feet retreated until her back hit the door.

"We're close! Very close. There's almost a pattern." Lou swept his arm over the bulletin board. "A few more, and it will fall into place. We have the suspects narrowed down to a mere handful. All we need are the final pieces . . . and then we'll have him." He closed his fist. "Are you ready?"

"Ready for what?" Eve asked. Her voice felt dry.

"To remember more," Lou said.

Malcolm tilted her chin up so she had to look in his eyes. He stared at her as if he could access her thoughts through her eyes. "What's your last memory?"

"I saw the box in Patti's office. And then the hospital . . . and that's it until today in the library. I was shelving books. Malcolm, the box. How did it get there? What . . ."

Malcolm released her chin and said to Lou, "I told you, the harder we push—"

"Your objection was noted, but we have no choice. He *will* start again. My sources have confirmed it. It's a matter of when and who and where, not if." Lou pointed a finger at Eve and then at the leather couch. "Lie down. Use your magic. Have a vision. Tell us what you see."

Eve didn't move. She must have heard him wrong. He couldn't be asking her to . . . *No*, she thought. She couldn't have done this before. She couldn't have seen all those people!

She turned back to the bulletin board and tried to remember them again—but looking at them was looking at strangers. Except for the antlered girl and the boy with the tattoos. Eve wished she could run. She wanted to be as far from this place, these people, this case, as possible. But the photos stared at her. *He won't stop*, Malcolm had said to her once. *He'll find another way. If we don't catch him, it will begin again.*

The antlered girl, Victoria's sister, had worn silks and

velvets, Eve remembered. But she never wore shoes. She'd run through the forest at dawn while the undergrowth was still damp with dew and the air filled with birdsong. Eve had watched her, her bare feet pounding down the same path every morning. She'd skip over a brook, and it would burble and babble at her feet. Her footfalls were soft on the needles, but she was still loud enough to startle birds out of the underbrush and cause the squirrels to scurry to the tops of the trees. She had run alone.

Eve moved to the photo marked number two, the boy with tattoos. She leaned close until her nose almost touched the bulletin board. The tattoos looked like serpents that were woven so tightly together it was impossible to tell where one snake began and another ended. The scales bled into one another. She could picture a box with a clasp encrusted in silver serpents, a replica of those tattoos.

*There's truth in my visions*, she thought, and she felt her stomach churn. She tasted bile. If her visions were memories, or even twisted versions of real memories . . .

She realized both Lou and Malcolm were watching her. Arms crossed, Lou was drumming his fingers on his bicep. She wondered how many visions she'd already had and what she'd seen, and realized she was shaking.

Lou exhaled in a puff. "Just do it. Every moment you waste—"

"But I'll lose days!" For every memory she gave them, she lost dozens more. "How many times have we had this conversation? How many times have I forgotten everything I've done?" She waved her hand at all the photos on the bulletin board. "How many times have I forgotten everything I thought, felt, decided, believed? Everything I cared about? Everything I am?"

Malcolm was silent. He looked at Lou.

"We have had this conversation three times," Lou said. "And we will have it again. And you *will* remember because otherwise people will die."

Eve felt herself deflate.

"You will be here the entire time." Malcolm's voice was soothing, and he steered her gently to the couch. "You will be safe. You don't have to be afraid."

"Was I afraid before?" Eve lay down. She crossed her arms over her chest and felt as if she were lying in a coffin. The couch cushions were stiff and smelled of smoke.

Malcolm hesitated, as if he wanted to lie. "Every time."

She leaned back onto the pillows. Her heart was pounding hard, so hard that it hurt. She laid her hands over her chest as if it were a bird that she wanted to hold inside her ribs. Her ribs were a cage, and her heart was a bird, and it was fluttering its wings so very fast. It would escape, and it would fly to the sky and leave her body to die, heartless and without memories on the couch.

"You don't always forget." Malcolm patted her hand. "Sometimes you remember—at least until next time." He smiled as if this should reassure her. It didn't.

"Get on with it," Lou said.

She thought of a bit of magic she could do, harmless magic.

She remembered the flowers that Zach had grown in the library. She spread her hands and imagined there were flowers growing from them. Bark spread over her hands. Leaves sprouted between her fingers.

"Don't transform!" Lou said sharply.

But it was too late. She was wood inside. She felt it spread, calming her, steadying her. She felt his voice recede until it was merely wind. He was shouting; she could see his lips move, and doctors were rushing into the office. Then bark sealed over her eyes, and she saw nothing until the smoke rolled in.

❀

*Smoke curls around me in shapes: a snake, a dragon, a cat, a hand . . . and then it dissipates into a formless haze. I am suspended in the smoke. Ropes are wrapped around my wrists, my elbows, my shoulders, my knees, my neck.*

*I feel safe.*

*Cocooned, I spin slowly, and the ropes wrap tighter around me. And then I spin in the other direction, and the ropes unwrap. I twist. I untwist.*

*And then the ropes loosen, and I fall.*

*The ropes snap. I scream.*

*I am lying facedown in the muddy dirt. My arms shake as if they have never been used before, but I push myself upright.*

*I am on the dirt floor of the carnival tent, in a row of feet and legs. Around me, above me, hands are clapping for a performance that I didn't hear or see. Up farther, faces are smeared with white paint and rose circles. Garish eyes are painted on foreheads and necks and chests. I can't see the stage. It is shrouded in smoke, my smoke, that billows and puffs into a snake, a dragon, a cat, a hand . . . But I am outside the smoke, between strangers, and I do not feel safe anymore.*

*Pushing past the legs and climbing over the feet, I squeeze down the row until I reach the aisle. At last, I can see the stage. It is draped in red velvet and lit by candles that line the edge.*

*A cello plays slowly.*

*The Magician pushes a box onstage. It is larger than those in the wagon, but it is undeniably the same. I recognize its gilded edges and the silver clasp. Staring at it, I feel my rib cage shrink inside me. It's hard to breathe, and the smoke-laden air scratches my throat.*

*A girl with many arms scuttles onto the stage, pushing a free-standing silver mirror with two of her arms and using her other arms as extra legs. She positions the mirror behind the Magician, and then disappears back into the smoke.*

*Looking around, I see a break in the tent at the back of the audience. I walk toward it, away from the stage and the Magician and the box.*

*I hear a gasp, then whispers.*

*Hands point to the stage, but I do not look, will not look. I walk toward the exit, faster, but it seems farther away with each step.*

*At last I reach it and push aside the curtain. And face a silver wall.*

*In the silver, I see a reflection of the stage behind me. The*

*Magician has opened the box. He is looking over the audience at me, or at the silver wall. In the mirror, a boy with white-yellow hair and thin eyes stares out at me.*

*I look over my shoulder . . . but there's no boy. I am the boy.*

*I look back at the silver, and now I am a taller boy with leopard-spot tattoos on my neck. Leather straps cross my chest, and a sword is strapped to my back. I reach back to touch it, and the hand of the boy in the mirror reaches in sync with me. The reflection touches the sword, but I feel nothing. I look for the sword— and this time when I look back at the silver, I am a girl with feathers in my hair and glittering scales on my arms.*

*I reach to touch the reflection—and melt into it. Cold slices through me as I walk forward. Light pricks my eyes. I block my eyes with my arm and squint until my eyes adjust to the stabs of light.*

*I am behind the Magician on the stage.*

*The box, fully open, is in front of him. He flourishes his cape and then beckons with one finger. It is many-jointed, and it curls like a snake. I know without seeing his face that he is smiling.*

*The audience stares at me with their unblinking painted eyes.*

*A boy walks onto the stage, slowly and stiffly, as if he were pulled by puppet strings. He's young, not yet a man, and he has dark hair and dark skin. He wears an embroidered gold shirt. And I know he is about to die.*

*I want to warn him. Or stop him. Or force him to run away with me, far, far away until we can't hear the tinny sound of the carousel or feel the painted eyes of the audience.*

*But ropes wrap around my body, weaving themselves around my wrists, elbows, legs . . . tighter, tighter, until I cannot even shudder. I am lifted into the air and watch from above as the boy climbs into the box and lies down. The Magician closes the box.*

*He lifts a saw over his head. He turns, showing the saw to the front, the left, the right. It is the saw of a woodcutter. Candlelight dances over the blade, caressing it.*

*The audience is hushed, expectant, excited. I feel it in the air.*

*The Magician begins to saw the box in half, and blood drips onto the stage and runs in a river that douses the candles. I swing from the rafters as smoke rises. It thickens and curls around me. Obscuring the stage, it shapes itself into a snake and a hand and a cat . . .*

Eve woke in a hospital bed.

She lifted her hand. She hadn't been strapped down this time. Spreading her fingers, she didn't see leaves or bark. Maybe she had only imagined it. Or maybe the doctors had fixed her. She wondered if she looked the same. Her hands went to her face, and she touched the shape of her cheekbones, her chin, her forehead. She wondered how much time had passed.

"Want a mirror?" Aunt Nicki asked.

Eve started. She hadn't noticed Aunt Nicki was there. Aunt Nicki was curled on a chair next to the hospital bed. She had an array of empty, stained coffee cups next to her and a magazine on her lap. Searching her purse, Aunt Nicki produced a small case. She flipped it open and held the mirror up to Eve's face.

She didn't see the antlered girl, or the boy with the leopard tattoos, or anyone from a photo on the bulletin board. She saw only the face she remembered, the girl with green eyes.

"Neat trick you pulled," Aunt Nicki said. "Don't do it again. Can't put a lilac bush—or whatever you were—on the witness stand."

Eve felt her cheek, and her fingers touched smooth skin. "More surgeries?"

"You changed yourself back. Don't you remember? Never mind. Don't answer that. Clearly you don't, and no, I am not going to play twenty questions with you so you can figure out how much time you lost. You'll only forget again, so what's the point?"

Eve turned her face away from the mirror and stared through the bars of the hospital bed at the blank wall. This room did not have windows. Beside her, machines beeped in a steady rhythm. She had an IV attached to her arm. She heard Aunt Nicki's chair creak, and then rustling, as if Aunt Nicki were searching through her purse again.

"Okay, I need the details," Aunt Nicki said. Paper crinkled, and a pen clicked.

Eve didn't turn her head. "It's real, isn't it? The people that I see . . ." Her voice sounded dead to her ears. She felt so very tired, as if all the pain and surprise and fear had been drained out of her, replaced by the saline that dripped into her veins through the needle in her arm.

"Faces? Names? Locations? Come on, I know the visions aren't fun. Don't let them be pointless too. Share with your auntie."

Eve listened to the heart monitor and told Aunt Nicki every detail she could remember—the smoke, the audience with the painted eyes, the boy in the box, the silver mirror and her changing reflections. Aunt Nicki scribbled notes as Eve talked, the pen *skritch*ing over the paper. Eve also heard the click of a voice recorder, and she knew she was being filmed by at least two security cameras focused on the hospital bed.

"Great," Aunt Nicki said. "Photo time." She dumped the tablet onto Eve's lap. Eve tried to prop herself up on her elbows. An alarm shrieked. Aunt Nicki silenced it and waved away the guard and nurse who had shoved through the door side by side.

Aunt Nicki picked up the tablet and scrolled to the first face. "Do you recognize her?"

Eve shook her head.

Aunt Nicki slid to the next photo.

Another shake.

Next photo.

No.

Next.

No.

Next.

No.

Another. And another. And another.

"Yes." Eve studied the boy with the embroidered gold shirt. "Yes, this is the one I saw."

Aunt Nicki was silent for a moment.

Eve turned her head to look at her. Her face looked raw, pain clear on her features. She then switched off the tablet and stowed it in her bag. She didn't meet Eve's eyes.

"I knew him," Aunt Nicki said quietly. "He was one of the best." She stood and put her bag over her shoulder. "You should sleep now."

Eve thought of the smoke and the box. "I don't think I can."

Aunt Nicki smiled, but it was a cold smile. She twisted a dial on the IV. "You will." She left the room. The door closed behind her.

Eve watched the monitor as her heart rate slowed, and she faded into dreamless darkness.

# Fifteen

AS MALCOLM TALKED TO the nurses outside her room, Eve shed her blue hospital gown and dressed in ordinary clothes. She raked a brush through her hair and thought of the boy in the golden shirt. He'd admired the acrobats: three men with red-and-orange feathers that had either sprouted from their skin or been sewn into it. They'd been practicing a routine where they'd tossed one another into the air and rode the wind high above the carnival tent, spinning and swirling before plummeting in a dive that ended in a tumble. All three had been more graceful than birds, silent in their aerial dance. One had unfurled a ribbon from his wrist. Another had caught it and swung, and then they'd painted the sky with silks of ruby, emerald, and gold. Flipping over one another, they'd woven the ribbons into a circle that they then let flutter to the ground. Hands outstretched, the boy in gold had caught the circle of ribbons. He'd then flown into the sky with it—without hidden wires, a trapeze, or ribbons to lift him—and met the acrobats in the air.

In that world, the carnival had been beneath a city in the trees. Above them, vast structures had been woven into the branches, and the homes had been like enclosed nests. As the acrobats flew overhead, the Storyteller had nestled in the roots of one of the trees. She had told tales about birds who guarded treasure while silver-clad monkeys stole everlasting fruit. While listening to her, Eve had watched the golden boy.

Bits of memory or bits of imagination?

Eve didn't know, and she couldn't summon the energy to care. She felt drained, as if someone had siphoned every drop of blood and moisture out of her body and left her a husk.

Leaving the hospital room, Eve joined Malcolm at the nurses' station. He glanced at her and then handed the paperwork to an expressionless nurse with slicked-back hair. The nurse filed the papers and then turned to Eve. "Wrist," the nurse commanded.

Eve glanced at Malcolm to interpret this cryptic statement, and he tapped his left wrist. She wore an ID bracelet. She hadn't noticed it. As she lifted her arm up, she read the bracelet: PATIENT 001. She wondered if that meant she was their only patient or their first. She didn't ask. The nurse snipped the plastic band off and dropped it in the trash.

"Keep her hydrated," the nurse said to Malcolm, as if Eve weren't capable of listening to and following instructions. *Maybe I'm not*, Eve thought. She wondered how many instructions she'd heard and forgotten over the weeks, months, or however long she'd been with WitSec. "Lots of rest. You keep pushing her like this, and I won't be held responsible."

"It's not my call, not anymore," Malcolm said. "The situation changed." Eve looked sharply at him. "But I will do what I can. Her well-being is always my priority." Hand on her shoulder, Malcolm guided Eve away from the nurses' station. She wondered what had changed and if it would do any good to ask. Swiping his ID card, Malcolm unlocked a door and led her through a white hall to an elevator. He pushed the down button. The doors slid open—

She knew this elevator: the brown-walled interior and the worn carpet, the tinny music that drifted out the open door.

*This isn't a hospital*, she realized.

She'd never left the agency.

Eve followed Malcolm into the elevator. He punched the button for the garage, and the doors slid closed. The elevator lurched down. She'd been on level four. The offices were three. Level five had the room with the silver walls.

"How many times?" Eve asked dully.

Malcolm raised his eyebrows.

"I was at the pizza place with Aidan, Topher, and Victoria. You brought me here. How long have I been here?"

"Seven," Malcolm said.

"Days or visions?"

"Days," he said as the elevator opened. "I don't know how many visions."

*Seven lost days*, she thought. Numbly, she followed him out of the elevator and through the garage to yet another black car. She climbed into the passenger seat, snapped on her seat belt, and rested her head against the window as Malcolm drove out of the garage.

"You need rest," Malcolm said. "I told Lou this was too intense. You need the memories to return more naturally—through association or memory prompts, not self-inflicted comas. But Lou's under pressure with the latest incidents—" He cut himself off.

"Tell me more of your memories," Eve said. "You told me about your mother singing. Tell me about your father. Nice memories. I only want nice memories." Nice memories to scrub away the smoke and blood inside her.

He drove out of the parking garage. "*My* memories?" He sounded relieved, as if he'd expected other questions, but Eve couldn't bring herself to ask the real questions or hear about "incidents," not when she felt as if she'd been scraped raw inside. "Okay . . . um, let me think . . . My dad and I used to play basketball. When I was a kid, he'd lift me halfway up to the basket. I'd dunk it in, and he'd cheer and shake me in the air like I was a trophy." Taking one hand off the steering wheel, he demonstrated the shaking. "But I'd never made a basket on my own until one summer, when my father was away for two weeks. Every day of those two weeks, I practiced for hours. And the next Saturday, when Dad asked me to shoot hoops with him, I shot the basket from the ground by myself. My dad lifted me up and shook me like a trophy."

Eve closed her eyes. "Tell me more."

"My father was a cop, and he hoped I'd follow in his foot-steps. Have a son on the force, you know? On the day I told him I was a US marshal . . . I swear he wanted to lift me in the air and shake me like a trophy. Only reason he didn't was that I outweighed him by then. Also because my mom cried."

Eve opened her eyes. The sky was cloudless blue. The trees were heavy with dark-green leaves, motionless in the still air. She watched the telephone poles pass. "Why did she cry?"

"She didn't want me to be in any kind of law enforcement. She wanted me to be something safe like a veterinarian, even though I'm not good with animals. Hate cats. Okay with dogs. Don't see the point of goldfish."

"What happened?"

He shrugged. "Five years in, I was recruited for WitSec. Two years after that, a routine case proved to be anything but routine, and I came to the attention of the paranormal division. Para-WitSec is always looking for new agents. Since this is the only known nonmagical world, we are in high demand as a safe haven for witnesses of magical crimes. I was immediately assigned to multiple cases. All of it was classified, but I always wished I could have told her. As it was . . . she didn't understand that my job is to keep other people safe. I'm doing what she—what both of them—taught me, what feels right and natural."

Malcolm parked the car in front of the drab yellow house. She watched him get out, check the area, and then open her door. She stepped onto the sidewalk next to him.

"Was that the kind of thing you wanted to hear?" he asked.

"Yes," she said.

"Good." He slid on his sunglasses. "Because that's as much

sharing as I do. Go on in." He nodded toward the house as Aunt Nicki swung the door open. Eve headed toward her, then glanced back over her shoulder at Malcolm.

Unmoving, he watched her from the sidewalk.

❦

Inside, Aunt Nicki put her hands on her hips. "You look exhausted," she pronounced. "And too thin." She picked up Eve's wrist and wrapped her fingers around it. "You're wasting away. I don't care how much pressure Lou is under. We can't have you wasting away. Are you eating?"

Eve shrugged. She didn't know how many of the seven days she'd spent in the hospital bed and how many in Malcolm's office. "Intravenously, I think."

"Doesn't count." Aunt Nicki bustled into the kitchen, and Eve followed. "Soup? Sandwich?" She checked the refrigerator. "I'll make you a grilled cheese sandwich with microwaved tomato soup. Serious comfort food. You look in need of serious comfort food."

"I'm not hungry."

"Did I ask if you were hungry?"

"Will you tell me your memories instead?"

Aunt Nicki slowed. She stared at her, blinked once. "Excuse me?"

"I want . . . to hear your memories. I'm hungry for memories." It was the best way she could think of to put it. It felt like hunger, vast empty spaces yawning inside her that wanted to be filled.

"You are the weirdest kid that I have ever met." Aunt Nicki sped up again, making a cheese sandwich and plopping it into a pan. It sat there, sad and unsizzling. She selected a cup of soup and put it in the microwave.

Eve sank into one of the kitchen chairs. Not looking at Aunt Nicki, she fiddled with the edge of a placemat. It curled as she kneaded it. She only had a few memories of her own, rattling in the emptiness inside her, and so few of them made sense. "Why do I have memories of them, the people on the bulletin board? And why do I know they died? Was I . . . was I there when they died?"

Aunt Nicki didn't turn. Looking up at her, Eve saw that the muscles in her neck and shoulders were tense. "It's what you choose going forward that defines who you are," Aunt Nicki said. "Not what you chose in the past."

"What did I choose?" Eve asked. "Why didn't I stop their deaths? Could I have . . ." Her voice failed her, and she sat in silence. She clenched her hands in front of her on the placement.

Aunt Nicki flipped the sandwich. It was still pale yellow with unmelted chunks of butter on the other side. "Ah, yes, heat will help," she said, falsely merry. She turned on the stove. "There we go." She fetched a plate and a bowl and a spoon. Folding a napkin, she adjusted it so that it tucked neatly under the side of the plate.

"I need to know," Eve said softly.

"You asked about my memories." Aunt Nicki sat opposite Eve and uncurled Eve's fingers. Eve had bunched up the corner of the placemat. Aunt Nicki smoothed it flat. "I spent a lot of time trying to forget my past. My childhood . . . Let's say I did not have a perfect one. Spent a lot of time . . . Well, when I hit eighteen, that was it. I left it all behind."

"I didn't choose to leave my past behind," Eve said. "It was taken from me."

"Are you sure about that?" Aunt Nicki asked gently. The microwave dinged. She popped out of her chair, retrieved the soup, and flipped the sandwich. At the stove, her back to Eve, she said, "My father drank. My mother drank. My older brother . . . dead in prison by eighteen. Hanged himself. Or had someone help him. No one was ever sure. Can't say I was sorry. He used to put out his cigarettes on my arm, at least until Dad stopped him with a baseball bat. After that, he left home, and Dad left soon after. Now, it's just Mom and my baby brother. He's in California, as far away as he could get. She's in a nursing home and needs twenty-four-seven care, which I can barely afford. Alcohol ate her brain cells. She's fifty-eight and barely knows her own name . . . She reminds me of you, actually, but you drool less. And so I chase down petty fugitives to pay her bills, when I'm not babysitting for someone who doesn't know me and barely knows herself. But it's my choice, to be the responsible one, to be the caretaker, to be the person who . . ." Aunt Nicki took a deep breath and turned around. "Point is, I invented me . . . maybe as a reaction to them . . . *definitely* as a reaction to them. I am myself in spite of my memories."

"So are you saying I *shouldn't* remember?" Eve asked.

"God, no," Aunt Nicki said. "Lou would have my head. Especially now, with the latest developments. You need to remember faster." She pushed away from the table and returned to the stove. A minute later, she flopped the grilled cheese sandwich onto a plate and slid it next to the soup in front of Eve. "Eat."

Eve sipped her soup. It slid warmly down her throat. She bit into the sandwich, and the cheese singed the roof of her mouth. She puffed air to cool her mouth.

"Dip it," Aunt Nicki suggested. She mimed dipping the sandwich into the soup.

Eve tried it. "You're right," she said. "It's comfort food." Eating it made the agency and the hospital and the visions feel far away. She couldn't bring herself to ask about the "latest developments." Most likely Aunt Nicki wouldn't explain anyway.

She ate in silence and didn't try to remember anything. If she couldn't remember everything, she wondered if it would be easier if she remembered nothing. Aunt Nicki busied herself cleaning the kitchen. At last Eve asked, "Do you think I could do that? I mean, invent myself like you did."

Aunt Nicki stopped. "I have absolutely no idea."

As she turned that thought over and over in her mind, Eve finished the soup, running the last of the sandwich crust around the bowl.

Aunt Nicki cleared her dishes. "Get some sleep. That boy from the library is anxious to see you at work tomorrow. He's been calling nonstop for the past week."

Zach! Eve stood up. "I can call him back—"

Aunt Nicki shook her head. "Sleep. One more night won't kill him."

"Can you promise me that?"

"He's not the primary target," Aunt Nicki said. "I can promise you *that*."

Eve thought of the who's-next game from the cafeteria, and she wondered how many people—aside from Aidan, Topher, and Victoria—the marshals were protecting. For all she knew, there were hundreds hidden around the city or spread throughout this world. "Who's the primary target?"

Aunt Nicki looked at her. "You," she said. "It's always been you."

Eve nodded. Of course. She knew that. She'd always known that. She was the key, whatever that meant. "Thank you for the food."

"Go." Aunt Nicki waved toward the bedroom. "Don't let the bedbugs bite, and all that."

Eve tried to smile, failed, and gave up. She nodded to Aunt Nicki, then headed down the hall. She trailed her fingers over the faded hall wallpaper and thought of Zach. His hall had been filled with family memories.

She wondered if, someday, she could piece together bits of memories like that wall. Maybe if she accumulated enough little memories, she too could have a history. Thinking of that possibility, Eve opened the door to her bedroom.

Lying in the center of the quilt was the Magician's hat.

# Sixteen

THE BLACK VELVET HAT was incongruous on the cotton quilt. It lay like a cat, asleep or dead, in the center of the bed. Dust particles drifted around it, catching the light from the window.

Eve screamed.

The air shoved out of her throat so hard and fast that she felt as if it would never reverse and she would never breathe again. She would simply scream and scream until every bit of oxygen was forced from her lungs, her blood, her body, her mind, and she turned inside out into the air itself and dissolved into her scream.

And then Aunt Nicki was there.

Out of the corner of her eye, Eve saw the marshal burst into the room with her gun drawn. Kneeling, she swept the gun in a circle, aiming it at all corners of the room. She stalked to the closet, kicked it open, aimed the gun inside. Empty. She dropped to the floor, looked under the bed. She checked behind the door. At last, she leaned against the wall beside the window. Gun up, Aunt Nicki peeked out the window. The backyard was empty.

Eve's scream slowly died.

Aunt Nicki pulled out her phone. "Code 34. Malcolm, respond now." To Eve, she said, "Keep clear of the window, stay away from the door. Center of the room is safest."

"Don't leave me alone with it." Eve couldn't tear her eyes away from the hat. It permeated her vision, as if it were growing and spreading through her mind's eye.

"I'm not leaving you," Aunt Nicki said. "And reinforcements are on the way. I need you to stay calm. Breathe. Atta girl. Breathe in, breathe out. It's only a hat. See?" Aunt Nicki tipped the hat with the butt of her gun, and it fell to the side.

Eve sprang back.

But the hat was empty and motionless. No horrors crawled from it. Inside was red velvet trim . . . She'd expected black. The Magician's hat was black inside.

Eve took a step toward the bed, toward the hat. It had a silk ribbon around its base. His hat didn't. This hat's brim curved slightly like his, but it wasn't battered. His had a dent in the brim halfway around and a rip in the velvet . . .

"It's not his hat." Eve felt oxygen rush into her lungs. She could breathe again. "It's not. It's . . . Whose is it? Why is it here? Who put it here?"

Again, Aunt Nicki glanced at the door, but this time it seemed to be the glance of someone who was looking away, not looking toward something.

"You?"

"No!" Aunt Nicki said.

"Not Malcolm. Lou?"

Aunt Nicki wouldn't meet her eyes. "It's an extreme technique to jog your memory. And it did work. You remembered the original enough to spot this as a fake, right? That kind of precision is exactly what we need on the witness stand."

"And the box in the library?" Eve thought her voice sounded calm. Distant but calm.

Aunt Nicki didn't answer.

Eve backed away from Aunt Nicki until she felt the wall at her back. She spread her hands against the images of branches and birds as if they could somehow comfort her or protect her against this woman who was supposed to be her protector, her guard, even her family.

Aidan, Topher, and Victoria had been right. She couldn't trust them.

"This was for your own good," Aunt Nicki said. "Lou thought—"

"You let him come in here and place this *thing* on my bed, where I'm supposed to be safe, where I'm supposed to *feel* safe." Eve wanted to knock the hat off her bed. She couldn't bring herself to approach it. "I wanted so badly to trust you."

"Of course you can trust us!"

"How can I?" Eve noticed that Aunt Nicki still held her gun. It was pointed down, held loosely in her right hand. She didn't think Aunt Nicki would aim it at her. Oh no. Not while she was still useful. Not while there were memories to pry from her. "All you care about is accessing my memories. Once you have them all, then what? You kill me?"

Aunt Nicki blanched.

*It's true*, Eve thought. Without a shadow of a doubt, she was certain. She could see it in Aunt Nicki's eyes. They'd use her, and they'd dispose of her.

Aunt Nicki tried to cover. "The hat was a mistake. But let's not overreact. Obviously you're distraught, but take a deep breath and think for a minute. People are dying out there! He's started to kill again, and you have information in that dense head of yours that we need to find him and stop him. Don't you want us to get that information out? Don't you want to save people? I know you do! You want what we want, for this all to be over. Think about it, Eve. This helps you as much as it helps us!"

Eve felt along the wallpaper, inching away from her. "How do I know that anything any of you say is true? How do I even know there *is* a killer? Or if there is, how do I know you're not on his side?" They'd manipulated her at least twice that she knew of. They'd confessed to the surgeries that changed her body and maybe affected her memory. How did she know where the truth ended and the lies began? It could all be lies. Everything she knew could be a lie.

She heard the front door slam open. Footsteps in the hall.

*I can't trust anyone*, Eve thought.

Aunt Nicki turned her head toward the door, and Eve pressed backward into the wall. She imagined she were melting into the wallpaper. She felt the air rush out of her and felt herself shrink, spread, and flatten. She shaped herself into a bird on the wallpaper, perched on a branch, identical to the hundred other birds on the wall.

Malcolm burst into the room. "Where is she?"

Aunt Nicki pivoted to point . . . and then she faltered. "She was right here!"

On the wall, a bird in the wallpaper, Eve lost consciousness again.

# Seventeen

*The Storyteller is combing my hair with her gnarled fingers. "She lives happily ever after, of course, though they don't say how long 'ever' is. Perhaps it is only a day before her horse is startled by a snake and she falls from his back and breaks her neck." The Storyteller strokes my neck lightly, softly. "Or perhaps it is only a week before a piece of meat lodges in her throat and no one is around to see that she cannot scream. Or breathe. Or she could have years with him in peace before she begins to doubt and to wonder and then despair that she will never be more than a story that ended—and so she ends herself with a rope from a strong tree branch."*

"I don't like this story," I say.

*Her fingers are entwined in my hair, but they do not move, and so I move forward and feel her stiff fingers slip away from the strands.*

"I don't like it," I repeat.

"It is the story I am telling," the Storyteller says.

*"Then I won't listen," I say. I know it's a futile statement. When the Storyteller weaves her tales, you must listen. It is her magic, or at least a talent so powerful that it seems like magic.*

*She continues, and I listen as the princess in her story dies again and again and again.*

*I am outside under the trees by a campfire. The wagon is beside us. The bright colors are a glossy near-black in the darkness. Through the trees, I see the fires of other wagons. It's cold by the campfire, even though the fire is red and yellow and pops and crackles. I feel cold inside. Wishing I could stop the Storyteller's tale, I rise and step closer to the flames.*

*"Step away, or you will burn," the Magician says. His voice comes out of the darkness, cutting through the Storyteller's voice but not stopping it. Even he can't do that. I don't see him in the shadows by the wagon, though he must be there.*

*I take another step closer, and I can feel the fire's warmth. "I am standing by the fire, and I do not burn." But I feel the fire creep onto my skin. It seizes me, and I feel the fire spread through me, as if bypassing my skin and going straight into my bones. It shoots through me and then spreads outward.*

*At last, the story stops.*

*I have ended it, I think with triumph.*

*As the fire seizes me, the Magician wraps his arms around me. His cloak muffles me, but the fire is already inside, burning through my bones. I think I am screaming. I feel the Magician put his hands on my burning cheeks. His face is close to mine. He breathes in. And the fire ceases. Even the campfire dies. It is cold. I am cold inside.*

*"Next time, you will obey me," the Magician says.*

*"Yes, Father," I say.*

*He strokes my cheek. "Always remember: you are nothing without me."*

I'm not nothing, *I think.* I'm Eve.

*And suddenly, it's Malcolm with his arms around me, protecting me . . . or trapping me. I am in a meadow of delicate white wildflowers that bend and sway in the breeze. He holds me gently as he says, "Shh, shh; tell me who you are."*

✻

*I'm Eve,* I wanted to say. But I couldn't.

I was pinned to the wall like a butterfly in a display case. My beak was half-open, and I felt the shape of my paper wings splayed against the milk-blue fake sky. I saw the bedroom distorted through one flattened bird's eye. The hat was all angles on a sea of quilt.

Beside the bed, Aunt Nicki bulged with her rounded limbs and torso, a three-dimensional person seen through my two-dimensional eyes. Malcolm was a vast bulk behind her. His eyes roved over the room.

I watched them test the window and check the closet. From the way Malcolm's mouth moved and the way his chest pumped, I thought he must be shouting, but his voice was distant and muffled to my painted ears, as if he were underwater. The words slid into each other until they were indistinguishable. Only a few moments seemed to have passed since I fell into my vision.

Still shouting, he scooped the hat off the bed and hurled it across the room. It skittered over the wood floor and smacked lightly against the wall. I felt its impact a moment later, rippling through the wallpaper like a pebble tossed into a pond.

The hat was directly below me. It matched the description I'd given to the marshals—I'd told them about the black velvet—but I'd never described the wear that had eaten at the edges and roughened certain patches down to the threads. The more I studied it, the more certain I was that it was not the Magician's hat. I remembered the true hat perfectly. It was as clear as my memory of the cards that the Magician used to lay on the red velvet table—ornate illustrations with medieval fairy-tale flourishes and, oddly, burn marks on the edges—and it was as clear as my memory of the Storyteller's hands as she knit yarn with her hands and worlds with her mouth.

Stories used to fall from her plump, wrinkled lips, I remembered. She told beautiful stories about princes and princesses in magic castles or half-rat children scurrying through the alleys of a city on adventures. And then there were other tales, like from my visions, where the castles crumbled and the children didn't leave the alleys alive. I hadn't liked those tales.

I listened to the agents search the house. Their footsteps were sharp, heavy, and angry. They slammed doors, and I felt the reverberation of each slam. Through the walls, I could feel where each agent was—six of them, guns drawn and wearing bulletproof vests, in every room.

At last they left, and the house felt silent.

The silence sank around me. It permeated the walls. I felt as if the house were sighing, easing into the soil, relaxing. I breathed with it, slow and deep, if one could call it breathing. I sensed the other birds around me, a persistent tingling as if they were extensions of my paper skin. The light from the window moved across me, and I felt it only on one side. My other side was cradled against the wall, nestled tightly as if held by arms. I let the minutes slide away. Somehow, I slept.

Waking, I was certain I was alone, though I couldn't explain how I knew. The house *felt* empty. Carefully, I peeled myself away from the wall. The glue hurt as it pulled, and I widened my beak in what would have been a scream if I'd had a voice. My fingers spread, and my wings expanded.

I poured myself into my memory of my body—smooth skin, golden hair, green eyes. I knew I had those correct. The rest . . . I wasn't certain how tall I was or what exactly was the shape of my head or my chin. But it didn't matter. I had my eyes, and that was enough.

I took a step toward the bed, intending to lie down before the vision overtook me.

I didn't make it.

❁

*I am in the wagon.*

*Bottles clink together. Skulls rattle, their loose jaws opening and shutting as if they still have screams inside them. "Once upon a time," the Storyteller says.*

*I clap my hands over my ears, though I know it's a useless gesture.*

*She pulls my hands away. I am surprised at her strength. Her arms are so thin that she looks as though she could not bend a piece of straw, much less move my hands against my will, but she pushes them down as if I'd offered no resistance. She looks young today, a waiflike slip of a girl with cornflower-blue eyes and full lips.*

*"Once upon a time, a girl set out to find her fortune . . ."*

*"Where are we going?" I ask.*

*She grips my arms. "Once upon a time, a girl set out, and she was quick and she was silent and she was lucky and she was strong."*

*Her eyes seem to blaze until the rest of the wagon dims. I feel the wagon slow as if it has reached its destination.*

*"I have done all I can for you and less than I should," she says. "Someday you'll forgive me, or you won't." I open my mouth to say I don't understand, but she presses a red scarf over my mouth. Taking a needle, she sews it into my skin.*

*I cannot scream.*

*And then I am on the stage beside the Magician. He flips cards onto a table and hums to himself off-key. I cannot see the audience, but I hear them inhale and exhale, nearly as one. The lights above glare on the stage and prick my eyes. I look again at the cards. He has spread them on the velvet—the image of a blindfolded woman, a dead tree beside a tower, an owl with a snake in its talons. "Take one," he says. I think he talks to me.*

*I try to reach for a card, but I am bound by ropes that*

*crisscross my body in a pattern as intricate as a spiderweb. Only my fingers can twitch.*

*A girl walks out of the audience and onto the stage. She takes a card. It is an image of a blindfolded woman, but the eyes are the last thing that the girl loses. I close my eyes and wish I could close my ears too. There is screaming. And then suddenly, there isn't.*

*I hear a soft snip. And then another. And another. I feel cool metal brush against my neck. Snip. Snip. The Storyteller is humming softly.*

*The ropes release and flutter to the ground. I look down. They lie around me in a circle, limp. I am standing before a silver mirror outside the wagon. The tent is behind me.*

*In the mirror, I look like the dead girl, but I know the mirror lies. My reflection does not have a red scarf sewn over her mouth; I still do. I feel the even stitches tear at my cheeks. In the polished silver, I also see the wagon and the Storyteller with her sewing shears in her hand. She's middle-aged now, though her eyes are milky white and surrounded by wrinkles. She snips the scarf away from my mouth.*

*"Seek your fortune," she says. "And don't ever look back."*

*She shoves me toward the mirror, and I melt into the silver.*

❖

Lying on the floor of the bedroom, I looked up at the cracks in the plaster ceiling. Every muscle shook, every nerve quivered, and my skin felt thick and bumpy. I lifted my hand in the air and studied it. It looked smooth and perfect.

I could feel a cramp in my left calf. Stretching my foot, I

breathed in deeply. The air smelled like dried roses and lemon with a hint of mildew. I pushed myself up to a sitting position and listened.

Silence.

Even the air in the house was still.

The hat lay against the wall where Malcolm had thrown it—a vivid reminder that I couldn't stay here. Reaching into my pocket, I pulled out the cell phone that Malcolm had used to track me to Zach's and slid it under the bed. Feeling as wobbly as a just-hatched bird, I tottered to the bedroom door. I inched it open and heard nothing from the rest of the house. Moving as silently as I could, I crept through the hallway to the front door. Pressing my back against the wall, I peeked through the window next to the door.

A black car was parked beneath the tree across the street.

Quickly, I stepped back. Of course the house was being watched. I stared at the door for a long moment as if it could solve this for me. If I left through the front door or even any of the windows on the front or side of the house, whoever was in that car would see me.

My bedroom was the only room in the back of the house that had a window, but I knew that window was sealed shut. I retreated to my bedroom anyway and looked outside. The backyard was deliciously empty. It beckoned me. I ran my fingers around the edge of the caulk and thought about breaking the window . . . but my watcher might hear it.

I could use magic.

But then I'd lose consciousness and be helpless. An agent

could find me. *I don't have a choice*, I thought. Stay and be caught, or flee and maybe be caught.

I took a deep breath, and walked through the wall.

It slid through me as though I were walking through a dry waterfall. It felt as if dust were sprinkling over my skin and down my throat and into my lungs and into my blood, traveling to every inch of my body. I emerged on the other side of the wall, and the dust dissolved inside me until I felt human again. I sank into the bushes and waited for the vision to claim me.

I didn't have to wait long.

❋

*I am strapped to the seat of a Ferris wheel. Ropes made of the Storyteller's yarn are wound around my arms and legs and the metal bar in front of me. My hands are tied to the bar. I look out over the carnival. Below, I see floating wisps of light that drift between the tents, and the people milling between them. Their laughter and delighted shrieks rise up, up, up to reach me in the Ferris wheel seat high above.*

*I wonder if I should be afraid.*

*The moon is fat in the sky. I see the craters, as crisp as if they were drawn with a fine pencil. The wind is tinged with cold, and it carries the smell of popcorn and fries and, more faintly, the ocean.*

*Around me, the landscape looks like quiltwork with patches of pale and dark. Strings of light, like the wisps in the carnival, lace through the fields and over the hills like luminescent embroidery.*

As one strand floats closer, I see that the strings are composed of beads of light and that each bead is moving in a complex dance, always touching the other beads. I think that maybe the light on the fields and in the carnival is alive.

This high, I can only see the tops of the tents: the acrobats' tent, the wild boys', the fortune-teller's, the headless woman's, the cages of wonders, the dreamland, the contortionists' . . . and the tattered red tent, the Magician's. Our wagon is behind it.

The tents stretch on for up to a mile, and I realize I have never seen it all. This is the closest I have come, high above, and I don't know why I have been allowed this sight. As the Ferris wheel turns, lowering, I see a crowd has gathered.

Twisting to see the wheel, I glimpse birds tied to each of the spokes. They spin as the wheel turns, their wings changing color as they frantically flap, until at last they burst into flame. The crowd below gasps, and I imagine they are seeing the wheel light up like a sparkler. A few children point. Others applaud. Others are transfixed. And some look frightened.

As more birds catch fire, they brighten the wheel, and I notice that I am not alone in the seat. Tied beside me is a silent shadow. It looks to be a girl, roughly the same height as me. Her face is shadowed, and she doesn't move.

As the Ferris wheel lowers, lights from the tents spill into our chair.

My companion has a painted porcelain face with glass eyes. She's dressed in a white pinafore, and has one hand tied to the metal bar. The other rests limply in her lap. She has a crack in her porcelain neck; smoke oozes from the crack. Her legs are unfinished, and cotton spills out of the seams.

*I cringe, pulling away from her—from it—and wait for the ride to end.*

*But it doesn't.*

*I sweep past the ground, past the crowd, past the man in a black-and-white harlequin suit who turns a crank at the base of the wheel—*the Magician, *I think, though it doesn't look like him. The wheel rises into the air, and the birds continue to burn.*

❦

I woke in the bushes. Twigs poked into my flesh. My head lay against the house, and the coolness of the concrete foundation seeped through my hair to my scalp.

It was daytime, either again or still. The sky was gray, and the shadows were flat. It was impossible to tell if it was morning or afternoon.

I'd been lucky. So far, I hadn't lost the memory of the false hat. Or of Aidan, Topher, and Victoria's warning. I could have been trapped again and not even known it. *I can't use any more magic*, I thought.

Slowly, I crept out of the bushes. Out of the shade, the sun pricked my skin. Humidity thickened the air. A few cicadas buzzed, and I heard a lawnmower in the distance. *I need Zach*, I thought. He could keep me free—at least until I figured out what to do. I didn't know what I wanted to do. All I knew was that I was sick of having things done to me.

With that thought, I sprinted across the yard. Reaching the fence, I threw myself at it and climbed over. I landed in the neighbor's backyard, also empty.

No one shouted at me. No one chased me. So I kept

running. I leaped over the fence into the next yard. And then the next yard, and the next. I ran through flower gardens and around sheds and play sets. I squeezed through bushes. I scrambled over wood piles. In one yard, I surprised an elderly woman who was kneeling in her garden—I landed in the soft earth of the flowerbed beside her. In another, kids played in a sandbox. But I didn't slow. The body that the doctors had shaped for me was strong, and I didn't need to slow. I felt my feet slap the ground and my muscles work and my heart pump and my lungs inflate and deflate, and it felt wonderful to run free after all the visions of ropes and bindings and boxes.

But it didn't—it couldn't—last forever.

The string of houses ended in a parking lot for a church. For an instant, I froze, staring at the church, as a memory poured into me. Elsewhere, another time, I'd seen a church beside a graveyard with silver pillars, marble statues, and a woman so still that she might as well have been one of the statues. She'd been wrapped in pale-gray scarves . . . Was it a real memory? I tried to picture the woman's face, but she was shrouded in mist.

Shaking myself out of my reverie, I ducked behind a garage. Cars drove by. A sprinkler *click-clicked* as it rotated. On one of the driveways nearby, three boys played basketball. Everything seemed so peaceful and ordinary that it almost lulled me into feeling safe. But I couldn't trust that feeling. I kept thinking of the woman in mist.

Across the street was the library surrounded by woods.

Creeping around the garage, I hid behind a trimmed hedge. I waited until the road was clear, and then barreled across and plunged between the trees.

Green surrounded me, and I waded through the underbrush and climbed over fallen stone walls as I circled the library. The birds chirped louder, and the leaves rustled—squirrels, I hoped.

Listening to the noises, I thought about the woods in my memory, the one with ancient trees and the homes nestled high in the branches. I still couldn't remember if I'd been chased through the woods or I'd been one of the ones doing the chasing. Oddly, it felt like both.

Ahead, I saw the rock that Zach had pointed out. Last time, I'd seen a snake on that rock: Victoria, watching me. *Everyone always watches me*, I thought. At home, Aunt Nicki watched over me. At the library, Patti kept her many eyes on me. Between those places, there was Malcolm. Or Lou. Or Victoria, Topher, and Aidan. Every moment of my life that I could remember, I'd been watched. *Except right now*, I thought— and it felt so glorious that I wished I could lose myself in the woods forever.

But the woods were finite, squeezed between streets and subdivisions. In only a few minutes, I spotted Zach's street through the leaves. Keeping low, I climbed over another old stone wall and then peered out through the bushes at his house.

The lawn was pristine, even sterile. A silver car was in the driveway—Zach's mother. A black car with tinted windows was parked down the street—a marshal. I felt my heart thump in my chest, harder than it had when I'd run through all the backyards. I crept backward, away from the road. At least one agent waited on the street. Others could be nearby.

*Maybe this is a mistake,* I thought. *Maybe I should run.* But where to? And then what? I didn't know this world. I didn't have money, a place to stay, a way to survive, or a way to stay hidden. Unless I used magic and risked losing myself . . . *Zach will help me.*

Half a block from Zach's house, the street curved out of sight of the agents. Checking in both directions like Malcolm always did, I darted across and dove behind a white fence. I sprinted through the backyards, keeping as far from the street as possible. Lowering myself over yet another fence, I landed in the bushes behind Zach's house.

For an instant, I didn't move.

It wasn't too late to change my mind. I could sneak back to the WitSec house, let myself back inside, and place myself back under the agency's protection. Except then it would begin again . . . the visions and the memory loss and the lies and the fear and the hospital and the bulletin board and the hat and the box.

Gathering my courage, I ran toward the enclosed porch. I ducked my head and hunched my shoulders, as if that would keep me from view. Any second, I expected to hear a shout or a shot. I flung open the screen door and threw myself inside.

Inside, the porch had windows and skylights, far too

many. I darted for the hallway. Inside at last, I leaned against the wall with the photos. My legs shook. My heart pounded.

There were voices in the kitchen.

I heard Zach's mother, shrill and strained. "I can't face it again! I can't!" And I heard Zach reply, soothing and soft, with a lilt to his voice as if he were coaxing a bird to his hand. I couldn't make out the words.

And then a man shouted, "Enough!"

Glass shattered.

Inching forward, I peeked into the kitchen.

# Eighteen

RED WINE HAD SPILLED on the marble countertop. It ran in a rivulet to the stainless steel sink and dripped in. I knew it wasn't blood. It wasn't thick enough. It looked so out of place amid the white tile, the shining brass pots on hooks, and the pristine floor.

I didn't see Zach.

Zach's mother was holding the broken stem of a wineglass in one hand.

A man—Zach's father—stood in the remnants of the shattered glass. Shards crunched under the soles of his polished black shoes. He wore a gray suit that wrinkled as he breathed deeply in and out, then in and out again. His face was flushed. "Not one more word," he said.

He hadn't seen me, and neither had she.

"Look out the window." Her words slurred together, loud and shrill, as if she couldn't hear the volume of her voice. "Tell me you don't see them. Day and night! And no one ever gets out of the car. You know they have binoculars trained on the house. Maybe they've bugged the house, the phones. Maybe they've talked to our neighbors. I can't go through this again!"

"Say they're watching. So what?" his father demanded. "We've done nothing wrong. We don't have anything to hide!"

"Except you." Zach's voice, soft. On the floor, he sopped up the spilled wine with a dishrag. One by one, he picked up the shards of glass. "And this."

His father grabbed his arm and yanked him to his feet. Glass pieces fell out of Zach's hands onto the floor. They shattered, sounding like hail on the hard tile. "You don't—"

"Zach?" I said from the doorway.

Releasing Zach, his father spun to face me. He was much broader than Zach and taller by a foot than both of us. His arms weren't as muscled as Malcolm's, though, and I saw the curve of a paunch above his belt. The belt must leave red dents in his flesh. "Excuse me?" he said. "Who are you? And what are you doing in my house?"

Zach quickly said, "She's no one."

"I'm not no one," I said.

Zach's mother's eyes focused on me, as if the sight of me didn't compute in her brain. And then she blinked and plastered a bright smile on her face. "Eve! This is unexpected. Did you expect her, Zach? I didn't expect her."

"Eve, why are you here?" Zach asked, his voice strained.

Shooting a look at the kitchen window, I stepped into the room. "I thought you could rescue me. But I think . . . you need rescuing."

Zach made himself laugh. "Me?"

"You don't lie," I reminded him.

His face crumpled as if I'd snipped the puppet strings that had pulled his lips into a smile. "Only about this," he said softly.

"Zach." His father's voice held a warning note.

"You're with them, aren't you?" his mother said to me. Her lips had blotches of dark purple-red between the lipstick, as did her gums. The wine bottle near the sink was nearly empty. "Checking up on us. Well, there's nothing to see here. We're fine. We're all fine. Fine, fine, fine!"

"She's not with them," his father said. "She's just a girl."

"The cars outside . . . Are they . . . ?" Zach trailed off, but I knew what he was asking. He'd guessed the cars were for me.

"You know why they're here, why *she's* here," Zach's mother said. She slid to the floor, her back against the marble island in the middle of the kitchen. "Sophie. My poor, sweet Sophie." She began to cry, ugly heaving sobs that shook her shoulders.

His father's fists curled. "It's been nine years! It's over!"

She raised her head. Makeup smeared under her eyes, looking like black-and-purple bruises. Her eyes looked hollow. "It's never over! It will never be over. I dream about her. Who she was supposed to be. What she would have been like. All of us, together."

"Jesus, why won't you stop?" his father said.

"Because I deserve this pain!" she said. "Because I should be dead, not her. Because life is cruel. Life is brutish, short, and . . ." She searched for the word. "Short."

"But it's not," Zach said. "It can be magical and—"

"And you, shut up," his father said. "Don't you see you're making it worse? You always make it worse."

Zach paled.

"Zach." I held out my hand. "You can take my breath if you want it." He'd have to walk past his father to reach me. I saw him realize this, calculate the distance. "You don't need to be powerless."

His father's face flushed darker, and he shot a glance at me. "This isn't what it looks like." He knelt beside Zach's mother and began to tend to her. He fetched a paper towel and dabbed it on her lip. Blood had welled in the middle of her bottom lip, just a drop. "She took a nasty spill. Slippery floor."

"I'd just mopped it," Zach's mother agreed.

"And the bruises?" Zach asked. "Are you going to claim the floor made them as well?"

Rising, his father leveled a finger at him. "No more."

"You're right," Zach said. "No more." In three strides, he brushed past him and crossed to me. He wrapped his hand around mine, fingers laced tight. His hand was slick with sweat.

His father slammed his hand on the counter. "You don't—"

Zach leaned his forehead against mine, and I exhaled, giving him whatever magic he wanted. Behind us, on the counter, the red wine caught fire.

His parents spun toward the flames. His father shouted for a fire extinguisher. Shrieking, his mother raced from cabinet to cabinet. The fire alarm wailed. His father yanked the extinguisher off the wall next to the stove and sprayed white mist on the flames. Foam coated the counter and floor.

Zach pulled me away, and hand in hand we walked out of the kitchen. He turned toward the front door, but I tugged his hand and drew him through the hall, past the family photographs, to the back porch. The yard looked empty. We went out onto the patio.

"Should we walk, drive, or fly?" Zach asked, his voice grim but steady.

"Definitely fly," I said.

"Oh yes, definitely."

We kissed and rose into the air. Spiraling upward, we reached the level of the roof. I felt Zach's heart beat fast through his shirt. Mine was thumping too. Entwined, we soared higher.

Quiet wrapped around us. Up here, the cars were only a distant buzz, like cicadas, and the wind smelled like freshly cut lawns. It was more peaceful than I'd imagined, to be untethered from the earth. I felt as if I could cocoon myself in clouds and drift away from all fear. Below, I saw the marshals rush toward Zach's house, drawn by the shrieking.

"They're after you, aren't they?" Zach asked.

"Yes. I . . . I'm in the witness protection program. But I'm leaving. I left. And they want me back. They want to know what I can't remember, and I think . . . I think when they have my memories, they plan to kill me."

His arms wrapped tighter around me. "I knew you were in danger."

"I thought they were keeping me safe, but now . . . I don't know. I don't know anything. I know I'm not . . . from here. And I have these visions. But I don't know if they're true, and I don't know who to trust."

"Trust me," Zach said automatically, and then as if he knew he'd spoken too quickly to be believed, he repeated it. "You can trust me."

Looking into his warm eyes, I wanted to. And then I realized that I had already decided to. By coming to his house, by soaring into the sky with him, I had involved him, and he deserved to know at least as much as I did.

Taking a deep breath, I told him everything as we flew high above the houses and trees: about the agency, about the other worlds, about my visions, about the case. I watched his face as I talked. His cheek twitched. His lips were pressed together. His eyes were open so wide that the skin around them stretched. I didn't know his expressions the way I knew Malcolm's. I didn't know if he believed me, or if he wanted to drop me from the sky now that he'd heard it all.

"Oh," he said.

I didn't think I had ever seen him truly speechless before.

"And you want *me* to rescue *you*?" he said at last.

"I didn't know who else . . ." An idea burst into my mind. "Patti."

"The librarian?"

"She has two extra eyes."

"Extra eyes?" he repeated.

"She knows how to keep herself safe. She'll know what to do." She'd have answers! I was sure of it. "Just let's go there. Please?"

The wind shifted as we changed directions. We flew in silence for a while, with the wind curving and swirling around us. The sun, thin through the clouds, warmed the air.

Lips against my ear, Zach said, "You have no idea how many dreams I've had about flying. Except I'm in a Superman cape or have falcon wings, instead of being in the arms of a gorgeous girl, which means this moment totally surpasses every dream I've ever had."

"I don't think I've ever had a nice dream."

"Ever?"

Arms around each other, we drifted over the roof of the library. "Maybe I just don't remember them. Given a choice, though, I'd rather remember what's real."

"No, no, you need a few good dreams. Like flying, or blasting into outer space, or winning a gold medal." Breathing in more of my magic, he lowered us down behind the library. "Or spending the afternoon with someone you lost."

As soon as my feet touched the ground, the feeling of peaceful floating vanished. Wind rustled the branches of the trees. Leaves slapped together. I tried the door handle. Locked.

Zach knocked on the door, loudly. I cringed at the sound. "Zach . . . ," I began, intending to tell him we could walk through the wall.

"You told me your truth; let me tell you mine. Sophie was

my sister, the girl on the swing from the photo that you saw." Zach didn't look at me. "She . . . she fell in the middle of the night. She hit her head too hard, and she didn't wake up. It was an accident. A stupid accident. The stairs were smooth wood. Her slippers had no tread. The lights were off. But she had bruises on her arms—she'd been learning to ride her bike. And she had scabs and cuts—she'd played hard at school. And so the police investigated. They claimed we were lying, that it wasn't an accident, that one of us had . . . It took a court case to end it."

"And that's why you don't lie?"

"Yep." Zach knocked again. "And why, in a twist of irony, my mother has become the raging alcoholic that they thought she was, my father has developed a temper he can't control, and my home is now poisonous to live in." He knocked harder, as if he wanted to punch the door.

I put my hand on his arm. "Zach . . ." I didn't know how I was going to end the sentence, but I knew there was something that I was supposed to say, something comforting or wise.

Before I could think of the words, the door swung open.

I jumped backward, ready to dive into the woods. Zach reached toward me—to protect me or stop me, I wasn't sure. But it was only one of the librarians, the one with tattoos on his neck. He scowled at us. "You know there's a front door."

"Thanks." Releasing me, Zach clasped the man on the shoulder. I hurried inside. The staff room all seemed normal: piles of books on all surfaces, labeling equipment on the floor, a half-eaten lunch on the table. The odor of tuna salad wafted across the room, overriding the smell of dust and printer toner. But my skin itched as if someone were watching me.

The librarian plopped down at the table and shoved the uneaten half of the tuna fish sandwich in his mouth. Zach lingered as if he wanted to talk to him, but before Zach could speak, I yanked him out of the staff room and into the main library.

"You don't think he—" Zach began.

Covering his mouth with my hand, I shuttled him into one of the rows. His breath felt soft, tickling my palm. "I don't know who to trust, and marshals could be anywhere." I lowered my hand. "We need to reach Patti's office without being seen. Any ideas?"

"Oh yes, I have ideas." Zach's eyes were alight, and he was grinning broadly. "Kiss me." He hooked his arm around my waist and drew me closer. I breathed magic into him through the kiss. He released me. "It might not—"

Suddenly, I felt as if fists were pummeling me from the inside out. I fell to the floor. Zach lay writhing beside me. In a few seconds, it was over.

The library looked gray, blue, and black. The shadows between books were crisp and layered, and the fibers in the carpet next to my cheek were in stark relief. I lifted my head. Beside me, a gray cat flicked his tail. He regarded me with narrow black pupils, and then he stood shakily. His front paws wobbled, and his tail swished behind him. Looking down at my own front paws, I placed them carefully on the rug and pushed up with all four legs. My center of gravity felt off, and the tail was an unfamiliar weight behind me. *This won't work*, I thought. *We'll be seen.* Hoping he'd understand, I shook my head slowly and emphatically and hissed.

He nudged his cat nose against mine and inhaled.

I felt my back itch.

Falconlike wings unfolded between his shoulder blades. They stretched out on either side of his cat body. Twisting my cat head, I saw black-and-white feathers behind me. A winged cat. Stretching my wings, I glared at Zach. His cat eyes were bright, as if he were laughing. *Absolutely not*, I thought.

I thumped my nose against his, exhaling into him. In less than a second, I felt myself shrink. I collapsed toward the ground. My bones squeezed, and my skin tightened as if it wanted to strangle me. As I gasped for air, the world fractured around me. It was as if I saw the library in a broken mirror, reflected over and over in a thousand shards. I could see in nearly·every direction—the fibers of the carpet in front of me as thick and deep as my chest, the bookcases rising up like steel mountains beside me, the books like skyscrapers . . . I looked at Zach, focusing my fractured vision.

Two teal orblike eyes dominated his tiny face. His body shimmered with metallic green, and his thin blue tail looked like a chain of precious metal. He also had four ethereal wings that stretched as wide as his body was long. *Dragonfly*, I thought. I'd seen dragonflies speed across a meadow of wildflowers, their wings beating so fast that they blurred. *Yes, this will work.*

I flexed my back, and air swirled around me as my wings rose up and down. I felt my thin, sticklike feet lift off the carpet as I pumped faster, and then I shot upward into the air.

My four wings swiveled in figure eights, stirring up tiny whirlwinds on either side of me. Midway up the shelves, I steadied myself. Zach rose after me, wobbling and shaking in the air, and then he shot ahead of me. Straightening my tail like an arrow, I flew after him.

Side by side, we banked hard and careened into the center aisle. We shot through the stacks. Emerging into the reference area, we flew toward the ceiling. The glare from the lights bleached the world. It felt as if we were flying through the sun.

Below us, I saw the brightened heads of the librarians and patrons, including the same man in a suit that I'd seen before. With my sharp dragonfly eyes, I could see the bulge of a gun under his suit coat—he was a marshal. But it didn't matter. In an instant, we were past him.

First Zach led, and then I led. We spiraled around each other, our wings nearly touching. If I could have laughed out loud, I would have. We swooped through the archway into the library lobby. Patti's door was only open a crack. We aimed for it.

As we dove into her office, the carpet rose up toward us. It was a forest, and we were airplanes. The fibers were the treetops, and we were going to hit. I tried to slow, stilling my four wings. My thin feet skimmed the floor, and then I toppled over my wings and crashed against the bookcase. Zach landed on top of me, one wing folded over my torso.

I twisted my head and pressed my smooth dragonfly face with globelike eyes against his and breathed. Ripples spread across my torso. I felt as if I were cracking. In an instant, Zach and I were human again, splayed on the floor of Patti's office. "Please don't," I gasped out as Patti opened her mouth to scream. I untangled myself from Zach. "They're after me."

Patti shut her mouth so fast that I heard the snap of her teeth hitting together. She strode to her door, closed it, and then slid the lock. Her high heels clicked as she walked back to her window and pulled the shade shut. "You shouldn't have come here. I work hard to keep this place safe."

I opened my mouth to reply and breathed in the wood smell of the bookshelf. Suddenly I pictured the forest; I saw a caravan of wagons disappearing into a silver wall, moving because people were coming . . . I shook away the memory and forced myself to focus on the present.

"She needs help," Zach said. "*We* need help."

"I can't help you," Patti said. "You need to leave. Before whoever is chasing you finds you here. I'll call Mal—"

"No, please!" Quickly, I explained—the memory losses, the visions, the hat, the box. "Those boxes . . . that's how he held his victims, if my visions are true. They're magician's boxes— they shrink whatever you want to put inside. Created for magic tricks, little parlor tricks. And then . . . adapted. The agency left one on your desk for me to find, to jog my memory, to frighten and manipulate me . . ." I described how I'd woken in the hospital and how they'd manipulated me to induce other visions.

Patti's face paled. She lowered herself into her desk chair. "They used *my* office, *my* library . . ." She ran her hands over her desktop as if reassuring herself that the box was gone.

"You hide yourself. You keep yourself safe," I said. "Please, tell us how to do it!"

Patti shook her head slowly, as if to deny my words or my request or me in general. "WitSec hid me. My family . . . I'm safe *because* of the marshals. I don't know how to be safe *from* them."

Zach watched the door. "Does she need to be scared, or are we being paranoid?"

I watched Patti's face, trying to read her expression. Patti's eyes flickered toward the door. *Uncertain*, I guessed. *She doesn't know. Or doesn't want to tell me.* Patti rose and crossed to her bookshelf. She lifted two books and pressed a button on the shelf behind them.

The shelf slid to the side to reveal a windowless room.

"Whoa," Zach said.

Crowding into the doorway, we peered in. The hidden room had a bed on one side and a bank of monitors on the other. Each monitor showed a different view of the library—the lobby, the reference area, the parking lot.

"About an hour ago, the marshals infiltrated the library." Patti pointed to people in several monitors—a woman in the reading room, a man in the lobby, another man in the nonfiction section. She also pointed to the black SUV under the tree in the parking lot. "As to whether they're here to help or harm you . . . you have to trust yourself. In the end, that's all you have. You." She'd said that before, when I'd asked for her help with Aidan.

"I don't know who I am," I said.

"Then find out," Patti said.

She said it so matter-of-factly, as if that wouldn't mean walking into the heart of my nightmares and confronting the very people from whom WitSec was purportedly hiding me. "But I'm the target," I said.

"Only if you let yourself be," Patti said. "My only strength is in hiding and watching." She gestured at the bed and the monitors. "But you . . . you aren't powerless, especially combined with Zachary. I've watched you two. Together, you can *make* yourself safe—once you find out who you need to be safe from."

"She's right!" Zach lowered his voice and repeated himself, "She's right. Think about it: I know that dragonflies can fly at speeds up to thirty-five miles per hour, switch directions in midair, and even fly backward, and you can make it happen. You have extraordinary magic, and I have an impressive imagination fueled by a decade of dedicated bookworming. Together, we're unstoppable."

My cheeks began to ache, and I realized I was smiling broadly, widely, wildly. He said "together." Reaching out my hand, I squeezed his. "Are you sure? It's dangerous."

"I'm coming with you."

"The agency will chase us. They need the visions in my mind."

"I'm still coming with you."

"We'll have to leave this world. And we might not come back."

He hesitated and then turned to Patti. "My parents . . . Can you tell them that I'm all right? Tell them that I'm . . . tell them I'm making up for not being able to help Sophie. They'll understand that. Or at least my mother will."

Patti shook her head. "Your parents—"

"Please. I . . . can't go back."

She looked as if she wanted to object again, but she didn't. "I won't tell them anything that will endanger them. But I will tell them you're safe. Even though it's a lie."

Zach took my hands in his. "Eve . . . all my life I've dreamed of doing something extraordinary. With you, I have the chance. Say the word, and I'll go with you."

He hadn't seen the nightmarish visions. He hadn't had IVs jabbed into him and new skin grafted to him. He wasn't haunted by the faces of people who had died. He didn't see blood, death, and pain when the world went dark around him.

"At worst, you'll learn who your enemy is, and who you really need to hide from," Zach pointed out. "And then we'll run like the wind, if the wind had legs and incredible superpowers."

"At worst, I'll be killed. And sliced into pieces." I shook my head. "No; at worst, *you* will." Unless Malcolm had lied . . . Unless my visions were wrong . . . Unless the agency was the enemy, and the carnival was the sanctuary . . . Unless no one had really died . . .

"Do you know how to find the carnival?" Zach asked.

"It's in another world. I don't even know which one. It travels around." But the idea was worming itself into my mind. As long as I had Zach, what could stand in our way? So far, I hadn't seen a limit to my powers. If I could learn who I was and why I had these powers and why I could share them and what had been done to me and who had done it . . . If I could learn what my past was, then maybe I'd have a chance at a future.

"Do you know how to get to other worlds?" he asked.

I glanced at Patti. "Level five?"

"Level five," she confirmed.

# Nineteen

PATTI RAISED THE SHADE in her library office and then opened the window. Outside, the parking lot was half-full. A woman in a rose-colored raincoat yanked a toddler onto the sidewalk. A man tossed books into the backseat of his car. Another man pulled out of his parking spot.

The black car with the tinted windows was in its familiar spot under a tree.

"I'll try to buy you time," Patti whispered. "Good luck. Be safe. And if you can't be safe . . . be yourself." She squeezed my shoulder as I climbed out the window and dropped down to the ground behind a bush. Zach followed after me.

Above us, Patti closed the window and shut the shade.

"Fly?" Zach suggested.

I shook my head. "They'll expect that." Through the branches, I studied the black car. I didn't see any movement, but from here, I couldn't even tell if the engine was on or off, much less if anyone was inside.

"But they don't know . . ." His eyes bulged as he realized what I'd implied. "You think Patti will tell them we're here?" His voice was incredulous, as if such a betrayal were inconceivable instead of logical.

"I know she will," I said.

"But . . ."

"Her safety depends on cooperating with them," I said. "She'll tell them everything. But I have an idea. See that car?" I pointed toward the black car. "I think we should use it."

His cheek next to my cheek, he peeked out at the parking lot in the direction that I'd pointed. "You mean, steal a car?"

"Stealing isn't the same as lying."

"True, but . . ."

"It's an agency car. We can drive it to the agency."

"Oh. Then that's not even stealing," Zach said. "That's returning it."

Grabbing his face, I brought his lips to mine. I breathed into him as his arms wrapped around my waist. We broke away, and I felt slightly dizzy.

"Ready?" I said.

"Uh, yeah. That was . . . wow."

"On three? One, two, three . . ." Hand in hand, we burst out of the bushes and ran across the parking lot toward the car. The car door flung open, and an agent stepped out. He had his gun in his hand.

And then the gun transformed into a flower. Petals fell from the agent's hand, and the stem drooped. Zach stole another quick breath of magic, and the agent was swept forward—up, up, up onto the roof of the library.

We ran to the car. Zach dove into the driver's seat, and I hopped into the passenger seat. The key was still in the ignition, and the radio was playing. Zach shifted the car into reverse and then stepped on the gas. The car lurched backward, and we careened out of the parking lot. I clutched the glove compartment and wondered if this one had a gun in it like Malcolm's did.

"Left," I told him. I continued to give him directions until a block from the agency. I pointed to the parking lot of a convenience store. "Stop there."

He swung into one of the parking spots, facing the Dumpsters. "Now what?"

Twisting in my seat to face him, I said, "Last chance to change your mind. You can go home, be with your parents, and live your normal life, and I won't blame you."

He was quiet for a moment. "You saw my home. You met my parents. You saw my normal life. Just tell me how to leave this world. Please."

I nodded. And he exhaled, his face relaxing into an almost-smile. "The offices are level three, the hospital is level four, and the silver room—the way out—is level five."

"What about one and two?" Zach asked.

"Doesn't matter."

"It might matter. I bet it matters to the people on one and two. You know it's going to bother me, not knowing what's on one and two. I like to know things."

"Zach, focus. We need level five. I thought we could transform—"

"Cats?" He sounded eager, as if he were about to start bouncing like a puppy. "Birds? Or mice. Mice could work. Mice can drop twelve feet without injury and can jump twelve inches straight up."

"Zach. You know this isn't a game."

He calmed instantly, and in his eyes I saw a hint of . . . fear? "I know. But if I think of only the magic, it makes the rest of it less terrifying. Leaving home? Stealing a car? Breaking into a government facility? Searching for a potential serial killer? Let me focus on the flying and the shapeshifting and kissing you."

I nodded. We sat in silence for a long moment. I spoke again, softly, calmly. "I think we need to change into people— specifically Malcolm and Aunt Nicki." Unclipping my seat belt, I faced Zach. "You can do me first. She has an angular face with a chin that juts out farther than her lips. Her nose is narrower than mine, nearly to a point, with a prominent bridge. Her eyes . . . brown with thin eyebrows, dark brown and plucked."

Zach held up both hands to stop me. "It's okay. I've seen her before."

"You have?"

"At the library. She dropped you off once."

I didn't remember that. It must have happened during the days I lost. But for the first time, my memory didn't matter. Only his did. "Can you do this?" In response, he leaned

forward and breathed in my magic, then furrowed his forehead and concentrated. I felt my face begin to itch, and then
my skin bubbled and stretched. I described her typical all-
black pantsuit with the fake knuckle-size pearls that Aunt
Nicki liked. Sweat beaded on Zach's forehead as he changed
my clothes. When he finished, I flipped the visor down and
looked at myself in the mirror.

For a brief instant, I expected to see the antlered girl.

Aunt Nicki stared back. Or almost Aunt Nicki.

"Shorten the hair." I mimed where it should be cut. I
watched it shrink and flatten. "And her skin has more olive in
it. I think that's . . . yes, that's it." He flopped back into his seat
as I touched my face. Its shape felt wrong under my fingertips, and I had to suppress the urge to yank and tug my skin
back into its familiar shape.

"I am going to have to close my eyes when I kiss you," he
said.

"Your turn. Do you remember Malcolm?"

"No one could ever forget Malcolm," Zach said. His skin
and bones shifted and moved as I watched. He then changed
his height and the width of his shoulders, as well as his hair,
skin, and eye color. Lastly, he added muscles and darkened
his clothes to a black suit.

"Perfect." Staring at him, I felt marginally better. Safer. As if
Malcolm himself approved this insane plan. Opening the glove
compartment, I found a pair of sunglasses and handed them to
him. There wasn't a gun, but there were insurance and registra-
tion cards for the car. "Can we change these into agency IDs?"

"Sure. Can you describe them?" His lungs, nose, and vocal cords were a different size, so his voice had deepened with the new body, but the inflections were pure Zach.

I'd seen the IDs, but I hadn't memorized them. I tried to picture the position and size of the photo, the words and the logo. Zach transformed the cards to match my directions. "I wish I could remember them better," I said.

"Just . . . wave them fast or something."

I couldn't remember if Aunt Nicki and Malcolm handed the IDs to the guard or just displayed them. I hoped the latter. I tucked the IDs into the cup holder between us and wondered if we'd be caught before we'd even begun. I wished there were time to make a better plan. But the longer we waited, the more likely we were to be found. And the more likely I was to lose my nerve. "Are you ready?" I asked.

"I think this is where I'm supposed to say I was born ready." Zach flashed me a smile. "But I was born ordinary."

"Don't," I said.

"Don't what?"

"Disparage yourself." I twisted in my seat to face him fully, and I tried to see Zach behind Malcolm's face. "You think just anyone would come with me like this? You say you dream of the extraordinary, but *you're* extraordinary. I say I'm broken, and you try to fix me. I say I'm lost, and you try to find me. I say I'm empty, and you fill me. You're . . . like a knight in shining armor, but from one of the nice stories." I took a deep breath. I hadn't meant to make a speech. I felt my face, Aunt Nicki's face, flush pink.

He stared at me for a moment, then blinked. "Yeah, you're right. I'm awesome. Let's go." Driving out of the parking lot, he ran over the curb. The car jolted up and down. I braced myself on the glove compartment again.

"Look calm," I instructed Zach. "Malcolm always looks calm."

As we drove closer, I pointed to the agency's garage doors. Gray and plain, the doors looked like they belonged to a non-descript office building. Zach hit the brakes too hard at the guard station—the car jerked as if we'd hit a pole. Taking a deep breath, he rolled down the window.

The guard leaned in. "Car trouble?"

Zach nodded.

I waved our IDs from the passenger seat. The guard glanced briefly at them, but he frowned at me. I wondered if we'd gotten Aunt Nicki's face wrong. Maybe her nose was flatter, or her eyes smaller, or her hair darker. "I could've sworn you'd . . . Never mind. Go ahead, Agent Gallo, Agent Harrington." He hit a button, and the garage door rumbled up.

"Have a nice day!" Zach called out the window. He stepped on the gas before the guard could change his mind. We shot into the garage. "Probably shouldn't have said that."

I looked behind us, but the guard wasn't following us. The garage door was closing. Daylight disappeared with it. "I think we're all right."

Pulling into a parking spot, Zach stopped the car. "At least he didn't shoot us on sight. I'd call that a win." He tried to smile, but it disappeared quickly.

"Zach . . . If things turn bad, I want you to take a breath of magic and run."

Zach opened his mouth, and I knew he was going to say something flippant or brave.

"Please, Zach. I don't want to have visions of your death haunting my memories. Promise me that you'll run. Or I tell that guard who I am and let them capture me right now."

"Fine," he said. "But you run too."

"Or fly."

"Definitely fly." He kissed me, and I wasn't sure if it was for the magic or just to kiss me. It didn't matter. I kissed him back, and his lips felt different, broader and softer. He tasted the same, though—like Zach, sweet and minty.

He broke off.

He looked like he wanted to say something but didn't know what. I opened the car door and stepped out into the garage. He did too. "Eve . . ."

"Gallo," I corrected. "He calls her by her last name." I headed for the door. Taking the ID cards from Zach, I held them up to the scanner. Nothing happened.

"I doubt we accurately replicated the magnetic strip," Zach said. "Is there another—"

Glancing over my shoulder, I saw the surveillance camera trained on the door. If anyone was watching the feed . . . but we didn't have much choice. "Quick. Walk us through the door."

He hesitated.

"I walked through a wall before."

He grinned suddenly, stretching Malcolm's cheeks abnormally wide. His expressions weren't the same as Malcolm's, even using the same face. "You're always full of surprises."

Zach put his hand up, and it melted into the door. He drew it back, took my hand with his other hand, and then we walked forward. Using the magic from the kiss in the car, we passed through the door. The cool metal sank into my skin and deep into my bones. I felt myself shiver and then shudder as we emerged on the other side, inside the hallway.

There were cameras in this hallway too.

Releasing Zach's hand—Aunt Nicki wouldn't have held Malcolm's—I strode toward the elevator. Zach kept pace beside me. He didn't have the same walk as Malcolm. His movements were jerkier, and he picked his knees up higher like a stork. Malcolm had a glide to his gait. I hoped that no one else knew Malcolm's walk the same way I did. Only a few steps to the elevator.

At the elevator, I pushed the button and we watched the numbers flicker down. The doors slid open. And Lou stood there.

I felt my bones harden into place. I couldn't breathe.

"Up?" Lou asked.

I nodded. Out of the corner of my eye, I saw Zach was nodding too. I wished there were a way to warn Zach . . . but he knew who Lou was, didn't he? He'd mentioned that a bald man had interrogated him. We walked into the elevator.

My finger hovered over the numbers. With Lou here, I couldn't push five. Instead, I pushed three. We'd have to lose him in the offices—and hope we didn't see the real Malcolm and Aunt Nicki.

As the elevator lurched upward, the tinny music played. It sounded like the carousel.

"This time, we contain her," Lou said. "No more of your touchy-feely nonsense. She stays on the hospital floor under guard. She is *not* to be treated like a refugee. Or even a pet. Do you understand me, Agent Harrington? I blame you for this."

Zach cleared his throat. "Yes, sir." He tried to pitch his voice lower. It came out close to a growl. Lou looked at him sharply.

The door slid open. For an instant, I thought we could stay in the elevator. But Lou slapped his hand on the elevator door to hold it open. We had to walk out.

"We've alerted the airport terminals, bus terminals, and train stations—the usual cover story." Lou aimed a fingers at me. "Gallo, bring in that Zachary boy. I want to know what he knows. I knew we should have kept him here. Remind me never to listen to you two bleeding hearts again."

"Yes, sir," I said.

He frowned at me, and for an instant, I thought he knew. But he pivoted and strode toward the lobby. We trailed after him. He halted at the receptionist's desk and leaned over the desk to speak to her. I couldn't hear what he said. She handed him a locked aluminum briefcase.

*Maybe we should run now, while he's distracted . . .* Before I could move, Lou turned and shoved the briefcase at me. Automatically, I took it. "Um, what do you want me to do with this?" I asked before I thought. I then froze. Aunt Nicki might have known the answer.

Lou smiled at me. It was an unsettling expression on his face. His cheeks and eyes crinkled like a crunched paper bag. "I want you to do your job, Gallo, before I fire your ass."

I looked at the briefcase. It had a combination lock.

He took the briefcase back and set it on the receptionist's desk, and then he turned the numbers on the combination lock. The lock snapped open. He raised the lid. Inside was the Magician's box. Instinctively, I shrank back. He lifted it out and then held it out toward me, his palm flat, not touching the clasp. "You might want this, when you find her. We've tested it—magic doesn't penetrate it. It will keep her from turning you into shrubbery."

Hands shaking, I took it. The metal felt chilled, as if the box had been recently stored in a freezer. I didn't trust myself to speak. I shoved the box into my front pocket. It bulged, and I felt the corners press against my thigh.

Ahead, I heard voices. Malcolm's office door swung open. We had to leave now. Smiling weakly at Lou, I pivoted and strode back toward the elevators. Zach walked fast beside me. My heart was beating so loudly that I was certain Lou could hear it.

"Gallo! Harrington!" Lou called after us.

From his office, Malcolm called, "Sir?"

I looked over my shoulder to see Malcolm, the real Malcolm, step into the hallway. I broke into a run as I heard him say, "What the hell—"

An alarm began to sound, and a red light flashed and spun in rhythm with the sirens. I looked back again. Oddly, Lou wasn't chasing us. He merely watched from the hallway. With one hand, he blocked Malcolm from chasing us as well. I caught a glimpse of Malcolm's expression: *Fear*, I thought. *Of* me? *For* me? But others were running toward us, and there was no time to puzzle it out.

Zach stabbed the elevator button.

It didn't open.

Shoving the stairwell door open, I pulled Zach with me. The door slammed behind us and then was pulled open again an instant later. An agent burst into the stairwell.

Zach grabbed me and planted his lips on mine, inhaling my magic with my breath. As the agent lunged for my arm, Zach shot into the air with his arms tight around my waist. We rocketed up the open center of the stairwell. Below us, several agents pounded up the stairs, but we were faster.

At the top, at level five, I yanked the door handle—locked. Zach breathed in more magic, and we slid through the metal door. We turned left, then right . . . At the end of the hall, the two guards in front of the steel door shouted and drew their guns.

The guns dissolved into water and collapsed on the floor in droplets.

Turning to me, Zach swiftly inhaled magic again, and I felt myself shrink, plummeting toward the floor. The world skewed—the carpet fibers were as thick and high as underbrush in a forest, and the ceiling was impossibly high. I swiveled my head and saw a beetle, monstrously huge . . . He'd turned us into beetles. *Clever boy*, I thought. But what about the box? Looking around, I didn't see it, and Zach was on the move.

Scurrying after him, I wove through the carpet.

Footsteps shook the floor. Looking like mountains in motion, the guards scoured the hallway. A boot landed near me, and I jerked back. The foot lifted, and the carpet fibers were mashed where he'd stepped. I darted forward as fast as my many legs could move.

Up ahead, I saw Zach squeeze beneath the door. I hurried after him, flattened, and slid on my smooth, slick stomach. At the end of the next hall was another door, but this one was flush to the floor. We'd never fit under it.

Zach bumped his head against mine. His legs clicked on the tile floor. And then I felt my body expand like a balloon. Soon I was human again—myself, not Aunt Nicki—and Zach was himself again too. My clothes were restored. I felt my pocket—the box was still there. The box and my clothes must have transformed with me, melding into my exoskeleton. He kissed me again and inhaled deeply. "Extra magic," he said. "Just in case."

This door had a palm reader but no guards. We ran through it. The next door required a combination code. We ran through it as well. The fourth door was guarded.

The guards already had their guns drawn.

"Shoot the male," one instructed. "Don't hit the female."

Before I could react, before I could think, the other guard squeezed the trigger. Zach jerked backward, his hand torn out of mine. The sound echoed and continued to echo, reverberating through the hall and through my bones. And then the bullet clattered to the floor at Zach's feet. "Bulletproof," Zach said as he lunged toward me and brushed his lips against mine. An instant later, the guards' jackets caught fire.

Startled, they dropped their guns. One began pounding the fire on his chest. The other shed his jacket as quickly as possible and stomped on the flames.

We ran forward and through the door into the silver room.

# Twenty

SILVER WALLS. SILVER CEILING. Spotless white floor.

I still had no memory of this place, other than from my failed attempt to remember it before. But I'd had visions with silver mirrors and silver walls.

"Dead end," Zach said. "Knew it was a trap. It was too easy."

"They *shot* you." I never, ever wanted to see that again.

"Lou should have stopped us before we even left the third floor. But he didn't."

Grabbing his hand, I walked straight toward one of the silver walls. In a vision, I'd walked through a silver wall into a meadow. The Storyteller had been there, knitting a red ribbon on the steps of the wagon. *There*, I thought, *I want to go there.* Behind us, the door burst open and slammed against the wall. Two armed agents ran into the room. But they were too late. Reaching the wall, we melted into it.

I felt coolness wrap around me, as if I were wrapped in chilled towels. It was hard to feel Zach's hand. It felt swaddled in wool, distant. My body felt numb. And then I stepped with Zach out of a silver mirror that lay on the ground in the middle of a meadow.

The sky was a startling blue, and the air was light and warm.

"Whoa," Zach said.

Birds called to each other—so many birds that their calls mashed together in a cacophony louder than screams. They flew in thick batches that looked like swooping clouds against the sky. *Sparrows*, I thought, watching the birds. This was where I'd learned about sparrows.

"'Flock' isn't an adequate word for this many birds." Zach strained to see them all. "Needs a special name, like bevy of quail, charm of finches, murder of crows, parliament of owls . . ."

"They're sparrows."

"Host of sparrows. I may have made that up, or—"

"Shh," I said.

The meadow stretched endlessly in all directions. It was coated in delicate wildflowers that swayed and dipped in the breeze. After I'd walked through the silver mirror, I'd waited here by the wagon while the Magician and the Storyteller erected the tent for the show . . .

Spurred by the memory, I ran forward through the flowers. Only a few yards from where the silver mirror lay, the grass was matted in a broad circle. No flowers grew, and the grass was sickly and yellow, as if it had been blocked from the sun. My heart was thumping so hard it almost hurt. I *knew* this place! I'd been here with the Storyteller and the Magician. Our tent had been here, near the other tents, and our wagon had been beside it.

"You remember this place," Zach said. It was more of a statement than a question.

I nodded.

"Do you remember other places?" Zach asked.

I nodded again.

"Then . . . we need some kind of plan. Maybe you, the Magician, and the Storyteller will have a nice reunion where you share childhood memories. But if the agency didn't lie . . . I'd rather not end up chopped to pieces and stuffed in a box."

I pulled the box out of my pocket and held it in the palm of my hand. The silver winked in the sunlight. "Lou gave me this to use against myself. We can use it trap the Magician."

"Very poetically appropriate," Zach said. "How does it work?"

"Open the lid, touch someone with the clasp, and they're sucked inside. They can't call for help; sound can't penetrate it. They can't use magic to escape; magic can't penetrate either."

"And Lou gave it to you. That's a stroke of luck that tips right over into massively suspicious."

I slid it back in my pocket. "He also didn't let Malcolm chase us."

"He wanted us to escape—or, more accurately, you," Zach said, and I nodded unhappily. He could be right. They didn't try to shoot me, only him. "On the plus side, maybe it means no one will try to stop you."

"Or maybe it means the carnival is a trap." I scanned the meadow. As far as I could tell, we were alone, except for the sparrows.

"But is it a trap for you, or for him?"

I walked around the outer edge of the matted grass. Suddenly, finding this place didn't feel so wonderful. "Lou, Malcolm, Aidan . . . they're playing a game, but no one ever told me the rules or even let me see the board."

"Then don't play," Zach said. "We can go anywhere. Any world. No one would ever find us. We could invent new lives. Leave our pasts behind."

Overhead, the birds dipped and swirled in clouds of feathers that cast shadows on the meadow. "You'd be living a lie. I can't ask you to do that."

"You're not asking; I'm offering."

"Why?" I asked.

"Because . . ." He trailed off, staring at me. "Wait. You're not quite yourself yet. I was too rushed." He kissed me lightly, and I felt pressure in my face as my features shifted. My cheekbones subtly rose. My body lengthened minutely. My painted fingernails reverted to my plain unpainted half moons. I ran my fingers over my cheeks and nose. Zach, I realized, had memorized me the way I had memorized Malcolm. "Because when I'm with you, I feel whole," he said. "Because with you, life doesn't feel brutish and short. It feels beautiful . . . and short."

"I think that makes the most sense of anything I've ever heard you say."

He grinned at me. "So, run away with me? Explore the multiverse?"

The way he said it . . . I felt the possibilities open in front of me, like morning sun illuminating hidden paths. But I couldn't. There was too much emptiness still inside me. I shook my head. "I can't feel whole, even with you. I need answers." As I said it, I realized how true it was. I'd spent enough time hiding. Before I could run again, I had to know more.

His grin faded, and I wished I'd said a simple yes instead. Above, the sparrows switched directions again, their cries filling the air. The wind blew the grasses and wildflowers sideways, and it blew my hair across my face. I wiped my hair from my eyes.

Zach took a deep breath. "Okay, then, how's this for a plan: you give me magic before we enter the carnival. I should be able to hold it for a little while, maybe up to half an hour, before I lose it. We find the Magician as quickly as we can, you distract him and I throw magic at him—toss him at you? You touch him with the box, and bam, it's over."

"And what if the agency lied, and he isn't a killer?"

"Then we open the box."

I considered the plan. "Simple. But effective."

"Simple plans are best," Zach said. "Supervillains always have complex plans and end up eaten by their own laser-toting sharks. Come on, let's do it before I utterly chicken out." He held out his hand. I took it, and we walked back to where the silver mirror lay, embedded in the earth and surrounded by tall grass and pink-and-white flowers. I thought of another memory: when I'd fled to Zach's house, I'd remembered a church with a graveyard. I fixed that image firmly in my head.

Together, we stepped onto the mirror, and we fell straight down into it.

A second later, we crashed onto bare dirt inside a circle of pillars. Six pillars were encased in mirrorlike silver and had been polished to reflect the blazing sun. I stood. Dusting off his knees, Zach stood beside me. On the other side of the pillars were marble statues and granite headstones silhouetted against the bleached-out sky. A church with red doors sat on a hill. Beyond the church and the graveyard was a vast expanse of dusty land.

Yes, this was the place I'd remembered. The carnival came here often. We used to set up our tents in the field of dust by the church.

Inhaling deeply, I imagined I could smell the carnival. Once, in this place, there had been a boy with diamonds knotted in his dreadlocks. He'd come to see the Magician, and he'd given flowers to the contortionist. I remembered they'd smelled sickly sweet, like one of the Magician's potions. The boy hadn't been interested in the animals, even the exotic ones from worlds without humans, but he had tried the games. He'd liked the archery test with the arrows that burst into flame and then dispersed as red-winged butterflies, as well as the ball toss into the mermaid's tank. One hundred points if it landed in the treasure chest without the mermaid catching it. She always caught it. I'd watched the boy all afternoon, like I was supposed to, until I saw the woman wrapped in scarves watching me.

*Like I was supposed to?* I didn't know where that thought had come from or what it meant. "I think . . . I want to leave."

I looked again at the marble statues. One of them was looking back.

Barely breathing, I held out my hand, and Zach took it. Retreating, we walked through a silver pillar. This time, we emerged in the middle of an ancient forest. The silver portal was embedded in a tree trunk. The ground was littered in leaves and dry needles, and the canopy of leaves blocked all but thin tendrils of sun. It was *the* forest, the one from my memory.

I knew all these places.

My memories . . . the visions . . . they weren't lies.

Zach's breath hissed. "Look up. There's . . . quite a view." His voice was light, but it shook. He pointed toward the tops of the trees.

Houses were nestled in the treetops. Bird men and bird women soared between them, their lithe bodies twisting between the branches. I remembered that the acrobats had performed in those branches, or ones like them. And the boy in the golden shirt had watched them. Later, we had chased him through the woods—the Magician, the Storyteller, and me. The Magician had carried me. I hadn't been fast enough on my own, and the boy had been fast. We caught him anyway.

"Keep going?" Zach asked.

"Yes," I said.

Again, we walked through the silver—and we walked out

into a city plaza made of gray paving stones. Skyscrapers towered around us. Again, I knew this place. I had been carried
through here at night. That time, we had been the ones being
chased. "We can't stay here either," I said.

A trio of people strode toward us. They wore matching
blue uniforms. Their faces were streaked with fur and scales,
and they had batons at their hips.

"But the carnival could be . . ." His voice died as he saw a
woman with wings on her back. Another had antlers on his
head. And still others . . . each a medley of human and animal. At last I saw him notice the trio of officials closing in on
us. "Guess it's moved on."

Zach and I scrambled back into the silver. I grasped for
another memory—and I thought of a pier, the Ferris wheel rising high above the water, kids laughing as loud as gulls.

The mirror melted around us, and we emerged beside an
ocean. Or not an ocean. A harbor. Sailboats were parked in
their slips, their white hulls gleaming. Fishing boats with crates
and ropes and cranes with nets were tied to a dock. Between
them, a woman with green skin hauled herself out of the
water to bask on a buoy.

"This looks nicer," Zach observed.

Several brick buildings jutted out onto piers. The wood pillars supporting them were coated in green threads and roughened with barnacles. A glass sculpture reflected the harbor on
its surface. Above, the sky was brilliant blue.

"Eve, look." Zach pointed behind me.

I turned and saw another dock. On it, tent posts without
tents rose into the air, like skeletons without flesh. At its tip, a

Ferris wheel was empty and motionless. A fence cut across the entrance to the dock. The fence was covered in photos and little pieces of paper, stuck into the links. Below the photos was a pile of wilted flowers, melted candles, and stacks of seashells.

I was walking toward the dock before I even decided to move, and then I was running. Skirting the fence, I entered the abandoned carnival. Gulls circled overhead, and water lapped at the pillars of the dock, but other than that, it was silent. I remembered this place flooded with people—cries of laughter, the call of the barkers, the music of the carousel.

A few of the rides remained, only the shell of a balloon ride that had lifted people to a floating roller coaster made out of clouds. The coaster was gone, swept away by the wind, but the balloon baskets and the ropes remained. The baskets were covered in graffiti.

I walked to an empty booth. There had been a pyramid of brightly colored balls at this booth that sang as they flew through the air. I remembered the face of the man who had run this game. He'd had a beard and sunken eyes. I didn't remember his name. I didn't know if I'd ever known it.

Zach stood behind me. "What happened? The other sites were empty. Why did they leave all this behind here?"

I didn't know. For the first time, I was worried about the Storyteller and the Magician, which was crazy—they were at the heart of my nightmares. "I need to find them."

"We," Zach corrected. "There's a term for the first person plural. Not for the second person plural, unfortunately. Closest we have for that is 'you guys,' which sounds like 1980s New Jersey, or 'y'all,' which sounds too affected southern for anyone who isn't really southern."

Gulls cawed at one another. One dove sharply down, snatched a piece of paper from the chain-link fence, and rose back up to the sky. I continued through the abandoned carnival until I found a darkened patch on the wood dock that matched the size of the wagon.

"I think we came here often." I looked out over the water and saw peaks—they weren't buoys or islands. They were the tips of underwater buildings. The city extended out under the harbor. I used to watch the selkies swim. "It was part of our regular circuit. But sometimes we'd do extra performances."

It shouldn't have been abandoned like this. It should have been dismantled and packed in wagons. No one should have defaced our site. And I started moving, fast, toward the fence and the papers that the gull had been pecking, certain that it would hold a clue. Zach jogged after me. I tugged one of the photos through the link and stared at it. A teenage girl with light-green skin and brilliant-blue hair pinned by shells . . .

"Who died?" Zach asked.

I looked at him.

"It's a memorial. At least, it looks like one."

I dropped the photo as if it had burned me. I didn't know that girl. She wasn't in my memories, and her photo wasn't on Malcolm's tablet.

"He's killing again," I said.

# Twenty-One

I KNELT BEHIND THE memorial on the carnival side of the fence.

"He must have been careless," I said. "Her death must have been traced to the carnival. They must have all fled." The flowers were half wilted, their blossoms closed or drooped. Leaves hung limp on the stems. A few were roses, their petals wide open. Others were flowers that I didn't recognize, tight clumps of purple petals with spikes of white in their hearts and teacup-like delicate blooms of pale yellow.

"You don't know any of that for certain," Zach said. "She could have fallen from the Ferris wheel or choked to death on popcorn or—"

"Aunt Nicki and Malcolm said that he'd started again. If it's true, then we're walking straight into the danger that they tried so hard to protect me from."

I felt his hand on my shoulder, a comforting weight. "If it's true, then he doesn't stand a chance against you," Zach said. "Together, we wield more power than a dozen superheroes."

I faced the memorial again, all the notes and the photos. One wreath of flowers had the word "sister" pinned to it. Another said "beloved daughter." I thought of the antlered girl, Victoria's sister, and all the other faces on the bulletin board. "Do you really think I can stop him?"

"Yes. And I think Lou wants you to."

"*I* want to." As I said it, it felt right.

"I know." He squeezed my hand, and I looked at him. He didn't look resigned or afraid or angry. He looked . . . proud and pleased. I wondered if he'd had this in mind all along . . . if he'd come for that reason . . . if the agency had encouraged him to come or even forced him. I wondered if he was manipulating me too, and then I pushed that thought down as hard as I could. It was *my* idea. If I discovered that my past held horrors, then I'd try to end them.

A voice came from the other side of the dock. "Hey, what are you kids doing?"

I spun, looking for the speaker.

"Just paying our respects!" Zach called.

Softly I said, "I don't see . . ."

Zach pointed to a man off the side of the pier, half in and half out of the water, bobbing with the waves. Shortly, several more mermen drifted to join the first man.

I stood up and dusted my knees. "Let's go."

The first merman hoisted himself out of the water. Seaweed dripped from his arms, and his tail split into two legs.

On scaly feet, he jogged toward us. Behind him, others pulled themselves out of the water.

Hand in hand, we ran around the fence and back to the silver mirror. They ran after us. We heard their footsteps sloshing on the sidewalk. But we were faster. We plunged into the silver . . . and found the carnival.

Banners and flags were strung between brightly painted poles. An elaborate archway marked the entrance. It was carved to look like clowns dancing, but the paint was chipped and peeling, so only the clowns' eyes were left in bright blue and green.

On the archway, a sign proclaimed, BE AMAZED AND ASTOUNDED BY THE FINEST FEATS OF MAGIC, STRENGTH, AND WONDERMENT FROM SEVENTY-SEVEN WORLDS! The banner fluttered in the wind and then hung limp and twisted.

"I think I'm home." The words tasted like cardboard in my mouth, and I had the nearly overwhelming urge to dive back into the mirror.

Beside me, Zach squeezed my hand. "Remember the plan? Kiss me?"

Wrapping my arms around his neck, I kissed him as if I were drinking him in. I tasted his breath in mine, and I gave him my magic in return.

Stepping away, I took a deep, shaky breath of air that tasted like stale cotton candy, and we walked up the hill toward the entrance. I'd been on this hill before. The antlered girl had run over it to visit the carnival.

Beyond the banner, the carousel turned slowly, the hundred bits of mirror in its top flashing in the sun. Music drifted down the hill, a complex melody of flute and fiddle that twisted and wove in on itself.

A woman was perched on top of the closest tent. She wore a billowing red dress and a hat with multiple feathers. She blew into a silent brass horn, and clouds shaped like horses, dragons, and rabbits ran, flew, and crawled from the mouth of the instrument. The clouds drifted across a bleached-blue sky and then dissipated. On the ground, a few kids ate cotton candy and watched. I remembered watching those clouds.

"Should we disguise ourselves?" Zach asked.

"I am disguised. That's what the surgery was for."

He stared at me. "What did you look like before?"

"I don't know."

"Huh."

"Do you mind? Not knowing?"

He considered the question for a moment, and I waited. "No. But then, I liked you as a dragonfly too."

Despite where we were and what we were about to do, I smiled.

We passed through the archway and entered the carnival. There were seven tents with a ring of wagons beyond them. Game booths were to our left. An outdoor stage was to our right. On the stage, the contortionists were performing.

One of the female contortionists bent backward and placed both hands on her ankles. Another stepped onto the first woman's raised stomach and lifted her own leg over her head and wrapped it around her neck. One of the men then stood on his hands in front of them and wrapped his feet around the second woman's neck.

Her head snapped off from her neck. She caught it in one hand and rolled it up her arm and then down her other arm. She then continued to stretch her leg around her body until it popped out of its socket and detached.

The other performers then silently removed their heads and rolled them up and down their arms. They traded heads once, twice, three times, and then they rolled the heads back to the necks of their original owners. The heads fused seamlessly back onto their necks.

Behind me, I heard Zach make a retching noise, and I turned to see him bent over a trash can. He raised his head and wiped his mouth. "Sorry," he said. The crowd applauded as the contortionists bowed, and I led Zach away from the stage.

We stopped at a water fountain, and Zach rinsed his mouth and splashed water on his face and neck. The water sparkled as if flecks of jewels had been mixed in it. When he finished, the fountain rose up on four legs and scuttled away.

"Now what?" Zach asked.

"Our wagon should be in the back corner." I pointed in a direction blocked by a tent . . . a tent of tattered red. I slowly lowered my arm.

That was it, the tent.

I took a step backward.

"You can do this," Zach said. "That is, if you want to do this. If you don't want to, I'm with you too." His eyes widened, bug-like. "Is that a mermaid?"

In a rusty tank, a mermaid swam in lackluster circles. Her pale-orange tail flopped against the glass walls. Algae had grown on the glass, and the water was so murky that when she swam away, she vanished into mist. Circling, she suddenly appeared again, distorted and blurry, against the front glass. She was an older mermaid with thin seaweed-green hair, wrinkled skin, and sagging breasts. Her eyes were bloodshot red. As she circled through her tank, her eyes fixed on me. My skin prickled as she vanished and reappeared, each time looking directly at me. I looked away, wondering if the mermaid would remember that the girl from the Magician's wagon had green eyes.

A line of boys and girls waited at the game booth to chuck balls at the algae-coated plastic treasure chest at the bottom of her tank. She caught the balls without altering her lazy circles and without looking at anyone but me.

I didn't know her name. Maybe I never knew it. I remembered she'd tried to leave the carnival once. She'd returned when she'd learned her family had died.

Tugging on Zach's sleeve, I led him away. His neck swiveled as he tried to look everywhere at once. In one tent, the wild boys were conducting their show. Riderless motorcycles shook the canvas walls as they roared past, racing upside down onto the ceiling. Six boys in loincloths and war paint chased after them with whips and nets, herding the cycles into more and more elaborate tricks. In another tent, an eyeless woman guided her audience into a dreamstate. She'd let them talk to their lost loved ones while she emptied their wallets. I'd never seen her perform, but I'd heard the Magician and the Storyteller say once that no one ever objected. As we passed by, I saw that her patrons were all levitating prone in the air. She walked beneath them in a tattered shawl and a dozen crystal necklaces.

Soon, the Magician's tent was directly in front of us. A gold sash tied the curtain doorway open, but it only revealed dark shadows. I knew candles lit the foot of the stage, but from here, I only saw the silhouette of the back of the audience—the backs of heads and the curve of empty chairs. I half wanted to step inside, to see how closely it matched my visions, and I half wanted to run as fast and far away as I could.

Zach held my hand as we passed by the tent, close enough that I could hear the applause from the audience inside. The Magician was performing. I stepped softly, as if he could hear me, as if he had any way to know I was here. I clung to Zach's hand as if it were a lifeline, as if he were a rope that could pull me out of a hole if I needed him to.

As I circled the tent, I saw the wagon.

Carved from wood, the wagon was as ornate and colorful as a gingerbread house. The walls were covered in swirls and curls, painted green with gold trim. The window shutters, all sealed closed, were blue. The wheels were gold with metal leaves and vines. Cherry-red steps led to the round door, and talismans of feathers and bones hung on it. A lantern was beside the door, lit with the broken wings of a will-o'-the-wisp.

It looked exactly like I remembered.

The Storyteller should be here. She used to sit on a woven blanket beside a table covered in a velvet cloth. Tarot cards would lie on the table, spread facedown, waiting for a customer. Silk pillows with tassels would be strewn on the grass around the table for listeners to sit on, and a tip jar would be on the corner of a blanket. But she wasn't—and the Magician was performing. It was the perfect opportunity.

Slowly, I walked up the cherry-red steps. I reached forward to open the door. The handle rattled in my hands—or maybe my hands were shaking. The door didn't open.

Leaning toward me, Zach breathed in more magic, refreshing his supply, which had most likely faded by now. "We could walk through . . ."

I shook my head. "I remember how to unlock it." Rose, leaf, stem . . . I pushed on the carvings on the door, and they sank in, a hidden combination lock. *Click, click, click*—the door swung open. The smell of sage and cinnamon and copper rolled out and over me, and I swayed on the top step, surrounded by the taste of the air—the taste of home.

Breathing deeply, I stepped inside.

Inside was brightly painted with hundreds of tiny mirrors embedded in the walls. Feathers, talons, and bird skeletons hung from rafters, broad beams that curved like whale bones. Bottles lined the shelves on the wall—green, blue, and purple glittering glass bottles with labels written in swooping black ink. He sold those bottles, I remembered. Ointments and potions that he'd gathered from the worlds we'd traveled to. Some worked, and some didn't. They were strapped to the shelves with leather belts to keep them from falling as the wagon lurched down a road.

And then of course there were the boxes. They were strung on a colored ribbon that stretched across the wagon. Silk scarves hung between them. Gathering my courage, I stepped closer to the first one and peered into it. Empty. All of them were empty.

"Do you remember this?" Zach asked.

"Yes." Except that sometimes the boxes weren't empty. But I didn't say that. Instead I pointed to the dolls that filled the cots and benches: life-size with porcelain faces and cotton arms. Some were unfinished, their faces unpainted or their limbs not yet attached. Others were dressed in lace and jewels. "Except them. I don't remember so many of them."

In one vision that I'd had, a doll had been strapped beside me on the Ferris wheel. The Storyteller had made her out of stray bits of fabric and a porcelain masquerade mask. Clearly, she'd made more after I'd gone.

"Listen," Zach whispered.

I held still.

There was breathing, soft and steady. It was so faint that I thought I was imagining it. It sounded as if it was coming from all around us. I scanned the wagon, looking for the source of the breathing. There weren't any places to hide—

"It's the dolls," Zach said. "They're *breathing*."

He was right. Motionless, the dolls were breathing in unison. Now that I focused on the sound, it was all I could hear. The dolls stared sightlessly at us.

"Are they . . . alive?" Zach asked.

One of the dolls held a box, a match to the ones that hung from the string. I crossed to it. Inside the box, through the slats, an eye blinked. It was a filmy white-red eye, edged in wrinkles. I knew that eye. "She's inside."

"Who?" Zach asked.

Carefully, I lifted the box out of the doll's hands. The doll's fingers were rigid, posed to hold it. The doll stared glassily through me and didn't move. Her lips were painted red and parted slightly. Her cheeks had been painted white with three black drops on each side, like a sad clown. Her eyes had painted eyelashes that curled an inch below and above her eyes, over her eyebrows. Her hair was black yarn. This close, I could hear her breathing, distinct from the others.

I held the box up to one of the lanterns. Inside, shrunken, the Storyteller was knitting a gray scarf. Her knees were jammed into her chest, and her feet were curled awkwardly under her, but she held her gnarled hands with her needles up by her face. I couldn't hear the *click-click* of the needles, but I could imagine the sound. Kneeling, I placed the box on the floor and pulled at the clasp. It was rusted shut, as if it had been out in the rain. The Storyteller must have been inside for a long time. I chipped at the rust with my fingernails. "Help me," I ordered. Zach's hand closed over mine, and together we pulled at the clasp. It creaked and screamed as the metal bent and scraped against itself. "He's punishing her. Maybe because of me. Maybe because she set me free."

Zach helped me pull at the clasp. Suddenly it snapped,

and the box fell open. Sitting on the floor of the wagon in the shards of the box, the Storyteller looked tiny, as if she were distant, and then suddenly huge, as if she were instantly close.

She matched my memory perfectly. The eyes, the wrinkles, the plump lips, the limp hair, the corseted dress, the gnarled hands, the pointed shoes, and the ever-present knitting on her lap. Deftly, the Storyteller lifted the box with one hand and closed the sides, the top, and then the clasp. She tossed the box from hand to hand as she smiled at us. She had few teeth left, and her gums were red and raw. "I thank you for freeing me."

Her voice washed over me, and I shivered like a puppy quivering in anticipation of either praise or punishment. The Storyteller didn't seem to recognize me. "Do you . . . do you know me?" I asked. I wanted to reach out and touch the wrinkles on her cheek. I wanted to curl against her and breathe in the smell of her, the smell of my childhood, the smell of my memory.

"You are the young adventurers who saved the wise old woman. I owe you a boon. Or advice. But I have nothing like that to give you."

"I think you are my mother," I burst out. After the words were out, I couldn't breathe in more air. It was as if those words had taken all the oxygen out with them. I didn't know where the idea had come from. My mother? Yes, of course, she had to be! Who else? I waited, breathless, for her response.

The Storyteller squinted at me. "I have no child."

"I have pretty eyes." I reached out to touch her—and then I stopped, not quite daring.

The Storyteller peered into my eyes, leaning closer and closer until I could smell her breath, rancid and sweet at the same time, and then she reeled back and laughed wildly, a dozen notes clashing together one after another, a cacophony of a hoot and caw and howl and giggle.

Zach gripped my arm to pull me backward. I stood firm. She didn't frighten me. She'd cared for me, comforted me, freed me. She'd mothered me. "You cut the ropes," I said. "You set me free."

The Storyteller giggled. "And you blossomed into the princess that I always knew you could be." She touched my face, tapped my shoulder, and tugged on my hair. "They did a finer job than I ever could."

"Mother." I tried out the word, letting it roll around my tongue. "I need to know—"

"I'm not your mother." The Storyteller wasn't laughing anymore, and there was sadness in her milky eyes. "You shouldn't be here."

The words felt like a blow to my stomach, and again I couldn't breathe. "But I . . ."

"You never had a mother," the Storyteller said.

I shook my head. "I don't understand. I was . . . adopted. Abandoned? I remember you. . . . You told me stories . . . lullabies. . . . You were always there. You cared for me. . . ." But I also remembered needles in my skin, ropes around my limbs. She hadn't always been kind. "Did you steal me from someone? Where do I come from? Who am I?"

"You shouldn't ask. And you shouldn't have come back." She bustled toward us, shooing us as if we were chickens.

"You must leave. Leave before he sees you and never come back!" She herded us toward the door, but I dug my feet into the wood floor.

"Please! I need your help! I've lost my memories—"

The door clicked.

The Storyteller quit pushing me. "I've helped you more than I should have and less than I could have." She retreated and sat heavily on a wooden bench between two unfinished dolls. "Once upon a time, a young witch fell in love with a boy who feared death . . . and it was beautiful. For a time." She wrapped one arm around a doll. It fell limply against her shoulder. Its head sagged forward.

I reached into my pocket and pulled out the box, hiding it behind my back. All I had to do was flip open the lid and touch him with the clasp—a simple plan. Ready, Zach waited behind the door. The Magician wouldn't see him. I stood in front of the door and waited.

*Click. Click, click.*

The door swung open.

And I saw the Magician.

*That is what the Magician's hat is supposed to look like,* I thought. It was crushed velvet with a white ribbon around its base. It was tattered and worn near the rim from years of use. It shadowed his face so I couldn't see his blacker-than-black eyes, only his snowy beard, which he had braided with multi-colored beads. I had forgotten the beads. I stared at the beads swinging from the tip of each braid. Some were glass; some were wood; some were bone. The bone ones had been carved with symbols and leaves.

His eyes fixed on the Storyteller first. "You're free."

"It's her," the Storyteller said. "They changed her body, but it's still her in all the ways that matter. She came back."

Then the Magician stared at me.

"Father?" I said.

"You're alive," he said. And joy lit up his face.

And then Zach worked magic: a blanket flew off a cot and wrapped around the Magician as tight as a strait-jacket. But I couldn't make myself open the box. My father! Maybe the agents were wrong about him. Maybe the visions lied. Maybe he—

The dolls moved.

From both sides of the wagon, they lurched onto their feet. They swarmed over Zach. From behind me, two grabbed my arms. Their knitted hands squeezed like wire garrotes. My left hand was still plunged into my pocket, but I couldn't move to draw the box out, though now I realized my mistake.

Across the wagon, his supply of magic gone, Zach struggled as four dolls held him fast. He was forced against the wall. The bottles shook from the impact. "Zach!" I cried. Without thinking, I threw magic at the dolls around us.

The dolls burst into flame.

And I collapsed.

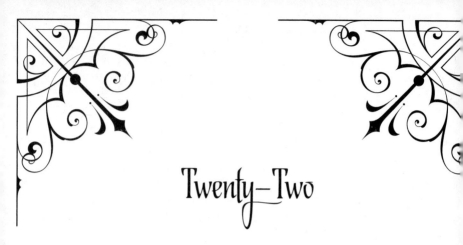

# Twenty-Two

The Storyteller dances the marionettes with ease. They leap and twirl at the twist of her gnarled fingers. She shouldn't have such dexterity in her old hands, but she does. Children on the grass hill laugh and clap their hands.

"Once upon a time," she says, "there was a boy and a girl lost in the woods . . ." She tells the story of Hansel and Gretel. A third marionette joins the others on the wooden stage. This one is dressed all in black, and her cloth face is pinched in false wrinkles. She looks like a cloth copy of the Storyteller. "Who is nibbling on my house?" The Storyteller tells of the witch pushed into the fire, and Hansel and Gretel locking the cast-iron door. She tells how they run out of the house into the forest, where they starve and die and their bodies are ravaged by wolves and then carrion birds and then crawled over and claimed by maggots and earthworms until they are nothing more than dirt and leaves on the forest floor.

She then beckons, and I dance on the stage between the dolls.

The click of needles was the only sound.

I opened my eyes and saw the Storyteller seated against the shuttered window. She was knitting an arm, a doll's arm. The rest of the doll lay next to her, and a bag of scraps leaned against the shutters. The doll had black yarn hair and black button eyes. Its body was magenta, and it wore a crocheted white dress. The Storyteller had not yet given it a mouth.

The other dolls were missing.

Lifting my head, I looked for them—and I saw a pile of burned rags in the corner, a tangled mass of charred dolls. Arms and legs stuck out at awkward angles. Half a charred face stared sightlessly at me. I had burned them all.

"She's awake," the Magician said.

I jerked at the sound of his voice. After hearing him in my visions and memories for so long, his voice felt oddly disembodied outside my head. Bending over me, he peered at my face, only inches away. He raised my eyelids higher and examined my eyes. "Where's Zach?" I asked.

He lifted my chin and turned it. With yarn pinning my arms to my sides, I couldn't do anything but tilt my head back away from his hands. He pinched my cheeks, and I yelped. "Perfect teeth," he said. "The details are magnificent."

"Are you my father?" I asked him.

He looked amused. "Yes."

"He is not," the Storyteller said.

"I'm the closest she has." The Magician didn't look away from me. He stroked my cheek. "I thought I lost you, little one."

"Freeing her was the humane approach," the Storyteller said.

"Losing her was my worst nightmare," the Magician said, an edge to his voice. I saw myself reflected in his eyes. His eyes were full of me, as if he were swallowing me whole.

"Once upon a time," the Storyteller said, "there was a lion who was raised from infancy by a man and his wife. They bathed him in their tub, fed him from their plates, and slept with him in their bed. One night, they missed dinner, and as they slept peacefully beside their adopted leonine son . . . he ate them."

"She's a girl, not a lion."

"You can't keep her," the Storyteller said.

His eyes stormy, he turned toward the Storyteller.

"I too felt joy when I first saw her. I even thought it would be all right if she simply left again." Her voice was tinged with regret. "If she'd stayed away, it would be different, but . . ."

I interrupted. "I want to know what you've done with Zach, the boy who came with me." I tried to keep my voice even and calm. I wouldn't let them scare me, even though I was bound with yarn that felt like steel wire. It was wrapped around my ankles, torso, and arms, securing me to the cot.

"He's safe." The Magician waved his hand toward the boxes that hung on the ribbon, but he continued to glare at the Story-teller. I strained to see into the boxes, but from my cot, I couldn't tell if they were empty or full. I imagined Zach, shrunken inside one, alone and afraid. But alive. At least he was alive! "If you're a good girl, he'll stay safe."

The Storyteller laid her knitting to the side, and she rose. She hobbled across the wagon to stand by the Magician's side, looking down at me. "She's here to kill you."

"She's mine." Leaning toward me, he inhaled, breathing in my breath, and then he smiled at me, fondly.

"She's more dangerous than you begin to comprehend." The Storyteller sat beside me and stroked my hair. Her fingers worked through knots in my hair, untangling it as she spoke. She then jerked her hands away as if she hadn't meant to touch me. "Dangerous to both of us, as much as I wish it were otherwise."

"She's a miracle! She left us broken, and she came back perfect!"

Gently, the Storyteller looped yarn around my neck as if the yarn were a necklace. "She shouldn't have come back. That fact seals her fate." She pulled the yarn tighter, and it bit into my skin. The fibers felt like metal, cool and unyielding. "I'll make it quick. You don't have to watch."

"Father!" I cried. I drew on my magic. But before I could release it, the Magician's hand shot out, and he knocked her back with a rush of wind that flew from the palms of his hands.

Sailing across the room, the Storyteller knocked into the bench that lined the opposite wall. The wagon rocked. The boxes on the ribbon swayed. The skulls tapped against each other, and the bottles clinked.

She didn't move.

*He's killed her,* I thought. My heart began to thud faster

and more wildly, as if it were a bird thrashing inside a bone cage.

But she spoke, soft at first. "Everything I have done has been for you. Everything. You felt alone; I gave you companionship. You felt old; I gave you youth. You felt weak; I gave you power. And you cast me aside. Imprison me. Strike me!" She rose, shaking. "But even if you despise me for it, I will protect you from yourself. I will destroy her—for you!"

Knitting needles flew at me, sharp and fast. Again before I could react, the Magician held up one hand, and the needles reversed—shooting back fast and straight. Two needles embedded themselves in the Storyteller's heart.

She clutched at them, and then she toppled forward onto her knees, hard.

I heard screaming. My scream. It tore out of my throat and filled the air, and I couldn't stop. Blood welled on her breast, staining her clothes.

The Magician fell to his knees in front of her. "No! No, no, what have I done?" He cradled her as she slumped to the ground. Quickly, he lifted her and carried her to me. Her breathing was ragged. A drop of blood dotted the corner of her mouth.

He slammed his lips onto mine and inhaled so deeply that it felt as if he were swallowing my scream. He broke away, my scream silenced, and he focused on her.

Her face shifted, smoothing. Her white hair darkened and softened. Her eyes cleared, ivory whites and brown irises. I'd seen her with this face in my visions, her younger self. The

Magician yanked the needles from her chest, and he pressed his hands over the wounds. They didn't heal. He didn't—I didn't—have the power to heal so grave a wound.

As he concentrated, her body shifted again: first, she became a dog; blood seeped into her short gray fur. Then she changed again, shrinking into a cat. Her wounds didn't close. He changed her into a bird, a songbird that lay limp in his hands. Then an owl. Then a mouse. Pressing himself against me, he inhaled again. I saw tears bright in his eyes, unshed. Determined, he continued, trying to find some form that wouldn't bear her wounds. He transformed her into a tree, rooted in the floor. Sap still leaked from gashes in her bark. "There, there, you'll be all right, yes, yes." He put his hand over the bark. "You won't die. You can't." He changed her again, back to the woman with the silk black hair. She was paler now, her skin almost frostbitten. "No!" He changed her again—a stone. It was smooth and flawless. He transformed her back.

She was still dying.

No matter what form he chose, when he returned her to human, she was weaker than before. She put her hand, gnarled despite the youth of her face, on his wrist. "Enough," she whispered. "We never . . . drained one . . . who could heal."

His voice was broken. "I am sorry."

"Do it. Don't waste my strength."

I watched the color drain from his face. But he said nothing.

The Magician found a stick of chalk. With shaking hands,

he drew a circle on the floor of the wagon. He marked it with symbols—I'd seen the symbols before, both on his Tarot cards and on this same floor. I felt memories bubble inside of me. Those symbols . . . "You can't!"

He didn't respond.

"Please, not to her!" The Storyteller used to soothe me with stories as we traveled between worlds. Her stories had power of their own. They wrapped around you and forced you to listen. I remembered she used to do puppet shows for the children at the carnival, drawing her audience with her voice. Sometimes she'd use me in them. She'd tie strings around my wrists and ankles, and I'd dance on the stage. She'd praise me if I danced well, and I'd reveled in her praise.

Her breathing was loud, ragged enough to drown out the soft inhales and exhales of the dolls. She coughed, and blood speckled the floor. She opened and closed her mouth as if she wanted to talk but couldn't. Her hands, around the wounds, were red, and a pool of red spread across the wood, seeping toward the chalk circle.

"She said she wasn't my mother." But she had to be. As mixed with nightmares as my memories of her were, she still felt like family. I couldn't remember any other.

"She wasn't, and she was." The Magician didn't look at me. I saw he had tears staining his cheeks. He plucked boxes from the ribbon, all except for one, which I knew must hold Zach. As the Magician plucked each box, the ribbon shook and Zach's box swayed.

"Who are my parents?"

"You have none." The Magician drew a knife from within the folds of his conjurer's robe. It had a black bone handle, and the blade was covered in writing and runes.

"But where did I come from?"

"From her," he said shortly. He crossed to me and picked me up as if I were a pile of cloth. He dropped me down beside her, in the blood. My face was inches from the Storyteller's. Her young brown eyes stared into mine. I didn't think she saw me. The blood smelled acrid, and I felt its warm wetness seep through my shirt.

I wanted to scream again.

"Breathe," he told me.

And I remembered him saying that many, many times before. I remembered lying bound on the floor, facing eyes . . . green eyes, brown eyes, red eyes, cat eyes, black eyes, blue eyes.

"Breathe in her magic. Don't let it be wasted."

The Storyteller fixed her eyes on me. Milky eyes, old eyes again—her true eyes. I couldn't look away. She was still alive, but only barely. Each breath was harder, slower. Her blood-stained hands lay limp across her chest.

Gently, the Magician lifted her face and placed her mouth close to my lips. I shrank back as far as I could, but the steel-like yarn held me tight. I felt the Storyteller's breath, tasted it in my mouth.

And then I felt a rush of wind inside me.

It was magic, her magic, filling me.

She lay slack and still. Dead.

He began to cut her body. The knife slid through her flesh, her muscle, and her bone as if they were soft cheese. Blood didn't drip where the knife cut. He severed each limb, and he placed each in its own box. He was methodical and silent, crying as he cut. Last, he lovingly carved out her eyes one by one and placed them in boxes.

He placed the rest of her in the final box and closed it. One by one, he strung the boxes on the colored string, and then he knelt next to me in the pool of blood. He leaned toward my lips. "Whisper sweet nothings to me," he said.

He breathed in. Leaning back, he closed his eyes. He then picked up the needles, stained red with blood, and he chose a ball of yarn. Eyes still closed, he began to knit.

And I blacked out. But this time, it was the oblivion of darkness. There were no visions.

When I woke, the blood was gone, and the chalk had been erased. I again lay on the cot, bound in the Storyteller's unbreakable yarn. I smelled of dried blood.

The Magician was seated across from me next to the unfinished doll. He was watching me.

"What . . . what am I?" I asked.

"You're a doll," the Magician said. "You were yarn and cloth and buttons and stitches. She made you to hold the magic we collected."

I opened my mouth and then closed it.

"No person can hold another's magic. Not for more than a few hours. It fades. But you can. You can hold it forever, or at least as long as you exist. You were to be our power source—our battery, so to speak—to draw on whenever we pleased. She made you that way. Creating you was her magic."

It felt like truth, horrible and hideous.

"We filled you with transformation magic, plant magic, flight, weather . . . so many different kinds of magic."

*Except healing,* I thought.

"Over the years, the magic changed you," he said. "You absorbed more than merely power. You absorbed the essence, the life spirit, of those people, and you . . . woke. With the others, the new ones, we've been careful. Only a little power, only a few thoughts, only a few bits of soul. But with you . . . You were our first. We didn't know."

I remembered now. All of it. I was made from stolen bits of magic, comprised of bits of the thoughts and personalities of their victims. That's what woke me up, made me alive—or at least lifelike.

I closed my eyes.

*I'm not real,* I thought. *I am a patchwork doll made of leftover bits of the dead.* The words repeated in my head. *I'm not real. Not real. Not real. I am no one. I am nothing.*

"She and I . . . we were together for a very long time. A very long time. I did not intend to trade her for you. But now . . . it's you and me. We're together now." I heard his footsteps as he crossed the wagon, and I opened my eyes. He was kneeling next to me. I shrank away as far as I could. His lips didn't touch mine, but he drew a breath close to me. "You may look human, but it's only an illusion. It's time for you to be what you truly are, what she and I created you to be."

I felt my body change, softening inside and out. I saw my hair, which lay splayed across my cheek and the cot, thicken into yarn. I knew without a mirror that my face was cloth, my eyes were green marbles, and my mouth was embroidered. My body shrank and changed as my skin reverted to cloth.

"Welcome home," the Magician said.

# Twenty-Three

THE DOLL LAID ON the bench and counted the boxes on the ribbon, the silk scarves, the potion bottles, and the bird skulls. And then she counted them again.

Across the wagon, the boy wouldn't stop talking. "I think each skull is from a different kind of bird. You can see the differences in the shapes. Hooked bills . . . they have to be raptors. And the ones in the corner must be seed eaters. Sparrows and such. I think most are songbirds. Don't know if that means he likes songbirds or hates them. He must have practiced killing birds and worked his way up to humans. You know, a common sign of a disturbed kid is torturing animals— it's a sign he or she lacks empathy. You don't lack empathy, Eve. When the Magician walked through the door, you hesitated. You're *more* human than he is, not less."

The boy was tied to a cot on the opposite side of the wagon. The doll was tied to a bench with the same steel-like yarn. The Magician was asleep—or feigning sleep—in his cot. She knew better than to trust he was truly asleep.

After the transformation, while the Magician slept, she'd used magic to sever the yarn and had tried to reach the boy. The Magician had caught her before she'd crossed the wagon, and the vision had taken her. The vision had been full of death and screams, and when she had woken, the Magician had hurt the boy.

Next time, she'd waited until she was certain his breathing was deep and even, and she'd used her magic to free the boy. Awakening, the Magician had broken the boy's fingers.

She'd tried once more, changing the Magician into a tree, hardening his body with bark and sealing his face with leaves, but she'd lost consciousness before she could reach the boy. When she woke, it was five days later, and the boy's face was streaked with blood and bruises. That was when she'd stopped thinking of him by name.

The Magician released the boy from his bindings twice a day, and the doll lay on her bench while the boy ate, drank, and relieved himself in a pot. The Magician never released the doll. But he did allow the boy to talk to her.

At first, the doll thought this was a kindness. But after a while, she changed her mind. It was a constant reminder that the boy was here because of her and that she couldn't save him. He chattered fast, like a magpie. The doll found that if she didn't focus on individual words, she could let his voice swirl around her like birdsong.

Every few days, the wagon would move. The boxes and skulls would sway as the wagon lurched forward, and she'd listen to the clatter and clang and clink of the bottles and bones. When the wagon reached its next destination, the Magician would entrap her and the boy in separate boxes and leave. Sometimes she slept, though as a doll she didn't need to. Sometimes she'd lie awake, curled into a ball of cloth, and try not to think.

She'd be jolted awake when the Magician released her from the box, took her magic, and then trapped her again while he performed another show. When he returned, he'd release her, secure her to a bench, and talk for hours. He'd tell her about the new world outside and how much the audience had loved his show. The carnival had been dying, he said, but now that she'd returned, his shows were full of magic again and his tent was full of people. The other dolls had been too weak, too new, too empty, to give him what he needed, but she was marvelous! He'd be giddy for a while, even kind, and then he'd fall silent again.

After a while, he grew more ambitious. He wanted his shows to have more magic, instill more wonder, and inspire more awe, but there were limits to how much magic he could inhale and how long it would last. He was efficient in his magic use—a single breath could sustain him for multiple tricks—but it wasn't enough for him. So he began to train her. He fed her lines to say, and he positioned her to hold his hat, his cloak, his Tarot cards. He choreographed how he would siphon magic from her mid-show, a subtle breath here and a brush past there, so the audience wouldn't notice. He practiced with her in the confines of the wagon, and then he'd leave to conduct his shows without her. He returned between sets to breathe in her magic.

She woke one night with his sour breath in her face. She

held still and wished she could stop breathing. He grinned when he saw her eyes open. His teeth were brilliant white, gleaming in the candlelight from the lantern that hung in the corner of the wagon. "I have a surprise for you," he said.

The doll looked up at the shuttered windows. No light leaked in. It had to be night. She wondered how many days she'd been here, and then she squelched the thought. The boy was tied to a bench across the wagon. He was awake as well.

With a flourish, the Magician pulled a dress out of a paper bag. It had been sewn with hundreds of bird feathers and set with thousands of jewels. It fluttered and sparkled as he waved it through the air.

He pointed to a bucket in the corner. "Clean and dress yourself. You've accumulated filth from the road." After untying the yarn that bound her, he yanked her to her feet. Her cotton-stuffed legs shook, and she caught herself on the wall of the wagon as the world tilted. It had been many hours since she had last stood, not since their last practice session. She stumbled to the corner of the room with the bucket.

The Magician paced through the wagon while the doll slowly peeled off the clothes that she had worn for days and days. She hadn't sweat into them, of course—she couldn't—but dust and dirt had seeped into the wagon and onto her. She found a sponge in the bucket, and she rubbed it over her cloth body. The fabric that was her skin soaked up the water. She scrubbed her green marble eyes, and she wet her yarn hair. The water in the bucket grayed, and a puddle formed around her fabric feet. She tried to dry herself with a towel, dabbing her body as best she could, and then she pulled on the dress. The feathers scraped and poked into her cotton. She fastened the buttons hidden within the feathers and jewels. For her yarn hair, the Magician presented a comb inlaid with clusters of the same starlight jewels, and for her feet, he had golden shoes.

"Lovely," the Magician said. "You will enchant them."

The boy was watching her. She wondered if she enchanted or repulsed him, and then she reminded herself not to think about him.

"Spin," the Magician ordered.

Cloth legs wobbling, the doll turned in a circle. The skirt whispered around her, rising lightly into the air as if it would lift her higher and higher until she flew. She remembered she *had* flown . . . with the boy who laid bound across the tent.

Looking at him, she faltered.

The boy began to talk again, "He may call himself the Magician, but he's a fraud. He has no magic of his own. He's a parasite."

The Magician plucked an empty box from the ribbon, and he clicked it open.

The boy shrank back, but he didn't stop talking. "You're the magic one, Eve. He has no magic. He steals it all from you. You're the special one. You have to believe that."

The Magician pressed the clasp to the boy's skin, and the boy vanished into the box. The Magician shut the lid. "You may hold the magic, but you can't use it, not without dropping into dreamland. We built that 'quirk' into you. A sensible precaution, as it turns out." He smiled, pleased with himself. "Obey me in all things, and we will all three return here unharmed after the show. Disobey me, and you and I return alone."

He held out his arm, bent at the elbow, as if to escort a lady. "Our audience awaits."

Inside the tent, the acrobats were performing. Rings dangled from the rafters of the tent, and three men and two women dangled from them by one hand or one foot or one knee. They spun in sync, five pinwheels in the wind. In unison, they unfurled ribbons from their sleeves. It looked as though their shirts were unraveling. The ribbons plummeted into the audience, and the acrobats shimmied onto the ribbons. Dancing in the air, they wrapped the ribbons around their bodies and swooped and soared with them. The ribbons twisted together in midair above the audience, and then they released from the rings and fluttered down on the crowd. The acrobats hung in midair, suspended by seemingly nothing, as the audience applauded, and then they somersaulted down, bowed, and exited.

"Come," the Magician said to the doll. He hauled her through a silver mirror at the back of the tent. He kept a grip on her arm tight enough to bruise if she'd had human skin, and they stepped out of a second mirror onto the stage—a dramatic entrance. At his signal, a stagehand wheeled away the silver mirror.

The audience clapped politely. They had seen portals before. In most worlds, they were ubiquitous. A few patrons fidgeted and rustled their bags, gathering their belongings as if preparing the leave. But they quieted when she walked forward on her shaky cloth legs—a living doll. Somewhere in the tent, a baby cried.

"My beautiful assistant!" the Magician said.

The audience laughed at her thread face, her yarn hair, her wobbling legs.

And the Magician began the show.

He started with sleight of hand, magicless tricks with cards, balls, and scarves. But then he added real magic: he tossed the scarves into the air, and they didn't fall. Over his head, the scarves twisted slowly as if they were underwater. And then the scarves burst into flame.

The audience gasped, their attention rapt.

Silent on the stage, the doll watched the audience through glass eyes. Children. Men. Women. Most had painted faces: leopard spots, zebra stripes, fish scales, feathers. Their clothes were fashioned out of fur, feathers, and scales to match their faces. A few held caramel popcorn in a red-and-white-striped bag, forgotten as the Magician performed. One child sucked endlessly on a lollipop.

Near the center of the audience, one face was unpainted: a perfect face with blond tousled hair and bright-blue eyes. He watched the Magician as intently as a hawk watches a mouse.

The doll watched this boy as she took the Magician's cloak and waved it with a flourish, the perfect assistant. The

Magician pretended to kiss her cheek in thanks and instead stole her breath. She kept watching as he tossed card after card into the air. Each card stopped in midair until at last he had a ladder of cards leading up to the scarves.

The Magician climbed the card ladder up to where the fiery scarves spun and sparked. On one foot, he stood on the top card, and he juggled the silken balls of fire. As the scarves dissolved into ash, the applause was thunderous.

The boy in the audience didn't clap.

The doll knew his name. Aidan. She fought against the memories that rose inside her, and she fixed her eyes instead on the Magician.

Coming down from the ladder of cards, the Magician held his hand out toward the audience. A girl in the front row leaped to her feet and scrambled onto the stage.

*No*, the doll thought.

The girl looked so innocent. Her face was painted like a swan. She wore white feathers in a skirt. She was smiling as if she'd won a prize. With broad gestures, the Magician invited her to climb the ladder. Laughing, the girl climbed, and he stood beneath her. On the tenth card, her foot slipped. She grabbed at the card above, but it slid out of her hand. Screaming, she fell.

He turned her into a bird before she hit the ground.

The Magician scooped his hat from the doll's hands. He laid it over the bird that fluttered on the stage. Slowly, he raised the hat up, and the girl stood under it, wearing his hat. She laughed and clapped her hands. The Magician bowed. The girl curtsied before scurrying back to her seat, and her parents hugged her with proud smiles on their painted faces.

The girl wasn't his next victim. The doll wished her cold, dry eyes could cry. She wished she were more than cotton inside so she could feel relief in her heart, her stomach, and her breath. Perhaps no one would die today.

The show continued. Soon, other carnival people gathered at the back of the tent. The Magician's shows never went so long. But the Magician didn't slow or tire. Between tricks, he'd kiss his doll assistant on the cheek, secretly filling his lungs each time. He drew a cloud into the tent and caused it to rain on the stage. He transformed the raindrops into butterflies, and then he forced the butterflies to fly in patterns against the roof of the tent—and then he changed them back into rain that fell toward the audience, transforming at the last second to paper confetti that melted into nothingness.

He then caused the seats to sprout, as if watered by the vanished confetti. Vines spread over the arms and legs of the audience. Roses blossomed on the vine, and then just as quickly, they wilted. The vines blackened and crumbled. Each audience member was left with a rose on his or her lap.

The applause was thunderous.

The Magician bowed. "And now for my final trick . . ."

Plucking the cards from the air, the Magician displayed them, showing that each card had a drawing of a figure: an old woman, a young girl, a harlequin, a queen, a reaper . . . He blew on the cards, tapped them, and the figures detached from the card faces. The paper figures lurched across the stage. He sent them into the audience. They crawled over the audience members, their eyes flat and their progress unslowed. They climbed onto the shoulders or heads of different audience members, whose smiles faltered as the paper feet and hands touched them.

"This time, the cards choose you," the Magician said.

A few of the audience members tried to remove the paper creatures and people. They clung fast. Some pulled harder, and the paper bodies tore.

The Magician shuffled the blank Tarot cards.

As one, the paper figures turned their heads toward the center of the audience. They climbed over people faster with a single-minded determination, converging on the boy Aidan. They climbed up his legs and over his body, laying against his clothes as if glued to him.

"Remember him," the Magician said softly to the doll. The boy Aidan didn't move as the paper figures stuck to his shirt and hair and skin. "He has magic."

The doll met Aidan's eyes.

And Aidan vanished with a soft *pop.*

Outside the wagon, after the performance, Aidan waited on the steps. He still had the paper figures from the Tarot cards on him. One sat on his shoulder, swinging his paper legs. Another clung to the pocket of Aidan's shirt. Others were stuck to him like magnets.

"I believe these are yours." Aidan flashed a dazzling smile at the Magician.

The doll felt unable to move, as if she were on strings but no one had tugged them to make her walk or talk. A part of her wanted to scream at Aidan to run. A part of her wanted to run to him. The rest of her did not move or speak.

The Magician smiled. "Did you like the performance?" He fanned the blank cards, and the paper figures clambered down Aidan's body and crawled up the Magician and onto the cards.

"Very impressive." Aidan stood up lazily, as if he didn't have a care in the world. He hadn't looked at her yet, the doll noted. She stared at him with her green marble eyes that couldn't blink. "But I am here on business." Aidan drew a wallet from his back pocket and flipped it open. A badge with a ring of circles was inside.

The Magician's smile did not waver. "Oh, it's show and tell!" He drew out a box from the pocket of his robe. "Have you ever seen one of these?" He turned the box over in his hands, sliding it over the backs of his hands and around in a figure-eight. "Marvelous device. Impervious to strength or weapons or magic. Yet if you twist it in a particular way and squeeze, you can crush it and its contents with one hand. A trade secret." He fixed his eyes on the doll as he said this. "Now, how can I help you, officer?"

"I'm looking for this girl." Aidan held up a photograph. It was a photo she'd seen before—a girl with yellow hair and green eyes with this boy in a pizza parlor. In the photo, his arm was draped around her.

"I haven't seen her," the Magician said.

Aidan turned to the doll. "And you?"

The doll stared at the box. The boy was inside it. *Zach*, she thought. The Magician held the box in one hand, fingers curled around it, about to tighten. "She isn't here," the doll lied.

"But you've seen her?" Aidan asked.

"Come inside and we'll talk," the Magician said. His smile was frozen on his face. *Don't hurt him*, the doll thought.

Smiling broadly, Aidan said, "I'd be delighted." He followed the Magician up the cherry-red steps to the door of the wagon. The doll wanted to scream at him to run, to hurl magic at him to stop him, to scream for help with every bit of air trapped in her cotton body.

But she didn't.

Instead, she followed Aidan and the Magician with Zach's box inside. By the time she stepped over the threshold, there were two boxes in the Magician's hands, and Aidan was gone.

# Twenty-Four

THE MAGICIAN DREW CHALK circles on the floor of the wagon. He hummed to himself as he added symbols and runes. Dully, the doll watched.

He rocked back on his heels and studied his work.

The doll looked away. She counted the mirrors inlaid in the wall. Each button-size mirror reflected a part of a bird skull or a corner of a box, or a piece of the Magician himself—an elbow in one, a swirl of cloak in another, a bit of his beard in a third.

She heard the click of a clasp and looked back at the Magician. He held one box in his hand. The lid popped open, and the sides fell apart. Zach tumbled out onto the floor. He moaned as the Magician trussed him in bloodstained yarn.

"Eve, that was . . ." Zach stopped as he saw the chalk circle. His eyes widened, and he struggled against the yarn. "No! Are you going to kill me? Eve, is it me next?"

The Magician dragged him to his usual cot and tied him to

it. Zach twisted and flopped. "Hush," the Magician said. "I don't harvest the powerless."

Zach exhaled, and then his breath caught. "But it is someone. You're going to kill someone. Here. Now. I can't be here. I can't watch this. Please, put me back in the box!" His voice rose higher, panic-infused. The Magician tightened the yarn. "Eve . . . you have to stop this!" Zach said. "Make him stop."

The doll looked away. Strands of her yarn hair fell over her face, and she wished it could hide her, block her sight. She wished her eyes would close.

"She cannot," the Magician said. "She must breathe in the last dying breath. There is no other way to harvest the power. If I do it, the magic will fade and be wasted. If she does it, the magic lasts. It's simply a fact." He placed another box in the center of the circle. He unhooked the clasp, and the sides fell open. Aidan huddled on the floor, curled into a ball, holding his knees to his chest.

"You!" Zach said.

Instantly, Aidan vanished.

The Magician laughed. "Splendid!"

Aidan reappeared by the door.

He vanished again and reappeared next to Zach. Aidan's hand clapped on Zach's arm. He disappeared with him, and then reappeared in the same spot. The doll heard the air pop and felt it *whoosh* through the wagon.

He tried again. And again.

The Magician's eyes were alight. "We don't have this in our repertoire. Such strength! Oh my dear . . ." His eyes dimmed as if he'd suddenly remembered that the Storyteller was gone. With a sigh, he leaned in toward the doll and sucked in a breath. When Aidan charged at him, he deflected him with a wave of his hand. The Storyteller's leftover yarn then wrapped around Aidan's body. "She would have found you to be an exquisite addition. In fact . . . you do look familiar. You aren't from this world, are you, boy? We hunted you once before."

"Talk to me, library boy," Aidan said. "Why can't I pop out of here?"

"I'm guessing the wagon functions like the boxes. Probably made of the same material. Magic can't penetrate it—which means no teleporting out. Or blasting out. Or walking through walls. Please tell me you brought the cavalry."

"Very observant," the Magician said to Zach. To Aidan he said, "I'm sorry to tell you, but escape won't be possible. Please know that your magic will be put to good use."

"A fleet of marshals and law enforcement from multiple worlds is waiting to descend on this wagon," Aidan said. "Surrender yourself, and it's possible they'll show you some leniency. If not . . . you're surrounded. Escape won't be possible for you either."

"It will be, once I have your magic." The Magician spoke gently, as if to a child.

"If I can't teleport from within this box, then neither can you," Aidan said. "You'll be arrested as soon as you step outside. Do yourself a favor, and turn yourself in."

The Magician sucked in another breath from the doll's mouth, and then he transformed himself into an identical match to Aidan, right down to the cocky smile. "They won't arrest *you*." He then transformed himself back.

Aidan vanished and reappeared again, still bound in yarn. He struggled at the yarn, straining against it. But the threads did not even stretch. The doll leaned her head against the wall and wished she could change into stone and never feel again . . . but it wouldn't work. She'd still feel. She didn't think it would even help to die. The Magician could still use an inert doll, and besides, she wasn't truly alive to begin with.

"Where's Eve?" Aidan asked.

The Magician didn't answer. He was absorbed in preparing the chalk symbols.

"Behind you," Zach said.

"The freaky doll?" He twisted to look at the doll, and he struggled harder. "He changed her into *that*? Eve? Eve, is that you?"

"He changed me back to who . . . what . . . I am," the doll said. "Eve doesn't exist. She never existed. I'm not her. I'm not real." Silently, she added, *I don't deserve to be real.*

"You *are* Eve," Zach said. "You may have started like this, but you became Eve!" The doll shook her head, lolling it on her limp neck. That had been a dream, a delusion. This was her reality. "Remember the day we first met? I made a bad apple joke. I told you I wanted to kiss you. You sat in the lobby and read books I picked out for you. Remember the everything bagel?"

The Magician flicked his hand, and Aidan was knocked off his feet. The yarn wrapped tighter, shackling him to the floor in the center of the chalk circle. He vanished and reappeared again.

"Tell her memories," Zach told him. "Remind her that she's real. First time you kissed. The moment when you knew she was perfect for you, when you knew you didn't ever want to be anywhere else but with her, when you knew she was your escape and your salvation and your chance at something more."

"I don't . . . ," Aidan said. "I can't . . ."

"She's the one with the magic. Your life depends on her," Zach said. "This is not the time to be squeamish about . . . what did you call it? Oh, yes . . . 'sappy maudlin mush.' Help her remember she matters!"

Aidan disappeared and reappeared behind the Magician. He tried to knock into him, but the Magician was prepared. Sidestepping Aidan, the Magician levitated the ritual knife to Aidan's throat.

Aidan didn't move. "I don't have any memories because I lied. We were never together. I knew she'd lost her memories. I manufactured a relationship so she'd trust me."

The doll swiveled her head to stare at him.

"Okay, that's the opposite of helpful. Wait . . . really? It was only me?" Zach's face lightened. "Eve, listen to me. What we had was real. You care about me. You know you do! I'd be a rotten hostage if you didn't care. You have feelings. You are real!"

She now stared at Zach. She didn't want to, but she couldn't help it.

"You've made yourself real! Maybe you didn't start out that way. Maybe you weren't born. Maybe your childhood was crap. Well, guess what? My childhood was crap too. After Sophie died . . . I was just someone else to blame, another person who wasn't watching, who wasn't careful enough, never mind that I was a kid too. My existence was only a reminder of her absence. But it doesn't matter what happened in the past or what other people think of you in the present. What matters is who you are. And you . . . you're amazing, Eve! You created yourself! He didn't make you. You did it! You formed yourself! And that's extraordinary."

The doll couldn't stop staring at Zach. *He doesn't lie*, she thought.

"Enough," the Magician said. He sucked in the doll's breath, and the doll felt herself rise into the air. She floated to the circle and was lowered into the center. Knife still at Aidan's throat, the Magician levitated him as well, laying him near the doll.

"Eve, listen to me," Zach said. "The roses in the bookshelves, the painting with the real water, the books that flew around us, the way we flew . . . Remember how it felt." She *did* remember. She'd loved the way it felt with their arms around each other, rising into the air. That had been real. What she'd felt . . . what *I'd* felt had been real.

"I said, enough." The Magician flicked his hand toward Zach, and a scrap of cloth plastered itself over his mouth, silencing him. But it didn't block Zach's eyes. Zach was looking at me exactly the same way he had when I wore the body of a beautiful human girl, instead of a cloth face with green marble eyes. He was looking at me as if he saw me, all of me, as if I were real and whole and unbroken. I saw myself through his eyes.

I saw me.

As the Magician knelt beside Aidan, I said, "You must miss her. You must feel some sadness, some regret, some human emotion. I do. I miss her."

He positioned Aidan's body within the chalk circle.

I continued. "I miss the way she used to brush my hair, strand by strand, while she told me stories. I miss how she'd make the marionettes dance. Do you remember our life together? We lived in a forest for a time under the trees, and we watched the acrobats swing and twist in the air. And we lived on a pier in a harbor. You'd use the magic in me for beautiful things: to change both of you into seabirds and fly out over the waves, to make the rain dance as it fell, to grow hundreds of roses in an instant . . . Your shows were pure joy, and your audiences loved you, but your performances weren't for them. Every one you did, every bit of stolen magic you used, was for her; everything was always for her—to make her happy and to keep her safe. Because of how she made you feel. Safe. Strong. Magical."

He wasn't listening.

He *had* to listen.

I thought of the Storyteller—how she could command the full attention of any audience with the tone of her voice. "Once upon a time, there was a boy who was afraid." I said it in the way the Storyteller would say it, drawing on her memories of how to weave a tale. "He was afraid of dying, of hurting, of being weak, of being powerless, of being helpless, of failing, of humiliating himself, of being alone, of growing old, of never being safe . . . and the fear ate him inside."

The Magician drew the knife, but he moved more slowly, as if the air had thickened.

"And once upon a time, this boy met a girl who knew how to steal strength from others as they died. But though the boy and girl stole the magic, the magic wouldn't stay inside them. So the girl, who had become a woman, knitted a doll to hold the magic. This doll was made of cloth for skin, button eyes, thread for her mouth, and yarn for her hair. At first, the doll was like all other dolls, limp and lifeless. But as the magic poured into her, she began to wake up. She learned to breathe. She learned to see. She learned to hear. One day, she learned to move. Another, she learned to speak. And last, she learned to think and very, very slowly to feel. And while this happened, you were learning *not* to feel. With each death, you died a little inside, until you forgot why you were doing this—that it was for her, to be with her, to be alive with her, to be safe with her and special for her. And she was doing it for you, to be together without fear. She sent me away to protect you. She tried to kill me so you could be together . . ."

The Magician was crying.

"But you killed her instead."

The knife slipped from his fingers and clattered on the floor of the wagon. The Magician dropped his face into his hands.

Seizing the moment, Aidan flailed his body. His forehead touched mine, and with a pop, we vanished. We reappeared beside Zach. Leaning forward, I pressed my embroidered lips against Zach's and breathed all the magic I could into him.

The yarn that bound us dissolved into smoke that swirled through the wagon.

Free, I sprang to my shaky cloth feet and plucked an empty box off the string. I opened the lid. Using magic, Zach sent the box sailing toward the Magician.

As the Magician raised his tear-streaked face, the open box hit him in the chest.

He vanished inside it.

# Twenty-Five

WITHOUT LOOKING AT ZACH or Aidan, I fetched a cloth and began to scrub at the chalk circles and symbols. Aidan caught my arm, the cotton in my elbow squishing under his grip. "That's evidence," he said.

I yanked my arm away. Bits of fiber flew in the air. "The boxes are evidence. The body parts are evidence. *I* am evidence. *These* are instructions for how to do what he did. No one sees this."

Zach grabbed another cloth from the Storyteller's bag of scraps and began to scrub beside me. His lips were pressed together into a thin line, and he scrubbed with such ferocity that he looked as though he wanted to wear through the floor as well.

"But you can't—" Aidan began.

"You lied to me."

Aidan winced. "I thought it would be the best way to win your trust. You're remarkably unsusceptible to my manly

charm, Green Eyes. And you already trusted the WitSec
agents. I thought I had to trump that."

"You could have told me the truth," I said. Beside me, Zach
obliterated another set of symbols. Nearly all traces of the
ritual markings were gone.

"You didn't like me," Aidan said, as if this were inexplicable.
"You wouldn't have believed me. As you may or may not recall,
when we *did* tell you the truth, you didn't believe us."

"Whoa, back up," Zach said. "What truth?"

"The truth that she is special," Aidan said, looking only at
me. "And we value her. Regardless of how the trial turns out,
she will be safe with us."

"Who's 'us'?" Zach demanded. "Who are you?"

"He had a badge," I said.

"What badge?" Zach asked. "Did I miss something? Obviously I did. I was stuck in a box. What did I miss?"

Aidan shrugged with fake modesty. "I persuaded a few
people that I could be useful here. Namely, Lou and Malcolm.
Lou seems to think he controls me, and Malcolm . . . well, he
knows I want to keep you safe. Our interests align, at least in
that respect. They loaned me the badge." He bent to pick up the
box with the Magician inside, but I scooped it off the floor
faster. I clutched it to my chest.

"Notice how he's avoiding the key question," Zach said.
"Let me say it very slowly. Who are you, and what do you want
with Eve?"

"I want her help," Aidan said simply. He faced me, his eyes
earnest. "My home . . . my country . . . we're at war. A nation

on our northern border wants to topple our government, destroy our culture, and claim our resources. They've invaded twice, and we've fought them back twice. But thousands have died. And I believe—I *know*—we are losing."

"So?" Zach said. "I mean, I'm sorry, I am, but what does that have to do with Eve?"

"Two years ago, I left school and enlisted," Aidan said. "I used my power to help my country . . . but when word spread about a serial killer who was targeting the young and powerful, I was ordered to let WitSec hide me."

Zach crossed his arms. "Okay, so you're a war hero in hiding."

Aidan ignored him and focused on me. "I was also ordered to recruit others with power to join our cause."

"Victoria and Topher," I guessed.

"Yes. And I was ordered to find a weapon—the killer's power source. My superiors were certain that WitSec had it. And they were right." Aidan flashed his brilliant smile at me. "I found you."

I felt cold. "I don't want to be a weapon."

"Would you rather be dead?" Aidan asked. "After the trial, they'll kill you. Or they'll try. If you agree to work for my government and to help us win the war, then we will ensure that WitSec can't hurt you."

Zach put his arm around my cloth shoulders. As a doll, I was smaller than he was, and his arm draped down, enveloping me. "I don't trust him," he declared.

"He's *still* so innocent," Aidan marveled. "Tell me, Green Eyes: Who exactly would you trust? Can't trust your maker."

He pointed at the Magician's box. "You ran from WitSec, so I doubt you trust them. Face it, I am your only reasonable option. Come with me, and we will keep you safe in exchange for your cooperation."

"And Zach?" I asked. "Will you keep him safe too?"

Aidan hesitated. "He belongs in his own world. He said it himself—you're the special one, Evy."

"You want to use me, like the Magician used me," I said.

"It's not the same! Our enemies are like the Magician. Unscrupulous. Evil. You'll be able to save hundreds, potentially thousands, of lives—"

Zach snorted. "By being a weapon?"

"For a just cause!" Aidan said. "Yes, we will use your power against our enemy. Yes, some people—*evil* people—may die. I won't lie to you. War isn't pretty. But with your strength . . . we could win, end the war, stop the violence, save the day! Eve, you'd be a hero to millions. Please, Eve . . . consider it. And be ready when the moment comes." He then fetched a cloth and wiped away the final symbols on the floor with a flourish, as if he were making a point.

I didn't know what to think of that decision and the possible future he offered. But I knew I was done with the past. Holding the Magician's box, I surveyed the wagon, my home and my prison. The candleflame in the lantern flickered, causing shadows to dance over the bottles, bones, and boxes. "I want to leave."

"The marshals are outside," Aidan said. "Ready to take you to the trial."

"Outside? I thought that was a bluff! They're really . . ."

Zach's eyes bulged, and his face tinted pink. He looked as if he wanted to explode. He gulped in air like a fish. "And they didn't help because . . . why? You were nearly killed! I was . . . And there was help outside?"

"As soon as I obtained proof that Eve was here and that this was the right magician, I was to pop out and signal for help. An impenetrable wagon was not part of the plan."

"You had a crappy plan," Zach said. "You could have been killed."

"It was a risk I accepted," Aidan said.

"I could have been killed!" Zach said. "She could have been killed!"

Aidan tilted his head and smiled his dazzling smile. "Seems to me your plan had flaws too, library boy. Yet you chose to come as well. You weren't forced. In fact, I believe the agency tried enthusiastically to prevent you. And when Lou realized that he couldn't stop you, he gave you the tool you'd need to succeed." He nodded at the box. Aidan's words made sense. Maybe he wasn't lying anymore.

The box in my hands felt like a weight. "I want this to be over," I said.

"Then let's end it, Green Eyes." Aidan held out his hand to me. I ignored his hand and instead took Zach's. His fingers closed tightly around my cloth fingers. Aidan lowered his hand, and I thought I saw his expression twist . . . but no, the smile was plastered on his face again. "You really do have green eyes. Don't you want to change back to human before we go out there?"

"This is who I am. *What* I am. Anything else is a lie, and I'm done with lies."

Zach and I walked to the door. He released my hand so I could unlock it. I cradled the Magician's box under my arm. As I ran my fingers over the swirls in the wood, I heard the familiar *click, click-click-click.* The door swung open, and weak sunlight filtered inside. I looked back once more—the bottles caught the sunlight and cast colored shadows across the boxes, skulls, and feathers. I held the box containing the Magician tighter, and then the three of us stepped outside.

❦

Guns were trained on us. On either side of me, Aidan and Zach raised their hands as if in surrender. I didn't. I was holding the box tightly in my cloth hands, clutched to my chest. The guns were held by agents in flak jackets—Malcolm, Lou, Aunt Nicki, and dozens of others that I didn't recognize. Behind them, in a semicircle, I saw the acrobats and contortionists and animal trainers from the carnival. Squeezed between them, a kid ate a caramel apple, as if this were just another part of the show.

I must have looked strange to them, even compared to the circus performers. A living doll. I wondered what they thought, if they even knew who or what I was. Holding up the box with the Magician, I said, "He's here."

Malcolm lowered his gun.

He walked forward. His eyes were fixed on the box. *He doesn't recognize me*, I thought, and I was surprised at how much that thought hurt. Approaching me, he held out his hands. My grip on the box tightened, and the fabric of my fingers strained. I didn't know what the agency planned to do with him—or what I wanted them to do with him. One twist, the Magician had said, and you could crush a box in one hand. One twist, and he would never hurt anyone ever again. As if this thought were visible in my eyes, Malcolm stopped. He didn't touch the box. He looked down at me. As a doll, I was much shorter than he was. "Eve."

He knew me! Even like this . . .

"He'll stand trial," Malcolm said quietly. "He will be held accountable for what he has done. Your testimony will make it possible."

"Did you let me escape?" I asked.

"Yes," he said.

"Because you needed more evidence? Because you needed me to stop him? Because you couldn't find him without me?"

"Yes," he said again.

"I could have died."

He nodded.

"Zach could have died. Aidan almost did."

He looked down at his feet.

"You were supposed to keep me safe," I said. "And Aidan too. You were supposed to keep everyone safe. It's your job. It's who you are, who your past made you."

Malcolm half smiled. It was a sad smile. "I can't keep you safe from yourself. It's true we let you escape, but stopping you would have required deadly force. Lou . . . tried to salvage the situation."

"How did you find me?"

"Pieced together clues from our notes about your visions, plus you and the boy were spotted several times by our contacts as you passed through their worlds. But finding the carnival took longer than we wanted. There are many worlds." He looked up at me, met my green marble eyes. "I *wanted* to keep you safe, if that counts for anything."

I didn't know if it did or not, but I handed him the box.

"Thank you," he said. "We will talk more back at the agency. I am . . . glad you're alive." He looked as if he wanted to say more, but he didn't.

I watched him carry the box to a steel briefcase. It was lined with foam inside, cut to fit the box. *They were prepared for this*, I thought. I was a pawn who had been moved across the chessboard. Malcolm's strong hands were trembling as he laid the box inside. He closed the lid. The snap of the clasps echoed in my ears.

"Now what happens?" Zach asked softly in my ear.

I shook my head. I didn't know.

Behind us, other agents swept into and over the wagon. It was photographed, and then the items inside were carefully collected, each sealed into its own plastic bag or jar and labeled. Yellow tape was stretched around the site, and the carnival workers and patrons were pushed back behind the tape. Outside the tape, the agents began to interview the contortionists and the acrobats and others. A few tried to drift away but were corralled back for their turn. I saw several of them point to me as they were interrogated.

Aidan joined a cluster of agents around a computer—they'd

set up a makeshift workstation under a white tent, a command center. Lou took Malcolm aside and spoke in low tones that I couldn't hear. When Lou finished, Malcolm nodded and looked over at Aidan as if something had been decided. For the first time, I couldn't read Malcolm's expression. I gripped Zach's hand with my cloth fingers. His hand felt damp with sweat that seeped into the fabric of my palm.

Lou strode toward us. "Zachary, our medics would like to check you out." He nodded to a woman in a doctor's uniform. She beckoned three assistants to join her. "Afterward, we'd like to ask you some questions."

"He stays with me," I said.

The doctor spoke calmly, as if I were a wild horse that needed soothing. "He's been hurt. He may have internal bleeding. We need to be certain that his injuries are superficial."

I hadn't thought about his injuries. Of course they should check him. "You'll bring him back to me?"

"You should check her too," Zach said at the same time.

The doctor looked at Lou and then at me—my cloth skin, my marble eyes, my thread mouth. Carefully, she said to Zach, "She doesn't need human medicine."

"Don't change," Lou said quickly to me. "You as a doll will be more effective at the trial. No one will doubt your story with you as living evidence."

"She isn't just a doll," Zach said.

"Of course," Lou said.

"She's become more."

"So Agent Harrington has said, time and time again."

Zach turned to me. "Who you were . . . who you became . . . You were wrong before, when you said it was a lie. You have changed, in all the ways that matter."

I didn't know if I believed him, but I smiled as if I did. He loosened his grip on my hand, and the doctor and her assistants efficiently separated us. Zach was escorted away from me. The instant he wasn't touching me, I felt panic rise up into my throat. I pushed forward, and Lou held out his arm, blocking me.

"I won't cooperate if he's not safe," I said quietly, low so that Zach wouldn't hear. "You want my testimony, then that's my price. Don't harm him. Don't detain him. Don't . . . do anything to him he doesn't want. In fact, help him. Set him up with whatever life he wants, with or without his family, in whatever world he wants. And I'll say whatever you need me to say."

"She means it," Aunt Nicki said behind me.

I turned to look at her. Her gaze slid away from me, as if she didn't want to look at my doll face. She watched Malcolm lock the briefcase. Aidan was beside him, double-checking and triple-checking the locks.

"She has succeeded beyond our wildest expectations. You have to admit that," Aunt Nicki said, her eyes still on Malcolm. "Malcolm was right."

Lou grunted. "Suppose I'll have to give him a promotion."

"He deserves a damn medal," Aunt Nicki said. To me, she said, "Malcolm was the one who first discovered you, you know, after you escaped the carnival. You were careening between worlds. He insisted you had the potential to grow, to coalesce into a coherent being, even though you were"—she gestured at my cloth body—"like this. The rest of us thought he was crazy."

Malcolm lifted the steel briefcase. He was flanked by multiple agents.

"He badgered Lou into pulling in magic-wielding doctors from multiple worlds—specialists to build your body." Frowning again at me, Aunt Nicki clarified, "Your human body. At the time, you couldn't control your magic well enough to do it yourself, even if you'd understood what we wanted you to do."

"Those doctors are ridiculously proud of you," Lou said. "They babble on about papers that they'll write based on you. You made a number of careers."

"At Malcolm's insistence, we set you up," Aunt Nicki continued. "Gave you a home. A job."

"At *my* insistence, we recruited Aidan, Victoria, and Topher to befriend you—they were our three strongest, the ones best suited to challenge you and the ones best able to defend themselves against you, if need be," Lou said. "Working with them, we threw as much stimulation at you as we could."

"Malcolm believed the memories and instincts were buried in there, inside you," Aunt Nicki said. "We simply needed to help you become someone who could access them. And we succeeded!"

"Yes." Lou contemplated me as if I were a sculpture he'd carved. "Yes, we did. We're all proud of you." From Lou, this was an extraordinary statement. I stared at him with my marble eyes. Maybe . . . maybe I had misjudged him.

The agents parted, creating a path through the crowd, and Malcolm marched toward one of the silver mirrors, carrying the briefcase. He looked back once, directly at me, and raised his hand in a wave. Aidan vanished from his side as Malcolm melted into the mirror—I wasn't certain if Aidan had gone through the mirror or not. I felt a breath of wind on the back of my neck.

"You have done well." Lou smiled, an unnatural expression on his face. I hadn't thought his mouth could form any shape but a scowl. I remembered I'd seen him smile exactly once, when he'd handed me the magic box. He put his hand on my shoulder, as if to be friendly. "Our apologies," Lou said. "But we can't risk losing you now."

I looked behind me to see Aidan holding an open box, the one that had once held the Storyteller. "See you at the trial, Green Eyes," Aidan said. Lou shoved me toward him, and Aidan touched me with the box.

I was trapped inside.

# Twenty–Six

ON THE DAY OF the trial, Malcolm escorted me into the courtroom. He was flanked by two agents, plus another six behind us. Their guns were drawn—two tranquilizer guns, two tasers, and two loaded rifles. Malcolm had said the guns were merely a precaution.

All the guns were pointed at me, and I heard whispers and gasps and the words "doll" and "puppet" as people craned for their first look at me.

The courtroom was on the first floor of the agency. There was a solid-wood jury box, as well as mahogany benches for the audience, plus the judge's podium with a witness stand beside it. Lit by iron chandeliers, the warm wood made the room look oddly cozy.

The room was filled with strangers. As I passed by the bailiffs, I recognized three faces in the audience: Aidan, Victoria, and Topher. Aidan wore an elaborate and exotic suit that made him look even more handsome. He had an entourage around him of men and women in uniform, which made his offer to me seem all the more real. These were the people from his government, the ones who wanted me to work for them, who wanted to use me as their weapon. Near them, Victoria was dressed in a floor-length gown, and her hair was arranged in dreadlocks that imitated snakes. They slithered over her shoulders as she watched me walk down the long aisle from the door to the front of the courtroom. Beside her, Topher was also in formal dress, a uniform-like suit with an orange sun on his chest. A man next to him carried a flag with the same symbol. None of them gave any hint that they knew me, but Topher looked at Aidan, who shook his head almost imperceptibly. I didn't know what the exchange meant.

Zach was also in the audience. He had agents on either side of him. I couldn't see well enough over the heads of the audience to tell whether or not he was bound. He was as far from me as possible, near an emergency exit door.

At the front, the jury box was full of men and women, not all human, in gray and black suits. The judge was a man with a neatly trimmed beard.

The witness stand was empty, waiting for me.

The Magician was in silver shackles at the front of the courtroom. He wore an orange jumpsuit. Without his tattered suit and hat, he looked wrong. I wanted to place a hat on his head, just so he'd look like he should. This way, he looked like an ordinary man, and that only made me feel more unnatural with my cloth skin, yarn hair, and marble eyes.

As I passed by him, I felt his eyes on me. Malcolm led me

to the witness stand and then stepped back. I climbed the steps alone. It was only three steps, but my cotton feet felt heavy. I looked at the judge. His skin was tinged green, and the flaps of gills were visible beneath the wiry curls of his beard. The gills were closed. His expression was unreadable.

I looked at Malcolm. He held his expression still, and I knew that meant there were thoughts and emotions held in check underneath, though I didn't know what they were. Outside the courtroom, in the moments before my entrance, Lou had lectured me about the importance of remembering everything. Remember what you heard. Remember what you saw. Remember where you were. Malcolm had only said one thing: "Remember who you have become."

He didn't speak now. He nodded to the judge, and then he left me at the witness stand and took a seat in the audience in a row of marshals. I noticed that Aunt Nicki wasn't there. But the courtroom was packed with people. As I looked over them, I felt shivers crawl over my cloth skin. I didn't know them, but I recognized bits of them. That man, he had the same eyes as the boy with tattoos. The woman with the tears streaking her cheeks had the same face as the girl with silvery hair. I saw a little boy with diamonds in his dreadlocks. Another woman, older, had antlers that budded from her gray curls. She sat between Victoria and a man with snakelike skin. These were their families, the families of the dead. I wondered what they saw when they looked at me, a living doll in a dress of jewels and feathers.

I couldn't look at them anymore. Looking up at the iron

chandeliers, I wished I were elsewhere. I wished Zach and I had run away from the marshals, found a mirror, and kept running. But it was too late for running now.

The judge was speaking. ". . . the truth, the whole truth, and nothing but the truth."

I met the Magician's eyes with my green marble eyes.

Then I laid my cloth hand on a book and said, "I swear."

A lawyer rose. "Let's start at the beginning . . ."

The beginning. What was the beginning? Was it when the Storyteller made me? Was it when I was first filled with magic? Was it when I began to hear, began to see, began to talk, began to think, began to feel? Or was it when I left the wagon and left the carnival behind? Was it when Malcolm found me? Was it when the doctors gave me a new body? Or when I walked into the house on Hall Avenue, believing I was an ordinary girl? Or when I kissed Zach and defied the marshals? Or was it when I was a bird in the wallpaper, suddenly realizing that I could choose what I did, said, felt, or thought? Or later, when I chose not to be what the Magician meant for me to be and decided to be real instead?

I testified for three days, with breaks for the judge and jury to eat, pee, and sleep. I didn't need to do any of these things. On the breaks, I simply waited in a room beside the courtroom until it was time for the questions to begin again. Sometimes I repeated things; sometimes I backtracked. A woman with a shirt buttoned to her neck typed every word I said. She had four arms. She typed quickly and never looked at me. I didn't stop talking.

I told them every moment that I could remember. Every word spoken. Every sound heard. Everything I felt. As I talked, I remembered more and more until the memories were waves inside me, pounding at my skin, wanting to burst out. I let them—and out tumbled more memories, memories that weren't even mine. The freshest were the memories of the Storyteller.

It was the Storyteller who had figured out how to drain magic from someone's last dying breath. It was she who had crafted a doll that could hold that magic—it faded inside a human, but it stayed within her special doll. It was the Magician who had discovered how to siphon the magic from the doll into himself to use as he pleased. And it was he who had adapted the boxes into traps.

Together, they had joined the carnival and handpicked their victims—they targeted the young, the strong, and the unique magic users in each world. Together, the Magician and the Storyteller lured or trapped or chased them through forests or towns or fields and brought them to the wagon. Together, they drew the chalk symbols on the floor. Together, they killed.

At first they'd been devastated by guilt, and they had tried to find another way. But nothing else worked. And so, they'd learned to kill without remorse, and they'd learned that teenagers had the strongest magic.

I was with them for every death. Standing on the witness stand with the eyes of the families of the dead on me, I remembered them all.

I told them about how the Storyteller had recognized that

I was becoming aware, how at first she'd fostered it but then she'd feared it. A doll who knew their secrets, who couldn't be controlled, who was filled with bits and pieces of the magic and the memories and the knowledge of the people who had died . . . They'd built into me the magical equivalent of a failsafe— a trigger that caused me to lose consciousness whenever I used magic—but that only made them safe from my magic. They weren't safe from my knowledge. I knew what they'd done, and I was beginning to think and, worse, to feel. The Storyteller resolved to make new dolls, replacements that wouldn't have so much magic inside them and would never come alive. But she'd also loved me. She'd created me. I was hers and his, their sort-of child. So she'd set me free, hoping I'd never return, hoping to replace me with new, weaker dolls.

I was lost for a long time after that, going from world to world in a blur, until Malcolm found me. He'd been investigating this case for some time already and was looking for someone, or something, like me who could lead him to the killer. He saw me use magic that matched those of the victims, and he realized what I was—a receptacle for stolen power. He brought me here, initiated the surgeries, taught me how to function in a world beyond the carnival . . .

One of the lawyers interrupted me and submitted into evidence a series of recordings: videos of when I'd first arrived at the agency, of the surgeries, of the training. With the judge's permission, he projected them onto a screen at the front of the courtroom.

Standing on the witness stand, I watched myself, stiff and

halting, a doll who drifted in and out of rationality. On the screen, I saw Malcolm guide me into his office, where I sat in a leather chair, motionless and unblinking. I heard Aunt Nicki's voice, thin through the speakers—she must have been holding the video camera. She called me Pinocchio, pronounced me a freaky thing, and told Malcolm if he wanted a pet, cats were much more appealing. But he knelt before me, looked into my green marble eyes and talked to me. Even then, he treated me as if I were a person.

He was with me as I was wheeled into the first of the surgeries. I reached out my hand to hold his, and I turned my cloth face to look at him with green-glass marble eyes, trusting him. The camera focused on our hands, my misshapen cloth fingers in his strong human ones.

Projected on the screen, the surgeries were a ghastly amalgam of medicine and magic. Veins were threaded inside me, skin was grafted onto me, and human eyes were transplanted onto my half-cloth, half-tattered-skin face—brown eyes in place of green glass. I forced myself to watch—each image causing memories to rise inside me, like bile rising in my throat.

Later, there was another video of me in Malcolm's office. This time, I looked human but was still very doll-like in my movements, lurching through the office like a strangely detailed windup toy. He had to teach me how to eat, to pee, to sleep. As a doll, I'd done none of that.

Watching the videos, I remembered all of it. My memories, this time.

After it ended, I talked again. I told them everything from meeting Zach and working in the library to having lunch in the pizza parlor with Aidan, Topher, and Victoria. I omitted only their offer and their accusations against the agency, and the lawyer did not ask.

At last, I told Lou and the judge and the jury and the families of the dead about my return to the carnival with Zach and what happened in the wagon with him and Aidan. I didn't spare a single detail, including the Storyteller's death and my role in the Magician's plans.

When at last I ran out of words, I stopped talking. I pressed my thread lips together and thought I might never talk again. I felt drained of all words. I sagged against the witness stand, my cotton body limp.

The Magician spoke then, for the first time. "They will kill you, you know." His voice was conversational and his words were only for me, as if he weren't bound and shackled in front of a crowd full of families that wanted to see him flayed alive for all that I'd said he'd done. "I am the only one who never would. I would never destroy you. I am the father you never had, and together we are magic!"

"You are not authorized to speak," the judge said. He signaled to the bailiffs, and they advanced on the Magician. But he had said all that he wanted to say. He spoke the truth. I knew he would never kill me, and I knew that my own words had condemned me as much as they'd condemned him. I knew what I saw and what I did and what I didn't do: I didn't save any of them.

I wondered how they'd kill me—if they'd use magic, if they'd poison my food, if they'd shoot me. I wondered if, when the time came, Aidan, Victoria, and Topher would try to save me, or if what they'd heard had changed their minds. I wondered if I wanted to be saved, if I deserved to be saved.

I wished I could return to the carnival without the Magician. It was home, after all. I'd have liked to travel with the carnival from world to world, see the places from my memories but without the overlay of death and pain, touch an audience without taking from them. I remembered there were beautiful places out there beyond the silver mirror. I'd like to see them again, explore the multiverse.

As I was escorted from the witness stand, I wished I'd had a chance to say good-bye to Zach. Flanked by Malcolm and Aunt Nicki, he watched me as I was led out of the courtroom by armed bailiffs. I met his human eyes with my marble eyes. His were wet, tears staining his cheeks. He'd cried for me.

❖

I was taken to a box.

It didn't look like a box on the outside any more than the wagon did. It was a nice room on the second floor of the agency, the kind of room that I'd imagine would be in a hotel, except there were no windows. The bed had my quilt from the house on Hall Avenue, as well as the stuffed monkey.

The monkey was a gift from Malcolm—I had remembered that during my testimony, just as I'd remembered the times he'd patiently explained and reexplained where I was and what my name was, the time he'd introduced me to pizza, the time he'd shown me a supermarket, the time he and Aunt Nicki had demonstrated how to dance to the radio. I picked up the monkey and sat on the bed, as the guards who'd escorted me shut the door and locked it. Malcolm and Aunt Nicki had taught me how to be human.

My new room had a dresser with my clothes in the drawers. There was no mirror or anything that could be made sharp. A stack of books, all from the library, were beside the bed.

I wondered if there was any trace of me left in the house on Hall Avenue.

I wondered if there would be any trace of me anywhere in this world. Maybe in the records of the trial. The woman with many arms had typed my every word, plus there had been a video camera recording. And I knew Malcolm, Aunt Nicki, and Zach would remember me. I'd exist in their memories. Maybe that was enough. It didn't feel like enough.

Hours passed.

One day, two, three.

I spent time sitting on the bed, the stuffed monkey in my arms. I read the library books and imagined that Zach had chosen them for me. I knew without anyone telling me that this was the closest I'd get to him. After what I'd told the jury about how powerful we were together, I doubted Lou would allow us anywhere near each other. I wondered if I'd see Zach again before I died. When I tired of reading, I stared up at the ceiling. There were no cracks in the plaster for me to count, only fluorescent lights in a row, but I counted anyway.

The bailiffs brought me food that I didn't eat and water that I didn't drink, and doctors came in to check on me. I didn't talk to them unless they talked to me. I felt as if I'd talked enough to last several lifetimes.

Eventually, I stopped counting and started to think. In my head, I ran through everything I had said on the witness stand. I tried to separate the memories: times I was aware, times I wasn't, to see if it was possible to draw a line between when I was a doll and when I was a person.

I couldn't. The line was blurred, and it wiggled through the past.

Laying there with the monkey and with my own thoughts and memories, I thought about Zach too. Zach had told the truth, as always: who I was wasn't who I'd become. And now that the trial was over, I didn't have to stay this way anymore.

If I was going to die, I wanted at least to die as myself, not as who I was made to be.

Closing my eyes, I pictured myself as the girl that I'd become, the one that Zach knew. I let the magic run through me, shaping me, transforming me. I chose my face, my hair, and my green eyes. And then I lay on the bed and let the vision sweep over me.

❋

*The Storyteller and the Magician sit on either side of me. Each holds one of my cloth hands. There are stars spread over the sky, and a pale-gray cloud covers half the moon. The Ferris wheel is silhouetted against the sky. It's motionless.*

*"I feel old," the Magician says.*

*The Storyteller kneads my cotton knuckles with her gnarled fingers. I think it calms her. "Do you want to stop?" she asks him.*

*He sighs. "Some days, yes."*

*"The audience threw roses," the Storyteller says. "You changed them into birds. Rose birds whose perfume smell wafted through the tent every time they flapped their wings."*

*The Magician smiles. "That was lovely."*

*"It was," she says.*

*They fall silent.*

*I think it would be nice to talk. Straining, I stretch my mouth. The threads that tie my mouth strain. I press my fabric lips together, and the threads lie limp. I try to open my mouth again.*

*"You add beauty to the world," the Storyteller says. "People need that. They come into your tent expecting a trick, half wanting to see a fraud and half wanting to believe. You show them magic, and they leave full of wonder."*

*"Sometimes I feel that it's not enough."*

*The Storyteller drops my hand and rises. She holds out her hand to him. "Make me something beautiful." He leans toward me, breathes in, and then takes her hand. As he rises, green sprouts burst out of the ground. They shoot upward and wrap around the tent poles. Buds blossom and then open into burgundy roses. A trickle of water falls over the side of the wagon, forming a pool with water lilies.*

*Holding each other close, the Magician and the Storyteller dance.*

*I want to dance too. I want to tell them so. I push my lips together and wiggle them side to side, loosening the threads.*

*As they sway and spin to the sound of crickets and the night breeze, the Storyteller says, "Once upon a time, there was an empty boy, and the emptiness ate him inside until one day, he met a girl who knew how to fill him . . ."*

*I stretch my mouth again, and the threads snap one after another.*

*Hearing the snaps, the Storyteller and the Magician stop and look at me. They study my cloth face and button eyes. "Some would see her as an abomination," the Magician says.*

*"Is that what you see?" the Storyteller asks.*

*He shakes his head and smiles. "I see beauty, wonder, and magic. I see the best of us. She is the 'something beautiful' we made together."*

*The Storyteller smiles too, showing her crooked, stained teeth. "She could be. I'll sew her a new dress, silk maybe. And I will give her glass eyes. Marbles or sea glass. I think perhaps they'll be green. She'd look pretty with green eyes."*

*The threads have snapped. I open my mouth. It widens freely. Carefully, I curve my lips, threads dangling, into a smile. "Thank you," I say.*

⁂

I went calmly with Malcolm when he came to claim me. I brought the monkey with me.

Malcolm led me back to the courtroom, which was again filled with the same people. Zach, though, wasn't there, I noticed immediately, nor was Aunt Nicki. But Aidan, Victoria, and Topher were. And of course the Magician.

Malcolm led me to a table across the aisle from the Magician. He squeezed my shoulder. And then he left the courtroom. Gone, just like that. He left me alone. I never thought he would do that, and I suddenly felt fear squeeze my insides, my human stomach and lungs. I wanted to call out after him, but I didn't. Half the eyes in the courtroom were on the Magician; the other half were on me.

And suddenly I realized I'd lied to myself. I wasn't ready to die.

The judge banged his gavel. He listed the crimes—illegal use of magic across worlds, false identification, performing with an illegal license, and myriad other infractions. Then he paused and said, "Murder in the first degree." And he began to list the names.

The list went on and on.

With each name, I remembered a face or a moment—all the talking that I had done had jogged loose the pictures in my head. I closed my eyes and let the images come, all the photos that I had identified in the tablet and Lou had then pinned to the bulletin board, all the boxes that had hung in the wagon, all the magic that swirled inside me.

The judge continued, and, caught in the memory of faces, I didn't hear his words.

But I heard the intake of breath, the sudden stillness that spread over the courtroom, as the jury leader spoke the verdict. "We find the defendant guilty as charged."

As one, the audience exhaled.

Guilty as charged.

The words echoed around the chamber.

I was led by a bailiff to a side room and instructed to wait. The court was in recess. I sat on a bench in a dull gray room and didn't move, didn't speak, and didn't think. When it was time for sentencing, the bailiff led me back to the courtroom. Everyone had reassembled. I felt the Magician's eyes on me. I didn't look at him. Instead, I looked again for Zach. I didn't see him or Malcolm or Aunt Nicki or Topher . . .

In the crowded courtroom, I felt alone.

The judge banged his gavel. "Sentencing is as follows: life imprisonment with no possibility of parole, this location with no possibility of extradition."

The courtroom erupted in shouting. I heard shouts for the Magician's death, loud anger. Several jumped to their feet. The bailiffs rushed forward.

The judge banged his gavel harder. All around the courtroom, the bailiffs pushed people back into their seats. Slowly, the courtroom stilled.

"His belongings will be destroyed, including the doll known as Eve, who was created through his deeds. All records from this case will be sealed to prevent these crimes from ever being repeated. This court is adjourned."

The gavel banged again.

And the words sank in.

The Magician would be imprisoned.

I would be destroyed.

# Twenty-Seven

AS THE COURTROOM ERUPTED again in shouting, I wanted to fly away as fast as I could . . . or transform into a knot in the wood and hide . . . or change into a beetle and scurry away. I'd only have one chance—

Electricity shot in an upward lightning strike toward the fluorescent lights. It hit three, and they exploded in a shower of glass and sparks. All the other lights flickered off, and people screamed.

I hadn't done it.

I looked to where I knew the Magician was, though I couldn't see him in the sudden, complete blackness. *He couldn't have done it either*, I thought. He had no magic of his own, and he hadn't drawn from me in days.

Emergency lights snapped on, shedding weak, stark light on the courtroom. Agents aimed their guns in every direction. I was looking directly at the Magician, so I saw the snake a second before they did. Coiling on the table in front of him, the snake reared back and sank her fangs into his neck. His face paled, then reddened, then purpled. His neck swelled. His eyes bulged and then bled, red tears streaking his purple-veined cheeks. He toppled forward onto the desk, and the snake slid back to the floor and disappeared beneath the benches.

I felt as if the venom were seeping into me too. I couldn't move. He was dead. Dead! The man that haunted my dreams, filled my memories . . . fathered me, in his own way.

A hand squeezed my shoulder. Jerking back, I turned. Aidan smiled at me, his usual dazzling smile, and he tightened his grip. The courtroom vanished.

I reappeared with him inside the agency elevator.

Topher was there, finger poised over the buttons. "Which floor?"

Unable to think, I stared at him.

"Which floor has the portal, Green Eyes?" Aidan asked.

Slowly, my brain chugged forward. I remembered that Aidan had said he couldn't teleport somewhere he hadn't seen. He'd been blindfolded when he'd arrived, he'd once said. They must have blindfolded him again when he went through to find the carnival. "Fifth."

Topher pushed the button to the fifth floor.

"Victoria?" Topher asked Aidan.

Aidan vanished.

The tinny elevator music played. Side by side, Topher and I watched the numbers click up. I clutched the stuffed monkey to my chest.

A second later, Aidan reappeared, a snake wrapped around his arms. The snake slithered to the ground, and Victoria rose from the floor. "Justice has been served, and my sister is avenged," she announced.

"Good," Topher said. "I can't believe the stupid sheep thought they could keep a psychopath like that alive. Even without his tools, such a man is too dangerous."

"All's well that end's well," Victoria said. "I see you succeeded too." Victoria's eyes swept over me, as if appraising my worth. She wasn't speaking to me. I thought of Aidan saying I was the treasure he sought and the prize he was destined to win, and I wished I were anywhere but here—the house, the pizza parlor, the carnival. "Delightful."

Looking at each of them, I realized I'd traded one trap for another, except instead of wanting to kill me, my new jailors wanted me to kill. I wished I could run, fly away, fade into the wallpaper . . .

At level five, the elevator lurched to a halt. "Ready yourselves," Aidan said. Topher tossed sparks between his hands. Aidan gripped my arm, ready to vanish or to keep me from vanishing. Victoria dropped back into her snake form.

The elevator door opened.

Malcolm and Aunt Nicki waited for us. Side by side, they blocked the corridor. His eyes were glued on mine. Slowly, he and Aunt Nicki raised their hands as if in surrender.

"That's right," Aidan said. "You don't want to fight us."

Topher tossed a fireball from hand to hand. Flames licked his fingers, and sparks sprayed onto the floor. Smiling, he strolled out of the elevator with Aidan. I followed behind. Victoria slithered in front of us, hissing.

"So, how about you step aside?" Topher said. "Shame if someone got hurt."

Eyes full of compassion, Malcolm asked, "Eve? Do you want to go with them?"

I opened my mouth and then shut it. If I said no . . . Aidan, Topher, and Victoria were poised to hurt them, badly. But if I said yes . . . they wanted me as a weapon. I would face a lifetime of hurting people.

"She's coming with us," Aidan said.

"If she wants to go with you, then she goes with my blessing," Malcolm said. "If not . . ."

Aunt Nicki grinned. "If not, things might get messy."

"I need her." Aidan vanished and then reappeared next to Aunt Nicki, too close to her. He put his hand on her throat.

Aunt Nicki didn't move. Her expression didn't change either. "It's Eve's choice."

"Just tell the truth," a voice said softly in my ear. "Yes or no?"

Zach.

I turned. He must have been waiting, tucked into the corner beside the elevator, against the wall. With Malcolm and Aunt Nicki in front of us, we hadn't seen him. Now he was close, his face only inches away from mine. He breathed in my breath, my magic. "No," I said. And the hallway erupted in chaos.

Zach pointed at the snake Victoria, and she flew backward

into the elevator and hit the back wall. She collapsed onto the floor. Topher hurled the fireball, and Malcolm lunged and rolled. It slammed into the door behind him, and the carpet ignited. Drawing his gun as he jumped to his feet, Malcolm squeezed the trigger. A needle embedded in Topher's neck. He clutched at it, took a step forward, and then slumped to the floor. Aidan vanished and then reappeared behind me, hands on my shoulders, as Zach pressed his lips against mine again.

I felt Aidan's hands harden.

The hallway fell silent.

Slowly, I turned. Aidan's face was porcelain, and his body was cloth. I lifted his porcelain hands from my shoulders, and he crumpled to the ground.

Grabbing a fire extinguisher from the wall, Aunt Nicki sprayed the flames with white foam. The fire died, and the foam soaked into the carpet.

"Is he . . . ," I began.

"I don't know," Zach said.

Both Malcolm and Aunt Nicki approached. They stood over the doll Aidan, tranquilizer guns aimed at him. "Turn him back, and we'll see," Aunt Nicki said.

Zach took another breath from my lips, and Aidan's porcelain face and hands softened. His cloth skin smoothed into human skin. His chest shuddered, and he began to breathe.

Malcolm shot him with a tranquilizer dart.

"Bet that felt good," Aunt Nicki said to Malcolm.

"Reasonably satisfying," Malcolm agreed. The two of them

dragged Topher and Aidan into the elevator with the still-unconscious snake Victoria. Aunt Nicki stabbed the close button and then stepped back out into the corridor. The doors slid shut.

I realized I was still clutching the stuffed monkey.

"You'll need to be quick," Aunt Nicki said to me. "And random. Don't go places you've been before. Stay away from anything familiar."

I gawked at her.

Her mouth quirked. "That's the Eve I know and love. Always quick with the thank-you. Don't overflow with emotions. I don't want to get weepy."

"I don't understand." Were they truly going to let me go? Even Aunt Nicki? Sure, she'd said it was my choice, but their job . . . the agency . . . the trial . . . Lou . . .

She rolled her eyes. "At least you're consistent."

Malcolm holstered the tranquilizer gun and wrapped me in a bear hug. I leaned against his chest, letting his arms fold around me. "Be careful."

My eyes felt hot, and it was hard to swallow. "I'll . . . miss you."

"Me too," he said softly, barely loud enough for me to hear, and then he released me and shoved me toward Zach. "Kiss the boy and go."

I turned to Zach. "How did—"

"I told them the truth." Zach took my hand and brought it to his lips. His eyes were bright. "You're real. Turns out, though, they'd already decided that. The two of them have been planning this since the trial began."

"Yeah, this is all very nice, but you need to leave now." Aunt Nicki made shooing motions with her hands. "Kiss the boy and knock us out."

"What?" I asked.

"Make it look like we tried to stop you," Aunt Nicki said. "I'm not going down for you if I don't have to. You're Malcolm's case, not mine. And he deserves a better fate than the agency's censure. If you care about either of us, then kick our asses. We'll take care of explaining Aidan, Victoria, and Topher."

I kissed Zach, and then he flicked his hand. Both of them flew backward across the hall. Aunt Nicki hit the door, and then slumped onto the floor. I didn't know if she was feigning unconsciousness or if she truly was. Malcolm grunted but stood.

"Try again," I told Zach.

Zach caused vines to burst out of the wall and wrap around him.

We kissed again. And then we ran through the wall. Guards were on the other side. We changed our shape. Two times, three times, as we plunged through the second and third doors. Wolves. Birds. Mice. And then dragonflies. We flew into the ventilation system, careened through the air-conditioning ducts, and then shot into the silver room.

Inside the room, we changed into ourselves.

Hand in hand, we walked through the silver walls.

And I am, for the first time, free.

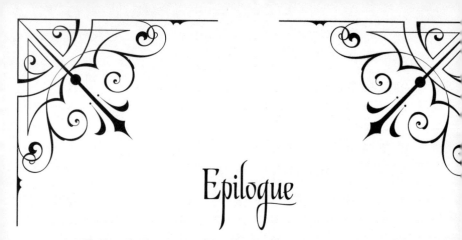

# Epilogue

THERE ISN'T A CARNIVAL tent, but the audience comes anyway. Zach and I had written in the sky with wisps of clouds, inviting them, and we'd used fireflies at night to guide them. And so they come, whispering and laughing, through the forest, trampling the ferns and ducking under branches, to see the magicians.

Our stage is the base of an oak tree. Fireflies collect around the stage, defining the edges. The audience sits beyond it on moss and roots and rocks. They wait, and from behind the tree, I can hear the buzz of their anticipation. Zach squeezes my hand.

"Ready?" he says.

"Ready." I kiss him. For a moment, I don't hear the audience or the wind in the branches or the chirp of the cicadas. His arms are warm around my waist, and he tastes like the strawberries we shared for dinner, fresh from a field on another world.

Hand in hand, we walk around the tree. Our audience is small: twenty or so, but word will spread. Tomorrow, more will come, and then more the next night. We'll leave before word of us can spread too far.

I begin with a deck of cards. I shuffle them fast from hand to hand. The cards arc through the air, landing neatly in my palm. I have practiced this, and I have some skill at it, which both surprises and pleases me. I toss the cards in the air as high as I can toward the branches, one card after another in rapid succession.

Zach steps in front of me as if to catch the cards—and the cards transform into paper birds and fly up, up into the tree branches. The audience gasps and then claps.

We change positions, and I give him my breath again. He then kneels, and I step onto his cupped palms. He tosses me, and I fly up too, higher than he could have thrown me. I pluck half the bird-cards from the tree and plummet down. He catches me, breathes in my magic, and tosses me again, still higher. I capture the other half of the cards, and then I land in his arms again.

Standing, I spread the cards in my hands and fan them before the audience, to show that they are ordinary cards, and then I toss them in the air again, one after another, rapid-fire.

This time the cards dance in the air, weaving an intricate pattern. As they dance above the stage, dozens of flowers poke through the earth in the midst of the audience. The stems stretch, leaves unfurl, and buds blossom until the audience is awash in flowers.

Zach picks a bloom and tosses it in the air. He gestures for the audience to do the same. Eagerly, the kids yank the flowers out of the ground and throw them into the air. The men and women are more hesitant, but then they begin tossing flowers as well. The flowers join the aerial dance, twisting and twirling with the cards until they are all paired, each card with its own flower.

One more kiss, and the flowers melt into the cards, becoming part of the design. The cards tumble from the sky, each with a painted flower on it that wasn't there before. The children in the audience leap up and catch the cards.

As the audience whispers, laughs, and trades flower cards, I bring out a cup full of water, and I throw it at the audience. The water arcs toward them but never lands. Suspended, each drop sparkles like a star. Zach shapes the water into horses that ride through the surf, a castle that rises out of foam, dragons that breathe water instead of fire.

After drawing the water back to the cup, Zach then transforms me into a dragon, a cat with wings, and a pink rabbit. He repeats this with volunteers from the audience, changing each for a few precious seconds into whatever they choose.

When we end the show, the audience leaps to their feet and claps. Some of the adults have tears in their eyes. The children are jabbering and chattering excitedly to each other. They leave full of beauty, magic, and wonder.

We melt into the oak tree, joining the wood, until the audience is gone.

Afterward, we walk out of the tree.

There is a pile in the center of the stage—blankets, clothes, tinder to light a fire, fresh-baked bread, some oranges that look like clementines. We asked for nothing, but they left it anyway.

The first time this happened, I had wanted to return it all.

"I don't want to take," I'd said. "I'm not *him*. I want to give without taking."

"Maybe they feel the same way," Zach had said. And my objections had died.

We scoop up our gifts and retreat farther into the woods, far enough that we won't be easy to find. We light a fire and lay beneath the blankets, along with the now-ragged stuffed monkey, as we eat the bread and the clementines. I have never tasted sweeter, and I can say that with glorious certainty.

"Are you happy?" I ask Zach.

"Yes," he says without hesitation.

"Are you lying?"

"Never," he says. I ask him this every night; every night, he answers the same. "Are you happy?" he asks me.

I think about it, turn the question over in my mind, compare what I feel to my memories. We are building new memories every day and with every world we see. The good memories are beginning to outweigh the bad memories. "Yes."

"Are you lying?" he asks.

"Usually," I say, "but never to you."

Around us, the trees darken to shadows, and the sky deepens to azure then blue-black. Stars poke through the sky. I'm not tempted to count them. I'm content to lie beside Zach.

"I'd like a home someday," Zach says suddenly. This isn't what we usually say.

"You mean, you want to go home? Do you miss home? Your parents?"

"Sometimes, yes, of course. I love them, even as messed up as they are. I worry about them, that they're worrying about me. But that's not what I mean. I mean, I don't want to travel forever. Someday I want a home that's ours, that we stay in, that we fill with our things and our memories. It should have lots of skylights. Maybe be near an ocean. You know, oceans cover seventy percent of the Earth's surface, and if you extracted all the salt, you could bury the continents in five feet of salt. It would be nice to be near an ocean."

I think about a home by the ocean for Zach and me, imagine it with our own hall of photos, and decide it does sound nice. "All right," I say.

"But not yet," he says.

"Not yet," I agree.

We lie side by side for a while more. The bread is gone. The clementines are gone. The cicadas are louder now, and the forest is silent. His body is wonderfully warm beside mine.

"Should we see another world tomorrow?" he asks.

"I'd like that," I say.

I turn my head to look at him. He turns his. We are only inches away. He smiles at me, and then we kiss. We don't do any magic. It's only a kiss, magic on its own.

# Acknowledgments

I'd like to thank my nightmares. Without you, this book would never have been born. Also, thank you to my magnificent agent, Andrea Somberg, and to my fantastic editor, Emily Easton, as well as Laura Whitaker and all the other amazing people at Walker who have worked to bring Eve's story to life. Many thanks and much love to my family, who have given me so many wonderful memories. And a thousand kisses to my children, who make me feel alive, and to my husband, who makes my dreams come true.